THE SAUCY LUCY MURDERS

CINDY KEEN REYNDERS

Medallion Press, Inc.
Printed in USA

THE SAUCY LUCY MURDERS

CINDY KEEN REYNDERS

DEDICATIONS:

I wrote this book for my mother, who sang
me salty WWII WAC songs as a babe in my
cradle, giving me a fine appreciation for humor.
I also wrote this for the laughter gods, with
whom we should all communicate daily.

Published 2007 by Medallion Press, Inc.

The MEDALLION PRESS LOGO
is a registered tradmark of Medallion Press, Inc.

Cover Illustration by Adam Mock

Typeset in Caslon 540

Printed in the United States of America

10-digit ISBN: 1-9338362-4-5
13-digit ISBN: 978-1-933836-24-9

10 9 8 7 6 5 4 3 2 1
First Edition

ACKNOWLEDGEMENTS:

Thanks to Cristina, Jordon and Brian for putting up with mom when I had my fingers glued to the keyboard instead attending PTA meetings. Thanks to my dad and the rest of my extended family for listening to me ramble about my "latest" story. Thanks to my husband Rich for his fantastic Sunday breakfasts which fueled my imagination. Most of all, thanks to my best friend and sister Shauna, who taught me to laugh at life again when my creative spirit went MIA and who was a major player in helping me write *The Saucy Lucy Murders*.

PROLOGUE

SUN GLISTENED BRIGHTLY THROUGH PINE AND spruce trees, and onto the champagne powder snow. Above, blue sky, scattered with lumpy winter clouds, arched like a dome. A roaring snowmobile skiffed across the frosty white landscape with two riders bundled in heavy coats, hats, mittens, and goggles. Their laughter rang out into the crisp air, echoing throughout the remote wilderness.

Someone crouched in the shadows on a ledge above the snowmobile, hidden by a boulder. With steady hands, the shadow-person lifted a high-powered rifle and took aim. As the snowmobile's occupants came into range, the shooter took a deep breath and pulled the trigger.

The snowmobile driver immediately slumped over the steering wheel and the vehicle veered into a snow-drift, spilling the occupants onto the ground. Blood spread out from the driver's head and onto the white powder, like a snow cone dunked in cherry syrup.

Neither occupant moved for a moment, then the smaller individual, who had been riding behind, scooted out from underneath the snowmobile's bulk and scrambled to their knees. Leaning forward, the individual examined the driver.

A scream pierced the silent landscape.

The shadow-person smiled.

CHAPTER 1

YOU NEED TO START DATING AGAIN, LEXIE. Otherwise you're going to dry up and turn into a prune with lips." Lucy Parnell plopped plump blueberries into the thick batter in the bowl she held and the occasional one into her mouth.

"Damn it Lucy, I refuse to go on another one of your heifer checks," Lexie Lightfoot returned. "Just because a guy has a pulse and all his real hair doesn't mean I have to go out with him."

Lucy rolled her eyes.

"Besides," Lexie continued. "The last time you set me up on a date, the guy wound up with a bad headache and an appointment at Stiffwell's funeral home."

Lexie gave the loaf pan in her hand another shot of flour spray and loudly thunked it down on the counter. Blind dates were pure misery. She hated them. Yet, despite her protests about being 'fixed up', her older sister constantly tried to play matchmaker.

"You can't blame that on me," Lucy shot back as she stirred the blue-specked concoction with a large wooden spoon. "And the sheriff ruled Hugh Glenwood's death a hunting accident. Case closed."

"Whatever. Lexie turned on the oven to preheat. "It was January—way past any hunting season we have around here. More like it was nearly Super Bowl time and Sheriff Otis, my dear brother-in-law and your chunky hubby, probably wanted to solve the murder quickly so he wouldn't miss any of the game or miss the bouncing boobies at half-time."

"For Pete's sake, Lexie!" Lucy's brows shot up. "Your mouth! Mother and Father would roll over in their graves."

Yes, they probably would, Lexie thought. The good Reverend Castleton and his gentle wife would never have dreamed of swearing or speaking in such colorful language. Lexie respected her family's desire not to swear, yet she couldn't break herself of the habit. She considered the occasional swear word or use of colorful language therapeutic.

Oh well, it was best to just ignore Sister Lucy's outburst. "I still say there was foul play involved," Lexie said, referring to Glenwood's death.

"You have always had an active imagination, baby sister." As usual, Lucy dismissed the man's death as nothing more than a sad mishap, then prattled on about the virtues of being a wife, mother, and pillar of the community. Things, she reminded Lexie, *she* had no hopes of attaining unless she became a Mrs. Somebody again.

Unfortunately, Lucy had chosen to start her crusade right before the starving lunch crowd came barging through the front door. Lexie cast a worried glance at the clock, hoping her sister would be done tongue-whipping her before the café got slammed.

Still yickkety-yakking, her slightly plump shape clad in one of her typical floral-printed shifts, ruffled apron, and sturdy brown work shoes, Lucy ladled batter into the loaf pans.

Lexie wiped down counters, rinsed dishes and loaded the dishwasher, oblivious to what her sister was actually saying. Man, that woman could ramble. No wonder Otis sent her off once a year to a religious retreat, no questions asked. He needed a break. His wife could talk the feathers off a peacock.

Lexie considered the unexpected turns her world had taken the last couple of years. She would never have imagined returning home and opening a café. But life was like a lake sometimes, the waves rippling in different directions depending on which way the wind blew. Whatever happens you have to be prepared for change.

So, after Lexie's divorce from Dan Lightfoot two years ago, she'd moved back home to tiny Moose Creek Junction. At first, she and her daughter Eva, then sixteen, had lived in a small apartment over the Loose Goose Emporium, and Lexie had clerked there. Six months later, Lexie and Lucy's parents passed away in a car accident. In their will, they passed the Castleton family home, an old Victorian, to Lexie and Lucy.

The accident shocked Lexie and Lucy to the bone. But after the sadness faded, Lexie suggested they convert the downstairs of the Victorian into a café and the upstairs into comfortable living quarters for herself and Eva. Lucy could work in the café and also share in the profits since she would be co-owner. Lexie also suggested they name the café in their mother's honor. Lucy loved the idea.

The Saucy Lucy Café was born with a simple menu—good old-fashioned soups and hearty sandwiches assembled with homemade bread. Or a customer could have a piece of pie and coffee. All made with Lucille Castleton's recipes. Lexie and Lucy's mother, despite her penchant for wearing support hose and bad wigs, had been a wonderful cook.

The Saucy Lucy Café was an instant success. Of course, it was the *only* sandwich shop in town, which translated into the only fast food available to local residents. Lexie supposed that might have something to do with it.

"Yoohoo, you're not listening to me." Lucy had popped the blueberry bread into the oven and now stared at Lexie, arms akimbo.

Lexie realized she'd been standing at the aluminum sink for far too long, scrubbing the bottom of it mercilessly.

Lucy made an exasperated sound. "Quit being so melodramatic, Scarlett O'Hara. It's time to join

the world of the living again. I know this nice gentleman who attends my book club meetings . . ."

Lexie rolled her eyes. Just what she wanted. To
date a man who crashed a book club filled with spin-
sters and housewives. He must be a real winner.

Lucy just wouldn't leave well enough alone.
When they were kids, she played overprotective
big sister like a mama bear protecting her cubs. Of
course, Lexie resented Lucy's constant interference
in her life. It was like having two mothers. Most
people had trouble with one.

Would she never stop meddling in her love life?
Lexie scowled. "Look Luce, I'm not interested in
the barf bags you introduce me to. All of them ogle
me like I'm a prize cow fresh from Fannie Farmer's
spread."

"You're too judgmental," Lucy said. "Remember, the Bible says, 'Judge not, lest ye be judged.'"

"OK, maybe not a prize cow. A well done steak,
then. And they talk to my boobs." She grabbed her
chest for emphasis.

"Goodness!" Lucy's face turned pink and she
cleared her throat. "You need to be thankful for
God's gifts."

"Right," Lexie said. "If I wore a push-up bra, I'd
smother myself."

"I'm only trying to fix you up on a simple date,
dear. It's not like I'm making you bungee jump off
a water tower. And so what if you're . . . ah, well
endowed. There are worse things. You could have

cancer or—"

"Leukemia or be blind . . . I know. Why won't you just leave me alone? Why do you think that marriage is a cure-all?"

"It's been an entire year since you had a date." Lucy shook her finger at Lexie. "And you know what our church says about being married. It's the only way to enter into the Kingdom of our Lord."

Lexie stared heavenward. "Forgive her, Father, for she knows not the hell pit of dating. Besides, who died and said the First Community Church of the Lamb of God is right about everything?"

"Lexie, don't be sacrilegious. You know Mother and Father wouldn't approve. Especially since Father was the reverend there for over twenty years."

"Mom and Dad don't have to worry about such things now, sis. They're in a better place." Lexie thought of the car accident that took their lives and closed her eyes, the pain of their passing still sharp to bear.

"They are always with us in spirit," Lucy insisted. "And they would want me to give you solid guidance. Please, stop by my book club picnic tomorrow and meet Henry. He's divorced, like you, and has two children a few years younger than Eva."

In her mind's eye, Lexie imagined a roller coaster ride headed for hell on a flaming track. Sure, she *wanted* to help raise more teenagers. *Uh, huh.* Just like she wanted to have all her fingernails pulled out. Slowly. One by one.

Eva had been tough enough at sixteen, especially after ex-husband, Dan Lightfoot, aka, The Undertaker, had made a fool of himself by running off with Davina Blakely, recent widow and resident rich bitch of Tidewater, California. That left Lexie to teach Eva the following lessons for the last twenty-four months— *All About Driving, All About Boys, and All About Why Your Father Ran Off with a Redhead with Blond Roots.* Of course, Lexie had red hair, just a shade lighter than Davina's, but her roots weren't blond. She came by her red hair naturally. Honest.

"Don't you have something else to do besides harass me, Lucy? Surely there's some juicy gossip you need to spread with your church cronies." In a burg the size of Moose Creek Junction, it wasn't difficult to know everyone's business. And Lucy, respectable churchwoman that she was, made it her business to know.

Lucy folded her arms and tapped her toe. "There is no need to be hateful, baby sister."

Why did Lucy have to try and fix everything in her life? Maybe because she had attained such a perfect little life for herself. Things were too comfortable for Lucy, comfortable and *predictable*. On the other hand, Lexie's life was like riding a warped seesaw. Nothing ever stayed the same. Two years ago, it had turned into a soap opera.

Lexie knew it was her own fault her life had turned out so crazy. Choices. It all boiled down to choices. But growing up in Moose Creek Junction, the daughter of a preacher at a church where everybody knows your name had been difficult.

Reverend Castleton's family was expected to set an example for the local citizens and behave with religious decorum. Lexie, the reverend's wild-child daughter, never fit the mold.

Lord have mercy on a sinner born to saints. Amen.

Lucy, however, was the perfect angel. Always a good girl, she'd done what was expected. She'd been active in sports and community groups, graduated from high school at the top of her class, then had gone off to college. Afterward, she'd come home and married a local boy, Otis Parnell, now town sheriff, and started a family.

In typical fashion, the more Lucy conformed to society's expectations, the more Lexie rebelled. Impulsive and headstrong, she started dating Dan Lightfoot against her parents' wishes when she was sixteen. She'd gotten pregnant at seventeen and barely graduated high school.

She and Dan got married, despite both of their parents' protests. In order to get away from everyone's disapproval, Lexie and Dan took off for California with baby Eva. There, he'd managed to finish enough college to get into the funeral home business. Unfortunately, in the end, Dan turned out to be truth-challenged and developed a wicked eye for the ladies.

Lexie played dumb to the truth for too long and it bit her hard in the end. In retrospect, she realized there were many things she should have done differently. No use crying over spilled milk, her mother used to say. Lexie had begun a new life and she had yet another choice in front of her.

Piss off her sister, or not? Lucy had a good heart and meant well, after all. How could Lexie fault her for that? She glanced at the clock again.

Ten to twelve. The doors will be banging open any minute.

Lexie's stubborn resolve melted. "Does this guy at least have a cute butt?"

"For Pete's sake, Lexie—"

"Well, does he? That would at least be one compensation."

Lucy shook her head. "Honestly, dear. You do have a crude streak in your soul. I have no idea what type of derriere Henry Whitehead has."

"So what's the point in me meeting him?"

Lucy tapped her sturdy, solid, gold band. "You know the church says the only way you can get into heaven is through the sanctity of marriage. You have to at least *try* to find a soul mate."

"Damn, you never give up, do you?"

"For Pete's sake, quit swearing," Lucy complained. "And quit making faces at me. It isn't ladylike. Remember what Mother always told us? It makes the wrinkles around your eyes set prematurely. You don't want to look like the Crypt Keeper, do you?"

How amazing that a 47-year-old-woman still

heeded her mother's voice, even if it was all in her head. Of course, Lexie still heard Lucille Castleton's voice in her head, too. No matter where you went, your mother was always with you. And Lucy did have a point.

Lexie pressed her palms against her hot cheeks, as if by holding them taut, she could smooth out any potential wrinkles, and maybe even salvage her thirty-six-year-old complexion from the damage of free radicals in the environment. *Am I stupid, or what?* Pulling her hands away, Lexie eyeballed one of the cellophane bags of veggie chips stacked on the counter. She had a nasty urge to bonk Lucy over the head with them.

"Look, Lucy. We don't have time for this. It's almost noon and the lunch stampede will be here any minute."

"You're putting me off."

Lexie glanced at the clock. *Five to twelve.* The front doorbell tinkled. Through the order window, she noticed a couple of teenage boys wearing dog collars, scrubby T-shirts and backward baseball caps atop mops of purple and yellow hair shuffle in and stare at the lunch menu written on a dry erase board.

Lexie tried desperately to fish for an excuse to refuse meeting this Henry guy. "Don't we need to finish the soups?"

"They're all finished and warming in the crock pots, and all the sandwich fillings are mixed and in the refrigerator."

"Can't we talk about this later?" Lexie pleaded with her eyes.

"I refuse to let my baby sister dry up and wither away in this . . ." Lucy waved her hand toward the café on the other side of the order counter. It was filled with plastic molded aqua-colored chairs and bistro tables, tie-die wall hangings, beaded curtains and trailing plants in macramé hangers. ". . . hole-in-the-wall, hippie-retro eatery. You need a life again."

"I like this hole-in-the-wall, hippie-retro eatery of which, might I remind you, you are part owner. I have a lovely apartment upstairs, I'm putting my daughter through college, and I keep plenty of home-grown bean sprouts on my table, so I'll never go hungry again. What more could a girl ask for?"

"A companion. You're lonely."

"I am?"

"You are."

Lexie blinked. "Thanks for telling me since I'm so clueless I couldn't figure that out myself. I could always buy a goldfish for company, you know. At least they don't flake out on you like men do."

"Not all men are flakes, dear."

"Sure could'a fooled me."

"Be nice." Lucy wore a cautionary expression, standing there so prim and proper as she patted down a stray hair that had come loose from her serviceable brown bun. "And you might try dressing a little nicer. It's as if you try to hide your attractiveness by wearing unflattering clothing."

Lexie glanced down her faded jeans, old blue T-shirt, and checkered apron. With her pony-tailed, frizzy, ginger-colored hair, she knew she must look like Little Orphan Annie. Well, she was definitely no Cindy Crawford. So what?

Just then two farmers in coveralls, plaid shirts, and green, John Deere ball caps walked into the café and stood behind the punk-rocker boys to read the menu. The boys, obviously having made their choice of sandwich, walked purposefully toward the counter.

Twelve o'clock. High noon. Showdown time.

Desperation shot like a jolt of lightening through Lexie. "OK, I'll go to your damn picnic and meet what's-his-name! Eva doesn't have any classes tomorrow so she'll be home tonight. I'm sure she won't mind covering for us at the café. Now will you please leave me alone?"

Lucy's brows rose. "Honestly, Lexie. Your language is atrocious. If Mother and Father could hear you—"

"That line is getting old, Lucy. How many times do I have to tell you to quit worrying about me?"

"You always were an ungrateful, spoiled brat and, unfortunately, you still are." Lucy sighed heavily. "However, if it is my lot in life to lead you into the fold, then I will. Even if it takes me until the end of my days."

"Oh, brother. Now who's being Scarlet O'Hara?" Lexie opened the refrigerator and pulled out several plastic tubs of sandwich fillings, stacked them one atop the other, and set them down by Lucy who was slicing crusty loaves of bread.

She stepped over to the counter, picked up a pad and pencil, and looked at the punk-rocker boys standing on the other side. One of them had so many piercings in his eyebrows and lips and nose that she hurt all over just looking at him. She suppressed a shudder and forced a smile. "May I take your order?"

The next morning, Lexie shuffled downstairs through the empty sandwich shop, and into the kitchen, eyes still glazed with sleep. *Coffee, coffee*, her mind chanted to a primitive rhythm known only to man, and she vaguely made out the Mr. Coffee machine beckoning to her on the counter. But when her toes recoiled at something cold and wet, she looked down.

"Holy mother-of-pearl!" An inch of water and soapsuds arched across the yellow and blue linoleum, as if the Great Lakes had taken residence in her kitchen overnight. Lexie's gaze instantly traced the pool of water back to its source. One of the dishwashers. "Eva!" She shouted over her shoulder, hoping her voice would carry up the stairs.

"What, Mom?" Eva called a few seconds later.

"I need your help. ASAP."

"What's wrong?"

"Just hurry. And bring every bath towel we own."

"Be right there."

While Lexie waited for Eva and the bath towels, she dragged out every dishtowel, tablecloth, and rag in the joint and threw them on Lake Superior. Then she grabbed a mop, sopped up the water and squeezed it into the sink. Lord, this was going to take all day.

Lexie struggled to figure out what in the heck must have gone wrong with the dishwasher. It'll probably cost an arm and a leg for the repairman to fix it. Just what she needed—another repair bill.

Eva finally appeared in the kitchen door, arms loaded with towels. "Eeeeewwww, what happened?" Her faded pink flannel bathrobe had obviously been flung on in a hurry, and her long, brownish-auburn hair was knotted in a loose bun atop her head. She sloshed across the floor toward Lexie. Having inherited her father's height, she was nearly a head taller than Lexie's petite five-foot-tall frame.

"I have no idea. But at least the floor will be squeaky clean when we're through," Lexie told her. "Throw down the towels then wring them off the back porch."

An hour later, Lexie stood to iron out the crick in her back. Finally, the floor was dry. Mom would have been so upset to think her linoleum could have been ruined. And heaven help the individual caught up in her wrath.

Wondering what in the world she could have done

to make the dishwasher go on the fritz, Lexie glanced over at the guilty beast. Then it all came flooding back. Eva had loaded it. A bottle of dishwashing liquid sat strategically close to the loading zone, with the jug of dishwasher soap nowhere in sight.

Eva walked in from the back porch, the screen door slamming behind her. "Phewww, what a mess. You're lucky I was here to pitch in. It's going to get hot outside so the towels should dry pretty quick."

Lexie nodded. "Hey, tell me something. When you loaded that dishwasher last night, what soap did you use?"

Eva walked over and picked up the dishwashing liquid. "This." Her brows quirked innocently. "Why?"

Despite her annoyance, Lexie checked her temper. Eva was completely clueless sometimes, but she'd meant well. "That's used for washing dishes by hand, sweetie." Lexie shuffled over, feet and toes withered beyond recognition now, and withdrew the jug of dishwasher soap from under the sink. "This is what we use for the dishwasher. OK?"

"Oops." Eva winced. "Sorry."

"Not a biggie." Lexie said. "I'm just glad to know the dishwasher only had a bad case of indigestion."

"Right," Eva said. "I'm gonna go hit the shower. Can I help you do anything else?"

"No," Lexie responded too quickly, then decided to change the subject so Eva wouldn't guess she was afraid of her help right now. "Say, how's your new roommate working out?"

"She's cool. College is cool . . . at least in the three weeks since I started. The cafeteria food sucks, though. Yours is much better."

Lexie warmed at the unexpected compliment from her self-absorbed teenager. "I suppose they do their best."

"Mom, it'd gag a maggot. And their mystery meat is totally disgusting. Like, it's not fit for human consumption." Eva brushed past Lexie and went upstairs.

"Kids," Lexie muttered to the sparkling clean kitchen. "Gotta love 'em."

Later, trusting Eva could manage to make sandwiches and ladle soup for the lunch crowd, Lexie drove across town to Lucy's book club picnic at the Moose Creek Junction City Park. Under an arching canopy of ancient elms and cottonwoods sporting the golds, oranges, and reds of autumn, she navigated her truck past treacherous potholes on the narrow streets. She wondered briefly when the annual "Potluck and Pothole Day" was going to be held.

As a kid, Lexie loved when everyone got together for a community potluck and road repair day. Kids ran around playing and eating while their parents worked with the local asphalt company filling and smoothing out holes in the road. Moose Creek Junction was definitely due for this event. She made a mental note to ask Lucy about it.

Tucking strands of hair behind her ears, Lexie stared at the parched brown lawns of the neat bungalows lining the sidewalks. It had been dry over the summer. Terribly dry. And now the small town was under strict water rationing because Mayor Gollyhorn had determined they could have a potential emergency situation if the winter ahead turned out as warm as the last few years. *Global warming. The end of the world . . .* Lexie didn't want to think of that. The end of the world, that is.

Lucy said that Gus Lincolnway, the reverend at the First Community Church of the Lamb of God was always harping on it, and how the evils of mankind were ruining the environment. Sister Lucy bought all that crap, but Lexie, the sinner, didn't. She believed the environment had various cycles. The current cycle happened to be dry and hot. It was that simple. *Amen.*

Lexie looked at the children again. Several of them were bouncing back and forth between the homes, chattering and having a bang-up time. She wondered if their mothers realized how lucky they were. That's what she'd always wanted. Loving husband, little house, white picket fence, two-point-five kids, a dog, a cat, and goldfish, maybe even a gerbil or a parakeet.

Never mind Women's Lib. She hadn't really planned herself a career, despite her parents urging, so when good looking Dan Lightfoot came along, promising her the world, her born-yesterday self had fallen right into his snare. They'd been high school sweethearts, prom king and queen.

Then she'd gone and gotten herself knocked up. Well, Dan had helped.

"No problem," Dan had said when she told him she was in the family way. At the time, his comment made her love him more because her delicate condition hadn't even ruffled a hair on his fair head. Somehow, with the world against them, they'd graduated high school and took off for California with their tiny baby. Dan managed to make it through funeral home school with student loans and Lexie working evening waitress jobs.

Unfortunately, any time something went wrong, even if there was real trouble looming on the horizon, Dan's trademark comment was always, "No problem." After a while, it became annoying, but Lexie learned to live with it.

Once Dan started his own business, Lexie became a stay-at-home mom. *Stay-at-home-mom*. What an oxymoron created by some dork. Lexie and Eva lived more in the car than they did at home. There were play dates and nursery school to shuttle back and forth to, then PTA meetings and school plays, flute recitals, room-mother commitments and pee wee soccer games, gymnastic and swim meets, and finally high school football games where Eva cheerleaded her little heart out wearing micro-mini skirts and school sweaters.

While Lexie concentrated on taking care of Eva, Dan worked late, sometimes into the wee hours of the morning. Lexie never complained, believing Dan had been building his business and their future. *Hah.* Sixteen years went by before Lexie, either clueless or in denial, realized Dan's 'duties' now included more than simply directing funerals.

Come to find out, Dan, The Undertaker, was also providing *too* much comfort for bereaved widows. Above and beyond the call of duty, to be exact. Lexie's storybook marriage crumbled; in fact, it had never really existed, except in her mind. Lexie filed for divorce and came back home to Moose Creek Junction.

So much for the little cottage and white picket fence thing. Eva, being of age to choose which parent she wanted to live with, left with Lexie, though she'd grumped about being uprooted in her sophomore year of high school. Dan had been so involved with the new love in his life, he'd barely noticed when his daughter moved away and barely kept in touch with her.

Coming back home after all this time was strange, to say the least. But like small towns, most things remained the same in Moose Creek Junction. People had gotten older, old timers had passed away. Yet they were subtle changes and it was like the same town and the same people Lexie had known years ago. Only thing was, she looked at life through the eyes of a former carpool and cookie mom, instead of a kid with scraped up knees and a runny nose.

Lexie had been so absorbed in her thoughts that, with a start, she realized she had arrived at the park. Pulling into a shade-dappled parking spot, she turned off the engine of her old truck. It shivered, made a popping noise and went silent. Sliding out, she stuffed the keys in her pocket.

Her gaze caught a cluster of people gathered near an ancient steam locomotive memorial. This was the place. *Why do I let Lucy get me into this stuff, anyway?*

As she scuffed through fallen leaves toward the pavilion, she scanned the crowd for this Henry guy. Men stood everywhere on the burned-out lawn, tossing horseshoes or flipping burgers at smoking grills. Which one was Sister Lucy's next victim? Lexie shook her head and plodded on.

Mountainous piles of potato chip bags were mounded at one end of the two picnic tables pushed together. Crusty brown rolls, salads, brownies, and other assorted goodies also decorated the red wooden planks. When Lexie spotted the ice chests full of sodas, she smacked her cottony tongue against the top of her mouth and made a beeline over to the drinks. Popping the lid of a diet lemon-lime, she took a cooling sip and scanned the crowd for her matchmaking sister.

Ah, there she was. Standing over by a group of women and gabbing. More like gossiping, Lexie figured. Lucy couldn't stand in a group of hens and not talk about the latest and greatest juicy tidbits. Bless her, she had her finger on the pulse of the town's latest happenings, such as whose bed whose boots were currently under. And that was putting it nicely.

A fly decided to dive-bomb Lexie's face and she brushed it away as she walked toward Lucy. How annoying. She could attract flies, but decent men ran from her like they had hot coals in their jockey shorts.

Whatever. She did not need a man in her life. That was the whole point behind why she did not need to be here today meeting Henry what's-his-name. As she drew closer to Lucy, the women's cackling voices drifted on the air.

"Hanna's Kincaid's baby sure doesn't look like his daddy, especially the older he gets," one of the women said, getting nods from everyone in the group.

"That's right," Lucy agreed. "Why, that child has jet-black hair. Bob is almost albino blond and Hanna's hair is not much darker. I'd say maybe the milkman's been delivering more than milk—"

Lexie cleared her throat, ignoring her devout churchwoman, gossip-mongering sister's last comment. "Hey, Luce. What's up?"

Lucy whirled toward her sister, brown eyes snapping. "You're late." Today she wore another floral printed dress, support hose just like Mom used to wear and her sturdy brown shoes. Her brown hair had been twisted into a perfect bun with a hairnet. This was Sister Lucy's usual uniform.

Lexie sighed. "My dishwasher went on the fritz and I had to do some extra clean-up. You know I wouldn't dream of missing out on the excitement of a heifer check."

Lucy glared at her.

"What's a heifer check?" One of the women asked. Her intricate beehive hairdo, shot through with glittery barrettes and hairpins, glistened in the sun.

Lexie blinked. Man, that beehive hairdo would be a very cool place for magpies to nest.

"Nothing to concern yourself about, Adeline," Lucy muttered. "It's just a private joke between sisters." Gripping Lexie's elbow, Lucy steered her away from the gossip circle.

"You are such an ingrate," Lucy complained to Lexie. "Here I am, trying my hardest to bring some sunshine back into your life, and you don't act even halfway appreciative."

Sunshine? Lexie didn't say anything until they stopped near a swingset resting in a sandpit. Annoyed didn't begin to explain the emotion she felt. But there was no sense in starting any arguments.

"I don't mean to come off as a sourpuss," she said. "I've just been burned in the men-department. It's a sore spot with me."

"It'll get better, dear," Lucy soothed. "Just give it time."

"Really, I'm tired of dealing with relationships. I think in my next life I'll come back as a caterpillar. Their lives are short, sweet, and to the point. They don't suffer like humans. And I really don't think they get all hung up about sex—"

"Really, Lexie! You're too much sometimes. Mom wouldn't like you talking about living other incarnations. It's not Christian and it's not civil."

"Well, neither is dating, sis. Dating is murder."

"For Pete's sake, there you go again being all melodramatic on me." Lucy rolled her eyes. "You're only going to meet Henry today. It may or may not go any further from there."

"Let's hope it doesn't." Lexie took another sip of her soda and looked around. "OK, so where's this Greek god you've been raving about?"

"Let's see." Lucy shaded her eyes, and scanned the crowd. "Ah, there he is. Over by the horseshoe pit wearing the green shirt. Let's go say hello."

Lexie looked for the green shirt, blinking hard when she found it. The man she saw was a true god. Tall and definitely good-looking, and probably near her age, his chest was broad and muscled and he had a chiseled, athletic build. *He'll probably think he's too good for me.* She suddenly felt chunky and unattractive in her old jeans and T-shirt.

Why hadn't she dressed a little nicer like Lucy was always telling her to? She could have combed her hair out instead of leaving it in a ponytail. And she could have put on a little more make-up than a dab of lipstick and blush.

As they walked toward Adonis, Lexie's gaze met his and he sent her a fantastic, dimpled smile. Her knees buckled ever so slightly. *Maybe Lucy finally hit on a good thing.* Lexie stopped walking once they reached Adonis, but Lucy tightened her grip on her elbow and pushed her forward.

Confused, Lexie said, "Wasn't that Henry back there by the horseshoes?"

Lucy looked over her shoulder at him. "Oh, no. That's Kent Braxton. Helen Braxton's husband."

After nearly drooling over the man, Lexie finally noticed the gold gleaming on his left hand. *Brother*. She should have known better.

With horror, she watched as they approached another man sitting underneath a tree, gut hanging over his belt as he sucked a beer. He, too, was wearing a green polo shirt. He shoved to his feet when he noticed their approach. Lexie noted his shirt was a tad too small, showing his hairy belly button. His grin was positively slimy. Lexie's dork meter started pinging.

"I'm gonna kill you," she muttered to Lucy.

"Don't be so quick to judge, my dear. He might clean up good. And some women might consider him cute in a Panda Bear sort of way."

"More like a troll sort of way."

Lucy jabbed Lexie's ribs with her bony elbow and Lexie sent one right back.

Once they were up close to Henry, Lexie's nostrils flared with the smell of . . . something. Something strange. And it wasn't grilled hamburgers, either. Maybe one of the toddlers running around needed their diapers changed. That had to be it.

He gave that icky grin again. "Hi, ladies."

Lucy smiled. "I'd like you to meet my sister,

Lexie. Lexie, this is Henry Whitehead."

Lucy released her death grip on Lexie so she could shake hands with Sister Lucy's latest victim. *Did I shave my legs for this?*

Whitehead's gaze lowered and he stared directly at Lexie's cleavage.

Her skin crawled with disgust. But what else could she really expect from a caveman?

"You two will have to excuse me a minute," Lucy interjected. "I've got to make sure we're not running out of soda." With a wink at Lexie, she disappeared.

Lexie wanted to sprint after her. Run away. Fast. But Lucy would kill her if she did.

"That sister of yours has got a heart of gold," Henry said. "Did you know she started the annual Christmas program down at the women and children's shelter?"

Lexie nodded, wondering if Lucy considered her sister a charitable endeavor. "Uh, so what do you do? For a living, I mean."

Whitehead puffed himself up, making Lexie think of one of those goldfish with the wobbly bubbles on their gills.

"I'm a sanitation engineer."

"Ah, I see." *A janitor.*

That horrible odor wafted Lexie's way again and her nose twitched. Looking for the possible source, she noticed a heavyset brunette staring daggers at them. Lexie nodded in the brunette's direction and asked Whitehead if he knew her.

"Ah, yeah. Shit. That's my ex-wife, Violet." He ran his hand through his greasy black hair. "I swear she's stalking me. It's creepy."

Ignoring Whitehead's she-devil of an ex-wife, Lexie took off her bracelet and fiddled with it. She'd purchased the turquoise and silver bauble several years ago at a southwestern jewelry shop, right after she'd found out about Dan and Davina. It cost over two hundred dollars and Lexie would never have considered buying something so expensive. But under the circumstances, she'd decided to splurge.

Lexie accidentally dropped the bracelet and it rolled toward a tree.

"I'll fetch that for you, honey," Whitehead said.

Honey?

As he bent over and picked up the bracelet, giving a loud grunt, Lexie caught a birds-eye view of his plumber's crack. And also another major whiff of the bad smell. *Gross.* Now Lexie knew where the odor had been coming from. She'd obviously been standing downwind from the definitely *not* cute-butted Henry Whitehead.

"Here you go." Whitehead handed over the bracelet. "It's very pretty. Where'd you get it?"

Lexie quickly gathered her thoughts, which had been out circling Jupiter. Wondering how a grown man could smell so foul, she slid the turquoise and silver southwestern band back on her wrist. "I got it on a trip to Mexico with my ex-husband about a million years ago."

He chuckled. "I like you. And you're not large at all. Not like I expected you'd be."

"Large?"

"You know . . . um, heavyset."

"You mean *fat*." The jerk-alert started clanging like a fire truck bell in Lexie's head.

Whitehead shrugged. "What's a guy to think? The way your sister talked, it sounded like you were hard-up for a date, and I just figured . . . well, *you know*."

"No, I don't know."

"No harm, no foul." He cocked his head to the side. Hey, I'm meeting some buddies and their dates at the carnival tonight. Wanna be my arm candy?"

"I'm busy," she responded in a pleasantly icy tone.

"Doing what?"

Think fast. "Uh, I promised my daughter I'd take her out to dinner."

"Can't you take her out another time?"

Lexie scrambled for something that sounded good. "Well, tonight's the . . . uh . . . anniversary of when . . . uh, Eva lost her first tooth."

"Wow, you still remember that?" His dark bushy brows, which were actually one large one, shot up.

"Yes. She's an only child, see, and we take the time to celebrate a lot of little 'firsts' together." Lexie's mouth was really dry, like a tumbleweed, and she took another sip of soda.

"I'm lucky if I even see my kids these days," Whitehead said. "And they only call when they want money."

Lucy sauntered up, an expectant look on her face. "So, how are you two getting along?"

"We've been having a nice little chat," Lexie said. "But I need to get back to the café." Lexie began to back away, intending to make like a ghost and disappear. *Fast.*

Lucy quickly death-gripped Lexie's shoulders. "Don't you two have big plans for tonight?"

An ambush! By her very own sister.

"Lexie says she's busy. It's the anniversary of when her daughter lost her first tooth and they're going out for a celebration dinner."

"Really?" Lucy fixed Lexie with her famous, *I'm the big sister and I know you're up to something,* look.

"*Really,*" Lexie repeated emphatically, praying Lucy wouldn't blow her excuse out of the water.

"It must have slipped your mind, Lexie." Lucy grinned. "The anniversary is *next* Friday. Remember?"

Lexie glared at her.

Whitehead grinned ickily at Lexie. "That means we're on for tonight."

Her heart flopped to the ground and rolled around like a tennis ball in a metal garbage can lid. *Why me, God?*

"Excuse me for a moment, ladies." Taking the dirty diaper smell with him, Whitehead trotted toward the restroom.

Lexie punched Lucy's arm. "Lying is a sin, you know."

"At least I can confess to Reverend Lincolnway. You, however, must live with your sin."

"Oh, brother."

"Henry's a nice man, Lexie. I'm sure you two will have an enjoyable evening."

"Depends on your interpretation of 'enjoyable'."

"Give him a chance before you draw and quarter him."

"Whatever. But I refuse to go out on any more charity-case dates for you."

You'll feel differently in the morning." Lucy gave a Cheshire cat smile, as though she'd just made the match of the century.

Lexie watched as Whitehead trotted back out of the restroom, hairy belly jiggling like Jell-O. "Somehow I doubt it."

Lexie practically flew back to the café. Eva had handled the busy lunch hour, so the afternoon consisted of stragglers and the time dragged. Thinking of the night ahead, Lexie's nerves tangled like loose rope in the Wyoming wind. Why, oh why had she agreed to that stupid date with Whitehead? She would much rather have her big toe removed. Make that both big toes.

She had half a mind not to even show up, but she knew once Lucy caught wind of her playing hooky she'd be in big trouble. No, it would be best for her to do her duty and go out with him this one time, then go underground. No more blind dates, no charity-case Casanovas. *Nada*.

Life was too damn short for this kind of misery.

Since it was so quiet at the café, Lexie left Eva in charge and headed to her back yard for some garden therapy. She retrieved her gloves from the shed and stared at her dry, dusty attempt to grow anything this past summer. With the water rationing restrictions, her garden was a pitiful version of its former glory and her sad harvest had hardly been worth the effort.

Oh, well. Chopping thistles and dandelions always calmed the soul. Forty-five minutes later, Lexie had half the garden weeded and she did feel a little better. After uprooting a basket of underdeveloped carrots for tomorrow's soup-of-the-day, she slipped back inside and went upstairs to shower.

She changed into a fresh pair of jeans, a blue short-sleeved summer sweater and went downstairs.

Eva, seated at the order counter, looked up from a zoology book she'd been reading. "Mom. Aren't you going to be late for your date?"

"Probably. And if I'm lucky, maybe he'll leave for the carnival without me. Too bad, so sad." Lexie snagged her purse from a closet.

"Is it all right if I use your computer while you're out?" Eva's brows arched questioningly. "I have to write a paper for history."

Lexie winced. She preferred Eva use the computer she'd sent her with to college. But that was forty miles away in her dorm room. What could she say? "Sure, go ahead. Do me a favor and don't fiddle with any of the settings. OK?"

"Sure, Mom. See ya later."

Lexie walked out into the backyard where long purple shadows stretched across the ground. She glanced at the weeded half of her garden, deciding she'd do the other half on Sunday when the café was closed. Making her way down a set of ancient, crumbling concrete steps, which she decided to get fixed soon before someone fell and broke their neck, she entered her old garage.

It had been built long after the Victorian had been erected—probably around the 1940s. It was dark and musty and in ramshackle condition, but it did the job of keeping Lexie's truck and Eva's little car out of the wind, rain, and snow.

As her truck chugged along the dusty streets, she resigned herself to suffering in silence through the evening. She'd insisted upon picking Whitehead up at his place. That way, she would be in control and had a means of escape if things got ugly.

Before long, she came upon the address of his man-cave, an old, pumpkin-colored house with scruffy, overgrown bushes. She had parked and was walking toward it when suddenly a dog leapt from behind a stand of tall, dry weeds, hackles raised and teeth bared. It was a big mutt with gray shaggy hair and a humped back. He made *Cujo* look well mannered.

"Nice, doggie," Lexie soothed as she backed up. Unfortunately, the more she inched away, the more the dog snarled at her.

"Back off, Tiny," a whiny male voice called out.

Lexie noticed Whitehead at the door, a piece of meat in his hairy hand. Tossing it to the mutt, Tiny snagged it between his fangs and scarfed it down with a gulp. Then he stared at Lexie again with beady black eyes.

"*Tiny?*" Lexie blinked in surprise.

Whitehead galumphed down the front porch steps. "Yeah, he keeps away the boogie man and my battle ax ex-wife. Unfortunately, he keeps getting loose." Whitehead grabbed Tiny's collar and led him toward the bushes, hooking the canine up to a thick chain.

Lexie released the breath she didn't realize she'd been holding.

Whitehead grabbed her arm. "Let's get a move on. Everyone's waiting for us."

At least he'd changed into a button-down jeans shirt that covered his hairy, Jell-O belly. He must have taken a bath, too, probably in Old Spice cologne. And while Whitehead's cologne scent was nearly overwhelming, almost enough to peel the socks right off your feet, it was definitely preferable to his former *eau-de-dirty-diaper* scent.

The carnival was its usual self. This was the first time since she'd come home Lexie had attended the cheesy affair that an even cheesier company brought to Moose Creek Junction every year. It offered the same glittery, noisy activities she remembered. Along with the same smells of corn dogs, greasy sausage, and powered sugar covered funnel cakes. Despite its tackiness, Lexie totally loved it. It was just too bad she was with Captain Caveman, the nickname she'd bestowed on Whitehead.

She managed to avoid going on any rides with him until he finally dragged her onto the Ferris wheel. She suffered through his fake yawn and ancient slither-arm-around-the-shoulders-trick by leaning forward and coughing, thus leaving his hairy paw to embrace nothing but air. When the ride finally ended, Lexie said she needed to powder her nose and vamoosed.

Managing to avoid Captain Caveman and his motley crew for the next hour, she snuck into the house of fun and hooted at her reflection in the freaky mirrors, hopped on a car that took her on a hilarious ride through spook alley, and finally wound up at Madame Evangeline's fortune telling booth.

The elderly gypsy woman, wearing a bright scarf and colorful long skirts, took Lexie inside her darkened tent lit only with candles and lanterns. She sat on a chair covered with silken, tasseled pillows and placed her hands palm down on the table in front of her. She waved her hand toward a chair on the other side of the table, indicating Lexie should sit.

Madame Evangeline closed her eyes and inhaled deeply of the patchouli incense curling around the room in snakes of smoke. She tossed her long black and gray hair over her shoulder and her golden earrings tinkled. Her gaze bore into Lexie like a drill.

"I have told your fortune before, have I not, my child?"

"A long time ago." A shiver crawled up Lexie's spine. Lucy would think she was a complete fool for coming here and listening to this stuff, along with being sacriligious. But what the heck. It was fun.

"I knew it was so," the gypsy woman exclaimed, black eyes flashing. "Back when you were but a child and untainted by the world's cruelties." She rested her hands on the crystal ball, long red nails like specks of blood on the glowing surface.

"What do you wish to know about your life, child?" she asked Lexie.

Lexie was basically just killing time to avoid Captain Caveman and gang, so it didn't really matter to her. "Whatever you see in the future for me."

Madame Evangeline closed her eyes. "I see danger. Danger that lurks in the darkness. Someone from your past seeks to destroy you with his or her jealousy. Be mindful of those around you lest you befall their snare. Beware the Greek."

Wait a minute—back up the train.

Lexie figured Madame E. would give her the standard line about marrying someone tall dark and handsome and having six kids. Not that she was in danger. That wasn't what she wanted to hear.

She pushed money toward the gypsy woman

and stood. "Thank you."

"Please, I'm not finished."

"Yes, you are." Lexie blew out of the tent like she'd been stung by a bee. Who believed that fortune teller crap, anyway?

Lexie ferreted out Whitehead at Mort's duck-shoot and dragged him home, despite his gripes that he wasn't ready to leave. She took him back to his pumpkin-colored house and deposited him on the front porch.

"Come inside for a while," he urged.

"No."

"Ah, come on. Just for a minute so we can talk."

Lexie finally relented and went inside with him.

Without warning, he leaned forward and embraced her in a hairy bear hug, then shoved his wet, bumpy tongue in her ear. Lexie struggled in his straitjacket embrace.

"I bet you probably haven't had any nookie in a long time, Lexie. I bet you're hot. And I can go at it all night—

"Cut it out, Whitehead." Lexie continued to squirm. "I do not want to make out with you."

But before she could make her escape, he planted a warm, slobbery kiss on her mouth. With a cry of disgust, she finally broke loose and pushed outside. She flew down the porch steps, wiping her lips on the back of her hand.

Whitehead followed her. "Does this mean you won't go out with me again?" Disappointment etched his face as Tiny started to growl from some-where in the dark bushes.

"You got that right. Go find somebody else to play footsies with."

Digging her keys out of her pocket, Lexie rushed to her truck. She peeled out, flinging tiny asphalt rocks in her wake. Rule number one of dating, she decided, was to stay in public places where men had to behave themselves. She fought back tears of frus-tration. What a hideous date. But at least it was over. Sister Lucy would pay for this humiliation.

Darkness closed around her truck like a black cloak as she drove home. Anxious to get there as quickly as possible, Lexie turned down Elm Street and stopped for a red light at the intersection. Her heart had stopped racing and she leaned over to turn up the radio to drown out her thoughts. When she sat back up, she noticed the pair of headlights in her rearview mirror. To her amazement, the headlights continued to approach, despite the red light.

She cried out when the vehicle smacked her old truck from behind and her head snapped forward, then back, like a rubber band. Her brain hammered like it had been bounced across the floor. Outraged, Lexie turned around to holler at the dark vehicle.

Amazed and still somewhat in shock, she watched as the mystery car, neat as you please, pulled out around her truck and shot through the intersection. Squinting, she tried making out the license plate. Nice try, no cigar. It was too dark and her head hurt like hell.

Butt wipes. They could have at least stopped to make sure she hadn't conked her head on the dashboard and swallowed any teeth.

The light turned green and Lexie still sat in a daze. A wicked bout of hiccoughs jolted her back to reality and she put the truck in gear and drove home. Should she call the cops? No. She really had nothing to report—no license plate, no car description.

Besides, this is what would happen if she tried to tell her brother-in-law, the sheriff. He'd sit back in his office chair, hands laced over his potbelly, chewing on a pen cap. To make it look good, Otis would nod occasionally and pretend to jot notes in dog-eared notebook. Then he would proceed to do nothing.

Hiccough. Hiccough. Lexie's hands trembled on the steering wheel, but she was really all right. And her old, dinged-up truck would live to fight another battle.

Only two more years, she told herself as she parked and went inside her house. Then she'd have Eva's car paid off and she could buy herself more reliable transportation. That wasn't so far off. She could keep her truck band-aided together till then.

"Eva, I'm home," she called wearily as she started up the stairs, her feet heavy as boulders and her knees still watery. In the small living room she walked past Eva who was plinking away on the computer. Eva didn't even look up when Lexie sighed and flung herself onto their old, overstuffed couch. Her mind reeling from the night's events, she stared like a zombie at a Venus flytrap atop Grandmother Castleton's antique fern stand.

"Back already?" Eva twirled around in the office chair, one leg crossed over the other. She stared at her mother with a perplexed expression.

"It was perfectly awful. Just like I expected." Lexie hiccoughed.

"What happened?"

"He was all over me."

"So, did he kiss you, or what?" Eva popped her gum.

"Slobbered me," *hiccough*, "is more like it. Then I went home."

Eva made a time out sign with her hands. "TMI, Mom. Too much info."

"You asked."

"OK, so he doesn't turn you on. But you're obviously a hottie. Consider yourself lucky that at your age you've still got it."

"At *my age?*" Lexie stared at her daughter.

Eva shrugged. "I just mean that you should be grateful. If you'd been a real hag or something he wouldn't have asked you out."

"Wow. I'm comforted." *Hiccough, hiccough.* Lexie stretched her legs out on the wicker coffee table. She sucked in her breath and held it, then forced burps. OK, so she sounded like a garbage disposal with a paperclip in crosswise, but this was a guaranteed hiccough killer.

"You know," Eva popped her gum again. "I

heard you have to date a hundred men before you find the right one."

Lexie stopped burping. She suddenly did not feel well. "A hundred men? I'd rather have a hundred root canals, thank you."

Lexie tossed and turned all night. By morning she was tired and stiff. When 5 a.m. rolled around, sleep was not an option. She decided the garden therapy must have taken its toll and she made mental note not to go at it with such gusto on Sunday. She did, after all, need to take into account her advanced years, as her daughter so kindly reminded her.

"Good morning, sweetie," she said to Eva as she shuffled into the kitchen, surprised to see her at the kitchen table hitting the books at this unholy hour of the morning. She headed for the coffee pot that was set on a timer. A rich hazelnut brew called to her, the aroma tickling her nostrils. "You're up way early."

"Morning," Eva mumbled around a mouthful of fruit loops, then swallowed. "I need to get ten chapters of this history book read by Monday or I'm dead."

"We wouldn't have been *procrastinating*, would we?"

"I got busy." Eva glared at her book.

Lexie imagined the busy part had something to do with dorm parties and such. "You need anything for your room? Junk food? Sheets? Stuffed animals? Voodoo dolls?"

"Nope."

Ahhh. She hadn't even caught the joke. "How about your roommate? Is she working out?"

Eva shrugged, her gaze plastered to the textbook. "OK, I guess."

Lexie poured herself a cup of coffee. Leaning back against the counter sipping the hot brew, she began to go over her to-do list for the day. Then it hit her.

I left my purse at Captain Caveman's place.

Crapola, she'd completely forgotten about it. Growling with frustration, she told Eva she'd be right back, ran upstairs and dressed, then drove over to his pumpkin-colored cottage.

As she approached, she wondered why Tiny wasn't barking his fat head off. She checked the bushes and spotted the dogless chain on the ground. He must have run off again. She knocked on the ripped screen door. No answer. *Ru roh.* Whitehead was probably still in bed. He'd think she was nuts for coming over so early. Oh, well, too bad. She really needed her purse.

The front door was ajar. Stepping inside, Lexie spotted her purse sitting beside the coffee table. *All righty then. I'll just slip in real quiet like, get what I need and beeline outta here.*

Feeling like a thief and sweating like a pig, Lexie tiptoed inside and snatched her purse. But as she turned to go, her eye caught something in the kitchen that froze her legs in place like pretzels in plaster castings. Her heart flip-flopped and started to play the tango.

In the middle of the floor, Whitehead lay in a pool of blood.

CHAPTER 2

LEXIE REELED BACKWARD AND LEANED AGAINST the wall for support. Unwelcome memories of her last date with Hugh Glenwood flashed through her mind. One minute they'd been laughing in the crisp winter woods, his snowmobile slicing through the trails while she rode on the seat behind, clinging to his waist. The next, he'd fallen sideways, tipping them over onto the cold ground.

She remembered screaming, then blood on snow . . . *crimson soaking into white.*

With a sudden jolt, she was back in the present. A small voice told her to do something, call someone for help. An ambulance?

Lexie had no medical training, but from the looks of Whitehead, he was no doubt beyond any paramedics' ability to resuscitate. His hairy skin had a bluish tinge and his lips were set in a silent scream. The front of his shirt was ripped and covered in blood.

Unable to stomach the sight any longer, she turned away, fumbling for her cell phone in a jacket pocket. She dialed 911 with trembling fingers. Struggling with a bout of hiccoughs, she told the operator how she had found Whitehead and gave her the address.

"I don't . . . I don't think he's alive," she told the operator in a thin, trembling voice, her hiccoughs escalating.

The operator promised to dispatch an ambulance from Westonville Medical Center and told Lexie to stay at the scene.

Lexie did not want to look at him again, so she stumbled into the front room and sat stiffly on his black vinyl couch. She wrapped her arms around herself to try and quell her shaking, then her nose began to twitch. Lord, it smelled in here. Henry had an even stranger odor than before. But of course, that was to be expected. He had an excuse to smell now.

How crude. Lexie mentally kicked herself for having such wicked thoughts of the recently departed.

Lexie managed to dial one more number on her cell phone. Moose Creek Junction's sheriff, Otis Parnell. He was pretty incompetent, but he was Lucy's husband, and he wore the badge. Also, he was the only law around for miles.

"Hello?" Lucy answered groggily.

Lexie hiccoughed. "Lucy?"

"Well, it's sure not the Avon lady at . . ." She must have glanced at the clock. "Six a.m.? Gracious, we're still in bed!"

"Something t-terrible has happened." Lexie hiccoughed.

"Lexie? What's wrong? You sound like a chipmunk on steroids."

"Otis needs to come over to Henry Whitehead's place immediately. I think . . . I think somebody murdered him."

"Lord have mercy." Silence thrummed on the cell for a second and Lexie heard her sister say something to her husband, then she heard Otis's corresponding grunt and a string of gruff expletives. "He'll be right over," Lucy told her.

Lexie flipped the cell phone closed and slipped it back into her pocket, numbness seeping into her limbs. Even her toes had gone numb and her mind reeled with disbelief.

Who killed Henry Whitehead? And why?

The man might have been a creep, but he didn't deserve to be murdered. Lexie's hiccoughing got worse and she held her breath. It seemed inappropriate to do the burping backward thing with a corpse in the next room, so she held off.

As Eva would say, this whole thing was *so* not good. Lexie was probably the last person who had seen Whitehead alive, besides his murderer, and Otis would rip her apart. Just thinking about it made hiccoughs ricochet through her diaphragm with a vengeance.

Suddenly, there was noise on the front porch and Lexie nearly jumped through the roof.

"Get your lazy butt up and answer the door, Henry," a female voice called through the open screen. "I thought you was gonna pick up the kids this morning!"

Whitehead's ex-wife, Violet, Lexie thought. Maybe she'd off'd him last night after Lexie left. She seemed resentful enough toward him, so she had the motive. But why would she show up on his doorstep this morning after she'd murdered him last night? Maybe to throw off suspicion? And what would she do if she found Lexie here?

Stop being paranoid, Lexie told herself, re-membering Lucy always complained she had a wild imagination. What did she know? She was no Sher-lock Holmes.

She walked toward the screen door, immediately recognizing Violet standing on the porch in a gray sweat suit and running shoes. The heavyset bru-nette gave her a she-devil look, just like the one at the picnic. She was indeed creepy, as Whitehead had said.

"What the hell's goin' on? Where's Henry?" Violet scowled. "Oh, I recognize you. You're one of Henry's new floozies, ain't ya?"

Lexie's face flushed with embarrassment. "This isn't what it seems."

"Geez, I knew Henry was a sleaze ball, but couldn't he at least lay off the broads long enough to pick up his kids like he promised? *Crud*. He was supposed to be over to my place a half hour ago."

Violet heaved herself inside.

"I don't think you should be here," Lexie said. "There's been an . . . incident."

"Sure, and I'm the queen of Sheba." Violet shoved her hands on her hips. "Hey, Henry Horatio Whitehead," she hollered. "Get your butt-skee out here." She smirked at Lexie. "He hates when I call him that."

Lexie noticed Violet's chipped front tooth and her dirty fingernails. As unpleasant as Violet was, and as much as she seemed to dislike her ex, Lexie still figured she would not want to see him laid out on the kitchen floor in a pool of blood. She was the mother of his children, after all.

"He can't," Lexie said.

"Can't what?"

"Come out here. Like I said, there's been an incident."

"Oh, I got it." Violet tossed her dark head. "You two had a hot and heavy night so he's sacked out cold in bed. Far be it from me to disturb his lordship. So do me a favor, toots, and go get the jerk for me."

The wail of a siren sliced through the air and Lexie decided there was no point in trying to spare Violet Whitehead any longer. She pointed into the kitchen. "Go get him yourself. He's in there."

Swearing like a sailor, Violet stomped into the kitchen, complaining about the filthy stench. Suddenly she fell silent, then stumbled back into the front room, her face drained of all color. "I knew he was a son of a bitch, but why'd you go and kill him?"

Lexie hugged herself and shivered. "I didn't. I found him like that."

"God damn." Violet shook her shaggy dark head. "I always told the butthead he'd better watch out where he poked his pecker or some pissed-off husband was going to fix his bucket." She blinked several times, made a gagging sound, and ran outside.

Lexie heard her dousing the bushes with her breakfast.

After what seemed like a million years, the ambulance from Westonville arrived and the paramedics hustled over to have a look at Whitehead. As they hovered above him with their medical equipment, Lexie slipped outside. The sunlight was a welcome relief and she breathed deeply of the fresh morning air.

She sidestepped past poor Violet, who was sitting on the edge of a brick planter chewing her nails and crying, and went out to sit in her truck. Swallowing over and over, she finally banished her hiccoughs. Then she glanced around, noticing that several of the neighbors were up and staring out their windows or standing on their front porches rubbernecking.

Lexie recognized Axel and Janie Dimspoon, who must have been at least in their eighties, exit the house next door. Dressed in thick terry bathrobes and slippers, they came up Whitehead's drive and approached Lexie with questioning glances.

"What happened?" Axel queried.

"An incident," Lexie said. "You'll read all about it in the paper." When they continued to look at her with prying glances, she added, "I'm sorry, I don't know what else to tell you." She watched as they shuffled back into their homes, shaking their heads and whispering to themselves.

The community had one small newspaper called the Moose Creek Junction Chronicle. Lexie figured it wouldn't be long before one of their reporters caught wind of trouble and came around snooping. And what a story this would be—murder in Moose Creek Junction. The second one in just a little over a year.

Otis' sheriff's car finally appeared, lights flashing and siren screaming, slamming over the curb and coming to a halt on Whitehead's lawn.

Lexie rolled her eyes. That man just had to make a dramatic entrance. He was so ridiculously proud of his position as town sheriff, Lexie wondered if he wore his tin star in bed. Probably rolled over on it and cut himself all the time. Maybe that's why he was so crabby.

Otis heaved himself from the car and slapped his hat on his head. His pig-like jowels working furiously as he barked at his skinny deputy, Cleve Harris, to call for back up from Westonville. Westonville was about fifty miles away, but it was much larger than Moose Creek Junction and had a decent sized police force that was a bit more accustomed to the occasional murder.

Otis scowled at Whitehead's house, then over at Lexie and pointed accusingly at her. "You," he ordered. "Don't go anywhere." He disappeared inside Whitehead's house with Harris trotting obediently after him.

The police backup from Westonville arrived a short while after that and hurried into Whitehead's house as well. Lexie tried not to think of what was going on. It was unreal. Like a television program or a movie.

Lucy pulled up in her blue Ford sedan and got out. She shuffled quickly toward Lexie in her sensible brown loafers, her print housedress flapping. "Are you all right, baby sister?"

"Of course. I find bodies all the time in my line of work."

"Don't joke. This is not funny," Lucy scolded.

"I don't think it's one bit funny, either. But this is making me crazy. Do you realize Whitehead is the second man you've introduced me to who has wound up dead?

"Oh, my." Lucy's face flushed and she began to fan herself madly. "Hot flash, you know. Happens when I'm upset."

"I thought it was just menopause."

Lucy pulled out a hankie and mopped her perspiration-dotted brow. "I am *not* going through menopause. I have got years before that happens.

Many, many years."

"Right," Lexie said.

"What happened? Did you and Henry have a fight? Did he make advances toward you?"

"He tried."

"Well for Pete's sake! You didn't have to off him."

"Lucy, I did not kill Whitehead. I forgot my purse last night after I left him at his house. This morning I came by to pick up the darn thing and I found Whitehead dead."

"This is not good, baby sister."

"No kidding it's not good. Do you think Otis is capable of handling another murder investigation?"

"I don't know. He got pretty upset when Hugh was shot."

"Well, if he botches this investigation, you might be visiting me at the women's correctional center down in Chamber City. Do you think you'll still be able to fix me up on dates then?"

A clanking noise drew their attention and Lexie saw the paramedics rolling Whitehead's sheeted body over to the ambulance. They hefted him up, shut the double doors and drove away.

As other uniformed officers looped yellow crime scene tape around Whitehead's house, Otis and another man Lexie didn't recognize walked toward her truck.

Otis introduced his wife and sister-in-law to Detective Gabriel Stevenson. He'd recently moved to Westonville and had just started work with their police department.

A solidly built male, Stevenson wore jeans, a worn black leather jacket, and a black Stetson. He had a neatly trimmed brown mustache and beard sprinkled with gray and a healthy tan complexion. The badge attached to his belt had a frightening legal glint to it.

Lexie and Lucy told Stevenson, "Hello," at the same time.

"Pleased to make your acquaintance, ladies," Stevenson responded in a deep, rumbling voice as he shook their hands. He removed his hat and ran his hair through wavy brown hair shot with gray.

"How well did you know Henry Whitehead?" Stevenson asked Lexie, his hazel eyes piercing.

"I only met him yesterday. We went to the carnival with some friends of his last night." Lexie couldn't help but check Stevenson out a little closer, noting that he was pleasant to the eye. There weren't many men as good looking as him in Moose Creek Junction. His looks made him a tad intriguing, although still frightening. He was the law, after all.

Stevenson scribbled in a notebook, then sized Lexie up again, his gaze questioning. "What time did you return?"

"I dropped him off here at about 9 p.m. Then I went home."

"Can anyone vouch for your story?"

Lexie nodded. "My daughter, Eva."

He jotted down something else, and Lexie

noticed Otis had produced a notebook and took notes every time Stevenson did. *Monkey see, monkey do.*

"Do you know of any enemies Whitehead might have had?" Stevenson leaned against Lexie's truck and crossed his long legs. "Someone who would be capable of murder?"

"Again, I barely knew the man. He did say his ex-wife, Violet, that's her over there sitting on the planter, was creepy. And then something weird happened on my way home from his house."

"Yes?"

"This car rear-ended me at the stop light, then took off."

"Why didn't you call me and report that?" Otis wet the tip of his pencil and kept it poised above his note pad. His jowls worked up and down as he chewed on what Lexie knew was most likely tobacco.

"I didn't have a license plate or a vehicle description. It was too dark."

Stevenson cleared his throat. "Ms. Lightfoot, I understand you're divorced. You and your ex-husband having any trouble?"

"Dan lives in California. I haven't heard from him in six months, and neither has my daughter."

"Is he a violent man?" Stevenson's brows raised. "Does he have a temper?"

Lexie went cold. "What are you implying?"

The detective shrugged. "Could be he's the jealous type. I have to ask."

"He's remarried . . ." Lexie trailed off, as if that answered Stevenson's question. There was a dark part of her life with Dan she chose to keep dead and buried. She didn't want to talk about it, especially not with the inquisitive and handsome detective from Westonville.

Stevenson wrote more notes and so did Otis.

"Stay around town, Ms. Lightfoot," Stevenson warned. "I don't really consider you a serious suspect. But I may need to question you again."

"Oh, I'll cancel my flight to London right away," Lexie returned.

Stevenson gave her a dark gaze. He obviously did not appreciate her attempt at humor.

"Let me know what the boys in your crime lab have to say, Stevenson." Otis puffed out his beefy chest, making his sheriff's badge glint in the sun. "I'll keep my eyes and ears open for any local leads."

"You do that." Stevenson took long strides over to Violet Whitehead, who was still weeping and blowing her nose in a crumbling tissue, and began talking to her.

"Whooeeee." Otis rubbed his fleshy neck. "Leave it to my sister-in-law to find trouble wherever she goes. This is the second man who's died after dating you. Any man in his right mind would think twice about sporting you around."

"Believe me, I never wanted this," Lexie muttered. "To heck with my purse. I should have stayed home this morning."

"We'd still need to question you, Lex," Otis said. "You were the last person who saw Henry White-head alive."

Lexie shook her head. "Lucky me."

"You gals can head home now." Otis pointed a pudgy finger at Lexie. "And you, stay the hell away from those hack reporters. Don't say a damn thing. Got it?"

Lexie nodded.

Once Otis had stomped over to join Stevenson in questioning Violet, Lucy released a giant breath. "Thank goodness. He wasn't as angry as I thought he would be."

"I'm sorry I spoiled his Sunday funnies."

Lucy ignored Lexie's last snide comment, which was just as well.

"He's a very nice looking man," Lucy said.

Lexie frowned. "Who?"

"Detective Stevenson. I wonder if he's married? I didn't see a wedding ring."

"Lucy Parnell, don't you ever stop meddling?" Lexie folded her arms across her chest. "I am not interested in Detective Stevenson. *Capisce*? Do not try to start your matchmaking again."

"Honestly, wouldn't you like to know?"

"No, I would not. All I want to do right now is go home. I just want to be with my daughter. And no more of you fixer-upper dates. Got it?"

"You're just upset, dear. Who wouldn't be?" Lucy smiled. "I'm still going to find out if Detective

Stevenson is married."

"Knock yourself out." Lexie climbed into her truck, revved up the engine and rattled home.

After Lexie told Eva about Whitehead's murder, the rest of the day went by in a blur. Except for the phone call from Barnard Savage, a ruthless reporter for the *Moose Creek Junction Chronicle*. He hammered Lexie with questions about Henry Whitehead and her relationship with him, and then brought up Hugh. Lexie said, "No comment," several times, and finally hung up.

Savage was a pure nuisance. She could see him now wearing his press hat and rumpled suit, notebook, and ever present stubby pencil he constantly wet with the tip of his tongue. Once he was onto a good story, he was like a chronic cold you couldn't shake.

She kept thinking about poor Henry on a slab in the Westonville morgue. Café customers came and went, but her mind barely registered the fact. All she could think about was who would have wanted Whitehead dead, and why?

Then she got to thinking about the car that had rammed her truck at the light. Who had been driving? Had they run into her on purpose? And did it have anything to do with Whitehead's murder?

Then there was Dan. Last she'd heard, he was still married to Davina and living in California. He wouldn't have returned to Moose Creek Junction to cause trouble for her, would he? Was he stalking her? A shiver danced up her spine.

All of the sudden, she realized what a mess she was in. Just like Otis had said. Good Lord, what if the police decided all the evidence pointed to her as the killer? What would she do then?

Better get a good attorney.

With what, she wondered. She had a little bit of money in savings, but not enough to pay for an expensive trial lawyer to save her neck from the gallows. Then again, maybe she could pay him or her with homemade bread and free meals at *The Saucy Lucy Café* for the rest of his or her life.

Don't borrow trouble, she heard her mother's firm counsel.

Good advice, of course. No one had said anything about charging Lexie with murder. Just further questioning. That made her relax.

Still, Whitehead's untimely death bothered her. She couldn't help but feel somehow responsible, though she had no idea why. She also couldn't shake the disturbing idea of wearing orange jumpsuits and visiting with Eva and Lucy through thick Plexiglas.

That night Lexie went to bed early. Her dreams were fitful and she tossed and turned, unable to sleep a wink. By two a.m. her bed looked like a battlefield.

Dragging herself out of bed, she showered, dressed in jeans and a T-shirt, shoved her tousled hair into a headband and padded downstairs in her ragged slippers to the kitchen. Once her coffee had begun to brew, she balanced her checkbook and paid bills. That done, she swept the kitchen floor, then got down on her hands and knees and scrubbed it with a vengeance, even though it was spic and span after the dishwasher escapade.

As soon as the sun came up, she went outside and began hoeing what was left of her garden. The second she started hacking at the dusty weeds, she knew she was going to be sorry. Her poor old, nearing-middle-age muscles, were surely going to let her have it once she was done taking out her troubles on the good earth. But what the heck? Maybe she'd be in so much pain she could keep her mind off the murder.

The sun had nearly melted her into a puddle and she was breathing pretty heavily by the time Eva came out and grabbed her by the shoulder.

"Mom . . . *Mom!*"

Lexie dropped her hoe and swung around to face her daughter. "What?"

"You're going at those weeds like a madwoman."

Lexie put a hand over her heart, feeling it hammer under her palm. "I am mad. Mad at life."

"Well, you're gonna keel over if you don't knock it off."

Feeling like a mutt who'd been caught digging holes in the yard, Lexie followed her daughter over to an ancient picnic table and sat down. Eva sat across from her, poured a glass of lemonade and slid it across the splintered wood.

"Drink," she commanded.

Lexie swallowed the cool, tart liquid. "Thanks."

"What's up?" Eva asked.

"Do you realize that Henry Whitehead is the second man I've dated who has died?"

"So?" Eva shrugged. "It's not like you're the black widow or anything. It's just bad luck."

Ah, the simplicity of youth. So untainted by the real world. Then Lexie remembered Madame Evangeline's warnings. Should she give them any consideration? Was someone jealous of her? Should she beware the Greek?

What Greek?

For goodness sake. It was silly of her to even take that fortune-telling nonsense into consideration. What was wrong with her, anyway?

"Mom?"

Lexie pulled herself from her deep thoughts. "Yes, honey?"

"Have you heard from Dad lately?"

"No. Have you?"

Eva shook her head, her chocolate brown eyes, the color of her father's, sad.

"He's probably just busy," Lexie reassured her.

"With Davina and their new baby, I bet. I'm sure she's had it by now."

"No doubt. Unless she has the gestation period of an elephant."

"So I could have a little half brother or sister and

I don't even know its name."

Lexie didn't say anything. She took another drink of lemonade.

"Why didn't you and Dad have any more kids besides me?" Eva tucked strands of hair behind her ears and stared earnestly at her mother.

Memories flooded Lexie's mind and she wanted to cry out, but she held back. Should she tell Eva or not? Her heart twisted.

"Mom, are you all right?"

Lexie nodded. Eva was eighteen years old, a college student. She was mature enough to handle the truth. It was time. "You had a sister. I named her Elena."

Eva's eyes went wide. "What happened? Oh, my gosh, I don't remember any little sister."

"You wouldn't. I was only four months pregnant when I miscarried. I fell down the stairs."

"I think I remember that, but I didn't know you were going to have a baby."

"You were only four, sweetie. You wouldn't have."

"I'm sorry, Mom." Eva reached across the table and took Lexie's hand. "That must have been pretty awful."

"It was. But I didn't just fall, Eva. I was pushed."

"Pushed? Who pushed you?"

"Are you sure you want to know?"

"Of course I do! I'll go kick their butt!"

"No you won't," Lexie said quietly. "It was your father."

Eva's eyes filled with tears. "Dad? He . . . he did that to you?"

Lexie recalled Detective Stevenson's question about whether or not her ex-husband was violent. She had lied. Lied to cover her own embarrassment that she'd put up with his uncontrollable temper for so long and made excuses for his behavior. She'd been so afraid to leave. So afraid of admitting to folks back home she'd made a mistake. And so very afraid of not being able to take care of Eva on her own.

Miserable, Lexie nodded. "He was angry about something I had said or done. It's been so long now, I don't even remember."

"He was mean to you a lot, wasn't he?"

"Yes." Lexie wiped hot tears from her cheeks with the back of her hand.

"I've known all along," Eva said. "I have memories."

"Of what?" Lexie was horrified. She thought she'd hidden her bruises, her fear, and her shame from her daughter.

"His yelling. His slapping and hitting. I remember him coming at you with a gun one time, threatening to shoot you. I remember him locking you out of the house. I cried because I was afraid you'd be cold."

"Oh, sweetie. You saw all that?" Lexie came around and hugged her daughter. "I tried to spare you the truth. And you knew all along. What a fool I was."

"Most of it happened at night when you both thought I was asleep. But I'd hear you two and wake up. I'd sit at the top of the stairs and listen. Then I'd sneak back to bed and cry myself to sleep. In the morning, I'd convince myself I'd imagined everything—that it had all been a nightmare."

Lexie took Eva's head between her hands. "I'm sorry. So sorry."

"I'm sorry, too," Eva said. "I wish I could have done something."

"You were a child. What could you do? But everything's all right now."

"I love you, Mom."

"I love you too, sweetie. So very much." They hugged for a while longer.

Then, sniffling a little, Eva went back in the house to pack. After dinner, she would be driving back to college.

Lexie sat back down and stared at her lemonade. She'd finally admitted to her daughter the awful truth about Dan's temper, who had known about it all along. It was like a burden had been lifted. A little light had been shed on the dark part of her past. Still, it was a place Lexie didn't want to visit often.

She had been backed into a corner with Dan for too long, with no way out. She did not like the feeling of being helpless. Which is how she felt right now. And if someone was killing her dates on purpose, maybe they'd have it in for her. Who knows when she'd be next on the hit list?

Lexie swallowed her unease. Surely, someone in this town had answers. While she knew very little about Henry Whitehead, other people must know more. The likely person to do the questioning would be Otis, but Lexie knew he'd leave that to the big guns in Westonville.

Which left Detective Stevenson in charge of working the case. He looked capable enough, but would he ask the right things of the right people? The man had only recently moved here. What did he know about anyone? It would take him twice as long to solve the murder as someone who knew the place intimately.

There was only one person who knew this town and its citizens like the back of her hand. Lexie's good-hearted, gossip-mongering sister. She'd know all the right people to talk to and all the right questions to ask. If Moose Creek Junction had a pulse, Lucy had her finger on it.

It was clear to Lexie what she needed to do next. She pulled her cell phone from her pocket and punched in Lucy's number. When Lucy answered, Lexie said, "Lucy. I need your help."

"I don't like your tone of voice," Lucy responded.

"I'm worried."

"About what?"

"Detective Stevenson's murder investigation."

"Let him handle it, dear. I'm sure he's good at what he does. He's single, by the way. Actually, he's a widower."

"Lucy, concentrate. I do not care about Stevenson's marital status. But I do care about his investigation abilities. What if he's no good? What if he never finds out who killed Whitehead? What if he decides *I* did it?"

"That would be impossible. The Westonville coroner will determine Henry's time of death, and I'm sure it will be hours after you went home."

"Still, don't you think it's weird? This is the second man I've dated who has turned up dead. What if somebody has it in for me? What if I'm next?"

Lucy was silent a moment. "I never thought of it that way."

"Well, I have. A lot. And I want to find out who's been doing my dates in."

"Otis will kill us if we start snooping around."

"He doesn't have to know. We'll be very careful."

"Still, I don't like it one bit."

"Picture me in an orange jumpsuit with a cigarette hanging out of my mouth," Lexie said. "Or, worse yet, pushing up daisies." When Lucy did not respond, Lexie said, "Fine, no need for you to get involved. I'll just check into this myself."

"Oh, stop. You are not going to jail and you are not going to die." Lucy sighed heavily. "You win. I don't think we'll find the murderer, but we'll do some of our own investigations."

"Excellent. Where do you think we should start? You know this town better than I do. I've been away too long."

The line was silent a moment while Lucy reflected. "At Nailed to the Wall, of course," she finally said. "Women are as loose-lipped over at Carma Leone's beauty parlor as teenage girls at a sleepover. We'll both have a set of acrylic nails put on while we listen to shop-talk."

Lexie was surprised. Lucy didn't wear make-up or perfume or anything that would enhance her looks. It was against her religion. "But isn't vanity a sin?"

"Of course, dear. And I wouldn't be caught dead there under normal circumstances. But we are, after all, on a mission to try and ferret out a murderer. God will understand."

Having one's nails done was far too sinful for a Sunday-go-to meeting gal like Lucy and far too long and painstaking a process for Lexie. But since they would be suffering for a cause, Lexie figured she would bite the bullet.

CHAPTER 3

WHEN LEXIE AND LUCY WALKED INSIDE Nailed to the Wall a few days later, the shop bell tinkled on the door. The place exuded a comfortable feeling with ivy-stenciled walls, floral wreaths and posters with perfect models in perfect clothes advertising the latest hairstyles and nail polish. The floor had thick, rose-colored carpet and there were plenty of mirrors for women to observe themselves after various cosmetic procedures. Unfortunately, it reeked of polish remover and other mysterious substances.

Upon Lexie and Lucy's entrance, everyone froze in the different stations of beauty treatment—massage, pedicure, manicure, and hairdressing—and looked up. Before long, low, tittering comments flowed across the room.

"Well, well, well," Carma Leone said as she walked in their direction. "Look what the cat dragged in. The preacher man's prodigal daughters."

"Hello, Carma," Lexie said, ignoring her former classmate's condescending remarks. "Nice to see you, too. It's been a long time." Carma graduated from Moose Creek Junction High School the same year as Lexie. But her looks had changed drastically over the years—for the better.

Back in high school, Carma had been tall and plump. Her hair had been greasy; she'd worn dorky glasses and perpetually slumped her shoulders. Now the ugly duckling had blossomed into a lovely woman with dark, exotic good looks and mysterious green eyes. Her black smock and black slacks emphasized her sleek, sophisticated look. Sleek and sophisticated like Cat Woman.

Carma's dark brows arched into an expression of curiosity and she folded her arms across her chest. "What brings you ladies here today?"

"Would you have time to do our nails this morning?" Lexie held up her ragged paws.

Carma's dark brows arched. "I'm dying to know why two little brown sparrows such as yourselves would care to have your nails done."

"I suppose that's our business, Carma," Lucy said. "Unless you'd rather we drive over to Westonville and pay someone else to do them."

Carma smiled, but her right eye began to twitch a little. "Actually, I have a cancellation this morning and so does Georgia. We'd be more than happy to take care of you."

"Thank you." Lexie wished desperately she

could give Cat Woman a piece of her mind. But it would be pointless to irritate Carma. They were here to soak up the latest gossip and she wasn't about to let her personal feelings ruin the opportunity.

"Georgia will do your nails, Lucy. Go ahead and have a seat at her station and she'll be right back. She just powdering her nose." Carma pointed toward a desk adjacent to hers and Lucy lowered into a chair.

"You're looking good," Lexie said to Cat Woman as she sat at her station. "And you seem to be doing good with your business."

Carma sent her an icy, insincere smile. "I'm so sorry to hear about your parents passing away. And your divorce. You and Dan always seemed so meant for each other." Her face took on a peculiar expression.

"Things change." Lexie fought down the sting of Dan's betrayal for the millionth time.

Carma started to buff Lexie's short, ragged nails. "And your daughter? How is she doing?"

"It was rough at first, with the divorce and all. But now she's fine. She's a freshman at Westonville University this fall."

"My, my, children do grow up fast. I understand you're a business owner, too."

Lexie nodded. "Lucy and I own The Saucy Lucy Café on Willow Street."

"I suppose I need to stop by there sometime and have a bite to eat. I hear it's excellent."

Huh? Lexie had seen Carma there a few months

ago, right after Eva's high school graduation in June. Maybe she'd forgotten. Or maybe Lexie had been mistaken. Oh, well. "Sure. Any time. I make a mean huckleberry pie you might want to try."

Carma rolled her eyes. "Like I need those kinds of calories."

Lexie laughed. "We'll make it a very small piece. That won't ruin your figure. By the way, how's your grandfather doing these days?"

"He died a couple of years back."

"I'm so sorry. I always enjoyed talking with him when I was a kid. Loved his army stories."

"Pops always was a real gas. He told the same stories over and over, but my mom and I just pretended we were hearing them for the first time. I do miss him. And my mother. She's gone now, too. I don't have anyone except my aunt and . . ." She cleared her throat. "Do you have any idea what color of polish you want?"

Carma's eyes filled with tears and she looked down. She got very busy with Lexie's nails, filing them with a vengeance.

"Red, I guess." Lexie felt a stab of sadness. Even though Carma had never been very friendly toward her, it was awful to lose a loved one.

About that time the absent Georgia made an appearance, sashaying into the room, her long, flowered muumuu flowing dramatically. "Thanks for being so patient, honey," the blond woman with dark black roots said to Lucy in a heavy southern accent.

She dropped her heavyset frame into her chair and reached for Lucy's hand. "I just couldn't hold it any longer. And y'all know it ain't healthy to hold off for *too* long."

"Of course," Lucy agreed.

"Poor thing," Georgia exclaimed. "Your hands are all red and chafed and those nails . . ." She shook her head, obviously in sympathy.

"They are a little dishpan red," Lucy admitted.

"It's downright good you came when you did, honey. Why, if these nails of yours had gotten any shorter or drier, I would really have had a tussle of a time to get you set up with acrylics." Georgia pulled out a nail buffer and began to run it across the nails on Lucy's right hand, then her left.

Lexie listened to the low buzz of voices in the shop while Carma worked on her nails, then heard Lucy pipe up. "Isn't it a shame about Henry Whitehead?"

"Ain't it, though?" Georgia shook her head. "I never would have expected such shenanigans going on in Moose Creek Junction. A genuine murder. Just think of it."

"It is awful." Carma agreed. "Of course, there's no excuse for killing someone. But I understand he didn't endear himself to a lot of people."

"Yup, call a spade a spade," Georgia said. "Why, I was talking to his poor wife Violet just last week. She's my neighbor, you know. And she was telling me about some of the things that went on in that marriage of theirs. Do you know that Henry wanted them to get into *swapping?*"

A lady under a hairdryer leaned forward, a few pink rollers peeking from beneath the hood. "Did you say shopping? What's so bad about that?"

"No, *swapping.* They do it in Denver and a lot of big cities like that. It's where husbands and wives go to parties with each other. They size each other up as sexual partners. Then the spouses agree to trade with each other for a night of . . . well, you can only imagine."

Lucy went white.

"Why, I think that's totally *Philistine,*" the hairdryer lady said. "No wonder poor Violet left him. What a deadbeat. Of course, that's no reason for someone to do away with him." Shaking her head, she slid back under the hairdryer and resumed reading a hairstyle magazine.

"How well do you know Violet?" Lexie asked Georgia.

"She's been my neighbor for nigh on ten years."

Lucy and Lexie exchanged a glance that acknowledged they had chosen a good place to come for gossip.

"Are you and Violet good friends?" Lucy asked.

"Good enough," Georgia drawled.

"Would Violet have gotten angry enough at Henry to do something desperate?" Lexie asked.

Georgia gave a questioning look. "Like *murder* him?"

Lexie shrugged. "Maybe."

Georgia shook her big, curly blond head with the black, need-to-be-dyed roots. "No ma'am, I don't think so. Not Violet. She just ain't the type."

Carma finished gluing the last acrylic nail to Lexie's real nails. Then she began to apply a smelly pink substance, brushing it out in perfect strokes. "You never know what people are capable of when they are pushed too far."

Lucy nodded. "They often go over the edge."

"True. But not poor Violet. She'd have been more likely to go into a convent than to kill someone," Georgia said.

Lexie wondered about that. Considering how Henry had mentioned *poor* Violet was a little creepy. And also how horribly she had mouthed off right before she heard Henry was dead. No, to Lexie she didn't seem like such a sweet innocent. Seemed like she had a few axes to grind with the ex.

"What about these *swapping* parties?" Lexie said. "Did Henry ever get Violet to go to any of them?"

"Violet claims it never got that far before she filed for divorce." Georgia said. "But she did mention Henry was living a pretty wild single life."

Lexie wondered who in the world would have found him attractive enough to go to bed with him let alone how to stand the smell. But, to each his own.

"Henry Whitehead had women parading in and out of his house day and night," Carma said. "He was an arrogant womanizer. He probably irritated a lot of people."

"Yes siree-Bob," Georgia said. "Henry White-head had become the Casanova of Moose Creek Junction. That's why Violet went for the jugular when they got divorced. She'd already gotten her revenge and a good divorce settlement. She really didn't have any reason to do him in."

"Maybe it wasn't as good a settlement as it seemed," Lucy said.

"Or maybe she was trying to cover up her own affairs," Lexie added.

"Violet? No, she's a good egg." Georgia started to glue the acrylic nails to Lucy's fingers. "But then, I'm a transplant from Hondo, Texas. I may not know shit from shinola about people up north."

Carma produced a new nail file and began the final buff on Lexie. "I've seen Henry hanging out at Mac-Greggor's Pub. Maybe he got involved with a married woman. Could be a jealous husband found out and de-cided to teach Henry Whitehead a lesson."

"I suppose that's possible," Lexie said.

"Now, enough with the cross examination," Carma said. "If I didn't know better, I'd say you two were trying to do your own police work."

The sisters fell silent, though they exchanged glances again that seemed to say, *No more questions. We learned plenty.*

A short while later, as Lexie and Lucy sat under the nail dryers with nearly identical red nail polish on their fingers, Lucy turned to her younger sister. No one else was nearby, and they could talk freely.

"What do you think about all this, Lexie?

"We have to become a couple of bar flies."

Lucy groaned. "That is so wrong. I don't know if going down there is a sin I can ever repent for."

"Wait a minute. You said God would understand the nails. Why not the bar?"

Lexie peeked at her vermilion nails under the dryer. It was too bad she wasn't going to a Halloween party. The red daggers on her fingertips would have looked super with a vampire costume.

"Oh, Lord."

"Come on," Lexie said. "How could it hurt to wander around and listen to people talk for a while? God would want us to do the right thing, which is to find Whitehead's murderer. Don't you think so?"

Lucy frowned. "God would want us to leave the detective work to the police, sister dear. He would not want us to endanger our lives."

"Fine then," Lexie snapped. "I'll do this by myself."

Lucy sighed. "Over my dead body."

After paying for the nail jobs, Lexie and Lucy discussed when they could set off on their next fact-finding adventure. Lucy had promised Reverend Lincolnway she would clean the church again and she knew it would take her several days to polish the wooden pews, wash stained glass windows and scrub walls. Any bar business would have to be conducted later in the week. They decided they would meet at MacGreggor's Pub on Friday at eight o'clock.

As far as Lexie was concerned, she would have rather gone to the bar sooner, by herself if necessary, to carry out the amateur investigation. But Lucy would hear nothing of it. She insisted that although the good Lord would no doubt be disappointed to see His loyal handmaiden frequenting a bar, despite her true purpose, she would not allow her baby sister to enter into the lion's den alone.

Lexie reluctantly agreed, even down to the pinkie promise she would wait until Friday before heading off to MacGreggor's. Pinkie promises were a serious thing between sisters, so when they locked little fingers, she knew she'd be in real trouble if she were to go back on her agreement.

Back at the café, she seriously considered ripping off the red acrylics. It'd be hell to prepare food for her customers with those things clamped on her fingers.

But it was almost lunchtime, so the little torture devices would have to remain in place for now. Before long, the crowd began to shuffle in and Lexie put on her best customer-service face, despite her anxiety about where she and Lucy's murder investigation would lead.

She nodded to her regulars who included old Ian Fletcher, a retired army type from the Vietnam War who liked to hunt and fish, and his wife Akiko, a tiny Japanese lady whom Ian had married a few years ago and brought to live with him in Moose Creek Junction. Rumor had it that Ian had met her in an Oriental massage parlor in Denver, but Akiko was a nice enough lady and Lexie never paid much attention to the jaw-flappers in town.

Lexie went out to their favorite table by the large bay window. Most people ordered at the window, but Akiko and Ian liked someone to come to their table. Since they were such good customers, Lexie accommodated them.

Akiko, about ten years younger than her husband, ordered her usual pot of green tea, an egg salad sandwich on honey oat bread and a piece of apple pie. Ian, probably in his mid-fifties, wore a plaid flannel shirt in his thin frame, frayed jeans, and boots, and had his hair tied back with a leather thong. A cigarette hung from the corner of his mouth as he muttered his order to Lexie. It was different from the usual of chicken salad on rye. In what seemed an unusually soft spoken manner for a former sergeant, used to barking orders, he ordered tuna on rye, along with a piece of peach pie and black coffee.

He must be branching out, Lexie thought, recalling Akiko had once mentioned to her that Ian moved and spoke quietly all the time. The reason, she told Lexie, went back to his army survival training. The men who'd served tours in Vietnam learned to move stealthily and speak as little or quietly as possible while they patrolled the thick jungles, praying the Viet Cong wouldn't detect their movements.

"*Konichi wa*, Rexie-*san*," Akiko commented in her pigeon English when Lexie brought their food. Akiko couldn't pronounce her els at all, so some of her words came out sounding strange. "You sick maybe? You eyes very sad."

"I'm just tired. There's been a lot going on lately."

"Ah, I see." Akiko tilted her head to the side, a lock of graying black hair falling out of her pixie hair cut. "Ian and I hear about that man who was, how to say . . ." She looked up at the ceiling. "*Murder?*"

Lexie nodded, not liking where the conversation was headed.

"We hear you two were, how to say . . ." Again she looked up at the ceiling. "*Date?*" She poked her husband, who was leaning back in his chair reading a newspaper. He grunted in response but didn't lower the reading material. Akiko narrowed her almond-shaped eyes. "Everybody in town knows about it. You be careful. Maybe not so many people come into café now. They afraid."

Lexie was stunned. What kind of wild gossip was going on in Moose Creek Junction? Would people really stop coming here to eat?

She couldn't survive without her café business. Surely folks wouldn't stop coming just because of some wild gossip. But as Lexie told herself that, cold reality hit her in the stomach. People were fickle. Still, so far things at the Saucy Lucy had been running smoothly and customers came and went just like before Whitehead's murder. Akiko probably didn't know what she was talking about.

"I heard about the murder, too," Lexie told Akiko. "And yes, I knew Henry Whitehead. But only briefly. We weren't dating. Not really."

"Ah, so sad that man die. Buddhist belief say that dead spirits live on in other things. Maybe he now exists as a tree or a bush or an insect. One does not know for sure, but one must always be prepared to respect all living things. Could be something like a drum is one of your ancient ancestors."

Lexie pondered that for a moment. "Does that mean maybe my dead mother lives on as a mixing bowl because she loved to cook?"

Akiko gave a slight bow. "*Hai*. Strange things happen in Buddhist belief. Bless your bowls before you cook. This will honor your mother."

Lexie briefly considered the idea of blessing her mixing bowls and how to go about it. Then the weird idea of Whitehead passing over and returning to earth as a flea popped into her head. Ah, she'd done it again! What a terrible way to consider the recently departed.

"I'll have to think about it, Akiko," she said to the little Japanese woman, putting the idea of Whitehead as a flea and her mother as a mixing bowl completely out of her mind. "Please, enjoy your meal."

Ian grunted again before putting down his newspaper and diving into his food. Akiko gave Lexie another slight bow, her tiny silver earrings tinkling against her faded pink cheeks. "*Sayonara*."

Lexie returned to the counter and quickly immersed herself in taking care of her other customers. She was still irritated at herself for buying into Akiko's Buddhist belief enough to consider a dead person as an inanimate object when the phone rang. Her last customer, one of the local farmers in coveralls and a green John Deere ball cap, picked up his order and sat at a bistro table near the soda machine.

Lexie figured the call was probably from Otis wanting to make good and sure she was behaving herself. It was about time for her brother-in-law to start harassing her for always being in the wrong place at the wrong time. He was definitely a cross to bear. Lexie wondered how her sister could stand living with him.

Hesitantly, Lexie put the cordless phone to her ear, grabbed a large spoon and stirred a crock-pot full of golden broth, tender white meat chunks, vegetables and fat, homemade noodles. "Saucy Lucy Café," she said into the mouthpiece. "This is Lexie, how may I help you?"

"We need to talk."

"Excuse me?" Lexie stopped stirring the chicken soup, her spoon poised in mid-air. "Who is this?"

"Detective Stevenson."

Lexie couldn't stop a trace of annoyance from creeping into her voice. "Well, hello to you, too. How goes the investigation? Have you found the murderer yet?" After Lexie said that, she wanted to smack herself. She sounded like a complete dork.

"We're making progress. And it appears we've found the murder weapon—we're still conducting tests. But it's important I speak with you ASAP."

Lexie's blood turned to ice cubes in her veins and she nearly choked. "Why?"

"Can't tell you on the phone. Meet me at the Westonville police station today."

"I'm covering the café alone this week."

"Then I'll come over to Moose Creek Junction. But I won't be able to get away till Friday night." The line was silent a moment. "Have dinner with me."

"Dinner?" Lexie squeaked. She had to admit, the prospect of him coming here seemed somehow safer. She had the impression that if she went to the police department in Westonville she'd get sucked into a deep, dark jail cell and never come out again.

"How about six?"

"I never said yes."

"You're still under suspicion, lady."

"All right," she agreed reluctantly, hating the way *under suspicion* sounded. "I just need to be done by seven-thirty. I have a . . . a prior engagement." Man, she definitely needed to find Whitehead's murderer so the police would leave her alone. It was getting too hot to handle.

"A date?"

"I think that's none of your business, Detective."

"It's my business to make sure you don't travel outside of Moose Creek Junction."

"Believe me, my brother-in-law would draw and

quarter me if I ventured beyond the boundaries of our fair little berg. I'm just going to MacGreggor's Pub. In fact, they serve some awesome buffalo burgers and steaks. We could have dinner there."

"You *eat* buffalo around here?"

"Never heard of buffalo burgers? Where are you from? The dark side of the moon?"

He chuckled. "New York."

"You're a long way from home, detective. Why did you move out here?"

"Be there Friday at six," he growled, and hung up.

Ru roh. Lexie sensed she'd ventured into the forbidden waters of Stevenson's past and he was not happy.

Lexie hung up in somewhat of a daze. The man, Deputy Dog as she referred to him in her mind, had ticked her off, but he'd definitely piqued her interest, too. How was it possible he could annoy her and intrigue her, all at the same time?

It was baffling.

CHAPTER 4

"MOM, COULD YOU SEND ME $50?"

Lexie hugged the phone to her shoulder as she slid into her jeans skirt, then leaned over to slip on her high heels. It was Friday and she had actually dredged up a skirt, low cut blouse, and sexy shoes from her closet for the MacGreggor Pub investigation, thinking the male patrons might be more talkative if they could see a little leg and cleavage.

Or was it because she was having dinner with Gabe Stevenson?

Brushing the latter idea from her mind, she concentrated on her daughter and her latest crisis, a little peeved by the tone of her greedy greeting. "Gee, and how are you dear? What was your week like at school? And did you miss me? Of course you did."

"Sorry, Mom. I just really need the cash."

Lexie straightened and clipped on hoop earrings. Studying her face in her dresser mirror, she applied makeup from a mostly untouched basket of cosmetics. "Well, I really need to know what's going on. I don't speak with you for a week, and out of the blue you call needing money? It doesn't sound good."

Annoyed, Lexie glanced at her watch. Stevenson expected her at MacGreggor's in a half hour. It was as if Eva had ESP and knew Lexie didn't have the time to argue. Still, she couldn't help but wonder what was up. She was a mom, first and foremost.

"Trust me. It's going for a good cause."

Like what? Save the whales?

Lexie sighed and fluffed her hair like the women in all those glamour magazines, then spritzed it with hair spray. "Hon, I asked last weekend if you need-ed anything. I would have bought it for you before you went back to school."

"But I *don't* need anything, Mom. The money is for something, um . . . different."

Oh my God. She's getting a belly button ring. Or maybe a tattoo . . .

Lexie's mind reeled for a minute. She wanted to ask Eva if that's what the money was for, but then she'd stew and fret if Eva confirmed what she feared. No, maybe it was better she didn't know what her daughter had planned. The girl was eighteen. Even mothers had to let go some time. But maybe if she changed the subject, Eva would forget about the plea for cash.

She took a deep breath. "I take it you're not coming home this weekend?"

"No. Zoe and I are going hiking in the mountains with a couple of guys tomorrow. Then on Sunday we're going to do some research at the library together."

"Zoe's your roommate, right?"

"Right?"

"Right."

"And the guys are . . .?"

"Just guys, Mom. They live in the same dorm."

"I see." Ah, the joys of watching your baby girl go off to a co-ed dorm at college. Would wonders never cease?

"Lighten up, Mom. It's not like I'm gonna run away and get married. We all just figured we'd get out and enjoy the warm fall weather. Living in the dorms gets intense, you know? And it smells weird, too. Kind of stinky and moldy."

"You're not dating either of these guys?"

"No way. They're both dweebs. But one of them has a cool four-wheel truck. So about that fifty dollars . . ."

Darn. Eva, precious child that she had always been, was not so easily distracted. "I'll get it to you in the mail tomorrow."

"Thanks, Mom. I'll pay you back."

"Don't worry about it, dear." Lexie knew Eva's part-time job at the college bookstore didn't pay much. "Just make sure that cause of yours really is worthy."

"Oh, it is, Mom. It totally is."

Lexie replaced the phone in its cradle, wondering about Eva. The girl's transfer from high school to college seemed to have gone smoothly and it appeared Eva was enjoying her higher education experience. It was just that with her being so far away, Lexie couldn't physically see her daughter every day and gauge how things were going.

For the first time since she was born, Lexie had to loosen the apron strings and trust Eva would make good choices. She had to trust she'd instilled good morals and provided a decent enough upbringing so the girl wouldn't wind up doing something crazy, dangerous, or stupid.

Right now, she wished Dan was still with her to discuss her fears and their daughter's future. But that wouldn't happen now. Dan's brain had left earth and landed on a whole new planet. Planet Davina. Lexie knew he didn't think much about Eva these days.

Lexie's friend back in California had sent her a card a few days ago updating her on happenings in her old neighborhood and the news that Dan and Davina's baby girl had been born. Leave it to Dan to let his daughter learn about her new sibling through a former neighbor, rather than talk with her himself.

Then again, maybe Dan planned on calling Eva. Did he still have a shred of human decency left in his shriveled, maimed heart? *Maybe donkeys really do fly*, a small voice told her. No, more than likely, Dan would leave the task to her. Lexie would be the one doing damage control. Eva would be hurt hearing the news second hand.

How could a little girl who had been the apple

of her daddy's eye not be hurt? Even if she was all grown up and in college?

Damn you Dan Lightfoot. Damn you to hell.

Suddenly Lexie remembered she had a dinner date with the law. She glanced at her watch again, seeing she had five minutes to make it over to Mac-Greggor's Pub for dinner with Stevenson. Mentally reminding herself to get a check to Eva in the mail tomorrow, she inspected her makeup one last time. Oops, maybe she'd overdone it a little.

I look like Barbie on Prozac.

But there was no time to worry about that. She put on her leather jacket and headed downstairs. Locking the door, she hustled to the garage and her truck, heels clicking like little steel nails being hammered into her coffin.

As she started up the old wreck, hearing the strange, but familiar, rat-a-tat-tat in the engine, she hoped Otis wasn't patrolling the streets. She'd have to step on it a little to get to MacGreggor's by six and she sure didn't need her brother-in-law stopping her for speeding.

Lexie wondered if he'd believed Lucy's story that the sisters were going to a movie in Westonville. Otis might not be the sharpest or the brightest crayon in the box, but he had an uncanny ability to sense whether someone was telling the truth.

Fortunately, she made it to MacGreggor's without incident, pulling into the lot off the street and parking way in the back of the building where no one would recognize her car. She walked toward the pub, fiddling with her fake nails and wishing she'd had the chance to rip the goofy things off.

As a last-minute thought, she undid the top two buttons on her blouse. She told herself it would have a good affect on the cowboys at the bar she intended to question. Hopefully, loosen their lips a little. That sort of thing.

"Parked kind of far away, didn't you?"

Lexie nearly jumped out of her skin when she looked up to see Detective Stevenson observing her with his intense hazel eyes. He wore jeans again, cowboy boots, a white button-down shirt and a tweed blazer. And she swore he was wearing Drakkar, a men's cologne that always made her weak in the knees.

Instantly she stopped fiddling with her buttons, heart pounding as she grappled for a sensible answer. "I, ah, figure my truck's safer parked in the back where it's not so visible to thugs."

"Last I heard, the criminal element isn't jacking too many '69 Ford trucks these days. In fact, last I heard, there's really not much of a criminal element in Moose Creek Junction."

Lexie smiled. "Except for the murderer we have running around loose. Or doesn't he count?"

Stevenson shrugged. "Sorry. I'm cursed with an observant nature. Guess it comes with the job."

"Well, call me a fool for being too practical, Detective Stevenson," Lexie said, nearly calling him

Deputy Dog. "But I don't believe it's a crime."

"That's a fact," Stevenson agreed. "By the way, call me Gabe. We might be working together for a while."

Good Lord, I hope not. Lexie was still a little hot from the detective's unwanted scrutiny, but decided it would be to her advantage to stay on his good side, so she didn't voice her thoughts aloud. Forcing a smile, she continued toward the pub.

In one long stride, Stevenson caught up and opened the door for her. "I really didn't mean to start off on the wrong foot with you, Lexie. I've got a crime to solve so we might as well get along."

Lexie met the detective's gaze. "What makes you think we're not getting along?"

Later, when they'd been seated in the restaurant area of the pub and ordered their dinner, Lexie ventured another question. "Tell me, Gabe. Why did you leave the high society crimes in New York for a bunch of backwater lawbreakers in windy Wyoming?"

He observed her silently for a moment, a muscle twitching in his cheek. "Police work in big cities is intense and I've got a daughter to raise."

"A daughter? How old?"

"She's 12. I had her in a private boarding school back east but she hated it so I got us moved out here to be together."

Sympathy twisted in Lexie's heart. "And her mother?"

He cleared his throat and his voice tightened.

"Passed away a few years back. Cancer."

"I am so sorry to hear that." Lexie instinctively patted his hand, then quickly pulled back, realizing what she'd done. "What's your daughter's name?"

A smile twitched at the corners of Gabe's mouth as he poured Lexie a glass of wine from the bottle he'd ordered. "Jade."

"Very pretty," Lexie said.

"Lexie, I wanted to talk with you about something important. Henry Whitehead was stabbed to death. We found the murder weapon."

Lexie took a sip of wine and felt it warming all the way down the length of her body until it tingled in her toes. Deputy Dog sure got to the point when he wanted to. "OK. What has that got to do with me?"

"Have you noticed any butcher knives missing from your kitchen?"

Puzzled, Lexie sipped her wine again. "No."

"I'm here to tell you one must be missing. It has your fingerprints all over it and it was found stuck in a tree trunk in Whitehead's yard."

"How do you know the butcher knife came from my kitchen?"

"It's a strong possibility."

Lexie cringed at the idea. Now the police must really think she was a murderer.

"Why are you telling me this if I'm a suspect? Wouldn't the prosecution want to drop that as a bombshell to incriminate me at a murder trial?"

"You're not on trial, Lexie."

"Not yet, anyway. But the way your investigation is going, it looks like I'll be wearing an orange jumpsuit any day now." The very possibility made her shiver, and goosebumps pimpled her forearms.

Then Lexie had a thought. "But Detective Stevens . . . er . . . Gabe, my fingerprints couldn't have been the only ones on that butcher knife. My daughter works at the Saucy Lucy sometimes and also my sister Lucy. Otis' fingerprints are probably on them too since we have Thanksgiving dinner at the café and he carves the turkey."

"Exactly. Which is why I set up this meeting, and why I'm not arresting you. There are several sets of prints on the knife; the evidence is inconclusive."

Lexie blinked. "And this is supposed to comfort me?"

"This is supposed to make you want to cooperate with me. Tell me anything you know about Whitehead. Anything at all you think might help."

"I barely knew him."

"Doesn't matter. Tell me what few things you know."

A server brought their dinner and they fell silent as he handed out the sizzling platters of buffalo steak and baked potatoes. When they were alone again Lexie told Gabe what little she knew about Whitehead, along with what she suspected, like how things didn't add up with his ex-wife Violet. It didn't seem like much.

After a bite of steak, Lexie asked Gabe, "What

is your theory on how my butcher knife wound up at the murder scene?"

"Somebody put it there."

"Really. But how did they get *my* knife?"

Stevenson dabbed his napkin to his lips. "It's obvious the murderer came into your kitchen and stole it. Could have been a customer who snuck in when you were distracted, or someone managed to slip in and steal it when you were gone. There's a million scenarios—just make sure to keep your doors and windows locked and maybe install some dead bolts."

Lexie made a mental note to do just that. "But why would someone go to all the trouble to take the knife from my kitchen? Why not use one of their own?"

"To implicate you. I believe someone wanted to make it look like you murdered Whitehead."

Lexie started to tremble. "They framed me? But why? I never did anything to anybody . . ."

"Do you have any enemies around here? And what about your ex-husband? Maybe he decided to come up and cause trouble. Otis also told me about Hugh Glenwood. I'm checking into that case to see if there's a connection."

Lexie felt lightheaded trying to absorb the incredible idea that someone would want to hurt her. "I don't have any enemies. At least none I know of. And Dan is on Planet Davina." Immediately Lexie realized what she'd said and warmth tingled in her cheeks. Gabe nodded. He looked like he was going to say something else, but the waiter arrived with their check and he kept silent.

Lexie's head swam with unanswered questions. Could Dan have sneaked up to Wyoming without her knowing and followed her around, then stabbed Whitehead, thinking he was her lover? Did he off Glenwood, too? Was he jealous of her, even though he was the one who'd had all the affairs while they were married?

The thought was eerie all the way around. More likely there was someone in town who had it in for her. Lexie bristled. Talk about feeling violated. This was her hometown. How dare somebody set her up like this?

Her stomach twisted with confusion, disbelief, and something she assumed might be shock. She finished her wine, then boldly poured herself more of the plum-colored liquid.

Why, she'd never had an enemy in her life!

Lexie stared through the window at the dark road outside awash with the pink tinge of street-lights. The buzz saw effect of the wine made her light-headed and for a second she thought she saw a dark figure. Then it vanished into the shadowy alley as quickly as she'd noticed it. Not much of a drinker, Lexie knew she was either tipsy or losing her mind. Sensing Detective Stevenson's steady gaze, she turned to see he'd grabbed the check and was concentrating on her.

Lexie took another sip of wine and looked him

right in the eye. "What?"

His brow wrinkled with concern. "Are you all right?"

"Good Lord." Lexie rolled her eyes. "The man tells me I'm being framed for murder and asks if I'm all right." She glared at Stevenson, feeling the effects of the wine on her tongue. "Of course I'm not all right. I'm scared stupid. What am I supposed to do now?"

"Don't panic. Stay calm."

"Easy for you to say," Lexie returned curtly.

"Watch your every move. Be careful. Keep your doors and windows locked, make sure no one follows you when you're driving."

"You're thinking of the person who hit me at the stoplight the night I left Whitehead's house?"

He nodded. "Possibly the murderer."

Lexie hiccoughed, then giggled, then felt helplessness wash over her. "Be careful. Sure, I'll be careful." The waiter appeared to clear away the table and just as quickly disappeared.

"Are you certain you don't know who was driving the car that hit you?" Gabe asked.

"No. Not a clue."

Lexie was really feeling loopy now. Heavens to Betsy, she was a cheap drunk. That's what happened when you didn't drink very often. One or two drinks, and poof! You're seeing pink elephants.

"See, at the time I was still upset about Whitehead groping me, so when this goober pulls up from behind and hits me, I wasn't thinking too straight. It was getting dark and I couldn't see who was inside the vehicle, and I sure as heck didn't get a license plate number."

Lexie sighed and templed her hands on the table. "Which reminds me, I still haven't had a chance to get that dent pulled out of my bumper."

"Good."

Lexie looked curiously at Deputy Dog. "Excuse me?"

"I'll take a look at it before I leave tonight. Could be some paint was left by the other car. I can scrape it off some and possibly trace the make and model."

"Be my guest. Scrape away." Lexie stood. "Since you're not going to arrest me, may I be excused from the table now?"

Gabe pushed his chair back and stood. "He reached into his tweed blazer and handed her a business card, one dark brow raised. "Call me if you think of anything that might be pertinent to the case. Or even just to talk."

"Sure." Lexie sensed he might have another interest in her besides the case. But she wasn't really in her right mind with the wine coursing through her blood, so she might be imagining things. Best not to assume anything.

"Are you sure you're all right? I could drive you home."

Lexie hiccoughed again. "Oh, I'm peachy, detective. Just peachy. And by the way, thanks for dinner."

No more alcohol for me, Lexie told herself firmly as she watched Deputy Dog saunter to the front desk to pay the bill, then exit the restaurant.

She sighed and walked over to the bar to sit and wait for Lucy on one of the padded stools. "Ice water, please," she asked the bartender, looking forward to a drink that would clear the wine from her senses.

It was important she get her wits about her. She had work to do.

The riot in Lexie's head settled to a dull roar as she drank the ice water. She tapped a fake fingernail against the glass while the dizziness receded to a small corner of her brain. Minutes ticked by on the bar clock and Lexie turned to look around at a darkened room full of tables with small candlelit globe centerpieces. Picking through the sea of faces and bodies in a haze of smoke, Lexie still did not see Lucy anywhere. Maybe she'd chickened out. *Figures.*

Disappointed, she slumped over her water and stirred the ice cubes with the thin red straw. A few seconds later, she felt a touch on her shoulder.

Heart pounding, Lexie whirled around, then relaxed. "Geez, Luce, you scared me half to death."

"Sorry, sis." Lucy stood behind Lexie clutching a flowered silk purse against her breasts like a shield. She wore a sparrow brown dress, brown loafers, and her typical sausage-effect support hose. "I didn't mean to frighten you. Gosh, your eyes are all bulged out like that Freddy Kruger fellow."

Lexie raised a curious brow. "I didn't think you watched trashy movies."

"I don't. I've only seen Kruger on the posters they put up at the theater. That's wicked enough for me."

"Pull up a seat," Lexie told her sister.

Lips pursed tightly, Lucy glanced around, undoubtedly praying no one would recognize her. Then she slid daintily onto a bar stool, still clutching the bag to her chest. "You look so different, Lexie. You're actually wearing a dress and it's so short you can nearly see . . . *ahem*." Even in the dark, her blush shone brightly. "And your makeup! My heavens! Mother would roll over in her grave. She'd say you look like a floozy."

Annoyed, Lexie ignored the comment. "How did the church cleaning go? Does it glow with the glory of God from stem to stern?"

Lucy sniffed with irritation. "It's finished and that's all I'll say. Have you found out anything so far?"

"Yes," Lexie said miserably. "I'll probably get a dead squirrel mailed to me in the next few days with a note that says 'you're next'."

"Heavenly stars! What happened?" Lucy produced a fan from her purse, snapped it open, and furiously batted away the cigarette smoke swirling around them.

Lexie shook her head. "I just had dinner with

Detective Stevenson and he told me some disturbing news. Whitehead was killed with a butcher knife that probably came from the Saucy Lucy Café."

"For Pete's sake!" Lucy gasped. "You're kidding!"

"Wish I was."

"Are we to be arrested?"

"No, nothing like that."

Lucy blinked. "But how can that be? A knife from our very own kitchen?"

"Gabe thinks somebody stole it. And he's pretty sure they wanted to frame me for the murder. He's also checking into a possible connection in Hugh and Whitehead's deaths."

"But why would someone do such foul deeds?"

"That's what we've got to find out before things get any worse."

Lucy also ordered an ice water from the bartender and sipped at it reflectively. "So Detective Stevenson came all the way over here from Westonville to tell you about the knife?"

Lexie nodded. "He wanted me to go down there to the police station, but with you busy at the church all week, I couldn't get away. He took me to dinner tonight instead."

"Oh, my. This is an interesting development indeed."

Lexie looked Lucy right in the eye. "Don't go getting any ideas. It was like a business dinner. Nothing more."

"He is good looking in a rugged, outdoorsman

sort of way," Lucy said in a dreamy voice. "And I positively adore that scruffy little beard of his. I wish Otis would grow one. It'd offset his bald head."

"Lucy, focus. I have absolutely no romantic interest in Stevenson."

"But you called him Gabe."

Lexie shrugged. "He asked me to call him that since we'd be working together on this case. That's all. Believe me, I've got enough trouble in my life without having a man around to complicate things."

"Oh, sweetie. You are in such denial," Lucy said.

"My life does not revolve around a man," Lexie said. "And, pray God, it never will. The last two times I dated guys they both dropped dead. Of course, somebody murdered them . . ." A shiver danced up her spine.

From the corner of her eye, Lexie noticed a tall man in a cowboy hat step away from the jukebox, and yet another country song began to blare. It brought Lexie back to reality.

"Enough with the mushy talk, Luce. We have a mission."

"Oh, my." Lucy's brow was speckled with droplets of glistening sweat. "I'm afraid I wouldn't know where to start. In fact, don't you think you got enough information from Detective Stevenson so that we can leave? Right now?"

"No. We need to get some of these cowboys to talk. See if they knew Whitehead or heard anything about him since this was a regular hangout of his."

"And how do we do that?"

Lexie took her sister's arm. "Let's go get a table."

The sisters found a likely place to sit. They lowered themselves into chairs and stared out at the sea of bodies meandering amongst the tables and chairs or swaying together on the dance floor.

After ten minutes, Lucy said, "How are we supposed to get anyone to come over and talk with us?"

Lexie shrugged. "I don't know. I mean, usually I'm like insect repellent when it comes to men."

"We need to think of something. I'm not sitting her all night sucking down smoke fumes and having my ears pounded by loud music." Lucy batted at the air again with her fan. "Besides, Otis will begin to wonder what's going on if I'm not home soon. Movies don't last that long."

Lexie smoothed her teased hair. "OK. Men are just a bunch of cavemen. Their agenda is pretty simple. Food. Women. Beer. We simply have to get their attention. I'd hate to think I dressed up like Barbarella for nothing."

"Goodness," Lucy said. "So, again I ask, what do we do?"

"Let's order a couple of beers."

"Alexandria! Alcohol is the devil's brew!"

"Settle down, sis. We'll just hold them for effect; it'll make us appear more approachable. We don't have to drink them. And wait a minute." Lexie reached into her purse, fumbled a bit, and pulled out a pack of cigarettes. "I almost forgot. I bought these at the gas station a few days ago. I thought they'd be perfect to have in here."

Lucy gasped and clutched her heart. "Is this absolutely necessary?"

"Smoking makes you look tough, Luce. Men like that." Lexie pulled out a cigarette for herself and gave one to Lucy. She produced a lighter, fumbled a little more and finally got her cigarette lit. Holding the end to her lips, Lexie pretended to inhale, then coughed, eyes watering.

Lexie lit Lucy's cigarette as well, but she only held it between her fingers as far away from herself as she could. Not very convincing, Lexie thought.

A waitress came by and Lexie ordered two beers. Before long, the waitress came back and plopped them down on the table.

"God forgive us," Lucy said. "Now that we have our props, what shall we do?"

Lexie cleared her throat and looked around, trying to observe some of the body language of the patrons. She crossed her legs in what she perceived to be a sexy pose and tossed her head. "I think we have to talk really loud," Lexie said. "Try to get a man's attention."

"Really," Lucy said. "This is too much."

"Don't forget to flick the ashes on that cigarette, sis."

"Disgusting," Lucy muttered as she tapped off the ashes in an ashtray and resumed holding her cigarette at arm's length with the tips of her thumb and forefinger.

"I know," Lexie said. "What did you find at the church when you were cleaning?"

"What did I find?" Lucy stared incredulously at Lexie. "Whatever do you mean?"

"Did you find dust balls?" Lexie said in a loud voice, then leaned toward Lucy and giggled stupidly, like she was drunk.

"Dust balls?" Lucy didn't get it.

"Come on. Maybe you found blue balls. Or maybe withered balls," Lexie said a little louder, feeling completely ridiculous. "Possibly hairy balls?"

"What are you talking about?" Lucy nearly shouted and glanced around. "You're embarrassing me!"

"Lucy, we've got to look like we're having fun."

"But this is awful!"

"It's harmless. We need to attract attention. Once we accomplish that, we can stop the nonsense. Either we make this work or we might as well forget about saving me from the bighouse. Do you want to talk to me through bars for the rest of my life?"

Lucy pouted for a moment, hand clutched to her heart again. Finally, she stubbed out her cigarette, stood up, and to Lexie's absolute surprise shouted, "Smelly balls!" Then she slid back down into her seat and fanned herself madly. "I can't believe I just said that! I'm losing my mind! The devil is definitely at work here."

"No, you're helping with the investigation is all," Lexie said. She pretended to puff on her cigarette, then stood and said, "Squishy balls, hot balls—"

"May I buy you ladies a drink?" Lexie recognized the tall, smiling cowboy from the jukebox. He was looking straight at her.

"Sure, thanks." Lexie exchanged a knowing glance with Lucy. Lucy blew out a breath of air, a relieved look on her face.

The cowboy caught a passing barmaid and ordered another round, then grabbed a chair and straddled it backward next to Lexie. "You ladies from around here?"

"Last I heard," Lexie said. "What about you?"

The cowboy winked at Lexie and they began to talk. Before long, two more men sauntered up and joined the group at Lexie and Lucy's table. Lexie pretended to be tipsy, but she kept the conversation at the level of simple flirting.

At an opportune moment, Lexie said to the jukebox cowboy, "Wasn't it a shame about what happened to Henry Whitehead?"

"And in our fair little town," Lucy added with a *tsk tsk.*

The cowboy from the jukebox, who had identified himself as Bob, put an arm around Lexie. It seemed he had a sweet spot for her and repeatedly asked for her phone number, which she refused to give. "Well, my mama always told me if you play with fire, you're gonna get burned."

"What do you mean?" Lexie asked.

"Whitehead was an old horndog. I heard tell he

practically had a revolving door installed on his house to accommodate the gals comin' and goin'. He wasn't much on looks or personality, but he went mostly after women who were bored with their men folk. Fed 'em the crap they wanted to hear, like how purty they was, and they fell lock, stock, and barrel for it." He took a swig of beer and gave a mighty guffaw.

The other men around the table nodded and grunted similar comments.

Lexie and Lucy exchanged knowing glances.

"Well, I guess that's OK as long as no one gets hurt." Lexie winked at Bob. Even though he kept asking her to go out with him, she had no intention of doing so. But it didn't hurt to flatter him a little in order to get more information.

"Oh, I wouldn't say no one was getting hurt," one of the men named Charlie said said. "Some of the gals Whitehead was messing around with were married. Eventually one or two of the husbands were getting wise to the bullshit. I know some of 'em were getting downright pissed."

Lexie twisted her hair around her finger in what she hoped was a fetching manner. "My goodness," she said to Charlie. "Do you know who, in particular?"

"I heard tell Ernie Howell was pretty hot about all the crap goin' on," Charlie said. "His wife Sophie really got messed up with Whitehead. Ernie threatened to go after him with a shotgun and a shovel. Swore he'd had enough of Whitehead foolin' with his wife and that he'd kill him with his bare hands if he didn't back off."

Lexie froze in place, her blood trickling like water through an icy, alpine creek. Was this the clue she and Lucy had been looking for? Had this Ernie fellow gone off the deep end? Grabbed a knife from Lexie's place, hoping to implicate her, and done poor Henry in?

"Where does Ernie live?" Lexie knew she had to keep fishing for more dirt, and Lucy gave her an encouraging nod.

"He ain't around these parts anymore," Charlie said.

"I heard he and Sophie moved to Denver," Bob said.

"Denver?" Lucy wrinkled her nose and batted her fan around some more. "What a horrible place to live. Too much traffic and crime."

Bob lit a cigarette and took a long puff, the end glowing red in the bar room darkness. "I heard Ernie was opening some sort of business down there."

"What kind?" Lexie asked.

"Not sure exactly." Bob shrugged. "But I think it had somethin' to do with magic."

"Magic?" Lexie folded her arms across her chest. "How odd."

"Well, he and Sophie's boys got into all those wizard books that gal from England wrote. And Ernie . . . he liked all that hocus pocus stuff, too."

"The move to Denver got Sophie far away from Moose Creek Junction and Henry Whitehead," Charlie added.

So there was another potential lead waiting in Denver, Lexie thought. It was time for a summit meeting with Lucy so they could make plans for their next fact-finding trip.

"Excuse me everyone. I need to . . . ah . . . powder my nose." Lexie decided nature's call was a good way to part company with the cowboys. "You coming, Luce?"

She exchanged a quick glance with Lucy who was earnestly discussing the First Congregational Church of the Lamb of God with Charlie. Leave it up to Sister Lucy to turn the investigation into a mission to save roughnecks from their heathenish ways. "Be right there, sis."

Lexie rolled her eyes and headed toward the ladies room. The blaring music and too many bodies pressed closely together made her dizzy. How could people stand coming here night after night? It would drive her insane.

Lexie headed down the dim hallway to the ladies room. Then with a fizzle and a pop, the lights went out. Just like that. Cloying darkness enveloped her like a heavy winter coat.

CHAPTER 5

DAMN," SHE MUTTERED, GROPING FOR THE wall. Unable to see anything, she wondered briefly if she should stay where she was, or try to go somewhere.

When someone grabbed her arm from behind, she thought it was Lucy who had slipped away from the cowboys. But it was soon obvious it wasn't her sister when whoever it was started to haul her toward the dim outline of the alley door.

Lexie's heart hammered like a tribal drum and she struggled in the stranger's grasp. "Hey, let me go! Whoever you are!"

A meaty hand clamped down hard on Lexie's mouth, instantly silencing her shouts. She was certain no one had heard her cry out because the dismayed howls coming from bar patrons would have drowned her voice. In the midst of the pub blackout, chaos and commotion ruled.

Panic plunged through Lexie when she smelled

a rank odor coming from her attacker. It was familiar, but she couldn't quite place it. She tried to shake free of the sure, steady grip. Her efforts were in vain. Lexie tried twisting from side to side to break loose but to no avail. Her attacker was taller and much stronger. She felt as weak as a rag doll in the spin cycle of a washer.

The more Lexie struggled, the more her attacker increased his hold, until she could barely breathe. He, or she, had glommed onto her like bubblegum to the back of a sneaker.

Panic sank wicked claws into Lexie. For a split second her body became paralyzed, then just as quickly adrenaline flowed—the fight or flight syndrome.

Loving faces flashed before her eyes: Eva, Lucy, her nephew Carl and even old patootiehead Otis.

Do something . . .

As she struggled with her attacker, feeling his hot, moist breath crawling on her neck, Lexie tried desperately to think of a way to break free. *My heels!* A pain in the butt to wear, they'd already worn saddle sores-from-hell on her feet. Then again, they might just save her butt.

Gasping for breath behind the meaty paw, Lexie brought her heel down hard on what she sensed was her attacker's instep.

Contact.

The creep gave a surprised, guttural gasp and let Lexie go. She instantly peeled away. Her eyes had adjusted to the darkness and she could just barely make out his bulk blocking the back entrance as he hopped around in pain.

There was no escape in that direction.

Heart slamming against her ribs and hiccoughs rising in her throat, she fumbled along the wall toward the ladies room. At last she located a handle, swung open a door and pushed inside. Darkness pervaded the lavatory stench, but faint blue neon light filtered through a small window inside one of the stalls.

Escape!

Hope flickered through Lexie and she headed for the light. Suddenly the ladies room door flew open, smacking against the cinderblock wall. Lexie squeaked in dismay and quickly locked herself inside the stall.

The creep started slamming against the metal frame with such ferocity Lexie truly believed it would cave in any second. Swallowing her panic, she stood on top of the toilet lid and tried to shove the window open.

It wouldn't budge.

Sobbing with frustration, she slammed her shoulder against the frame trying to loosen it, ignoring the pain. *Please, please, please,* she cried to herself hoping and praying she could get away before the creep out there tried to make her into a hood ornament. Again she tried to open the window and at last, to her shock and amazement, it wedged upward with a rusty squeak.

A grunt came from under the stall door. Lexie looked down and saw a dark form, dressed in what appeared to be a black hooded sweatshirt, slide in her direction. Quickly she hoisted herself into the open window, squeezed through, and dropped into the alley below.

She fell on the ground with a thud and felt an instant pain in her right ankle that crept its way up her leg like wildfire. After a swift look over her shoulder at the open bathroom window to make sure the creep wasn't on her tail, she limped through the gravel to the front of the building.

Lexie struggled to control her erratic breathing. She had to find Lucy. Find Lucy and get the hell out of here. She must have been nuts to ever think she could do her own detective work. Nuts or desperate. Now somebody was after her. They must not be happy she was asking questions of the locals.

Could she be getting too close to the truth?

Relief trickled through Lexie when she reached the entrance to MacGreggor's Pub. Surely her attacker wouldn't follow her here. After one more glance over her shoulder, she turned around and ran smack into a large body.

Gasping in dismay, Lexie stumbled backward. She yanked the shoe from her throbbing right foot and held the spike heel out like a weapon. "Take a hike, bucko. I've had just about enough of your crap!"

Suddenly the lights in the pub flashed on and yellow porch light illuminated the person standing in front of Lexie. Detective Stevenson. In all his lawman's glory. And he did not look happy.

Holy crap.

Lexie stared in embarrassment at the high heel clutched in her fingers. She tucked the shoe behind her back, feeling like a complete dork. After a couple of gulps, she swallowed her hiccoughs. "Sorry." She wet her dry lips with her equally dry tongue. "I thought you were someone else."

"Obviously." Gabe folded his arms across his broad chest and inclined his head toward the pub. "What's going on in there?"

She shook her head. "Nothing."

He snorted. "Something's up. Either Mac-Greggor forgot to pay his utility bill or somebody got hammered and flipped off the main power breaker."

"You'll have to ask MacGreggor." Lexie felt as trapped as a bug pinned on a science project board. She cleared her throat uneasily and glanced over her shoulder—still no creep. Looking back at Gabe she asked, "What are you doing here? I thought you'd be back in Westonville by now."

He ignored her question. "Is Bigfoot chasing you or something? You're jittery as a field mouse in a snake's cage."

Lexie swallowed hard. She'd have to watch herself around Deputy Dog here. There was no hiding anything from him. "I was just out for a stroll."

"By yourself?"

She nodded.

"And is it a common Wyoming custom to greet everyone you meet on your strolls by shoving a spiked heel in their face?"

"Uh, no. Like I said, I thought you were someone else."

"Who?"

Lexie shrugged. Darn it. All she needed was Westonville's finest to discover she and Lucy had been asking around about Henry Whitehead. Stevenson would tell Otis for sure, and their plans would be hosed.

Lord, she felt desperate. When she'd persuaded Lucy to help her with this investigation, it had seemed like the right thing to do. It had made complete sense for them to try and find out who had done poor Whitehead in, especially since Lexie was the last person to see him alive.

Now her plan seemed insane and dangerous. Especially in light of the recent attack.

Lexie leaned against the porch railing to take the weight off her throbbing foot. She hoped Gabe wouldn't guess how much pain she was in. "One of the cowboys in there just got a little carried away and I didn't like it," she lied. "Is it a crime to party a little on a Friday night?"

"For some reason, I get the impression that MacGreggor's Pub and horny cowboys aren't exactly your idea of fun." A muscle twitched along his whiskered jaw. "If I didn't know better, I'd say you were snooping around and asking questions about Whitehead's murder."

With a deep sigh, Lexie leaned over and put her shoe back on her throbbing foot, then straightened and stared up at the tall detective. "You know, if you were doing your job, you'd have found out that Whitehead had plenty of enemies around here. Instead of following me around, you'd be checking them out."

Gabe raised a dark brow. "What makes you think I'm not?"

"I'm still under suspicion," she finally said, hating the pout in her voice.

"You and several other people."

"But I don't like it."

"You'll live. Meantime, leave the murder investigation to me, Lexie. I'll chase the bad guys, OK?"

She nodded.

Gabe glanced down. "Go on home now and ice that ankle. It'll feel better in the morning."

Incredulous, Lexie intended to deny that her foot hurt. But the front door to the pub swung open and Lucy hustled out, a concerned expression on her face.

"Lexie, wherever have you been? It was awful! The lights went out and everyone went crazy in there." Lucy glared accusingly at her, support hose so tight her face was turning red. She smoothed down the front of her sad brown dress.

Lexie shook her head. "I told you to come with me when I went to powder my nose. But you were too busy playing Mother Theresa."

"Why you ungrateful little—" Then Lucy noticed Gabe and smiled demurely. "Why, Detective Stevenson, I didn't see you standing there. I almost ran into you."

He grinned. "Seems like lots of folks are running into me tonight. At least you didn't shove a spiked heel in my face."

Lexie's face flushed with warmth.

"What?" Lucy asked with large, curious eyes.

"Never mind," Lexie said. "Let's just go home."

"I'll walk you ladies to your cars," Gabe offered.

"No, we're fine." Lexie grabbed Lucy's elbow and steered her to her car trying hard not to limp. She decided to come back tomorrow and pick up the truck when her ankle felt better.

"What on earth is wrong with you?" Lucy asked. "Wait a minute! I know! You and Detective Stevenson had a lovers' quarrel. How exciting!"

"Knock it off," Lexie said. "We are not dating, therefore we cannot have a lovers' quarrel."

Lucy's face fell. "Then what were you two talking about?"

"Nothing," Lexie said.

They didn't say anything else until they got in the car and Stevenson had disappeared inside the pub.

With a sigh of relief, Lexie leaned back against the headrest. "Man, oh man, that was a close call." She pulled off her shoe and gingerly prodded the puffy flesh on her ankle.

"For Pete's sake." Lucy scooted around in the

driver's seat in order to face Lexie. "How did you hurt your foot? What happened?"

Lexie told her about the creep in the hallway, how she'd finally gotten loose and crawled out the bathroom window, then ran into Gabe Stevenson.

"I'm scared, Lucy. Somebody's out to get me. Probably they want to kill me, or get me locked behind bars forever. They must hate me pretty bad and I don't like it."

"I don't like it either, baby sister."

"Detective Stevenson knows we're up to something. He basically told me to back off."

"Then we've got to stop this sleuthing nonsense," Lucy declared. "Look at you! You were hurt tonight. It could have been worse than a sprained ankle, you know."

"I know," Lexie said.

"I think Detective Stevenson's right. And I think he likes you."

Lexie rolled her eyes. "Whatever. But I still want to talk to Ernie and Sophie Howell. It sounds like they might know something."

"Alexandria!"

"Stop calling me that," Lexie said. "You make me sound like the Queen of Egypt or something."

"Listen, Lexie. We are not trained to do police work. We really must keep our noses out of this investigation. What if Detective Stevenson tells Otis we've been questioning people about Henry's murder? I'm afraid he'll be quite unhappy with us."

"Stevenson won't say anything. I'm sure of it. He's just cocky enough to believe the little 'talking to' he gave me tonight will make me back off."

"And it should."

"But how can we pass up the chance to talk with the Howells? Besides, they live all the way in Denver and no one would ever know where we're going. We could be on a shopping trip."

"Lexie—"

Lexie took her sister's hands in hers. "Lucy, please. This is important to me . . . to both of us. I have to find out who hates me so much they would try to frame me. I don't think I can stand waiting forever for the police to poke around till they find the guilty party. They have no reason to be in a hurry, but we do."

"What's this 'we'? Why are we in such a hurry?"

"Akiko and Ian Fletcher came in for lunch at the Saucy Lucy the other day. She said a lot of people had heard about Whitehead and I dating—how I don't know. We barely knew each other. But she said everyone in town's nervous about eating at our place now. Like I'm going to do them in, too. It could be potentially disastrous for business."

"I never thought of it like that." Lucy removed her glasses and polished them on her dress, then slid them back on. "That isn't good."

"No kidding. You've got Otis to take care of you if the business fails. But I'd be out on my ear and Eva would have no money for college."

"Oh, dear."

"Oh dear is right. I'd be up shit creek without a paddle."

Lucy wrinkled her nose. "Goodness gracious, the things you come up with!"

"Well, it's true. So, what do you say? Will you take a field trip with me to Denver to visit the Howell's magic shop?"

"Do I have a choice?"

Lexie shrugged. "I could always go on my own."

"Over my dead body," Lucy said.

When Lexie got home she locked all her doors and windows, left a night light burning and sat wide awake in bed with her throbbing foot iced and propped on a pillow. She couldn't stop thinking about her dinner with Gabe, the conversation with the cowboys at MacGreggor's Pub and finally about the creep who had attacked her.

Much as she wanted to solve Whitehead's murder and assure her customers they had nothing to fear by eating at the Saucy Lucy Café, this amateur detective stuff was getting spooky.

She and Lucy couldn't let the attack tonight or Gabe Stevenson's warnings stop them from getting at the truth. It was too important. Her life and livelihood depended upon it.

At last Lexie fell into a fitful sleep, tossing and

turning until she nearly gave up. When she finally did nod off, she dreamed of being chased by black-hooded phantoms clutching large butcher knives. It was a relief when the harsh jangling of the telephone jolted her awake.

Despite the aspirin she'd taken last night to ease the pain in her foot, her head pounded like the California surf. Smacking her dry lips together and blinking in the gray morning light filtering through her bedroom curtains, Lexie sat up and reached for the cordless phone on her nightstand.

"Hullo?" she managed, wondering who could be calling so early in the morning.

"Lexie? Hi, this is Bruce."

"Bruce?" she repeated like a retarded parrot, the throbbing in her head slowly taking on jackhammer proportions.

"Cousin Bruce," he said with a little irritation. "Your Aunt Gladys' son."

"Oh, that Bruce. Sorry. I've got a really bad headache today. Maybe I'm getting the flu."

"Ah, the good old flu. I just got over a bad case of it myself a couple of weeks ago. An Asian strain, you know. A real killer."

Lexie's mind swam as she tried to recount the genealogy in her muddled mind. Aunt Gladys was her mother's sister and Bruce was her son. Ever since he'd put a frog down Lexie's shirt at the Fourth of July family picnic when she was ten, she'd never been able to stomach him. And to her knowledge, he only contacted Aunt Gladys' side of the family when he needed something.

Did he want something from her now? The idea didn't appeal much.

Lexie automatically tensed, dreading what that something might be. "How long has it been since we talked? About two years?"

"Something like that," Bruce said.

Lexie yawned. "So, what's the occasion?"

"I need to ask you a favor."

Lexie did not like the way the conversation was going. "What kind of favor?"

"I'm headquartered in Singapore right now. My company is working with some major investors over there and as district manager of the Far East division, it's crucial I be around for all final business transactions. Those won't be complete for about six more months."

"OK. What's that got to do with me?"

"I flew back to Denver about a week ago to visit Mother. She's in a nursing home there and, unfortunately, she's gotten herself into a patch of trouble."

Now Lexie was really tense. "Tell me already. I'm dying to know. How much trouble can a seventy-four-year-old woman in a nursing home get into?"

Bruce cleared his throat. "Plenty. One of the nurses found her in a, shall we say, compromising situation with one of the male patients."

"Compromising," Lexie intoned.

"They were having sex."

Lexie laughed. "Means they must be pretty healthy. The medical staff should be pleased."

"Well, they weren't," Bruce informed her dolefully. "The nursing home rules specifically prohibit intimate relations between patients. So Mother's been given the boot."

"They kicked her out?" Lexie was wide awake now. Aunt Gladys had always been eccentric and wild. Despite seven husbands, she'd never been able to settle down for long. But the family had always attributed her erratic nature to the fact she'd been a Las Vegas showgirl in her younger days and just couldn't quite get the exotic flair out of her blood.

"Mother and her, uh, boyfriend probably wouldn't have been in as much trouble if they'd kept their wild romp confined to the privacy of their rooms. But they got caught in the act on the recreation room pool table."

"Goodness, that is a little bit exhibitionist, even for Aunt Gladys. But leave it to her to find an octogenarian Romeo." Lexie raked a hand through her mussed hair. "So, why call me? What can I do?"

"The rest home will only allow Mother to stay another two weeks. After that, she has nowhere to go."

"You're kidding me? Can't you find her another home? Hire a nurse or something?"

"I've tried, but everything's full and there's not a private nurse to be found anywhere. I've got to be back in Singapore in forty-eight hours. I'm really in a bind here, Lex. Otis and Mother can't stand each other so I don't dare ask Lucy if she can stay at her place. Please, can Mother live with you?"

"That's not a good idea." Lexie thought about her and Lucy's amateur murder investigation. If Aunt Gladys came to stay the old bat would surely be in the way and her interference would compromise everything.

"C'mon Lex, be a sport. I know it would be a major imposition, but can't you help me out? Otherwise, I don't know what I'll do. I'll lose my job if I don't finish up with the Far East clients, and Mother absolutely can't live alone."

Lexie felt herself caving. "Does she still start fires?"

Bruce sighed. "When no one's looking, yes. But all you have to do is keep matches out of her reach and make sure she takes her medication."

Lexie closed her eyes and gathered her strength. Aunt Gladys wasn't just batty. She was a complete loon. A dingbat. A menace to society. "Bruce, I have no beds to spare. Just my old sofa. And I think she'd be pretty uncomfortable sleeping with springs up her butt for the next six months."

Not to be sidetracked, Bruce continued. "You're still living in your folks' house, aren't you? Doesn't it have an attic?"

"Yes, but it's full of storage."

"Clean it out. I'll foot the bill to have the place renovated into living quarters for my mom. I'll send you the same money for her room and board that I've been paying the retirement home. It'll be more than enough to take care of her."

"I don't know—"

"You know your mother would want you to do it."

Ah ha. Leave it to Bruce to use the old guilt trip. Still, Lexie was suddenly ashamed of herself. They'd been talking about poor old Aunt Gladys like she was a sack of potatoes to be stuffed out of the way on a shelf somewhere. She was, after all, family. She couldn't help that she'd lost most of her marbles long ago.

Bruce was right. If her mother were still alive, she would insist Lexie take her in, no buts about it.

Lexie also had to admit the offer was tempting since she'd been stewing about the cost of Eva's spring semester which was coming due soon. The extra money Bruce promised her would definitely come in handy. On top of it all, she'd get the chance to fix up that musty attic.

"Sure, Bruce." Lexie swallowed a hiccough that suddenly rose in her throat. "She can stay with me."

"You won't regret it," Bruce responded enthusiastically.

Lexie wasn't so sure.

CHAPTER 6

Two weeks later, Lexie, Lucy, and Eva stood in Lexie's newly refurbished attic evaluating the improvements. It had been impossible to find wallpaper and carpet and decent furniture in Moose Creek Junction. As a result Lexie had procured everything in Westonville.

True to his word, Cousin Bruce wired money right away for the project. The Carpinelli Brothers, who ran a local a carpentry shop, had done a nice job of renovation.

The cobwebs, dust bunnies, and broken windows that had recently graced the musty space were gone. Boxes of Eva's old baby clothes and toys had been stuffed into Lexie's garage. The clutter was replaced by a modest-sized sitting room with a floral patterned loveseat and a reclining rocker with a lace paneled window to let in wide beams of bright, October sunshine.

The Carpinellis had partitioned off a small

bedroom Lexie decorated with an antique sleigh bed and oval-mirrored dresser, along with a nightstand she'd found at the county flea market. She also purchased a large wardrobe for one corner of the bedroom since there wasn't enough room to install a closet.

The Carpinellis had polished the original hardwood floors until they glowed a warm honey-pine color. Lexie placed hooked rag rugs in the living area along with a large carpet covered with old-fashioned cabbage roses.

In one corner were a small drop-leaf table and two ladder-back chairs. A small refrigerator, microwave, and coffee pot sat on a butcher block in another corner. Ceiling fans with wooden paddles and antique brass accents hung in the sitting room and the bedroom.

Deep in thought, Lexie chewed her lower lip for a moment, then said, "I hope Aunt Gladys likes this. She's pretty particular where she hangs her feather boa, you know."

"Everything looks lovely, Lex." Lucy placed her hands on her hips, nodding appreciatively as she glanced around. "Aunt Gladys is lucky she has such a nice place to stay after that fiasco at the rest home."

Eva wrinkled her nose. "If I'd fixed this place up, I'd have gone with a retro look. Leather sofas and lava lamps and a black wrought iron bed."

"I thought this might suit Aunt Gladys better," Lexie explained. "Remember, she is in her seventies."

"And she was also a Las Vegas showgirl in her hey-day. Remember the photo album she showed us one time? It had pictures of her wearing all those lame' costumes that showed her butt. Oh, and those goofy headdresses and tasseled boob pasties she wore. Oh, my God!" Eva rolled her eyes dramatically. "You'd think she was actually proud of herself."

"Eva, girl, watch your language," Lucy scolded.

Eva darted an irritated glance at her aunt.

"Aunt Gladys made a good living as an enter-tainer, Eva," Lexie said. "She put Cousin Bruce through Harvard law school. It's nothing to be ashamed of."

"But Bruce is *such* a big loser! He's still living off fried rice and fish heads in the Orient. And now he's totally abandoning his mother."

"Lexie is only taking Aunt Gladys in for a few months until Bruce returns from Singapore to take care of her," Lucy commented.

Eva snorted. "Right, like I believe that. Bruce will never come to get her. He's made a life of stay-ing away from Aunt Gladys and her harping."

"Eva, honey. Honest, we're only keeping Aunt Gladys temporarily."

Eva threw her arms in the air. "Whatever, Mom. I just still can't believe she got herself in trouble at the rest home. She's pretty ancient to be doing the mattress mambo with some old fart."

Lucy made an outraged sound. She turned bright red, whipped a fan from her purse and began to wave it madly in front of her face.

Lexie squeezed Eva's shoulders, silently asking her daughter to spare her aunt from such bold, but truthful language. "Sweetie, I don't think there's an age when doing the, uh, mattress mambo, is against the rules. Unless you do it in a retirement home."

"Exactly," Eva said. "She is a complete Looney Toon."

"Eva, dear," Lucy interceded. "It isn't charitable to pass judgment on Aunt Gladys or her lifestyle."

"Whatever." Eva glanced around the renovated attic with a shrewd eye. "You don't think this place'll be a little too *Miss Daisy* for her? I mean, this is an old bag who takes shots of tequila straight up, screw the worm."

"Eva!" Lexie glared at her daughter.

"Well, that's what Dad always used to say. He never liked Aunt Gladys much."

"She never liked him either, honey." Considering her experience with men, Aunt Gladys had probably seen through Dan's good looks and smooth talk years ago. Why couldn't Lexie have done the same?

"Speaking of Dad," Eva said. "Have you heard anything from him lately?"

Lexie exchanged glances with Lucy. She'd told her sister about the letter she received from her friend in California bearing news of Dan and Davina's newest arrival. Lexie and Lucy agreed if Dan didn't soon tell Eva she had a baby sister, Lexie should.

"I got a letter from Ann Tollerton the other day.

She mentioned him."

Eva's expression brightened. "What did she say?"

"Ahem." Lucy walked toward the door. "I'm off to church, ladies. It's potluck Sunday, and I need to collect my chicken stew and chocolate pudding. I'll see you later." With that, she ducked out of the attic.

Eva stared after her Aunt, then turned to Lexie. "What's going on, Mom? What did Ann say?"

"Eva, sit down." Lexie steered her daughter to the sofa where they both plopped down. "Ann said your father and Davina had a baby girl."

"Really." Eva blinked, then turned to stare out the round attic window. "My bedroom's empty so I guess they can put the baby in there."

"Eva, are you OK?" Lexie patted her daughter's back. "I know this is a shock."

"Sure. I'm fine." Suddenly Eva put her face in her hands and groaned. "Jeez, Mom, why didn't he tell me? Why doesn't he talk to me anymore? I don't even know my little sister's name."

Lexie felt sad for her daughter. It must be hard to have been the apple of her daddy's eye for so long, then have him abandon her. What was he thinking?

"I'm sure he's just so caught up in this new life he's making some poor choices."

"Doesn't he love me anymore?" Eva asked miserably, looking at Lexie with tear-filled eyes. "Did I do something wrong?"

"Oh, no. It's not your fault. It was never your fault. You are a good person, a good daughter. Your father's apparently dealing with some emotional challenges. Give him time."

"You've always made excuses for him, Mom. And he was awful to you."

Lexie shrugged. "I married him and I stayed with him. That was my choice."

"Why didn't you ever leave him?"

"You were little. And you loved your daddy. I didn't want to spoil that for you."

"Oh, Mom." Eva hugged her mother and the two of them sobbed softly. After a while, Eva pulled back. "We're OK now, aren't we? We don't need him."

"I don't. But someday you may want to have a relationship with him again. He is your father, after all."

Eva stood and brushed away her tears with the back of her hand. "That doesn't mean I need him."

Lexie stood next to her taller daughter. Tall like her father. When he'd blasted off into the ozone layer with Davina, did he have any idea how much he would hurt his little girl?

"Don't make snap decisions, sweetie. We all have our disappointments, but life has a way of changing things as time goes on."

"Well, right now I don't care if I ever talk to that jerk again. He's got a new wife and a new baby so he obviously doesn't need to pay attention to me any more." Eva grabbed her jeans jacket and put it on, then turned to Lexie. "When are you and Aunt Lucy going to pick up Aunt Gladys from the funny farm?"

"We're leaving tomorrow. Can you still come

home and mind the café?"

"Sure. I'll be done with classes for the week and I'm not scheduled to work at the bookstore for a while."

"You are an angel." Lexie hugged Eva. She walked downstairs, watching as the girl got into her car.

Eva fished keys out of her purse and slid them into the ignition. "I want to take you out for your birthday Saturday night. Dinner and a movie maybe. Is that OK?"

Lord, that's right! She would be thirty-seven—she'd nearly forgotten. AARP would be knocking on her door before she knew it. She sighed. "Sure. We have to take Aunt Gladys, though."

"Not a problem. She'll get a kick out of what I have planned. Later."

Lexie waved as Eva drove down the dusty street, wondering why her daughter thought Aunt Gladys would get such a kick out of dinner and a movie. It wasn't like the old gal didn't get around, even in a rest home.

A gust of warm October wind blew dry brown leaves across the porch when Lexie went inside. In the kitchen, she made herself a cup of hazelnut coffee. She pulled mixing bowls and utensils out of the dishwasher and began to assemble the next day's café menu. Beef stew and the usual sandwich fillings, apple pie, and huckleberry muffins.

As she worked, she considered her revelation to Eva about Dan's baby. Had she done the right thing?

Eva had asked for the truth and she had told her. The girl was growing up and needed to understand life was not always kind.

She shifted her mind back to Aunt Gladys and the duty she had taken on. The woman was going to be a handful. But at least the trip to Denver to pick her up at the rest home would give Lexie and Lucy an opportunity to talk to Ernie and Sophie Howell.

For the past few weeks, Lexie had been calling around Denver to all the magic shops she could find, looking for the one Ernie Howell owned. She was about to give up when, on a stroke of luck, she'd run across his store—Houdini's Hideout.

She'd probably have to sell herself on the streets to pay her phone bill next month. No doubt it would make her face crack when she read the amount. But if they got enough information from the Howells to clear her name, it would be worth it.

Lexie was anxious to have Gabe Stevenson off her tail. Though, for some strange reason, a part of her was thrilled he might be interested in her.

Even if it was for all the wrong reasons.

The next morning at the ungodly hour of five a.m., Lexie—all showered and dressed in jeans and a sweatshirt—tiptoed into Eva's room to tell her good-bye. Then she went downstairs to the kitchen and had a bowl of cornflakes and skim milk.

Silently, Lexie took stock of things. Since Eva would be manning the fort she had made sure several freshly baked loaves of bread, sandwich fillings, and soups were on hand for customers. Eva would only need to keep the crock-pots warm and fill the orders.

Finished with her last minute evaluation, Lexie watched out the bay window for Lucy. When her sister drove up in front of the house, Lexie slid on a down jacket, scooped up her purse and hustled out into the frosty dawn air.

Lexie's truck wasn't fit to handle the long trip to Denver and there wouldn't be room for Aunt Gladys anyway. Lucy's vehicle, therefore, would transport them on their next undercover adventure, with the side trip to collect Cousin Bruce's mother from Mountain Shadows Rest Home.

A cloud of steam swirled from the tailpipe of Lucy's car as Lexie hopped inside. Teeth chattering, Lexie said, "S-s-sure glad your car's warm. You could hang meat outside. Think we'll run into any icebergs on I-25?"

"I really doubt it." Lucy said, laughing. She was dressed in a dark navy dress, dark support hose, and a pearl necklace. "Did you remember to pack your amateur spy kit?"

"The one with the secret decoder ring?"

Grinning, Lucy nodded.

"Nope. But I did bring Cracker Jack." Lexie pulled two boxes out of her purse.

Lucy rolled her eyes heavenward. "Lord have

mercy. You're going to make me fat as a cow."

"If the Lord has mercy, He will help us find the murderer so Stevenson can take me off his suspect list," Lexie said.

The sisters munched on caramel corn, not saying much. But Lexie could tell by the set of Lucy's lips that she was displeased by the inconvenience of not only having a sister under suspicion for murder, but also having to collect a crazy aunt from a nursing home. In her mind, Lexie agreed this wasn't the most pleasant of experiences, but what could she do?

Once it was light, the bright blue sky, slashed with a few wispy clouds, arched overhead like a huge dome. As the time went by, the temperature warmed and the sisters shed their jackets. Lexie rolled down her window, watching as waves of heat shimmered on the cars flying past.

Several hours later they reached Denver with its skyscraper horizon and Front Range mountain backdrop. It seemed summer hadn't left the big city yet, even though further north autumn's morning and evening temperatures had frosted unfortunate flowers into withered vines.

Lexie slipped the Denver city map from Lucy's glove compartment and studied the highlighted route to Houdini's Hideout. For a moment, everything was a jumble of numbers and licorice ribbon streets. Thank goodness someone had invented maps. Otherwise, Denver would remain an asphalt jungle to anyone who didn't live there.

"What exit do I take, for Pete's sake?" Vehicles zoomed past Lucy's car like popcorn in a pan of hot oil, and the corners of her mouth twitched nervously. "I'd like to know before the next century."

"Don't get your panties in a twist, Luce." Lexie scowled at the map. "We want exit three-twenty. It's coming right up."

"Finally." Lucy slid onto the exit ramp. "Right or left?"

Lexie glanced back at the map. "Right. I mean . . ." She held up her hands, noting the hand her wedding ring used to be on. "Left! Sorry. Take a left at the light."

Lucy raised her brows. "Are you sure which left you want me to take?"

Lexie nodded. "The left that goes this way." She gestured with her wedding ring-less hand.

Traffic was crazy as Lucy threaded her way through the narrow streets of downtown Denver until she got to a small strip mall near several rows of tacky older brick homes. Lexie noticed Houdini's Hideout as soon as they pulled into the pot-holed parking lot. "There it is," she told Lucy, pointing. "See the black top hat and the magic wand on the sign?"

"Here we are." The car rolled to a stop. "What do we do now?"

"Let's go inside and check it out. Play it by ear, you know?"

"Get ourselves into some innocent trouble?"

Lexie grinned and nodded.

Inside Houdini's Hideout were several aisles of magic equipment in fancy packaging. There were card tricks, strobe lights, fantasy gear, sweeping black capes, and top hats—you name it. Everything to warm the cockles of an amateur magician's heart.

It was a modest establishment . . . not extremely large, but not exactly postage-stamp-sized, either. Adding to the mystical atmosphere of Houdini's Hideout were its deep purple walls decorated with yellow star, moon, and sun decals.

The checkout counter was located on one side of the store where a small woman with a dark page-boy hairstyle was waiting on a line of customers, a few of whom were rambunctious little boys with stern mothers trying to keep them under control.

The world of illusion sported some pretty hefty price tags. So hefty Lexie would have had a difficult time affording even a small, disappearing coin box with her café earnings.

"Go look around and ask the lady at the counter some questions. Let me know what you find out."

Lucy patted stray hairs coming loose from her bun. "If you insist. But I really have no idea what this will accomplish."

When Lucy wandered toward the pageboy clerk, Lexie looked around for a bit, examining various items until she reached a small raised stage at the back of the store. Several people, both young and old, were gathered around a flaxen-haired man probably in his late thirties, wearing a top hat and cape, performing along to soft music. As Lexie watched, he did the white-rabbit-out-of-a-hat trick, and made several white doves appear in a cage, then disappear. Impressed, Lexie glanced around to see how he might have engineered such incredible feats.

The crowd clapped after the man's last trick, then a young boy of about ten wearing baggy pants and a baseball cap spoke up. "How did you do that, mister? I mean, that was pretty cool."

"Ah, a great magician never gives away his secrets," the man declared. He tapped a paperback book with his magic wand. "But for fifteen dollars and ninety-five cents, you can buy my book, *Ernie the Magnificent's Tricks and Illusions*. Guaranteed to give you instant success at being a great magician. That is, if you follow all the rules to a T," he added.

"Mom, can I get one? Puh-leese?" The youngster stared up at his mom with a long face and beseeching puppy dog eyes.

Mom clenched her jaw and shook her head at her son, mouthing a silent, emphatic, *No*, and ignored the boy's pouting disappointment.

Lexie stared hard at Ernie the Magnificent. Was he Ernie Howell? Proprietor of Houdini's Hideout and jaded husband of Sophie? She moved closer to the stage, intent on listening and watching.

"I need an assistant," Ernie declared, his gaze searching the crowd. Immediately a dozen hands shot in the air. "How refreshing. A crowd of eager apprentices. But for this particular trick, I need a grownup. You . . . the young lady with the lovely red hair." He gestured at Lexie with a patient smile. "Could I convince you to be Ernie the Magnificent's assistant for his next trick?"

"*Me?*" Lexie squeaked, moving slowly through the crowd. "I'm afraid I'm no good at magic, Mr. Magnificent."

"You don't need to be," Ernie the Magnificent continued, his chest pompously puffed. "Leave the illusions to the master."

Lexie cleared her throat and stepped onto the stage. "Uh, sure, Mr. Magnificent. Whatever you say."

Ernie rolled out a brightly painted coffin on legs and gestured at another table laden with wicked-looking saws. He made a grand sweep of his hand, indicating Lexie should crawl inside the coffin.

Lexie cringed. She really didn't want to do that. She wanted to disappear. Fast. Swallowing hard, she whispered to the master, "Uh, look, Ernie. Is this safe? I mean, I'm too young to die."

She thought of her upcoming birthday. Eva probably thought she was older than dirt. Heck, Eva probably thought she *named* dirt. Too bad. Lexie wasn't ready to be pushing up daisies.

Not just yet.

"I assure you, Madame, Ernie the Magnificent has never harmed an assistant yet." He took Lexie's arm and guided her firmly toward the coffin.

Lexie took exception to the *yet* part. What was that all about? She didn't want to be the *yet* assistant.

As the master helped her lie down inside the box, heart pounding like a jackhammer, she screwed up her courage. Ernie the Magnificent wouldn't risk his budding reputation by killing one of the volunteers in his performance, would he?

That would be very bad for business.

As Ernie closed the coffin lid, Lexie found her voice. "Uh, Ernie," she said softly. "Did you recently move to Denver from Moose Creek Junction?"

"I wish you wouldn't interrupt my magic trick, young lady," he whispered hoarsely. "Why do you want to know?"

"That's my hometown."

"Hmmm. Thought I recognized you." He clicked another lock into place. "Must have seen you around."

The master turned to face the crowd and said with a flourish, "And now for my magic saw trick. Watch closely, ladies and gentlemen. My magical powers are second only to the great Harry Houdini himself."

When he turned back to Lexie, she whispered, "Did you move from Moose Creek Junction? You and your wife Sophie and your two boys?"

He looked visibly shaken. "I'm in the middle of a performance here and my concentration shouldn't be disturbed," he returned in a low, irritated voice.

"What do you know about Henry Whitehead?"

His icy blue eyes got paler and wider, but he made no comment.

"He was murdered a little over a month ago," Lexie added.

The master's mouth worked open and closed, yet he still made no sound.

"I heard Henry had put the moves on Sophie, and that's why you moved away. To save your marriage."

The crowd grew impatient and Lexie heard them shifting restlessly. As for her, the wooden support around her neck was digging into tender flesh. She wanted out of this death box. Sooner than later. But curiosity outweighed discomfort.

"Why did you come here?" Ernie the Magnificent's nostrils flared and his face turned red as a tomato. "I don't know anything about Whitehead."

"Did you recently make a trip to Moose Creek Junction to confront him? Did things get out of control?"

"You're out of your mind, lady."

"But—"

Ernie whirled away from her, voice booming. "Observe if you will, ladies and gentlemen, the master's greatest feat. This will amaze and astound you. Watch closely as I send razor sharp saws through my lovely assistant here, yet she will emerge unharmed."

Lexie realized, too late, that the particular moment she had chosen to confront Ernie the Magnificent about Whitehead's murder was probably not the best. What if one of the razor sharp saws slipped? What if she became a grisly statistic in a sadistic magician's act? Lexie's heart hammered faster and she began to sweat buckets in the coffin.

Ernie nodded to someone in the wings of the stage, someone not visible to Lexie. The music swelled. Her gut clenched like a twisted rubber band. "Ernie, listen to me. Don't do this. I just want to get to the bottom of Whitehead's murder—" Lexie cringed and sucked in a breath as Ernie brought one of the saws down into the coffin.

Shhh-thunk. With deft movements, the master slid one of the wicked blades into place.

Shhh-thunk.

Lexie didn't feel a thing. Maybe she couldn't. She could be bleeding to death and no one would know. Is this what death felt like? Does death feel like . . . *nothing*?

Shhh-thunk. The last blade slid into place.

Tapping on the wooden surface, Ernie spun the coffin around a couple of times. Lexie wanted to vomit. She had not volunteered to have her brains scrambled. Or her limbs severed.

"Ernie, stop it this instant! I'm going to be sick," she shouted, her insides rising up in her throat. From her crazy, disoriented perspective, she could see Lucy in the crowd, her hands covering her mouth.

Make him stop, Lexie wanted to tell her sister. He's trying to kill me . . .

Suddenly the lights went out and the crowd gasped. Lexie gasped, too. She gasped so hard she thought she'd swallowed her tongue for sure. Man, she was tired of having the frigging lights go out on her. When the lights went out, bad things happened.

Finally the coffin quit spinning and came to a complete stop. Lexie heard Ernie, or someone, fiddling with the coffin in the dark. It sounded like the blades were sliding in the coffin again. There was the sound of a small explosion, and the lights came back on.

Billowy white smoke stung Lexie's eyes and made them water and she sneezed as she turned to look at the crowd.

Parents were coughing and waving their hands in front of their faces while the younger crowd was shouting, "Wow," and "Awesome," and talking excitedly about what a cool guy Ernie the Magnificent was.

Lexie didn't think he was so cool. She was getting claustrophobia. Where the hell was he, anyway? She wanted out of this moldy crate. "Ernie, I don't care how Magnificent you think you are. My assistant days are over. Ernie!"

"Hey, lady," one of the kids shouted, hands cupped around his mouth. "Chill out. Your coffin's unlocked. Get out yourself."

As Lexie started pounding on the thing, Lucy stepped on stage and pulled on the coffin lid. It finally opened and Lucy helped Lexie crawl out of her tomb.

Lexie shivered, brushing off her clothes. "Did you see where Ernie went?"

Lucy shook her head. "No one did. After everything went dark there was a small explosion, then the lights went on and there was smoke everywhere. Ernie disappeared."

"Creep," Lexie complained as they stepped away from the stage and regrouped in a small alcove full of magic books.

"Did you find anything out?" Lucy asked.

"Well, I'm pretty sure Ernie the Magnificent is Ernie Howell from Moose Creek Junction. But he sure didn't want to talk about it. Acted scared to death. And when I mentioned Whitehead, he nearly went ballistic."

"Not too smart, Lex. Especially when the master had you locked up tight in his coffin. With saws, no less."

Lexie folded her arms across her chest. "Unfortunately, that occurred to me when it was too late."

Lucy glanced around the room as though she might see the master hiding behind the curtains or lurking in the wings of the stage.

"What did you find out from Mrs. Magnificent? At least I'm assuming the woman at the counter is Sophie Howell."

"Oh, she's Sophie Howell all right. And she confirmed she's from Moose Creek Junction. There's only one thing."

"What's that?"

"She claims she's never heard of Henry Whitehead."

Lexie felt a lead weight in her stomach. "She must be lying."

"Probably. It appears neither Sophie nor her husband want to admit to knowing him. Makes them look a little guilty, don't you think?"

"Sure does." Lexie thought for a minute. "Do you think it was a conspiracy? That both Ernie and Sophie had something to do with Whitehead's murder?"

"It also could be that one or the other murdered him and they're covering for each other."

"People do strange things when it comes to affairs of the heart." Lexie remembered how betrayed she'd felt when Dan left her for Davina Blakely. All those years of her loyalty and devotion down the toilet.

Did Dan fall *out* of love with her and suddenly fall *in* love with Davina?

That didn't make any more sense than the idea that two people who had nearly divorced would reconcile and go out and kill the wife's ex-lover.

Why would they risk their futures on revenge?

"This is a creepy place, Luce. Don't you agree we've found out all we're going to about Ernie Howell and Sophie? "

Lucy nodded. "Amen to that."

"Then let's go collect Aunt Gladys."

Arm in arm, the sisters walked to the door.

Chapter 7

SUNLIGHT GLINTED OFF THE PINK STUCCO WALLS of the Mountain Shadows Rest Home, sprawling across an expanse of drying autumn grass like a crab in the sand.

Standing in the parking lot next to her sister, Lexie shaded her eyes from the bright sun with one hand and studied the wrought iron fence behind the building. It enclosed a large, tree-filled yard where the residents probably took walks and possibly played pinochle on good days. And complained that no one ever came to visit them.

A pang of sadness touched Lexie's heart and she hoped Lucy wouldn't see the emotion misting her eyes.

Lucy, of course, all-knowing sister that she was, was not fooled one bit. "What's wrong, dear?"

Lexie knew better than to hide what she was feeling. "I was just thinking about Mom and Dad. I miss them. Especially this time of the year . . . when the accident—"

"Happened," Lucy finished for her. She sighed and took out a crisp, lacy-edged hankie and wiped moisture from her eyes. "I know, me too. Who would have thought a stupid rabbit crossing the road would end it all for them? "

"I know. And Daddy would never hurt a fly so he must have swerved to miss it. If they'd only been wearing seatbelts."

"They never believed in them." Lucy paused. "Look at it this way, dear; they're at peace now. In a much better place than we are."

"But it's not fair," Lexie added softly, a quaver in her voice.

"I know, dear. I know. Look at the bright side." She nodded in the direction of the rest home. "We've still got good old Aunt Gladys."

They both moaned.

"So, how about you and Otis put Aunt Gladys in *your* spare room? I'm too young to die."

"That's not a good idea, Lexie."

This response from a woman who preached charity and compassion from sunrise to sunset? Lexie shook her head. "How in the world am I going to handle Miss Daisy-from-hell? She's as squirrelly as a sack of cats headed up the river."

"The Lord never gives us greater burdens than we can handle," Lucy returned.

"I think He made a mistake this time. Nobody can handle Aunt Gladys." Lexie hefted her purse on her shoulder. "We'd best go spring the grand old dame before she causes any more trouble."

Lucy looked heavenward, closed her eyes and said a little prayer. "Yes, let's go."

As they walked at an uneager pace to the front doors of the retirement home, Lexie figured Lucy could sally forth with such conviction since Aunt Gladys wouldn't be such a bother to her. What did she have to lose?

"Why do I feel like we're walking into the bowels of the beast?" Lexie asked.

"Maybe because the last time we saw Aunt Gladys, she set Mom and Dad's house on fire with sandalwood incense and tried to put it out with the garden hose."

Lexie laughed. "That's right. And remember how most of their good silver and crystal disappeared along with a couple of family antiques?"

"Yes, I do," Lucy said.

"Good gravy, Dad was pissed off," Lexie added. "He never wanted Aunt Gladys to come and stay with them again. He couldn't figure out how two sisters could be so opposite. Mom was always down-to-earth and calm, but he claimed Aunt Gladys was like a firecracker in a pork barrel."

Lucy *ts*, *tsked*. "You do have good insurance on your place, don't you?"

"Covers flood and fire," Lexie said with a nod. "And hopefully, all the holocausts Aunt Gladys can conjure up. Don't know about petty larceny, though."

"Say your prayers and keep your fingers crossed. Let's hope it won't be too long before Cousin Bruce comes to collect her."

"I won't hold my breath," Lexie said. "He's 45 and still can't manage to find his way home."

The sisters went inside and announced who they were at the front desk. A young lady named Rita assured them she would have a couple of attendants bring Mrs. Maplethorpe out to them right away and wouldn't they like to sit and make themselves comfortable?

Lexie studied the Navajo wall hangings and leather western art that filled the waiting area. Despite the décor, a persistent smell of disinfectant pervaded her nostrils—an attempt to mask something Lexie did not want to know about. The place made her feel weird. Like when your underwear twists up your crotch and you're too embarrassed to straighten it out.

Time ticked by and finally a serious-looking man, probably in his fifties, wearing tan Dockers, a button-down shirt, and striped tie approached them. "Pardon me, are you ladies Mrs. Maplethorpe's nieces?"

"Yes, we are," Lexie informed him.

His black and gray mustache twitched. "I'm Dr. Ravenwood, her physician. I'm sorry about the wait. I'm sorry to inform you your aunt is missing."

"Missing? As in *gone*?" How can that be?" Lucy produced a fan from her purse and began waving it madly.

"Dr. Ravenwood," Lexie said through clenched teeth, "aren't the residents watched closely?"

"Yes, they are. But I'm afraid Mrs. Maplethorpe managed to slip past our attendants." He wrung his hands. "This is terrible and I hold myself completely responsible."

The sisters stared at each other, then at Ravenwood.

Dr. Ravenwood's mustache twitched again. "I can assure the two of you this type of occurrence is very rare."

Lexie folded her arms across her chest. "How long has Aunt Gladys been gone?"

"The attendants saw her at breakfast, which is served at 8 a.m. every morning."

Lucy's jaw dropped, and she quickly shut her mouth.

"Two hours?" Lexie tapped her toe. "The woman's been missing for two hours, and you just now realized she's gone?"

Ravenwood stiffened, as though someone had run a metal rod up through his doctor's coat. "I assure you, we run a very reliable and reputable establishment. Despite our best efforts, on occasion mishaps occur."

"What are you doing to find Aunt Gladys?"

"Several attendants are combing the grounds at this very moment."

"What if she's not on the premises?" Lucy hugged her tapestry purse tightly to her bosom. "What if she's out wandering the streets of Denver? *Alone?*"

"Ladies, please don't jump to conclusions. Rest assured your aunt couldn't have gotten out the front door. We have video cameras monitoring the entrance twenty-four hours a day. The girls at the front desk would certainly have seen her. Right, Rita?" He nodded toward the counter.

"Absolutely," Rita-at-the-front-desk agreed. "Shelly and I would have stopped her from going anywhere." She turned to answer the phone.

"Your aunt has done this before. I'm sure we'll find her unharmed."

"She's disappeared before?" Lucy fanned even harder. "Oh, my."

Dr. Ravenwood clasped his hands behind his back. "She fancies the covered pavilions out on the grounds and that's where we found her last time. Mrs. Maplethorpe claimed she was having a rehearsal for one of her Las Vegas reviews—"

"Dr. Ravenwood, Dr. Ravenwood!"

Everyone turned to the little old blue-haired lady in a flowered housedress and sneakers who shuffled up to them holding tightly to a cane. Her chin quivered and her bright green eyes met the doctor's steady gaze. "Someone's up and died out in the courtyard. It's just awful."

"Oh, my." Lucy grasped the arm of her chair so tightly her knuckles went white.

Dr. Ravenwood put a hand on the elderly woman's arm. "Now, Hazel, did you take your medication this morning?"

She nodded excitedly. "I'm not seeing things, doc. Honest. And it wasn't just me who saw 'em. Bea and Norton saw, too. Saw 'em out the game room window. Somebody's layin' by the fountain, dead as a doornail. I swear."

"All right, calm down now. You go on back and tell Bea and the others to return to their rooms. I'll take care of everything."

Muttering to herself and shaking her blue curls, Hazel shuffled back down a hallway and disappeared.

"You'll have to excuse poor Hazel. She has delusional spells on occasion. She's apparently had a little setback today."

"Mrs. Maplethorpe's son completed most of the forms necessary to release her, and he's given permission for you two to check her out. But there is still some final paperwork to be completed before your aunt can leave." He nodded in the direction of a sheaf of papers on the counter. "While you ladies take care of it, I'll check on the . . . ahem . . . person in the courtyard."

"But what about Aunt Gladys?"

Ravenwood acted like he didn't hear Lexie's question as he exited out a pair of glass doors onto a flagstone patio.

"I can't believe this is happening," Lexie muttered incredulously. "Cousin Bruce was paying out the nose for this place, and they misplace their patients?"

"Excuse me, ladies," Rita-at-the-front-desk said. "Could I have one of you sign these forms?"

"I'll go look for Aunt Gladys while you John Hancock the paperwork," Lexie said to Lucy.

As Lucy walked up to the counter, Lexie slipped out the glass doors, walked across the patio and descended a set of wide stone steps. Hearing Dr. Ravenwood's agitated voice she paused, noting it seemed to be coming from behind an arbor filled with dry, crumbling roses and vines.

Lexie hustled around the arbor and stopped mid-stride.

Aunt Gladys lay on the ground, her cap of snow-white curly hair pressed against the lawn. She wore a tiger-stripe caftan, pink flowered flip-flops, black beads the size of walnuts, large hoop earrings and large black frame glasses. Her powdered and heavily made up face was still as a corpse's.

Uprooted golden and russet-colored Chrysan-themums lay around her in an oval, coffin-like shape. Lying extremely still, the old lady clutched a mum-bouquet in her red-nailed grasp, her eyes shut against the warm autumn sun, a mischievous grin tilting her plump, ruby-colored lips.

Dr. Ravenwood folded his arms across his chest, his expression stern. "For the second time, Mrs. Maplethorpe, get up. The ground is wet and you'll catch a cold."

"I'm dead. Leave me alone."

"You can't stay out here. You're upsetting everyone."

She opened one eye and peered at the doctor. "Why? You've killed me with all your stupid rules and regulations. A body can barely breathe in this concentration camp. You Nazi fascist pig, you."

"You have got to get up. Your nieces are here to take you home."

"And make me leave my Herman? I'm in love with him, you know. The only man I've *ever* loved," she added theatrically.

Lexie couldn't help but grin. Aunt Gladys had had seven husbands in her lifetime. She'd proclaimed true love for each of them and went through extensive grieving periods whether they died or she'd divorced them. Yessiree, Aunt Gladys was the queen of drama queens.

"This rotten flea-bag of a place is standing in the way of our true happiness." She opened her eyes wide and harrumphed loudly. "Nazis, Nazis, Nazis, all of you. Ach! Next thing I know you'll be herding all of us into a gas chamber!"

"Good heavens." Lexie ignored Dr. Ravenwood's scowl, pushed past him, and kneeled beside her aunt. "It's nice to see you, Aunt Gladys. It's been a long time."

Aunt Gladys' brown eyes opened wide. "Who the hell are you?"

Lexie blinked, a little taken aback by Aunt Gladys' vehemence. "Your niece, Aunt Gladys. Lexie."

Aunt Gladys' painted brows drew together. "My

sister's girl? *Leslie*? All the way from Moose Creek Junction?"

"*Lexie*, Aunt Gladys.   Short for Alexandria." Lexie took her aunt's hand, noting the dry, parchment-like skin covered in brown age spots.   About fifteen million gold bracelets rattled on her arm.

"Lexie, Leslie.   Same difference in my book." She sat up slowly with a grimace.   "What kind of a name is that anyway?"

"It's the name your sister gave me."

"Ah, Lucille Beatrice."   She smiled wistfully. "How is the old girl doing these days?   She still singing in the church choir?   And how's that pastor husband of hers?   Still fingering his prayer beads?"

Lexie's stomach twisted.   "She and my father were killed in a car accident.   Don't you remember?"

Aunt Gladys squeezed her eyes shut.   "Ah, yes. Her and Princess Di.   It's such a tragedy when we lose good people.   They say only the good die young. That must mean I'm bad.   Very bad.   *When I'm good, I'm bad.   When I'm bad, I'm even better.*"   She cackled.   "Mae West said that.   She was the best."   Aunt Gladys craned her neck and looked over Lexie's shoulder.   "Where's that big sister of yours?   Lucy? Dr. Demented here says she came, too."

Lexie stifled a chuckle, but it came out like a retarded snort.   "She's waiting for us out front.   We're taking you home to Moose Creek Junction."

"Oh sure, bury me in the armpit of America again."   She held up a long, bony middle finger.

"Where busybodies rule and normal people drool."

"Really, it's not that bad, Aunt Gladys."

Her brown eyes snapped. "Can't we go somewhere fun like Las Vegas? I can still dance, you know. I could hire on at the Flamingo. Teach those anorexic flailing floozies a thing or two." Aunt Gladys tried with difficulty to stand. Lexie quickly took one arm and Dr. Ravenwood grasped the other, helping to lift her up.

"Is Herman coming with us, too? Please tell me he is or I'll simply have a coronary." Aunt Gladys pressed a hand over her heart and stared heavenward.

Dr. Ravenwood firmly told her, "Herman's family picked him up yesterday. He is no longer a resident at Mountain Shadows."

Gladys shoved her hands on her hips. "He left me? Without even saying goodbye?"

"He went home to his family, Mrs. Maplethorpe. Just like you're going to."

"Bastard." Aunt Gladys jutted out her chin and fixed Dr. Ravenwood with a glare. "All men are bastards, you know. Including you, Dr. Demented."

"You're upset, madam," Dr. Ravenwood said with strained patience. He took Aunt Gladys' elbow and steered her back to the patio. "Let's get you to your room so you can get dressed."

Aunt Gladys smacked Dr. Ravenwood on the back of his head. "I am dressed, you nincompoop!"

Something plopped to the ground and landed by Aunt Gladys's caftan. She looked down and sucked in a breath.

"What's this?" Dr. Ravenwood leaned over to pick up a diamond-studded watch "I don't recall you having a watch like this, Mrs. Maplethorpe."

Aunt Gladys pursed her lips. "It's not mine, exactly."

"Where did you get it?" Ravenwood asked.

"I borrowed it from Minnie. You know, the poor old darling doesn't need timepieces these days. She's loonier than a . . . a loon."

"I take it you borrowed the watch without Minnie's knowledge?"

"I resent your implication that I stole it. Really, Dr. Demented. Perhaps you are losing your marbles. *Physician, heal thyself . . .*"

"I'm sure Aunt Gladys meant no harm," Lexie said. She met Aunt Gladys' gaze. "You meant to return the watch, right?"

"Of course." Aunt Gladys lifted a haughty brow. "I was merely polishing it."

"Dr. Ravenwood, will you please return the watch to Minnie for Aunt Gladys?" Lexie asked.

"By all means." Ravenwood pocketed the watch and took Aunt Gladys' elbow again. "This way, ladies."

As they walked into the retirement home, Aunt Gladys between Dr. Ravenwood and Lexie, she noticed how the old lady's frame was bent with age. Despite Aunt Gladys' feistiness, she still seemed frail. It was apparent the old gal would need protection, even it if was simply from herself.

A bad feeling washed over Lexie. Boy, oh boy, oh boy. She knew she was in for the time of her life with Aunt Gladys. Maybe the old lady would calm down and behave once she and Lucy got her home. But she wouldn't hold her breath on that one.

Gladys abruptly jerked away from Ravenwood. "Take your hands off of me, you whiny pervert! I'm not a thumb-sucking baby. I can still dress myself."

Dr. Ravenwood dropped his hands to his sides. "Of course you can. I apologize."

Aunt Gladys turned to Lexie. "And Leslie. If I'm to be staying with you, you simply must evict that boy-man who's been living with you all these years. I have trouble enough sleeping at night without Junior crawling around up on the roof, making all kinds of noise."

Boy-man? Junior? What universe was she living in? "Sure, Aunt Gladys. I'll get rid of him right away."

"Hmmph!" Mums drooping in her hands, Aunt Gladys pushed past the doctor, flounced inside and strutted down the hall to her room.

Dr. Ravenwood looked at Lexie and shrugged. "Your aunt is, shall we say, a most eccentric woman."

Lexie nodded, thinking that *eccentric* was putting it mildly. Man, oh man, oh man was she in for it. This was going to be one heck of an autumn.

She was under suspicion for murder. She was living with a certifiable lunatic.

Good Lord. She could only begin to imagine the fireworks once she got Aunt Gladys installed in her house and in her life.

It would be the Fourth of July all over again.

With Aunt Gladys signed out of the home, Lexie and Lucy loaded her bags and suitcases, which filled up the trunk and most of the back seat. At last, the three women belted up, took off, and headed north. With the unusually high fall temperatures hovering somewhere in the nineties, Lucy's air conditioning blasted away. Aunt Gladys in the back seat was blasting away, too, griping about the rotten nursing home and horrible Dr. Demented, all the while crocheting a purple afghan, gnarled fingers flying.

When the nursing home stories dried up, Aunt Gladys changed to long-winded stories about *sweet little Brucie* when he was a boy. *Sweet little Brucie my foot*, Lexie thought. If he was so sweet, why hadn't he come home from Singapore to care for his mother instead of pawning her off on relatives? She hoped he hadn't been lying when he said he'd be home soon to collect her.

No, change the hope. Lexie *prayed* he would be back.

Amazingly enough, the old gal continued to ramble for three hours. Three hours? How could anyone find that much to talk about? It just wasn't right. Just about the time Lexie thought she was going to pass out from the high pitched sound ringing in her ears, Aunt Gladys fell asleep, snoring loudly enough to wake King Tut.

Lucy gave Lexie a deer-in-the-headlights look as they headed into a restaurant. Lexie could tell that her patience was worn thin, too, because beads of sweat had popped out on her usually cool brow, and she was fanning her face. Another hot flash. If she wasn't menopausal, Lexie figured she would be soon, having Aunt Gladys around.

They returned home early in the evening without incident, except that both sisters were tone-deaf, thanks to Princess Runs-At-the-Mouth. Lucy helped Lexie settle Aunt Gladys in the attic apartment, then she gave Lexie a long-faced look that hinted heavily of her desire to leave. Lexie walked her to the door.

"Come by to visit often, Lucille," Aunt Gladys brightly told Lucy, waving one of her bony, be-ringed fingers before she threw a gauzy, fringed scarf over a lamp shade. "You're welcome any time."

At the front door, Lucy turned to Lexie, her forehead wrinkled in concern. "I'm worried. Maybe we shouldn't have taken Aunt Gladys in."

"*We* didn't. *I* did."

"You know Otis can't stand her. My house would be world war three if she stayed with me. But that's a minor detail."

Like clockwork, Sister Lucy listened each Sunday at church to sermons on the mount about being a good neighbor, loving thy fellow man and taking care of your own. Obviously, she only practiced what the preacher preached if it fit into her lifestyle. Funny, the things you learned about your family once you moved back home.

"I don't understand. How is the fact that Aunt Gladys has the potential to wreak utter havoc on my home a minor detail?"

"What about our murder investigation? How are we going to manage that with the poor dear lurking around, having to be watched every minute of her waking life? I think it's time to leave the police work to the police as your Detective Stevenson suggested."

"Number one, Gabe Stevenson is not *my* detective." Lexie shoved her hands on her hips. "Number two, I'll . . . I'll . . ." Lexie blew a hot, frustrated breath through her teeth. "I'll figure something out. I have to. I can't let my business go down the drain because I'm a murder suspect."

"Of course, dear. Of course." Lucy plucked nervously at the pearls around her neck. "I'll see you tomorrow. Remember, it's your birthday."

"Right. Thanks for reminding me. It's always been a dream of mine to turn into a thirty-seven year old divorcee supporting a child in college and having a crazy aunt living with her."

"Everything will be all right," Lucy said condescendingly as she patted Lexie's arm. "You'll see." Lucy headed off to her car in the lavender twilight.

Still grumpy about her sister getting off Aunt Gladys babysitting duty scot free, Lexie went back upstairs to make sure the old gal was comfortable. Demonstrating great restraint, she listened for another couple of hours to the woman's vivid memories of being a Las Vegas showgirl while she unpacked. When Aunt Gladys produced a candle and a lighter, Lexie quickly confiscated the loot.

"No, Aunt Gladys. No candles in the house."

Aunt Gladys batted her false eyelashes. "And why not, Leslie?"

Lexie pictured her house going up in flames and she swallowed hard. "Ah, I don't have a smoke alarm installed up here."

Aunt Gladys relaxed, but remained persistent. "When may I have my candle back?"

When pigs fly. "After I have a smoke alarm installed up here," Lexie explained.

"Very well then." Aunt Gladys began to hum another old show tune and Lexie busied herself picking up tossed plastic bags that had once held Aunt Gladys's hundreds of pairs of shoes.

After dinner, Aunt Gladys finally went to bed, claiming she was exhausted. Lexie cleaned up, started the dishwasher and went up to her own room, feeling like she'd weathered a tornado. Crawling between the sheets, she tried to sleep. Unfortunately, she tossed and turned all night, worried about Aunt Gladys and the myriad of shenanigans she might rain down upon her house.

At last Lexie slumbered, dreaming of a shadowy person chasing her with a butcher knife. Like a wild woman, she ran all over Moose Creek Junction, trying to escape the maniac. Unfortunately, everywhere she went, he stalked her, intent upon ending her life.

How could she get a decent night's sleep? She was still under suspicion for murder and there was a killer wandering around Moose Creek Junction. Even counting sheep could not counteract that niggling reality.

At 5 a.m., Lexie finally shot out of bed like a bolt of lightning, heart beating like a racehorse. The killer was still on the loose. He'd attacked her once. And since he apparently didn't like her asking questions around town about Whitehead's murder, he just might attack her again.

Even more disturbing she was still a murder suspect. What if people didn't come to the Saucy Lucy because they thought she really was guilty? God. And then there was Aunt Gladys.

What was she to do? Should she let the police do the investigating, even though they were slow as Christmas and she could lose her business before they solved the murder? Should she continue, despite the odds, to conduct her own amateur fact-finding missions?

Maybe if she were a religious person and prayed a lot, the Lord would part the heavens and give her a sign about what she should do. But she wasn't religious. She was afraid and desperate. And there was no apparent answer to her dilemma.

CHAPTER 8

WIRED TIGHT AS AN ANTIQUE BEDSPRING, Lexie showered and dressed then crept upstairs to check on her aunt. The old lady was snoring like a woodchuck in heat, her arm flung over her forehead and her shriveled breasts quivering beneath her gauzy pink nightie. Shutting the door to the bedroom, Lexie surveyed the attic apartment and Aunt Gladys' luggage strewn everywhere. She made a mental note to come up later in the afternoon and help organize her things in the chests and wardrobes.

Tip-toeing back down the stairs, Lexie mentally berated herself for any uncharitable thoughts she harbored about her loopy aunt. How sad to be old and alone and so annoying that not even your own child wanted to be around you. She should stop being so pessimistic and make some fun plans for the two of them to visit the local library and the museum and maybe even the botanical gardens in Westonville.

With Eva spending so little time at home, Lexie would have a companion to do things with when she wasn't working. They could rent videos and listen to music . . .

Lexie snorted. Who was she trying to fool?

This was Aunt Gladys she was talking about. The woman who spent more than twenty years on the Las Vegas strip as a showgirl with pasties on her boobs; the woman who had been married seven times and finally gone to truck driving school at age sixty-eight and handled big rigs for three years before her eyes got too bad. This was not your typical girlfriend type of companion, someone who would understand she was still saddened by her failed marriage and worried about her daughter adjusting to being a sister to a sibling she would probably never know.

And no, Aunt Gladys, who had always had a husband or boyfriend glued to her side, would definitely not understand the frustration of being celibate for two solid years without even so much as a whiff of testosterone coming her way.

Once she reached the kitchen and pawed through the refrigerator and cupboards, Lexie realized she was out of a few staples like coffee and butter. Her restaurant supplies were stocked to the hilt, but she'd been distracted lately and needed to re-supply a few of her own kitchen items.

With Aunt Gladys asleep, she felt it was safe to leave the house for a short amount of time. She drove over to Herb Musselman's grocery store and picked up a few more things since Eva would be back this weekend.

Driving home, Lexie reflected on everything that was wrong with her life. Man, she sure felt crabby all the time. Maybe that's what getting old did to you. Thank goodness she and Lucy had decided not to open the cafe on her birthday. She needed time to adjust to Aunt Gladys.

Back home, she put on a pot of coffee—butter rum flavor. She inhaled deeply and sighed; it smelled heavenly. Then she unloaded groceries and began putting things in cupboards. Trying to improve her outlook and attitude, she hummed, thinking that it seemed to work for batty Aunt Gladys. She really hoped the humming would brighten her mood because it suddenly occurred to her that black balloons would surely be a part of Eva's birthday present to her. *Oh-mi-god*, as Eva would say.

The ringing phone made her jump. Quickly she placed the celery in the vegetable drawer of the refrigerator and reached for the cordless. "Hello?"

"Lexie. Just called to check up on you. How are things going?"

Huh? Deputy Dog? Calling to harass me again, no doubt. This was not good. She had just lulled herself into a temporary state of semi-happiness, and now her hands were getting clammy and her breathing shallow. Darn that man anyway.

"As expected," Lexie responded. "You want to question me more, or what?"

"Do you want me to?"

"I'd prefer not." Lexie tensed her jaw. She'd be glad when this murder case was solved and Gabe Stevenson wasn't breathing down her back anymore. It was positively unnerving. "By the way, how is everything going down there at the police department? Find the murderer yet?"

"No. But I found out Henry Whitehead was involved with a woman named Sophie Howell. So I went to Denver yesterday to pay a visit to the magic shop she owns with her husband Ernie."

"And?" Lexie had a very bad feeling. Cradling the receiver on her shoulder, she unwrapped the roast she'd bought and plopped it into a crock-pot. Running water into a glass measuring cup, she added a package of dry onion soup and poured it over the meat. She finished by putting the lid on the pot and turning the heat to medium high.

"Come to find out, two women had been in to visit them a short while before I arrived. They asked all sorts of questions. One of them, a redhead, nearly got herself sawed in half she irritated Ernie so much."

Lexie pretended indifference. "Hmmm, imagine that."

"Lexie," he said in a low voice. "Didn't I tell you to leave the investigation to me?"

"What makes you think I was the redhead?"

"Otis told me you and Lucy were in Denver yesterday to pick up your Aunt Gladys."

"You didn't tell him we'd been to Houdini's

Hideout, did you?"

"You admit you were there?"

Lexie's grip on the phone tightened. "No. I just want to make sure you didn't tell Otis something that would make him angry with Lucy."

"I didn't tell him anything," Gabe said. "But it doesn't take a rocket scientist to figure out you were snooping."

Just then Aunt Gladys shuffled into the kitchen wearing fuzzy pink slippers with floppy bunny ears and a silky, zebra stripe robe with a feather collar. Her head, covered in pink sponge rollers, bobbed a little as she looked around the room. "Where in God's name am I? And who are you?"

Lexie put a hand over the receiver. "Your niece Lexie, Aunt Gladys. Lucy and I brought you here. This is my house in Moose Creek Junction."

"Moose Creek Junction?" Aunt Gladys wailed. "This place is cursed and everyone around town hates me. I'll die here."

"It's only temporary, Aunt Gladys. Bruce will be coming for you soon."

"Bruce?" Aunt Gladys fiddled with the large, square topaz ring on her right ring finger.

Lexie spoke in an authoritative voice. "Your son Bruce. He's in Singapore right now. You'll be fine here with me. No one is going to hurt you."

"What's going on?" Gabe asked.

Lexie took her hand off the receiver and whispered into it, "It's my aunt; she's a little confused."

"Leslie, Leslie . . ." Aunt Gladys still looked lost for a minute, and then she smiled and said, "Why, of course, now I remember where I am, dearie. Why are you shouting? I haven't lost my mind just yet. May I use your blender?"

From loony to lucid, all in a split second. Lexie was amazed. "What for?"

"I need to make my power breakfast drink. I have it every morning."

"Sure. It's right there on the counter."

Aunt Gladys tottered toward the refrigerator. Whistling yet another show tune, she dug through the contents and dumped eggs and milk into the glass container. Then she removed a small packet from her robe pocket and poured it in the blender as well.

"Lexie," Gabe said sternly in Lexie's ear. "Tell me what you found out when you went to Houdini's Hideout."

At that exact moment, Aunt Gladys flipped on the blender. Between the old woman's whistling and the blender's whirring, Lexie could barely hear herself think. She grinned, glad for Aunt Gladys' well-timed obnoxiousness. "Uh, I have to go now," she said loudly into the telephone.

"I can barely hear you," Stevenson shouted.

"We must have a bad connection," Lexie told him. "Thanks for calling."

She hung up, relieved to be rid of the intrusive cop. Her nostrils twitched at a strange odor and she glanced at Aunt Gladys. "What on earth are you making?"

"I told you, it's my power drink. It makes me feel like I'm 20 again." She poured the liquid into a clear glass, sat down at the table and began to chug-a-lug.

Lexie grimaced at the oatmeal-colored concoction. She decided she'd rather feel a 150 years old than consume that barf. "We're going to dinner tonight, Aunt Gladys. Do you have something decent to wear?"

"Of course, I do. Your aunt is no common chippie." She nodded at the crock-pot. "What's cooking?"

"Pot roast for Monday's soup special."

"Soup special?" Aunt Gladys thumped her chest and burped.

Lexie wrinkled her nose. "Lucy and I run a restaurant here. I named it after Mom: The Saucy Lucy Café. I use a lot of her special recipes."

"How nice. The preacher's wife has a restaurant named after her." Aunt Gladys took another sip of her drink, leaving a film of the substance on her upper lip. "What's the occasion for going out to dinner? You tired of your own cooking?"

"Eva's taking me out for my birthday." Lexie took her coffee and sat down at the table with Aunt Gladys.

"Ah, little Eva. She still have those precious strawberry blond pigtails? I should go out and buy her some pretty ribbons and maybe a doll."

"Eva's eighteen years old now, Aunt Gladys. She's not into ribbons and dolls anymore, though it's a nice thought."

"Hell's bells. The girl's all grown up." Aunt Gladys shook her head. She reached toward the middle of the table and picked up the ceramic salt and pepper shakers shaped like tiny poodles. They had also belonged to Lexie's mother. "She got any beaus?"

"She dates off and on. But there's no one steady." Lexie wondered if the poodles were long for this world since Aunt Gladys, who had a slight problem with kleptomania, had taken a fancy to them. She made a mental note to hide the poodles and put out a cheap set of shakers.

"I see. What about you? Does Junior still live here or did you finally kick him out?"

"You mean Dan?"

"No. I knew you dumped that scum-sucking turd a long time ago. I'm talking about the boy-man. I thought I heard him on the roof last night, but I wasn't sure."

"I don't know anything about a boy-man, Aunt Gladys. You probably just heard the wind."

Aunt Gladys shook a finger at Lexie. "I know what I know, Missy. And one way or another, we'll have to do something about Junior if he keeps stomping around on the roof."

Lexie rubbed her forehead, already tired of dealing with Aunt Gladys' delusions. And the woman had barely been home 24 hours. "Sure, Aunt Gladys. If Junior becomes a problem, I'll call someone out here to get rid of him."

"Very well, then." Aunt Gladys sipped at her

foul-smelling drink. "He ran off with another woman, didn't he?"

"Who? Junior?"

"No, silly. Dan. I knew he couldn't be trusted."

"You only met him at the wedding and a few other times. How did you know?"

"His eyes, dearie. I could always see the shiftiness in his eyes." Aunt Gladys cackled. "He's a liar, that one."

"I wish I'd seen it coming," Lexie said. "Could have saved myself a lot of heartbreak."

"Your Dan is a bastard, that's for sure," Aunt Gladys said. "I told your mother he was no good. She knew it and so did your father. But no one could convince you."

"I know," Lexie said, miserable. "I ruined my life by marrying him."

"Oh, fiddlesticks! You just made a mistake. You'll survive. And you're much better off without him, I say. Dan-the-flim-flam-man. That's all he was."

Lexie chuckled, warming to Aunt Gladys, despite her demented ways. "I suppose you're right. But he's making Eva miserable. He hasn't talked with her in months."

Aunt Gladys shrugged. "She'll survive, too. There's nobody who gets through this life without dealing with a few hard knocks. Lord knows I've had enough of my own."

"I'm sure you have."

"Did you know I've been married seven times?"

Aunt Gladys burped again. "Half of the old farts up and died on me and the other half I divorced. You'll find yourself another man soon enough, dearie. Like they say, there's lots of fish in the sea."

Lexie tapped the side of her coffee cup, glad the horrible fake nails had loosened and fallen off weeks ago. "Not a lot of eligible men in this town, I'm afraid. And I'm not sure I want to suffer with the antics of another testosterone junkie."

"Ah, one will come along before you know it and snap you right up. You'll see."

"I don't know that I want a man to *snap me up*."

"Of course you do. All women do. You just need to find the right one. And when it's right, it's right."

"All I know is that every time I date a man, they wind up dead. Murdered. It's happened twice now, Aunt Gladys."

"Murders in Moose Creek Junction?" Aunt Gladys batted her dark eyes.

"That's right."

Aunt Gladys licked at the filmy mustache on her upper lip. "Well, you are related to me, dearie. As I said before, I had a lot of men die on me, too."

"But were they murdered?"

"Who knows? A couple of them were into the mob. Someone could have put hits out on them." She shrugged. "It happens."

As difficult as it must have been, Lexie imagined Aunt Gladys had grown accustomed to losing husbands since she'd had so many. She was a salty old gal for sure.

"No more talk about people dying," Aunt Gladys insisted. "I know what we need."

"What's that?" Lexie sipped her coffee, which by now had gone cold.

"A hairdo from Winkie. If he's still in town, that is."

"Winkie? Who's *Winkie*?"

"Winfield Hightower. He used to do my hair before I left this godforsaken dirt hole. Even spending all those years in Las Vegas, I never found anyone as good. He's a true artist."

"Imagine that in this backwoods town," Lexie commented.

"He's gay, of course," Aunt Gladys added. "But that kind of comes with the territory, doesn't it? He was gay before it was fashionable. So I'd say he is a *true* gay man. Not a flash-in-the-pan gay man." She giggled at her own joke.

"Funny, I've never heard of him." Lexie figured that in a town this small she would have heard someone mention a gay man named Winkie.

"He may not have the beauty shop any more. Where's your phone book?"

Lexie grabbed it from the counter and handed it to her. Thinking about the nail escapade with Lucy, she said, "I don't think I want anyone messing with my hair."

"Nonsense. It could use some conditioning and a good trim." She squinted at Lexie's hair and ran her fingers lightly through it. "Even a bit of color. I can see some gray, you know. This is not a good way to catch a man, Leslie."

Releasing a breath of frustration, Lexie said, "Why does everyone insist I look for a man?"

Aunt Gladys rolled her eyes. "Lighten up, Francis. Don't you ever want to have sex again?"

Lexie's face burned with embarrassment. Aunt Gladys might be an eccentric nutcase, but she did have a point.

When Aunt Gladys called Winkie, she found out he was still in town. The instant she requested an appointment, he'd come right over, anxious to wield his scissors on a favorite customer and talk about old times.

Lexie and Aunt Gladys sat dutifully in the kitchen on high stools as Winfield Hightower, hairdresser supreme, put the finishing touches on their hair. He reached over to lightly fluff Lexie's washed, trimmed, and freshly ginger-colored hair with pudgy, be-ringed fingers. Then he held up a hand mirror for Lexie to look at her reflection.

She winced. There were still tiny crows-toes at the corners of her eyes. Nothing Winkie could do about that.

"Simply fabulous!" Winkie exclaimed as he stood back in his black and tangerine smock. He held aloft a comb with one hand, stroking his chin as he studied his most recent creations.

"Thank you," Lexie said. "My hair does look nice."

"Nice indeed, Winkie." Holding an identical hand mirror, Aunt Gladys touched her own hair which he'd pouffed into a cap of shimmery white curls. "I'm so glad you're still in town. You're the best. How much do I owe you?"

He beamed, cheeks rosy beneath his cropped, salt and pepper hair. "Nothing, love. It's just fabulous to have your radiant self back in town. Didn't you simply love Vegas?"

Aunt Gladys giggled. "Oh, yes. I danced there for years and met seven husbands there. Yessiree, Las Vegas will always be in my blood."

"Well, you simply *must* come to me to have your hair done from now on, girlfriend." He brushed off his smock with a flourish.

"But you're retired."

"Officially. But I still do hair for special clients."

When someone knocked, Winkie's dog, a tiny Yorkshire terrier named Muffin, began *woof-woofing*. He flew off his purple silk pillow in a corner of the kitchen and dashed madly around in circles.

Eva entered the room carrying a boom box and looked around. "Mom, I didn't know you'd gotten a dog. And what'd you do to your hair?"

"The dog belongs to Mr. Hightower." Lexie cleared her throat. "Winkie, this is my daughter Eva."

Eva greeted him, still looking slightly surprised.

He gave a little bow. "Charmed, I'm sure."

"Mr. Hightower is a friend of mine from when I used to live here. Look!" Aunt Gladys pointed to her head. "He just did our hair. Isn't it grand?"

"Awesome," Eva said.

Blushing from compliments, Winkie swept up the hair on the floor.

Aunt Gladys stood, took off her cape and set it aside. She gave Eva a hug. "My goodness, how you've grown up, Agnes."

Eva sent Lexie a frustrated look. "Eva, Aunt Gladys. It's Eva. Nice to see you again."

Lexie took another look at her hair in the hand mirror. Not bad for an old broad. She slid off the stool and removed her cape. "Aunt Gladys and I need to clean up a bit and we'll be ready for dinner. We're going to MacGreggor's, aren't we?"

"Nope." Smiling, Eva hugged the boom box closer and punched a button.

Loud music blared and a tall man in a Zorro costume, complete with black mask and cape, slid into the kitchen. Chest muscles rippling, he gyrated around the room, slashing a fake fencing sword in the air.

Muffin barked madly and Winkie picked the dog up, *shooshing* it as he scooted to the back of the kitchen.

"Eva!" Lexie watched in shock as the male dancer leapt around her. "What is this?"

"Your birthday present, Mom!"

Aunt Gladys' brows furrowed and she shook an

arthritic finger at Zorro. "Are you the boy-man who lives on the roof?"

"No way," Zorro shouted, then laughed richly.

"Good, then we can really have some fun." Aunt Gladys clapped in time to the music. "Whee," she shouted. "This reminds me of the all male review at the MGM!"

Lucy entered the room and her mouth dropped. She hugged her handbag to her chest. "What in heaven's name is going on?"

Eva set the boom box down and smiled. "This is just what Mom needed for her birthday, Aunt Lucy!"

"Birthday present, indeed. This is a spectacle!" Lucy returned, her face red as a tomato.

Just what I needed?

The more Lexie watched Zorro in his tight black costume, the hotter her face became. How embarrassing. Even her own daughter must realize she'd gone without sex for so long she could qualify for born-again virgin status. This was awful.

Wait a minute, Lexie thought, hopes brightening. No doubt this is where the extra money went she'd given Eva. Better this than a nose ring or a tongue stud. All was not wrong with the world.

Eva took Lexie's elbow, guided her into the eating area of the Saucy Lucy Café, and sat her in a chair. Zorro danced seductively in her direction. His hips gyrated in front of her face and spicy-cologned sweat flew from his hard, lean body. As he swept his cape around and slashed the air with his sword,

Lexie tried to catch her breath.

"Oh, my . . . oh, my!" Lucy had taken her fan out of her purse and was once again waving it madly in front of her face.

Eva grinned from ear to ear and Aunt Gladys was ecstatic, clapping and whooping like a wild person, encouraging the young man to, "Take it all off!"

Winkie eyed the male dancer intently, fingering the gold hoop in his ear as he clutched his little dog to his chest.

At last Zorro peeled away his cape, hat, and his clothes, piece by piece.

Lucy caught Lexie's attention. "Do something," she said. "This is simply outrageous!"

Lexie shrugged. What was she supposed to do? It was Eva's birthday surprise—how could she ruin it? And it really was harmless enough, though she was sure that by now Lucy's support hose must have melted into her sturdy brown loafers. What a story she'd have to tell patootiehead Otis!

Lucy glanced uncomfortably at her watch several times, trying pathetically to ignore Zorro when he brushed up against her. Her face turned incredibly red and she whipped her fan at him. "Shoo," she shouted. "Go away!"

Grinning devilishly, he moved on to Eva for a little playful seduction, while Lucy resumed fanning herself.

With a final flourish, he tore off his belled trousers, tossing them aside. When he swept past Aunt Gladys, she produced a bill and stuffed it in his g-string. Lucy put a hand to her forehead and plastered herself against a wall like an insect caught in spider web.

Zorro's oiled six-pack rippled as he danced his way over and straddled Lexie's lap, shaking his package in her face. Of course he stared at her cleavage while all of it was going on. Oh, well, Lexie thought. You only live once and she was, after all, the birthday broad. She pulled a bill from her jeans pocket and stuffed it in his g-string.

But he didn't go away. He continued with his dance for what seemed like hours, though it probably lasted only minutes. At last he leaned over, handed Lexie a card and whispered in her ear, his warm, moist breath caressing her cheek. "Call me later, baby. I love to do it with older women . . ."

Lexie's jaw dropped and her face prickled with wildfire. Did he really think she would call him? Not on her life. Good Lord, he could be her son!

Zorro jumped away, did a few more twists and gyrations and when the music stopped, he bowed deeply for his audience. While everyone clapped, with the exception of Lucy, he got dressed and waved to everyone. Winking at Lexie, he disappeared through the front door.

Eva turned down the music. "I'll order pizza for dinner if that's OK with everyone."

"That's fine with me," Lexie said.

"Splendid," Aunt Gladys squealed. "I haven't had pizza since Brucie put me in Dr. Demented's castle of torture. They're all crazy there, you know."

Lucy reached into her purse, fished out a small wrapped package and handed it to Lexie. Then she smoothed down her dress and patted her bun. "I think I need to go home," she said breathlessly. "I've had a little too much excitement for one night. I do believe my blood pressure's up."

Screeching tires, a loud thump, and a hoarse scream drew everyone's attention.

Muffin started barking, jumped out of Winkie's arms and ran around in circles. Everyone rushed out of the house and onto the porch.

Beneath the dim streetlights, Zorro lay on his back spread-eagled on the asphalt, his cape spread out behind him. Nearby, black tire tracks slashed across the road.

Winkie, who had managed to collect Muffin, clutched the growling mutt to his chest and said, "Oh, my God. The boy's been hurt."

CHAPTER 9

"HE'S BEEN RUN OVER," LEXIE CRIED AND RAN over to him with Eva on her heels. The two of them knelt beside Zorro.

The fine hairs on Lexie's neck stood on end as she looked at the blood pooling beside his head. She swallowed a wave of hiccoughs. Who could have done such an awful thing? Fighting squeamishness, she gently lifted his wrist and checked for a pulse. It was there, but very faint.

She leaned closer to him, held the back of her hand near his mouth and felt faint puffs of air. Thank God he was breathing, although it was very shallow. "He's alive," she told Eva. "But he needs help. Fast. Go inside and call 911, then Uncle Otis."

Eva sprinted back up the porch steps and inside the house.

Lucy hustled up beside them as fast as her sturdy loafers allowed. She looked down at Zorro, clasped her hands and began to pray, mutters of contrition filling the air.

"Lucy, Zorro needs blankets right now. Not prayers."

"Of course," she said, eyes popping open. Once again, as fast as her sturdy loafers allowed, she hurried back to the house.

Aunt Gladys tottered up next with Winkie at her side. "Why is that young man napping in the street? He has such a fine looking a—"

"Aunt Gladys!" Lexie gave her aunt a warning glance.

"Oh my, he's bleeding!" Aunt Gladys backed away, eyes wide. "My, oh my, oh my. I think I need my pills. I think I'm going to faint."

Winkie, still holding his growling dog, took Aunt Gladys' elbow and patted her on the back. "It's going to be all right, love. Help is on its way."

"But it's happening again!" Aunt Gladys shrieked. "It's the Castleton curse! That's why I left this place. It's horrible!"

"Could you take my aunt inside?" Lexie asked Winkie, wondering what in the world the Castleton curse was. "She's upset."

"Of course."

Aunt Gladys gibbered incoherently as Winkie guided her back to the Victorian, talking softly to console her. Eva came back outside followed by Lucy, arms loaded with blankets. Both of them headed into the street.

"The ambulance is on its way and I got a hold of Uncle Otis, too," Eva said, once she arrived at Lexie's side.

Lucy helped arrange the covers on Zorro.

"Eva, do you know Zorro's name?"

"Elton Briarhurst. He goes to Westonville University, too." She choked back a sob.

A thought occurred to Lexie. "Would Elton be a member of the *Dr. and Mrs. Miles Briarhurst* family who live in Marble Canyon in that huge mansion on the hill?"

Eva nodded. "He's their son."

Lexie groaned. Dr. Briarhurst was a famous surgeon with a golden pocketbook and tons of influence in the little town of Moose Creek Junction, Westonville, Denver, and probably the Great Beyond.

"Why would a kid whose parents are filthy rich take a job as a stripper?" Lexie asked.

"He's majoring in drama, Mom. He figures this helps him learn to get into character."

Lexie leaned close to the young man again. "Elton, can you hear me? Elton, Elton?"

He moaned, but didn't respond. In the distance, the sound of an ambulance siren pierced the air.

Otis pulled up in his sheriff's car, lights flashing. He got out of the vehicle and walked up to them. "Is he dead?" His brow knitted with concern as he knelt beside Zorro.

"No, but he's in bad shape," Lexie responded.

Otis mopped his forehead with a crumpled

handkerchief, turned to examine the tire tracks and stood up. "Jumpin' catfish. What happened?"

"We were having a birthday party for Mom, Uncle Otis," Eva said. "When Elton left, someone . . . someone ran over him!"

"Is he your boyfriend?" Otis asked.

"No. He was here to—"

"*Ahem.*" Lucy gave her niece a stern look.

"Ah, he was here to, ah . . ." Eva looked at Lexie for help.

"He was here to *entertain* us," Lexie finally said.

"Oh?" Otis raised a brow. "With what? A juggling act?" He shoved a cigar in his mouth and lit up, sending a curious look at them all.

"Otis, I really wish you wouldn't smoke those disgusting things," Lucy said. "Besides, it's not healthy to do that around a wounded person."

Grunting, Otis tossed the cigar on the asphalt and ground it out with his boot heel. "Somebody better tell me what the victim was doing here."

"Exotic dancing," Lexie finally said.

An ambulance roared up the street and stopped beside them, silencing any further questions Otis might have had. Lexie stood beside Eva and put her arm around her daughter's quaking shoulders. Lucy came up behind them and patted Lexie on the back.

"It's going to be OK," Lexie said, trying to reassure her daughter as much as herself.

While they watched, several attendants hustled

from the emergency vehicle and clustered around Elton. They checked for his vital signs, then started an IV. An old yellow VW bug drove up and parked by the curb across the street. Barnard Savage, wearing his usual uniform of press hat and rumpled suit and cigarette stub hanging from his lip, jumped from the car. He whipped out a camera with an enormous flash and took several photos. Then he took the pencil stub from behind his ear and jotted notes down on a pad, his tongue wetting the tip of the lead every so often.

Just as the ambulance team carefully shifted Elton onto a stretcher, Gabe arrived in his Westonville Police squad car. He exited his vehicle, a concerned expression on his face as he took long strides toward Savage and spoke with him in a gruff voice. Savage gestured wildly, apparently trying to justify his presence.

Otis, always one to join in, hurried over to stand beside Gabe and Savage, no doubt adding his two cents to the conversation. He hitched up his pants as he pointed an accusing finger at the reporter.

"Is he going to be all right?" Lexie asked one of the ambulance attendants standing nearby.

"Can't say for sure," he said. "Check with the hospital in a while. They'll be able to give you a condition update."

The attendants lifted Elton's stretcher and loaded it onto the ambulance. Lights flashing and siren blaring, it headed for the Westonville Hospital.

Lexie shuddered. *Please let him be all right.
Please. He's so young.*

Lexie hadn't noticed before, but her rubbernecking neighbors were out in force. Standing
in bathrobes on their doorsteps, they whispered
amongst themselves, craning their necks to see what
had happened.

"Show's over, folks," Otis called out to them, his
face set in hard lines. "You all go on back inside."
He turned to Lexie, Lucy and Eva. "You three,
don't go anywhere. Stay put."

Gabe walked over to his squad car and talked
into the microphone of police radio for a bit. Lexie
could hear the garbled responses and static blaring
back at him. Then he put on gloves and walked
around the crime scene bagging bits and pieces of
evidence and taking pictures.

While the detective went about his work, Otis
came over with his notebook and wet the tip of his
pencil. He asked the women several questions,
scribbling furiously to document the information
they provided. He had just finished the grilling session when the detective walked over. He'd removed
his gloves and put his camera back in the squad car.

Lexie took an uneven breath. Gabe wore a
tweed jacket, a white button down shirt, jeans, and
a cowboy hat. Man, he looked good. Despite the
confusion and shock of the evening, she felt an attraction, complete with a warm flush in her cheeks.

Here I go again!

Why in the world she would react to Gabe like this at such a time? What was wrong with her? Besides, he was the enemy. He still believed she might be connected to Whitehead's murder. It was absurd for her to be thinking like that about him.

Lexie's head began to hammer. Why was this happening? Why were people always getting hurt around her?

Gabe tipped his hat to them. "Are you ladies all right?"

"Yes," Lexie answered. "A little shaken up, but fine."

"Good. Otis told me there was a celebration going on when the incident occurred?"

Eva nodded. "My mom's birthday. And then this happened. It's just awful."

"Who was there?" Gabe asked.

"The three of us," Lexie answered. "Also my Aunt Gladys and her friend Winfield Hightower. He's inside getting her calmed down. She's pretty upset."

"I can imagine," Gabe said. "Did you see anyone or anything out of the ordinary?"

"Nothing," Lucy said. "By the time we all came outside, Eva's young man was lying in the road."

"He's not my young man, Aunt Lucy," Eva spat. "He's just a friend."

Lucy shrugged.

"Detective Stevenson," Lexie said, her face getting warmer. It would be best to use a more formal tone with him. Otherwise, Sister Lucy would start planning a spring wedding. "What can we do to help?"

"Nothing, really. Just be ready to answer any more questions we may have later."

"Do you think the person who hit Elton might be the same person who killed Whitehead?" *And attacked me*, she thought silently.

"It's hard to say," Otis answered.

Gabe folded his arms across his chest. "Otis is right. We'll have to do some more investigating before we know that for sure. But it is possible."

"Lord have mercy," Lucy said.

"If you want to pray, sis," Lexie said, "now would be a good time."

On cue, Lucy clenched her eyes shut and clasped her hands reverently.

"May I speak with you privately for a minute, Lexie?" Gabe asked.

Still praying, Lucy opened one eye and glanced curiously at Lexie.

Lexie ignored her. "Sure," she told the detective. She patted her daughter's arm reassuringly. "I'll be right back, sweetie."

Gabe and Lexie walked over by an ancient elm tree and a patch of rosebushes covered with worn and faded autumn blooms. "I didn't want to say this around your sister and your daughter because I didn't want to concern them."

Lexie froze. "What?"

"I'm worried. I think you're in danger."

"I've figured that much for a long time now.

What am I supposed to do?"

"Quit nosing around about Whitehead's murder. That's my job."

Lexie stiffened. "I've been far to busy with my aunt lately to go snooping around."

He lifted a dark brow. "Good. Because you only complicate things when you get involved."

Lexie released a frustrated breath. "Are you insinuating that what happened tonight is somehow my fault?"

"Absolutely not."

"Then what are you saying?" Lexie asked.

"Nothing." His mouth quirked. "Just watch your back and mind your own business. It's for your own good."

Lexie shoved her hands on her hips. "Are we done talking, Detective?"

"Yes."

"Good night, then." Lexie stormed back to Lucy and Eva.

Otis walked up to Gabe and they shook hands. Then the detective got into his squad car and drove off.

"Does that police guy, like, have the hots for you, or what?" Eva asked. "'Cause if you're getting hooked up, I want to know."

"I knew it," Lucy said with a grin.

"Stop it, you two," Lexie grumbled. "There's nothing between Detective Stevenson and me."

"Shut up," Eva said. "He called you by your first name."

Lexie shrugged. "He's working on a murder investigation and I'm a witness. Nothing romantic about that."

"Let's get going, Lucy," Otis said when he walked up beside them.

"What about my car?" she asked.

"I'll drive you over tomorrow to pick it up."

"Talk to you later," Lucy said to Lexie. She waved tiredly and walked with Otis over to the sheriff's car. A few seconds later, they were gone.

Lexie gave Eva a big hug. "Thank you for the birthday party, hon, even if it didn't turn out the way we wanted."

"I'm sorry, Mom. I feel so responsible for what happened to Elton."

"You're not. It was a terrible accident. No one was at fault."

"I guess," Eva said miserably.

"It was just an accident," Lexie repeated sternly. "And we'll call the hospital in a bit to check up on him. Now, let's head inside. I don't know about you, but I'm exhausted."

When Lexie finally crawled into bed, sleep refused to come. She'd called the hospital earlier to get a report on Elton's condition and they said he was out of surgery, but still in critical condition. Lexie couldn't stop thinking about him. And worrying.

Fitful dreams kept her tossing and turning. She woke several times and stared at the ominous shadows lancing across her bedroom. The night was warm, despite the fact it was October. At last Lexie glanced at her alarm clock on the bedside table. *Midnight*. What an unholy hour to find herself awake.

A fine sheen of sweat caused her thin nightgown to cling to her limbs, so she got up and opened her window wider. A warm breeze caressed her face and body, relieving the sticky sensation. Taking a deep breath, she studied her neighbors' dry, withered lawns stretching like silvery material beneath the streetlights.

With the west still in the grips of a severe drought, Lexie wondered if it would ever get cold enough to rain or snow. No doubt they would have another brown, parched Christmas—just like last year. She stared up at the moon's luminous, smiling face, imagining it mocked the waterless situation.

Well, she didn't think it was one bit funny. And it was awfully hard for an avid gardener such as herself to have a decent crop of anything besides weeds in these conditions. Hopefully, the weather cycle would change again, for the better, and the drought would finally end.

Thump, thump.

Lexie looked up at the ceiling. The sounds seemed to have emanated from the attic. *Aunt Gladys*. What on earth was she doing? Had she fallen out of bed? Or perhaps she'd left her tiny television blaring.

Lexie reached for her bathrobe and headed into the hallway, figuring she'd better go upstairs and make sure the old loon was all right. She'd had an upsetting night and maybe she couldn't sleep either.

Creak, creak . . .

The ancient stairs complained as Lexie padded barefoot to the attic. At the top she stepped into a short hallway and reached the door to Aunt Gladys' room. Even with all the renovations, Lexie's nostrils twitched with the musty odor of century-old walls.

Lexie heard Aunt Gladys' voice. And it sounded like Winkie was with her. What were those two doing at this time of night?

Lexie rapped on the door. "Aunt Gladys? What's going on?"

No answer. A dog barked.

She raised her hand to knock again. "Aunt Gla—"

More barking—Muffin no doubt—and the door swung open.

It took a couple of moments for Lexie's eyes to adjust to the inky blackness. Then she saw Aunt Gladys bathed in candlelight wearing a purple caftan covered in gold stars, golden, curly-toed slippers on her feet, her snowy white hair covered by a purple turban decorated with a tall ostrich feather. She clenched a cigarette, which was tucked into a long holder.

The scent of spicy incense wafted into the hallway and Lexie sneezed.

"Shhh, you'll scare them away, Leslie."

Lexie blinked. "Scare who away, Aunt Gladys?"

"The spirits."

Oh, my. "The spirits? What spirits?"

Winkie pulled the door open further and scowled at Lexie. "The spirits who were telling us what is going on in this wicked, wicked little town." Muffin, who rested comfortably in his arms, yapped at Lexie. You couldn't really call the rat-dog noises coming from the mutt real barks.

"OK, you two are busted. I heard weird sounds up here."

"Oh, don't worry. It wasn't the boy-man—he must be out of town tonight. It was probably just Winkie moving his chair," Aunt Gladys said.

Yap yap.

Ignoring Winkie's rat-dog, Lexie pushed her way past the culprits and entered the room. She didn't see anything out of order in the cozy quarters. Aunt Gladys' curtained alcove with the bed looked fine as well as the little sitting area with the sofa and over-stuffed recliner.

The round cupola nook, however, where Lexie had positioned the antique drop- leaf table she'd re-finished, along with two ladder-back chairs, looked suspicious. A board game of some sort covered the surface of the table with a thingie-ma-bob over-turned on the top of it.

Lexie noticed the lacy curtains were pulled back, revealing a zillion twinkling stars in the dark autumn sky. Along the windowsill sat several chunky pillar candles, all ablaze with flickering light. The burners nestled next to them were filled with tiny cakes of smoking incense.

Lexie whirled toward Winkie and her aunt. "Are you two insane? Do you want to set this house on fire again, Aunt Gladys?" Put those candles out this instant!"

Yap yap yap yap . . . yap yap!

"Oh, *pish*, *posh*," Aunt Gladys spoke over the rat-dog's protests. "Your sister Lucille is right, dear. You're too melodramatic for your own good." She took another puff on her cigarette.

"You shouldn't be smoking either, Aunt Gladys." Lexie folded her arms across her chest. "You know what the doctor said."

She shrugged. "Dr. Demented is an old hack with a cork up his butt. I don't give a hoot what he thinks." Aunt Gladys stood by the drop-leaf table, her purple silk robe flowing gracefully around her as she sank into a chair. She frowned at the board game. "We had just gotten to the good part, Leslie. Now you've ruined it."

Yap yap yap! Muffin's beady eyes glared at Lexie.

"Winkie, will you *please* tell me what kind of monkey business you and my aunt have been up to at this time of night? In the dark? And can you get that dog of yours to be quiet?"

Winkie stroked Muffie's silky head and the rat-dog's annoying *yap yaps* turned into low growls. "You've heard of a Ouija Board, haven't you?"

"A what-gee what?" Lexie looked back and

forth between Aunt Gladys and Winkie. "I have no idea what you're talking about."

"A Ouija Board," Aunt Gladys said again. "Pronounced *wee-gee*. Didn't you ever play it when you were a kid?"

"No."

"Of course you wouldn't have," Aunt Gladys said with a nod. "Your father, the preacher, would never have allowed such a device of the devil in his home. How your mother stood his holier-than-thou ways all those years, I'll never know."

Lexie threw her hands in the air. "Would somebody please tell me what a *wee-gee* board in the middle of the night and trying to set my house on fire has to do with anything?"

Winkie took her arm and steered her toward the drop-leaf table. "Sit," he commanded gently, prodding her into one of the chairs.

Against her better judgment, Lexie did as he asked. She studied the strange looking board with the thick black letters and the plastic what-cha-ma-call-it lying on top. "Once more, will somebody tell me—"

"The Ouija can conjure spirits from the Great Beyond." Winkie matter-of-factly plopped Muffin on his special pillow. He dragged a stool over and sat beside Aunt Gladys.

Lexie wrinkled her nose. "What?"

"Dead people, Lexie." Aunt Gladys smashed her cigarette butt into an ashtray. "In fact, we were just talking to Morris Van Scoy. He told us to call him by his nickname, though."

"Huh?" Lexie stared at Aunt Gladys. Good Lord, the old gal had really flipped her lid this time.

"Mortie had this house built in 1898," Winkie said. "He was a banker."

"Rich, too," Aunt Gladys said. "He brought his wife and five kids out here from Indiana. The railroad had just arrived and Moose Creek Junction was booming. He thought he could get even richer."

"Unfortunately, his wife missed her family back in Indiana," Aunt Gladys said. "She got addicted to laudanum and it drove her crazy."

"She killed herself in 1906," Winkie added. "Poor Mortie was so sad. He had to raise the kids by himself."

"He'd invested a lot in this town," Aunt Gladys said. "But when the railroad pulled up stakes and left, Moose Creek Junction was left with only a few wheat and cattle ranchers."

Winkie templed his fingers on the table. "Mortie lost everything, so he sold this house and moved back to Indiana in 1911."

"It's obvious where the Castleton curse came from," Aunt Gladys said. "Mortie's wife, Hortense, is still haunting this house. She brings disaster upon everyone who lives here. Your grandparents bought this place, and a few years later they drowned in Gun Smoke Lake in a freak accident. They left the house to my sister Lucille and her husband—your parents, Lexie—and look! They wound up dying in a tragic automobile accident. I was even affected from my sister marrying into the Castleton clan—look at all the husbands I lost! Now, Lexie," she said, staring deeply into her niece's eyes, "the curse has come to haunt you. It's the cause of all those murders you told me about."

Lexie shook her head. "You're kidding me, right? This is a joke."

"This is no joke, Leslie. Mortie told Winkie and I some very interesting things. By the way, he likes what you've done to the house. Figures everyone else would like it, too."

"Everyone else?"

"Everyone who has owned the house, you know. It's been owned by many people, or didn't you know that?"

"Whatever." It was all nonsense and she had to admit it had her spooked. "OK, so you two think you talked to someone who has passed on. I acknowledge that. Now it's time to put up the board game and call it a night."

"I don't want to," Aunt Gladys whined. "You're so mean. And I know you don't like me staying here. Why, you'd rather I went back to that lunatic asylum with Dr. Demented and the panty thief."

Lexie rolled her eyes. "Panty thief? What panty thief?"

"It was humiliating." Aunt Gladys *harrumphed*. "No one could catch him, though we were certain it was one of the attendants sneaking around. When we were out of our rooms exercising or having game night, he'd ransack all the ladies' drawers, pulling out their panties and sniffing the crotches. I caught him once, the sneaky little turd. It was disgusting."

"No way," Lexie said. "Mountain Shadows is an expensive place. The staff would never allow such a thing to go on."

"You think they actually cared?" Aunt Gladys tapped a be-ringed finger on the table. "People's jewelry turned up missing. You better believe the panty thief was stealing that, too. I'm sure he gave half of it to the staff so they'd keep their mouths shut."

Lexie reached over and patted Aunt Gladys' age-spotted hand. "Honestly, you've got to quit imagining such things. Did you take your medicine this evening?"

"Of course I did! And I'm telling the truth." Aunt Gladys started to cry.

"Now look what you've done." Winkie patted Aunt Gladys' back soothingly and Muffin growled at her from atop his special silk pillow.

Lexie felt awful. "Please, you've got to calm down, Aunt Gladys. Otherwise, you'll wear yourself out and get sick. Then what will Bruce think about you staying with me?"

"Do you think he gives a hoot about his old mother? *Pffft.*" Aunt Gladys flicked her red-nailed, be-ringed fingers at Lexie. "All he cares about is making money. Hand over fist. Or whatever way he can. That's all that matters to him. The curse has affected him, too. I'm just a nuisance to him, you know."

Lexie's anger melted into a puddle of guilt and she was instantly sorry for her aunt. The poor old lady—what a sad life she'd led—despite all of her fame on the Las Vegas strip. "Can't you and Winkie play parlor games another day?" Lexie asked Aunt Gladys in a more sympathetic voice. "It's awfully late."

Aunt Gladys sniffed and dabbed at her eyes with a lacy handkerchief. "No, actually late at night in the dark is when the spirits—"

"Aunt Gladys, you've got to stop this," Lexie warned. "You need your sleep."

"No, hear me out. This is when you get them to really talk. In fact, you should hear what Mortie has to say. Maybe Lexie should play, too?" Aunt Gladys looked up at Winkie.

Winkie smiled and clapped his chubby hands together. "Splendid idea. But she has to *believe*."

"Believe what?"

"That the spirits are real. That they are communicating with us."

"I don't care if you think you talked with Houdini. I think we all need to call it a night."

"Just play with us for a little bit," Aunt Gladys pleaded. "At least to humor an old lady. Remember what Shakespeare said?"

"No, I do not remember what Shakespeare said. I hated reading Shakespeare."

"I don't remember it exactly. But here goes." Aunt Gladys squeezed her eyes shut. "It was something about, 'There is more to heaven and earth,

Horatio, than you and I have dreamed possible . . .'"

"Whatever," Lexie said. "Horatio obviously didn't have to get up in the morning to clean house and do laundry like me."

"Just play it with us for a little while. If the spirits will even talk to us with you in the room, that is. Then I promise Winkie and I will blow out the candles and call it a night. Right?" Aunt Gladys glanced up at Winkie.

"Absolutely."

Lexie sighed deeply. "Fine. If it'll get you two off my back. But not for too long. OK?"

"Certainly, dear," Aunt Gladys agreed.

Aunt Gladys flipped over the plastic thingie-majig on the Ouija board and positioned it just so. "You have to place your fingertips on the planchette," she told Lexie.

She watched as Aunt Gladys and Winkie delicately touched the plastic what-cha-ma-call-it that she now knew was called a planchette. She did as they did, just trying to get the nonsense over with so she could go back to bed. Though she seriously doubted she would be able to get any sleep.

Aunt Gladys took several deep breaths. Then she said, "We ask only to speak with those spirits from the light. Those who have no intention to do us harm or cause evil to come upon us."

Lexie rolled her eyes, then an eerie chill brushed her cheeks as a gentle breeze came through the open window, rippling the long lace-curtain panels.

"Mortie," Aunt Gladys said in a soft, questioning voice. "Are you there?"

All was quiet in the room for a few moments, except for the sound of the rustling breeze and Muffin's little doggie breaths. Then the planchette thingie-ma-bob began to move under Lexie's fingertips. Ever so slightly. It slid up to the word *NO* printed at the top of the board.

"Come on. You guys are pushing this thing," Lexie whispered harshly.

"We are not," Aunt Gladys protested in a low voice, her eyes snapping in the dim light. "This is real. Try to be a little open-minded, Leslie. You never know what you may learn."

Winkie cleared his throat. "Are you a good spirit or a bad spirit?"

The thingie-ma-bob slowly spelled out *G-O-O-D*.

"Have you come to do us harm?" Winkie asked.

N-O, the thingie-ma-bob said.

Lexie started to hiccough and Aunt Gladys glared at her. "Hold your breath, Leslie. You'll scare them."

Lexie tried, but the hiccoughs continued to shake her frame.

"What is your name?" Aunt Gladys asked the spirit.

M-I-N-K, the planchette spelled out.

"Did you live in this town at one time?" Aunt Gladys asked.

The planchette pointed to the word *YES* printed at the top of the board.

"Do you know what is going on in Moose Creek

Junction?" Aunt Gladys asked. "Why people are being murdered?"

YES.

"Can you tell us who is doing it?" Winkie coaxed. "Can you give us a name?"

The planchette spelled, *E-V-I-L; J-E-A-L-O-U-S-Y; H-A-T-R-E-D.*

Lexie started to shiver.

STOP SHIVERING, LEXIE, the planchette spelled out.

Aunt Gladys and Winkie gave her annoyed looks. Lexie only shivered harder. How did the Ouija board know she was scared and shivering? Honestly, this thing was weird. Meanwhile, hiccoughs continued to rack her frame.

"Mink," Aunt Gladys said. "Can you give us the name of the murderer?"

C and D, the planchette spelled out

"Does this person live in town?" Winkie asked.

YES.

"Are they nearby at this very moment?"

YES.

"OK," Lexie said between hiccoughs, removing her fingers from the planchette. "I've had enough. It's time," *hiccough*, "to put this thing away."

"What can we do to stop the murders?" Aunt Gladys asked the board, ignoring Lexie.

C-A-N-T, it spelled out. *G-A-B-E D-O-E-S N-O-T K-N-O-W. D-A-N-G-E-R, D-A-N-G-E-R, D-A-N-G-E-R!*

CHAPTER 10

LEXIE'S HEART FROZE IN THE MIDDLE OF HER chest.

"Enough." She reached out and flipped over the thingie-ma-bob on the board.

"You do believe us now, don't you, Leslie?" Aunt Gladys' eyes went wide. "I tell you the Ouija is *real*."

"It's late." Lexie stood. "Time for everyone to call it a night."

"Aren't you even curious about what happened? Especially after what the spirits just told us?"

Lexie rolled her eyes in frustration. First the gypsy woman's warnings, and now the Ouija board. It was getting ridiculous. Although after everything that had happened, she did wonder about the mumbo jumbo. Was someone really out to get her? Who?

She pressed her lips into a firm line. Despite her questions, she couldn't let Aunt Gladys know her thoughts. Someone in this family had to maintain their sanity.

Aunt Gladys reached across the table with her arthritic fingers and gripped Lexie's hand. "You heard the Ouija. We're all in danger. What shall we do?"

"Keep the doors locked," Lexie said. "And get a good night's sleep. I think we're getting ourselves creeped out for no reason."

Aunt Gladys pouted. "But we were just getting to the good part."

"Sorry."

"Old people don't need so much sleep," Aunt Gladys insisted. "It's a proven fact."

"Well, this old person does." Lexie yawned and raised a brow at Winkie.

Winkie cleared his throat. "Uh, right. We'll get together again soon, dear," he said to Aunt Gladys, patting her hand. "Old Muffie needs his doggie sleep, you know." Winkie pushed his stool back into a corner and scooped the little Yorkie off his pillow.

Once they'd gone downstairs, Winkie rescued his trench coat from the hall tree and put it on, then wrapped a lavender cashmere scarf around his neck. "Some of my friends at the Sunrise Center are getting together for a bridge game tomorrow after lunch. Why don't you come, dear? Meet the gang, and all."

Aunt Gladys scowled. "Really, Winkie. Me? Play bridge? Not likely."

"It'll be such fun. Give you something to do, you know." Winkie gave Aunt Gladys a pleading look.

It would get her out of my hair, Lexie thought unkindly. Then she mentally scolded herself. Just because Aunt Gladys was a handful didn't mean she should be so cruel. Someday, she could be in the same position. Hopefully, not, though. And hopefully, she wouldn't be such a nuisance to everyone when she got to be seventy-something.

"Oh, hell's bells. What else have I got to do? Leslie will take me. Won't you, kiddo?" Aunt Gladys turned to stare at her niece.

"If that's what you'd like," Lexie said, trying to keep the excitement out of her voice so Aunt Gladys wouldn't be insulted.

"It's all settled then," Aunt Gladys told Winkie. "I'll be by tomorrow afternoon."

"Too-da-loo!" Aunt Gladys called to Winkie as he left. "Good night," she told Lexie, then climbed the stairs.

"Make sure to get those candles in your room blown out," Lexie told her. "I'll be up in a minute to check on you."

Aunt Gladys turned another pout on her. "You don't need to come up, Leslie. Do you think I'm incapable of doing even a simple task like that?"

Lexie shook her head. "No, just forgetful."

"Hmmph," Aunt Gladys said, and disappeared up the stairs.

Lexie went into the kitchen and brewed herself a cup of tea, hoping it would calm her frazzled nerves. At this late hour, the house seemed to creak louder than usual and shadows in corners seemed menacing.

Damn Aunt Gladys and her ridiculous Ouija board. The whole incident had gotten her spooked enough she probably wouldn't get a wink of shut-eye. But she couldn't sit up all night jumping at noises and staring at shadowy corners in the kitchen. She had to try and get some rest, even with all the strange events.

Wearily, Lexie climbed the stairs to the attic. It was extremely dark except for the nightlight plugged into the hallway outlet. Fighting off her unease and the sense that someone was watching her, Lexie peeked into Aunt Gladys's room. All the lights were out except for a small bedside lamp and, thankfully, all the candles were extinguished. A faint aroma of cinnamon-scented wax and smoke tickled Lexie's nostrils.

Satisfied her aunt was safely asleep for the night, Lexie went back to her room and sank onto her bed. She squeezed her eyes shut and in her mind's eye saw Henry's bloody corpse on the floor of his house. She fought off that image, then saw Elton lying broken and bleeding in the middle of the street.

What was happpening? And why was it happening to her? Was it coincidence? Lexie had too many unanswered questions hammering in her head. And her temples were beginning to throb.

She huddled under the covers and tried to force herself to sleep. It didn't work. She rolled on one side, then the other, then onto her back. Feeling too warm, she kicked off her blankets, only to have the chill of the night urge her to bury herself again.

Finally, sleep came. But it wasn't an easy sleep. Once again, phantoms with butcher knives chased her. Frantic, she managed to fight them off. Then a car tried to run her down. She ran blindly into a heavy mist, trying to escape. But her legs became heavy, as though they'd been saturated with glue.

Stuck to one spot, she watched the car coming, coming—approaching her like a nightstalking beast. It looked like the dark sedan that had slammed into her at the light the night Whitehead died. She tried hard to see inside the vehicle, see who was driving.

But all she could make out were flashing eyes in a sea of blackness. They were staring death at her. She screamed, yet no sound came out of her mouth. Nevertheless, the silence around her spoke to a deep part of her soul, telling her something she didn't want to know.

Someone wanted her to die.

Lexie bolted straight up in bed to a room filled with bright sunlight. "What time is it?" She whirled to see the cow-shaped alarm clock with the black-and-white Holstein paint scheme Eva had given her when she was in the fourth grade.

Good Lord, it was 10 a.m. *Holy mother of pearl.* Flying out of bed, Lexie threw on a pair of jeans, loafers, and a T-shirt. Then she hustled down the stairs, rubbing sleep out of her eyes as she slipped her hair into a ponytail holder.

In the kitchen, the delicious, decadent smell of chocolate attacked her nostrils. Bowls and spoons cluttered a counter also dusted with sugar and cocoa. Aunt Gladys stood there in her purple caftan, humming to herself and sliding a pan from Lexie's oven. She shuffled over and set it on a cooling rack. "Morning, Leslie. Have some breakfast. I've made plenty."

"Hi, Mom," Eva said without looking up. Sitting at the table, with a plate of brownies in front of her, she was reading Homer's *The Iliad and the Odyssey*. She munched on one of the chocolate squares and sipped from a tall glass of milk. "Thanks, Aunt G. These brownies are great."

Aunt G? Lexie smiled at the nickname Eva had given her. It was rather quaint. Then she shivered as nostalgia washed over her. Eva looked like she was about ten, except that back then, her favorite reading material had been anything written by Laura Ingalls Wilder or Clifford the Big Red Dog books.

How had the time gone by so quickly? Now that little girl was walking the lofty halls of Westonville University. Lexie had to be in a time warp—like an episode from the Twilight Zone.

She blinked, bringing herself back to the present. "We've got to get ready for customers, Eva. They'll be here soon."

Eva gave her an annoyed look. "Chill, Mom. It's Sunday, remember? The day of rest? The café is closed."

"Oh, I forgot." Good Lord, was Aunt Gladys' dementia catching? Lexie rubbed her eyes, trying to focus her fogged brain. "I couldn't sleep last night and I'm still groggy."

"The boy-man must have kept you awake." Aunt Gladys stared gravely at her. "I heard him dancing on the roof, too. You simply must have an exterminator come out and do away with him."

Lexie and Eva exchanged glances.

"I'll have someone check into it, Aunt Gladys."

"When?" The old woman's eyes went wide.

"Soon."

Aunt Gladys nodded. "I'll make you some of my special drink if you'd like, Leslie. It keeps me on the straight and narrow." Aunt Gladys tapped her forehead. "No old-timer's disease going on in here."

Except that you can't remember my name or where you are half the time. "No, thanks." Lexie went over to her coffee maker and reached into the cupboard above it, producing hazelnut brew and filters. "I just need caffeine."

"You swill too much of that poison," Aunt Gladys said. "No wonder you can't sleep."

"Caffeine's not the problem, Aunt Gladys. Besides, whoever heard of eating brownies for breakfast?" She gave her aunt a hard look. But Aunt Gladys didn't catch on. She was busy cutting up another pan of decadence. *And making my life crazier than it already is.*

While she drank her coffee, Lexie called the Westonville hospital to check on Elton's condition. At first they wouldn't give out any information. Out of desperation, she lied and told them her daughter was secretly engaged to Elton and that the girl was beside herself with worry.

"Why, I'm nearly his mother-in-law," she pleaded with them. Finally the hospital clerk relented and told her, coldly, Elton was still in intensive care. Lexie put the phone down, a strange numbness flooding her limbs.

"How is he?" Eva asked expectantly.

"Not good, sweetie."

Eva put down her brownie and her face went white. "I was hoping . . . I just had a feeling . . ." She shook her head and her eyes teared. "This is so awful."

Guilt prickled Lexie like a cactus. She still felt as if Elton's accident was all her fault. If he hadn't been at her birthday, stripping for a gaggle of wide-eyed women and a gay man, he might never have been hurt. Lexie felt like the wind had sucked the very breath out of her lungs.

"Just keep hoping, Eva. That's all we can do. Pray and hope. And stay occupied to keep our mind off things we can't change."

"How do we do that?" Eva asked.

Lexie tied on an apron. "We clean house."

"Ughhh." Eva got up and walked to the door. "I think I have to get back to school."

"In a few hours." Lexie grabbed her daughter's arm before she escaped, spun her around, and crushed another apron in her hands. "At the moment I could use your help."

Lexie put all of them to work including Aunt Gladys. It not only kept their minds off poor Elton lying in the hospital, but it kept her charge out of trouble. The three of them scrubbed tables, swept and mopped floors, vacuumed and dusted. All was going well and the place was starting to sparkle, except Aunt Gladys was full of unwanted advice.

"You and Lucy should put your restaurant tables over there," she said, and proceeded to rearrange everything to her satisfaction.

"Only an owl with a microscope could read that menu," Aunt Gladys added. "The lettering needs to be bigger." With arthritic fingers, the eccentric old woman proceeded to rewrite the specials and the prices on the whiteboard with a thick erasable marker. Lexie didn't think the new menu looked any better than her uneven writing, but whatever.

Upstairs in Lexie's apartment, the human whirlwind named Aunt Gladys continued to rearrange and suggest new ways of doing things, and generally had her way until Lexie was ready to crawl down a drain and hide.

Aunt Gladys was a terrorist; Lexie, the hostage. Why didn't Sister Lucy have to suffer through this, too? It wasn't fair.

For a woman Aunt Gladys' age, she was amazingly strong and agile. It was a shame Cousin Bruce kept her locked away in retirement homes. She seemed capable and strong-willed enough to take care of herself except for her occasional spells of forgetfulness.

Lexie prayed silently she would be relieved of Aunt Gladys soon. How long could she stand having the old lady around, bossing everything she did and going on about the boy-man? In the end, Lexie would be the one who would wind up having to be put in a home. Though she knew Cousin Bruce couldn't hear, she muttered a few epithets.

They were cleaning up in Lexie's apartment when the grandfather clock her father had given to her and Dan for their tenth anniversary bonged out the time.

Aunt Gladys's feather duster froze in space and she wailed, "Oh, my, didn't I have something to do today, Leslie? I just don't remember . . ."

"That's right—Winkie's bridge party is this afternoon," Lexie told her, temporary freedom looming precipitously.

"Hell's bells, I'd better go get ready." Aunt Gladys's bent form shuffled over to the stairs and up to her room. A short while later she shuffled back down dressed in bright red slacks and a pink silk blouse. Around her wrinkled column of neck she'd tied a tiger-striped scarf and looped five or six strands of colorful beads. She lit a cigarette and puffed smoke into the air, her hoop earrings tinkling. "I'm ready to go, Leslie."

Lexie wanted to lecture her about smoking, but decided to let it go. She was too excited to get a few minutes to herself. This was pretty bad; the old gal had only been here a couple of days and already Lexie was desperate to pawn her off somewhere.

"I'll be back in a bit," she told Eva who was on the floor sorting through a plastic box full of nail polish.

Lexie fished her keys from her purse and Aunt Gladys followed her down to the garage where she helped her aunt into the old Ford, then climbed in on the driver's side. The ancient truck chugged and clunked its way through the bungalow-lined streets, pitching Aunt Gladys and Lexie to and fro inside the cab.

"What? You can't afford a decent vehicle?" Aunt Gladys complained as she clutched the seat with arthritic fingers. "Ach, my brains—they're scrambled like eggs. Where in Satan's name are you taking me anyway, girl?"

Lexie sighed with impatience and shifted into a lower gear. "To the Sunrise Center to meet Winkie. Remember the bridge party he invited you to?"

Aunt Gladys' eyes went wide. "That's right. A card game for old people. What fun I'll have," she said dryly. "But I guess it's better than rearranging furniture."

The old gal fell silent and watched the passing scenery outside her window. Lexie, glad for the reprieve, glanced outside, too. It was another dry and unusually warm day for autumn. In the distance, the Teton mountain range hulked in shades of sienna. Rocky peaks shot up into the air, unforgiving and barren, except for a thin frosting of snow at the top; too far up to do the thirsty landscape any good.

Wind whipped mercilessly around the truck; it rarely stopped around these parts. People said there were two seasons in Wyoming. Wind and more wind. And if you ever sighted a Jackalope, a rabbit with horns, it meant you would have good luck. Although if you believed in Jackalopes, maybe Santa Claus still climbed down your chimney, too.

Before long, Lexie pulled up to an old cinder-block building that had once been Lubbie's Gas and Grub and still had an ancient red pump displayed in front. In its former glory days, before the Con-oco station took up residence, it had been a hub of the small community. People had come from miles around to have Lubbie fill-'er-up and discuss the latest wheat prices and cattle ranching problems.

Lubbie's had still been around when Lexie was a girl and she recalled meeting friends there for sodas and gum. Some of the kids convinced old Lubbie to sell them cigarettes. Lexie recalled huddling with classmates behind the station and puffing away on the contraband smokes. She'd really hated the way it burned her throat, but she'd wanted to fit in. And of course, when she got home, her parents could smell the odor on her clothing and she would be grounded.

Lexie also recalled that a year or so before she'd graduated from high school, the gas conglomerate had bought out Lubbie's Gas and Grub and built a truck stop outside of town. Lubbie, probably in his seventies or eighties, had retired. In the years since then, the old gas station had been renovated and turned into a meeting place for Moose Creek Junction's senior citizens, so Lexie supposed it still served as a meeting place, only in a different capacity.

Today, it was the answer to Lexie's prayers. The old folks would babysit Aunt Gladys while she got an hour or two of peace and quiet.

"Thank God we've finally arrived," Aunt Gladys exclaimed theatrically, waving a hankie in front of her face as she opened the truck door. "The fumes from this beast were about to suffocate me. Any longer and I would have gotten black lung."

She slid unsteadily from the truck and shuffled her bent form on pencil-thin black heels past the *Sunrise Center* sign, a wooden creation with the letters burned on it dramatically sitting in the middle of the winter brown lawn. A stagecoach image had also been burned into the sign along with mountains and a sun.

Lexie got out of the truck and followed her aunt inside; glancing briefly at the vinyl couches and fake potted ferns. A recreation area with pool tables and shuffleboard was off to the right where a large table surrounded by a group of elderly people sat. It sure looked different from when it had been Lubbie's.

Aunt Gladys and Lexie approached an attendant sitting at a desk by the door, a sturdy looking young man with a head full of closely cropped blond hair. He seemed familiar for some reason, but Lexie couldn't quite place his looks. It was something about his brown eyes, she decided, which were very closely set and nearly hidden behind thick, round glasses. He didn't seem quite right, either. "My aunt's here for the bridge game," she told him. "Does she need to sign in?"

He gave a lopsided grin. "Is she a thhh-enior thhh-itizen?" he asked in a slurred voice.

Down's Syndrome, Lexie thought. How wonderful he was able to be so functional. And he had a certain sweet innocence about him. "Yes, she is."

"Mr. Jack," the young man called.

A man in a checkered shirt and worn jeans came out of an office and moved up behind the boy, patting his back. His blond hair was shapped into silvery spikes, similar to a military haircut. And though his face had a no-nonsense appearance, he was pleasant enough and even nice looking, Lexie thought. He reached across the desk to shake her hand. "I'm Jack Sturgeon. The director here at Sunrise Center." He nodded at the young man. "This is Danny. He helps me out here once in a while."

Danny grinned widely.

Lexie smiled back at Danny, then at Sturgeon. "My name's Lexie Lightfoot," she returned, a slight tingle shooting up her arm when his flesh touched hers. "This is my aunt—"

"Mrs. Gladys Maplethorpe," she told him with a red-lipsticked smile, as if to impress him with her importance.

Jack Sturgeon shook Aunt Gladys' hand as well.

"Gladys," Winkie Hightower trilled as he got up from the table and strode in their direction. Dressed all in black again with his golden earring shining, he addressed the director. "Gladys is a dear friend of mine. I invited her for our afternoon bridge game."

"We're glad you could join us," Sturgeon said.

Winkie led Aunt Gladys over to the table and introduced her.

"I'll be back to pick her up my aunt when the game is over, Mr. Sturgeon," Lexie said.

"Jack—please call me Jack." He smiled, his white teeth shining. "I'm sure she'll enjoy herself. We have a friendly group of seniors here." He smiled. "Don't worry; she's in good hands."

Oh, but Lexie did worry. However, once she was back in her truck, she breathed a sigh of relief. Maybe this was going to work. Wouldn't it be nice to think she could bring Aunt Gladys over here a few times a week and get a break?

Back home, Lexie prepared chicken soup and beef stew and put them in the refrigerator to be reheated for tomorrow's café menu. Then she went upstairs to her living room and sank into her recliner. Reaching into a basket to retrieve the afghan she'd been crocheting, she glanced at Eva sitting on the floor in front of the boob tube watching MTV, toes separated by cotton balls as she painted the nails shiny black.

"Honestly, Eva. That's a hideous color."

"Whatever," Eva responded.

Lexie sighed and concentrated on her project. She'd started the afghan last summer for Eva before the girl left for college. She was close to finishing and hoped she'd get it completed in time for Eva to take back to her dorm room when she left in the evening. At about age 13, Lexie learned to crochet on her own, after her mother had tried to show her . . . how many times? She'd always been too impatient to follow directions. One day her mother had given her an afghan kit and suggested if she wanted to learn to crochet, she should do it by following written instructions.

The afghan pattern turned out to be granny squares and Lexie fell in love with the color of the yarn in the kit. Despite her penchant for fidgeting and restlessness, she managed to teach herself the art of "knotting string" as her father called it. She tried to pass the crocheting skill on to her daughter. Eva, having inherited Lexie's restlessness, preferred mall shopping and talking on the phone. Maybe someday she'd carve out a few domestic skills, but for now, she remained Lexie's wild child.

Ignoring the MTV blare of what kids these days called music, Lexie managed to complete the final few granny squares, now her favorite pattern.

She'd carefully chosen yarn in her daughter's favorite colors—a deep ocean blue, a sky blue, and a butter yellow to add contrast.

As she stitched the granny squares together, Lexie imagined Eva covering up in the labor of love every night while she was away at school. She was probably making too much of it, but it made her feel good to send her child off with an extension of a mother's protective spirit. All that energy put into an afghan. Man, what a goony bird she'd become. *Sheesh*.

Lexie's eyes suddenly got heavy, and she caught herself falling asleep with her crochet hook held in mid-air. Leaning back in her chair, she dozed. The next moment the phone rang. Lexie's eyes popped open.

"You'll have to get it, Mom," Eva insisted, her fingers and toes splayed. "I'm all wet."

Lexie shoved aside yarn and hooks and hustled over to the phone, snatching it from the cradle. "Hullo?"

"Lexie?"

"Yes."

"This is Jack. You need to come and pick up your aunt right away."

"Oh, is the bridge game finished so soon?"

"Not exactly."

Lexie's heart flip-flopped. She had a really bad feeling. "Is there a problem?"

"I'd prefer to discuss it with you in person."

"I'll be right over."

Good heavens. It had only been a couple of hours since she'd dropped off Aunt Gladys. What kind of trouble could the batty old broad have possibly gotten into in that short amount of time? Lexie put on her shoes and gathered up her purse.

Eva stopped blowing on her glossy black toenails and flipped hair out of her face. "What's up, Mom? Where are you going?"

Lexie paused at the door. "To rescue the Sunrise Center from Aunt Gladys."

"Oh-mi-God. What's she done now?"

"Who knows? And you'd better quit blowing on your toes or you're going to hyperventilate and pass out."

"Whatever." Eva ignored Lexie. Shaking her head, Lexie hurried out to the saggy-roofed garage to climb into the truck. Teenagers. Couldn't live with 'em, couldn't disown 'em. Now she had Aunt Gladys to stew over. Again she wondered what possible kind of mischief the woman could have gotten herself into in two hours.

Plenty, a small voice said.

CHAPTER 11

LEXIE'S TRUCK SPUTTERED AND COMPLAINED all the way to the Sunrise Center. For the millionth time, she prayed the temperamental vehicle would stay spit-glued together for a couple more years until she could get Eva's car paid off. *Please, please, please . . .* It was rotten to be at the mercy of a heap of metal and rubber.

The second Lexie walked inside the senior citizen center, she sensed tension rippling through the air. Young Danny stood at the desk, a frightened look on his face, wringing his hands. In the recreation area, the elderly folks groused at each other in loud voices and Jack Sturgeon stood nearby, restraining one woman with short, steel gray hair and equally gray clothes. Winkie Hightower stood not much further away, restraining Aunt Gladys in similar fashion.

Lexie winced. Maybe she should have worn full

body armor for the battle. Poor Danny looked pretty upset, muttering to himself and rocking back and forth. Feeling sorry for him, she reached into her purse, searching for the piece of peppermint candy she'd picked up at a restaurant and was saving for a bad-breath emergency. Handing it to him, she said, "Here you go, Danny, don't worry. It'll be OK."

Danny stared at her with wide eyes and shook his head. "No, no, no. I'm not supposed to take candy from strangers. That's what my mom and Granny said."

"But I'm not a stranger. You and Jack met me earlier, remember?"

His brows knitted in intense concentration, and he said, "Right!" He eagerly unwrapped the candy and popped it into his mouth. Despite the piece of sweet comfort, he resumed wringing his hands while watching the frantic geriatric scenario across the room.

Lexie hurried over. "What's going on?"

"Gladys Maplethorpe is a cheat and a liar," the lady in gray proclaimed, chin quivering.

Lexie looked at Jack.

He swept his hand toward the group of assorted seniors. "I'm afraid your aunt convinced everyone to switch from Bridge to Poker. Things got a little confused."

"No confusion here," Gray Lady spouted. "The old cow straight up cheated!"

"Did not!" Aunt Gladys roared.

"Did to!" Gray Lady shouted.

"Alice, calm down." Jack gave Gray Lady a stern look. "I'm sure it was all a mistake. Remember your high blood pressure. Don't upset yourself."

"He's right, Alice," Winkie added. "Gladys didn't mean to make anyone angry. Did you, dear?"

Aunt Gladys slowly shook her head, but steam practically emanated from her flared nostrils.

Alice shoved her hands on her hips. "But—"

"I'm so sorry for the misunderstanding," Lexie interrupted. She looped her arm through Aunt Gladys'. "We're leaving now."

Winkie and Sturgeon talked to the elderly group, calming them down, as Lexie dragged her fuming aunt out into the reception area.

"That woman's deranged," Aunt Gladys proclaimed. "She needs to be in a loony bin. Why, all we were doing is playing a good old-fashioned poker game and she doesn't even know what a full house is. In fact, none of them did. It's practically a crime."

"Not everyone spent twenty years in Las Vegas gambling every weekend, Aunt Gladys. And not everyone was married to Marty the card shark like you were. Now, let's go home."

As they went outside, Winkie came up and took one of Aunt Gladys's hands, speaking quietly to her. Then a short, pot-bellied gentleman hurried to her side as well, a grin tilting his lips. He had a cap of curly silver hair that gleamed in the sunlight, and he wore a green suit jacket and slacks with a matching green-striped tie. Though his clothing was obviously of good quality, the colors were a little bright and Lexie decided he looked like a leprechaun straight from the Emerald Isle.

"I know you weren't cheating, doll," the leprechaun man told Aunt Gladys in a cultured, almost English accent, eyes twinkling merrily. "You're just good at cards. Alice is only jealous."

"Thank you, Frenchie dear," Aunt Gladys said as she stared adoringly at the portly fellow.

"May I call you sometime? I'd love to escort you to dinner."

"Of course. I told you I'm staying with my niece Leslie, didn't I?"

"Right." He nodded. " I'll call you there." He smiled at her, then shuffled back to the group in the recreation room.

"Who was that?" Lexie asked.

"Ferdinand Duckworth the second," Winkie said, hugging himself. "Gladys thinks he's simply divine. And so do I."

"He's rolling in the dough," Aunt Gladys informed her. "He inherited millions."

Men with money. Aunt Gladys drew them like magnets. "What's a millionaire like Frenchie doing in Moose Creek Junction?"

"He made big bucks in the perfume industry and has been all over the world, even France, of course. He's retired now and decided to settle in Moose Creek Junction for a quiet, simple life where he wouldn't be bothered with high society. Can you even begin to imagine the life he's led?" Aunt Gladys fanned herself theatrically.

"Good gravy," Lexie responded. So, Moose Creek Junction had once seemed pretty harmless to him. Did Ferdinand Duckworth II still think so? After Henry Whitehead's murder and Elton's accident?

From the corner of her eye, Lexie noticed Donna Roos, the local realtor's wife, striding in their direction amid a whirlwind of dry leaves skittering across the sidewalk. A slobbering boxer at the end of the red leather leash she clung to was walking *her*, more than she was walking *him*. When she passed them, Lexie nodded.

Donna, however, merely glanced at her, raised her pinched face, and pressed her thin lips into a hard line. The dog and Donna kept on walking as though Lexie were invisible.

Something clicked in her mind and she remembered reading an article in *The Moose Creek Junction Chronicle* about the recent frightening drop in the local real estate market. Since the early nineties, when recreational mountain property around Rawhide City and the Ice Queen Resort skyrocketed, investors had purchased property further south in Moose Creek Junction where prices were more reasonable. But the property sales boom had mysteriously stopped.

Oh my gosh!

Were people blaming her for the plummeting property values? Did they think no one was buying land because there was a murderer on the loose and it might be her? Even though no one could prove Lexie had anything to do with Henry's death and Elton's accident, she was associated with the incidents. That alone made her suspect, especially to small town minds. A sense of unease washed over her and she tried to ignore it, but to no avail.

It was absolutely unfair for people to treat her like this. How could they be so petty?

Despite Lexie's outrage, she realized Donna's ridiculous snub wasn't worth worrying about. She had other matters with Aunt Gladys to attend to, and she focused on helping her blabbering aunt get settled into her truck.

Winkie spoke with Aunt Gladys in sympathetic tones and gave her a peck on the cheek.

"Thank you for your help with Aunt Gladys, Winkie," Lexie said as she shut the passenger door, still able to hear her aunt's prattling.

"Do try to convince the poor dear to get some rest this afternoon," Winkie said. "She's gotten herself in such a dither and it can't be good for her health."

"I'll see what I can do," Lexie said, "but she's pretty hard headed."

"Just like always." Winkie put his hands on his hips. "I'll call her later to see how she's doing."

As he walked back into the Sunrise Center, Jack Sturgeon left the building and approached Lexie.

"I'm so sorry about what happened," he told her, an apologetic look on his face.

Lexie shrugged. "Don't worry about it. My aunt has a way of irritating people. It's just what she does."

"Well, for what it's worth, I'm sorry it ended this way." He smiled. "And I know it may not be the best timing, but I'd like to see you again."

Lexie fought to keep the surprise out of her expression. "I suppose it could be arranged," she managed to answer. Oh, brother, she sounded like she was setting up an appointment to have furniture delivered!

"How about a movie Saturday night?"

Finally, a date Sister Lucy didn't have to set up for her. Jack Sturgeon had all his hair and teeth, too, and he hadn't salivated over her cleavage. Lexie was stunned. "Um, sure. How about I meet you at the old Jefferson Theater for the main feature?"

"Great." Jack winked, then turned and walked back into the Sunrise Center.

Lexie watched him go, still amazed. Miracles *can* happen, she told herself.

Still concerned about what to do with Aunt Gladys, but looking forward to her date with Jack, Lexie hopped into her truck and drove home, barely hearing Aunt Gladys' complaints. On a whim, she pulled into the Loose Goose Emporium parking lot underneath a canopy of tree branches covered with dry brown leaves.

"What are you doing?" Aunt Gladys grabbed onto the cracked dashboard. "You're driving like a maniac. I'd be better off hoofing it around town on a skateboard than letting you play chauffer."

"We need toilet paper. You just stay put while I go grab some." Lexie ignored Aunt Gladys' look of irritation when she got out of the truck.

The Loose Goose Emporium—why Fred and Bertie Creekmore had decided on that name was beyond Lexie—was housed in the old red brick DeLacy building originally built in 1885. It sported typical Victorian gingerbread trim, cupolas, a wrap-around porch, balconies, and many beautiful stained glass windows. The building had survived a vast assortment of incarnations as well as fires, floods, blizzards, and drought, though the present lack of rain wasn't the first dry spell Wyoming had ever suffered.

First built by one of Moose Creek Junction's founding fathers as an upscale home in one of the finer neighborhoods of the time, it had later become a mercantile and dry goods store, then a restaurant, another time a dress shop and for a while the town library. But the DeLacy building's most infamous incarnation by far was when it was called the Saddle Up Saloon.

Men from all walks of life frequented the Saddle Up: bankers and lawyers, outlaws and ruffians alike. For a price, Hattie Bookman's gals entertained them for an hour, or for the night, and her ladies didn't come cheap. They shimmied their buxom shapes into beautiful Parisian gowns, swished ostrich fans and served their clients the finest liquor and food. Men came for miles around to visit the saloon and partake of its delights.

The existence of the world's oldest profession was common in frontier towns and Moose Creek Junction was no different. As long as the girls paid their monthly fines and didn't cause trouble, the local law enforcement looked the other way. Besides, Hattie's loose women gave all the good ladies of society a night or two off while their husbands were otherwise engaged. It also helped that the shady ladies were philanthropic, sharing their wealth with the Orphans' Society, the Ladies' Sewing League, and other charitable organizations. The soiled doves also had purchasing power and were good for the local economy.

At the moment, the Loose Goose Emporium, while not having such a notorious reputation as the Saddle Up, filled a niche in Moose Creek Junction society. There was a large grocery store in Westonville if you had the time to make the 45-minute trip. For quicker errands, one could find plenty at the Loose Goose; milk, bread, eggs, cereal, Hamburger Helper, a small assortment of meats, canned goods, and necessary paper items. Actually, Bertie made it a point to stock a little of everything from personal hygiene items to cosmetics and a small supply of clothing. Since the Loose Goose had gone into business in the early seventies, nobody had an excuse to suffer without the necessities.

Lexie glanced at the over-sized wooden goose on the store sign. She remembered staring at it as a little girl and wondering if a real goose had posed for the portrait or if someone had painted it from memory. Why that had mattered to her, Lexie didn't remember. The goose looked tired and worn from age, just like she was.

Inside she took a small plastic cart from the front of the store that of course had gimpy, squeaky wheels—par for the course—then made a beeline for the paper goods and chose a 24-pack of bathroom tissue. A sudden thought occurred to her and she swerved down another aisle to the office and art supplies where she picked up a stack of velvet-backed paint-by-number kits. She headed to the wooden checkout counter that used to be the bar and still had a large, ornate mirror from the Saddle Up days hanging behind it.

"Well, as I live and breathe, if it isn't the town floozie herself." Violet Whitehead tossed her brunette head at Lexie and grabbed another chocolate from the box sitting next to her, popping it into her mouth. She licked her chubby fingers then chewed furiously on the candy. After she swallowed, she stared at Lexie and spat, "Stolen anyone else's husband lately?"

Lexie wrinkled her nose at the smell of chocolate candy and cheap perfume that floated from Violet's blue jeans and black embroidered peasant top, both of which were too tight and made her look like a lumpy sack of potatoes. She didn't know the woman well, but what she'd seen of her, especially today, hadn't given her a good impression. No wonder Henry Whitehead hadn't been thrilled to have her as his wife and his affections had wandered. Harpie was the word that came to Lexie's mind to describe Violet Whitehead.

"Excuse me?" Lexie blinked.

"Everyone knows how you entice men with your innocent, smarmy looks and teasing. It's all over town so you can't fool me. Even my poor, stupid Henry got duped."

Lexie put her items down on the counter with an emphatic thump. "Last I heard, you and poor Henry were divorced. I don't make a habit of dating married men. In fact, I rarely date at all."

Violet snorted and wiped her fingers on her jeans. "Right, and I'm Anna Nicole Smith," she screeched. "You date enough that men are falling at your feet, literally. *Dead.*"

"Look, Violet, I didn't come here to chit-chat with you about what you think you know. I just needed a few things."

"*I just needed a few things,*" Violet mimicked sarcastically. "Well, I'm so freakin' glad I got to wait on you I could just croak. If it weren't for you, my Henry would still be alive and paying his child support. And I wouldn't have to be working my ass off to wait on sissy-prissies like you."

Lexie was getting ticked off and couldn't stop from giving an angry retort. "Hey, I work for a living, too, Violet. Most of us around here do. Get off your high horse about how bad you have it."

Bertie Creekmore came out from a back room, expression dour. Her face was gaunt and her brownish-gray frizzy hair screamed for conditioner. She wore black from head to toe on her skeletal frame and seemed sad.

Bertie tapped the ancient cash register with a long finger and glared at Violet. "What's going on? It sounds like a wrestling match out here with all the shouting."

"Sorry," Lexie said. "I'm just trying to buy a couple of things and Violet's unhappy with me."

"What did I tell you about harassing the customers?" Bertie said to Violet.

Violet, properly chastised, hung her head. "That you'd let me go if I didn't quit."

"Shall I give you notice, then? Hmmm?"

Violet's face turned as purple as the flower she was named for.

Lexie was irritated, but she really didn't want to be a part of Violet loosing her job, too. "It's OK, really, Bertie. I think Violet's just having a bad day. Don't fire her."

"Lexie's right," Violet said. "I really didn't mean anything."

Bertie gave a loud sigh. "I don't need you chasing off my customers, mind you. I'll give you one more chance. Otherwise—"

"I know, I know," Violet said. "I'll behave myself. I promise."

Violet rang up Lexie's items and Bertie said, "I

don't know why you're still so defensive about that
ex-husband of yours anyway, Violet. He was a no-
good and I knew that boy was going to get himself
in trouble. I saw all the women he had parading in
and out, day and night, night and day. It's amazing
he could lift his head off his pillow, let alone get it
up any more."

Lexie suddenly realized the Loose Goose Emporium was right across the street from Whitehead's
place. Bertie and Fred had downsized from their
home and now lived above the store in the small
apartment she had once rented. Even with the bird's-
eye view, Bertie needed good eyesight or a pair of
binoculars to see much. Lexie placed a bet on the
binoculars. "You saw him a lot?" she asked.

"Oh, yes. I imagine he was dead on his feet at
work with all the nonsense he had going on at his
place. Loud music and goings on till all hours of the
morning almost every day. He constantly left his
curtains wide open and I could see . . ." she trailed
off and cleared her throat, obviously rethinking her
choice of words. "*People* told me they saw all manner
of wild parties and, well, *sexual* activities going on.
Why, he was a regular neighborhood nuisance. It's
funny his landlord didn't kick him out long before
somebody offed him. If you ask me, it's good rid-
dance to have him out of here." She colored brightly.
"Of course, it's not nice to speak of the dead that
way, but Henry Whitehead was not a pleasant person. I bet it was one of the neighbors hereabouts

who did him in."

"Did you see anything unusual the night of the murder?" Lexie asked anxiously. She paid for the items Violet rang up on the ancient cash register, picked up the brown bag. Had Bertie attacked Whitehead with a butcher knife? Or had one of her neighbors?

Lexie mulled it over a moment. That theory was pretty far fetched, although still a possibility. Whoever killed Whitehead probably killed Hugh Glenwood and hurt Elton. Bertie had no reason to do that.

Violet was right about one thing—she did have a penchant for getting the men around her hurt or killed. It wouldn't exactly win her the sweetheart award.

"Nothing more unusual than the usual." Bertie tapped her sallow cheek. "Except for that dark, foreign-looking car. That was definitely not usual. I'd never seen it before and I haven't seen it since. Of course, I told the police all about that. And then them reporters called like crazy askin' questions. 'Bout ripped the phone off the wall, I did."

Lexie's radar flicked on. Could it be the dark car that followed her home from Whitehead's house the night he was killed? "Did you get a license plate number?"

"Good gracious, no. It was too far away and my eyes are getting pretty dim, you know." She shook her head. "A shame about that Elton fella," Bertie said. "I hope he gets better soon. The Briarhursts are none too happy he's laid up in the hospital. I hear he's not good."

Lexie didn't comment because she didn't know what to say. She still felt the sting of guilt over Elton's accident. "You ladies have a good afternoon," she said, trying hard not to let Elton's condition get her down. Surely he'd get better. He just had to.

Carma was entering the store as Lexie left, sleek, smooth, and cosmopolitan as ever. Her black designer jeans, green silk blouse, and snakeskin boots definitely did not fit in with the flowered housedresses and red, windblown complexions of most of the women in this town. Carma looked even thinner than before and her make-up and dark hair were flawless, giving her a New York model sort of look. She gave a brief, "Hullo," and narrowed her exotically lined eyes at Lexie.

"Nice seeing you," Lexie returned, feeling a blast of ice come from Carma. Her long purple nails gripping the door caught Lexie's attention and she wondered how the woman could even use the phone with those evil lances. They were ridiculous, but then Lexie supposed she had to advertise her trade somehow. One of the main things Lexie remembered about Carma from high school was she believed everyone should see things her way.

"You simply must come to the next book club meeting with your sister, Lexie," Carma purred. "We read the most fabulous books; the next one we're going to read is that new murder mystery everyone's talking about." Her eyes gleamed. "And elections are coming up soon. If you join, you can vote for Lucy as the new president. She would be fabulous."

Carma was sure into the word *fabulous*. Lexie guessed her usage of the adjective made her feel superior to the townspeople she no doubt considered hicks. Funny, Carma had been born and raised here. Why she felt she was so far above everyone was beyond Lexie. "I didn't even know she was running."

"That's because she doesn't know herself. But she will, you can be sure." She laughed. "There's no one else who can fill Susannah Averill's shoes when she resigns this year."

"Sure, I'll think about coming sometime," Lexie responded. In a pig's eye, she thought silently. Someone would have to literally hog tie her and drag her screaming to the Moose Creek Junction Book Club and sign her up as a member. She would rather swallow rat poison than sit through an hour of that torture.

Carma certainly thought a lot of the club and herself. Another thing Lexie remembered about Carma from high school was that she had been mousy and withdrawn—a true loner with no real friends. These days, she was outspoken, irritating and still believed everyone should see things her way. She remained a loner and from what Lexie knew, had few friends. No doubt people became annoyed when she bossed them around. The book club was probably her only opportunity for social interaction.

Lexie wondered what Lucy would think about being involuntarily elected, by none other than

Carma Leone, to the presidency of the most gossipy group of women in town. Of course, Lucy gossiped with the best of them, and while she hated that trait in others, she couldn't see it in herself.

"You do that," Carma said, a smirk on her face.

What was up with her? Lexie said good-bye and hustled back outside, a funny feeling washing over her. Inside the truck, she handed the bag to Aunt Gladys.

"You've been gone about a million years," Aunt Gladys growled.

Lexie buckled up and started the sputtering truck. "I got you a present. Not the toilet paper."

Aunt Gladys glanced inside the bag and pulled out the bathroom tissue. "What in God's name did you buy these silly things for?"

Lexie drove down the street, refusing to let Aunt Gladys get to her any more. "To keep you busy and out of trouble while you're staying with me. You got a better idea?"

Aunt Gladys peered inside the bag again. "Hell's bells, paint-by-numbers? I can't even paint my own toenails let alone those little peckers with colored pee pots. These things are for digits and midgets."

"You'll learn." Lexie gripped the steering wheel tighter as she turned a corner. "Here are the rules. You're not allowed anywhere unless one of the family is with you."

Aunt Gladys snorted. "I'm under house arrest?"

"Call it what you like. I'm trying to keep you

out of trouble. You're also not to light candles in your room and I insist you stop smoking in the house."

"Well, fine, you friggin' Nazi. You didn't say anything about smoking in your rattletrap truck, though." Aunt Gladys promptly produced a cigarette, lit up, and proceeded to pout and puff, pout and puff.

For heaven's sake, Lexie thought as she rolled down her window for fresh air. The name of the game was survival. Hopefully, Cousin Bruce would soon arrive to collect his mother and life could resume some sense of normalcy. Lexie and Lucy could get back to their investigation, unless Deputy Dog or patootiehead Otis had managed to finger the murderer by then, which she doubted very much.

It was impossible to go sleuthing with Aunt Gladys in tow and Lexie was dying to check out a few things, especially after Elton's accident. Gabe Stevenson would not appreciate her nosing around, but tough. Once Cousin Bruce came to collect Aunt Gladys, she planned to snoop to her heart's content.

The week passed uneventfully, except for a dark car that kept cruising by Lexie's house. On a couple of occasions, Lexie thought she saw it following her. Every time she looked up again to try and get a license plate number, the car vanished. She called Otis to let him know about it, but he was unwilling to do anything unless she had a license plate number. Lexie maintained a vigilant watch for the vehicle, hoping sometime she could get a good enough glimpse.

Business was slow at the Saucy Lucy. Lexie hoped it was just the time of year and people were busy preparing for the upcoming holidays. No matter how she tried to rationalize the situation, in her heart she knew it was a bunch of hooey, as Aunt Gladys would say. In a small town like this, word got around fast and she was afraid people really were staying away because of Whitehead's murder.

It was an unsettling and disappointing thought. How could she take care of her family if her business went down the toilet? The money Cousin Bruce had wired would help keep food on the table and bills paid for a while. But that was it: Once it was gone, what would she do?

Lexie was up early Saturday morning, ready to start the workday. She showered and dressed and as she was putting her hair up into its usual ponytail, she noticed the lovely orange and red sunrise that illuminated her room. She crossed to the window and looked outside at the neighborhood, bathed in an ethereal, golden glow. No doubt it's going to be another warm day, she thought. Lexie was about to move away from the window when she noticed the dark car parked by the curb across the street.

It was back!

It was impossible to determine the make, model

or license plate numbers from this distance so, heart hammering, she hustled downstairs and slipped outside. By the time she reached the curb, her lungs were slamming against her ribs and the car was nowhere to be seen; as if it had never been there. Maybe I'm losing my marbles, she thought. *Maybe the dark, mysterious car is all a figment of my imagination.*

She was under so much pressure these days— could be she was cracking. Then again, Bertie Creekmore had mentioned she'd seen a dark car parked at Whitehead's house the night of his murder. Lexie sensed there was a connection between the strange vehicle and recent weird activities. Without being able to get a good look at the vehicle or license plate numbers, Otis couldn't help her and she figured Gabe couldn't either.

Annoyed, Lexie went into the kitchen, put coffee on to brew, then rummaged through her larder and produced flower, sugar, spices, and other baking supplies. She prepared the day's menu with a vengeance. At least for the time being, cooking would take her mind off the confusion.

Fingers and flour flew and by the time she was done, she had produced six loaves of bread consisting of oatmeal raisin, sourdough, and rye, all set to rise on the counter. She switched on the two large commercial ovens to preheat, and stirred together a big pot of golden colored corn-bacon chowder for the soup special. The chowder smelled heavenly by the time she started to put the finishing touches on a couple of apple and peach pies.

Bringing with her a whirl of orange and yellow leaves and a warm breeze, Lucy walked in through the back door. She left it open and latched the screen door. "Phew, it's hot in here. We need some air."

"Good morning," Lexie said, wrinkling her brow in consternation. For once, Lucy's complaints couldn't be attributed to menopause. The weather was still unseasonably warm and it was alarming. If this wound up being another dry season like last year, the mayor and city officials had plans to institute further water restrictions. That would ruin her chances for a garden with fresh vegetables for the café. She might as well kiss off all the hard work she'd put into getting the Victorian's lawn, shrubs, flowers, and rose bushes to flourish. It was frustrating to even think about.

Lucy set her purse down and slipped a white frilly apron over her dowdy brown and yellow housedress. With her sturdy brown loafers, support, hose and hairnet, she was in perfect uniform. "What's with the prune face? You look like the Crypt Keeper again."

Lexie frowned harder. "I hate this drought."

"Stop with the long face, already. We'll live. People throughout time have dealt with water problems all over the world." Lucy washed her hands at the sink and dried them on a paper towel. "Guess what?"

It was like when someone says; *knock, knock,* and you're supposed to say, *Who's there?* Lexie decided she was supposed to play the game. "What?"

"Doc said the gout in my big toe is nearly gone."

Lexie blinked. "I didn't know you had gout."

"Didn't want to bother you, but I've been having pain in my right foot. The medication he put me on has helped, thank the Lord."

Lexie shoved her hands on her hips. "Why didn't you tell me you were hurting? I would have insisted you take some time off."

"And spend more time at home where Otis can fuss at me?" She hooted. "For Pete's sake, I'd rather stand around with a sore big toe than be at the man's beck and call to run errands, thank you very much. Besides, you can't manage this place all alone."

"I still feel awful. I thought I saw you limping a little this week—I should have asked you about it."

Lucy shrugged. "All's well that ends well. How's the dragon lady doing today? Has she started any fires or stolen anything?"

"She's not up yet, I'm happy to say. Are you sure you can't take a turn having her at your house? She's driving me batty."

"Sorry." Lucy held her hands out in supplication. "Otis would have my head on a platter. It simply wouldn't work."

Lexie sighed, irritated by her sister's missing sense of family duty. When the phone rang, she picked it up and said, "Saucy Lucy Café, this is Lexie. May I help you?"

There was a moment of silence, then someone at the other end of the line hung up. Lexie stared at the receiver, puzzled.

"What happened? Wrong number?"

"Don't know." Lexie plugged in the corn chowder crockpot and pulled out the chicken and dumpling soup and beef stew tubs from the refrigerator and poured them into other crockpots to warm. "They hung up without saying a word."

"That's odd. Maybe it was one of those recorded telemarketer calls. Sometimes they get mangled up."

"Or maybe it was Barnard Savage. He'd do anything to get enough information to spin stories about all the awful things going on." The odd feeling she was being watched began to churn in Lexie's stomach.

"Ick." Lucy shivered. "That leech of a man."

The phone rang again and Lexie gave it a dirty look. "Maybe I ought to unplug it."

"No," Lucy said. "I'll get it. If it's Savage, I'd like to give him a piece of my mind. She picked up the receiver and said, "Look, you, mind your own business and quit hounding us!"

Suddenly she quit speaking and her face went white. She slammed the receiver down on the cradle as if it had bitten her.

"What?" Lexie wiped spills off of the stove.

Lucy put her hands to her cheeks and leaned back against the counter. "That . . . that person, or whoever it was on the phone said, '*Go back where you came from or you'll die!*'"

Lexie's fingers went limp and she dropped the sponge. "Oh, my God."

"I'll tell Otis. He'll know what to do." Lucy picked up the phone and called her husband at the office. She jabbered at him for a few seconds about the threatening call and hung up.

"What did he say?"

"That he'd have someone at the department tap your line. Stalkers have to stay on for a certain length of time in order for the calls to be traced. He said the last one probably wasn't long enough. But if they call back . . ."

"Dear Lord, let's hope they don't." Lexie put a hand over her racing heart for a few seconds.

"Let's get these pies finished," Lucy finally said. "It'll get our mind off the strange calls."

The sisters turned their attention back to the pies. After pinching the edges on the crusts, they sprinkled the cream-colored pastry with a mixture of cinnamon and sparkling sugar. The preheat lights had gone out on the ovens and Lexie popped pies in one of them. Lucy put the properly risen bread loaves into the other.

Glancing at the teapot-shaped clock on the wall, Lexie decided everything should be done about the time customers began to arrive. That was *if* they had any customers.

"You know you're taking home some of this food if we don't get any customers today."

Lucy raised a brow at her. "Why wouldn't we get customers?"

"Just a feeling I have." Lexie thought of the

strange looks she'd been getting from the towns-people lately. "People are concerned about the murders and Elton's accident. It's like I'm tainted. They must think I'm involved in all of this."

Lucy waved her hand. "They're all just super-stitious. They'll get over it."

"What is everyone saying at your book club? And by the way, Carma Leone says you are going to be the next president."

"President?" She shuffled uncomfortably and began to wipe counters. "Over my dead body. I like the book discussions, but I don't have time for their nonsense full time. The ladies think Henry's mur-der and Elton's accident are unfortunate."

Lexie grabbed a broom and started sweeping. "What are they saying about *me*?"

She was quiet a moment. "That it's too bad you're caught up in the middle of all the trouble."

"Truthfully." Lexie cocked her head.

Lucy sighed. "You're determined to drag it out of me, aren't you?"

Lexie nodded.

"Well, the ladies start to whisper whenever I come into a room, but I've overheard snippets of con-versations." She sighed. "They think pretty much what you suspected."

"I knew it!" Lexie leaned on the counter and put her head in her hands.

"It'll be all right, Lex. Everything will blow over soon." Lucy patted Lexie's back, mothering her as always. "You'll see."

"In the meantime," Lexie said, looking up at Lucy, "plan on taking home some food. Aunt Gladys and I can't possibly eat it all. In fact, you and Otis may have to plan on feeding us when the café goes belly up and Cousin Bruce's money runs out."

"There you go again, being all melodramatic. Things simply cannot be all that bad." Lucy stared into space for a moment then snapped her fingers. "Say, didn't you tell me you have a date with Jack Sturgeon tonight?"

Lexie leaned back on the counter and rubbed her eyes. Leave it to Sister Lucy to think a date would cure everything. "That's right, I do. I was so concerned about that mysterious car parked in front of the house this morning I completely forgot."

"It was out there again?" Lucy made a frustrated noise. "Did you get any plate numbers or the model? Otis will want to know."

Lexie shook her head. "By the time I got outside, it was gone."

"Just keep a look out, dear. I have confidence the police will eventually take care of the situation. These things take time." Lucy shook her finger at her in a motherly fashion. "Now, about this date . . ."

Lexie suffered through Lucy's lecture, about the millionth one, about how she needed a man in her life, etc. She was looking forward to the date with Jack, nevertheless, she intended to keep her excitement under control. It would be a pleasant evening. She didn't want to read more into it. Eva volunteered to drive home from Westonville this afternoon and keep an eye on Aunt Gladys while she was gone. A break from the lovable looney would be a welcome relief.

She had to admit though, as Lucy preached to her about the church's stand on marriage and morality, she did miss male companionship. Not just the physical part, although that had its benefits. She missed having someone to share her day with, someone to discuss her thoughts and feelings with. Hopefully, Jack really was as nice as he seemed, but only time would tell if they continued to see each other. A delicious shiver of anticipation traveled up her spine and she instantly quelled any further anticipation.

Maybe I should be concerned about my track record with men, she thought to herself. Violet Whitehead really had a point when she'd accused Lexie of causing trouble for the men she got involved with. An inner voice warned her to put off dating anyone until Whitehead's murder was solved.

Who knew how long that might take?

"What I want to know," Lucy was saying, "is how you managed to get a date with the most eligible bachelor in town?"

"He asked me."

"Hallelujah."

"It is surprising," Lexie said.

"He's a widower, you know. His wife died of leukemia. He cared for her up to the very last."

"He sounds like a good guy."

"Oh, he is. Which is why all the single women in town are after him. He hasn't dated since Emma died, so I didn't think he was ready yet. It's been a year."

"It'll be nice to get to know him."

Lucy clasped her hands. "You have to tell me all about your date tomorrow, you know."

Lexie rolled her eyes. "Nosy."

"Who loves ya, baby?" Aunt Gladys, wearing a leopard print caftan and enough beads to sink a ship, entered the kitchen. She danced around and sang, clapping and kicking her long legs in the air.

"Oh my," Lucy said. "Do you think she thinks she's back on stage in Vegas?"

"Probably." Lexie shook her head. "There's no telling with her."

Exhausted and out of breath, Aunt Gladys suddenly stopped and her face melted into a royal pout as she glanced around the kitchen. "Where the hell am I? What kind of bar is this?"

"Aunt Gladys," Lexie said firmly. "Remember, you're staying with me."

Aunt Gladys glared at her. "Hell's bells, you could at least put cocktail peanuts and appetizers out for the patrons. I'm hungry as a mule train."

"Do you want me to make you some eggs or pancakes for breakfast?"

Aunt Gladys shook her head. "Good God, no. I have to have my special shake." She tapped her forehead. "Keeps me sharp as a tack up here where it counts."

Aunt Gladys proceeded to bulldoze her way through a few cupboards then bellied up to the counter and mixed eggs, milk, and her special drink powder. She pushed a button and the blender whirred into action. Before long the gray, unappetizing drink came to life and Aunt Gladys seemed happy as a clam as she poured it into a tall glass, humming to herself.

"For Pete's sake, is she like this all the time?" Lucy asked.

"Ninety-nine-point-nine percent of it," Lexie told her.

Noon came and went; yet there was no familiar *ring-a-ling* from the bell on the door to announce customers. An hour went by, then two. Aunt Gladys, cussing and fussing, pulled out her paint-by-numbers and busied herself at the kitchen table dabbing color on a black velvet picture of a mountain stream. Lexie and Lucy stirred around the kitchen, waiting and watching for signs of life and trying to be hopeful.

No one came to have soup and sandwiches at the Saucy Lucy Café.

Finally the front door bell tinkled and Akiko shuffled inside and sat at her usual table by the bay window.

"I'll take her order," Lexie told Lucy and hurried out to greet the soft-spoken Japanese woman.

"Good afternoon, Akiko." Lexie smiled at the tiny Oriental lady, order pad in hand. "What can I get for you today?"

"*Konichiwa, Rexi-san*," Akiko said with a slight

bow of her short, dark-haired head. She wore black slacks, a white silk brocade blouse with a Mandarin collar, and diamond stud earrings. "I want soup special and what kind of pie you make today?"

Lexie told her what was on the menu.

"Ah, so. Very good. That is what I have. And coffee." She grinned. "My Eng-rish getting better, eh?"

"Absolutely." Lexie scribbled in her note pad. "And your husband? Is he joining you?"

"He no come," Akiko said with a sad expression, shaking her head. "Ian be-rieve in curse rike everyone else."

Lexie frowned, cold numbness seeping through her limbs. "Curse? What curse?"

"He say it bad to come here."

"But *what curse* is he talking about?" Lexie insisted.

"Everyone say this place evil. First reverend and you poor mama die in car accident. You go out with Mr. Grenwood and he die, then Mr. Whitehead die, and now that poor boy get hurt."

Lexie clutched the order pad so hard her fingers throbbed. "Oh no . . ."

"I say is only bad karma, not curse," Akiko said, trying to reassure her.

"The Ouija board warned you about the curse, Lexie," Aunt Gladys said as she shuffled into the café. "It could all be a bunch of hogwash. If people would use their noggins more and flap their gums less, they'd realize there's nothing going on here. Somebody's just pissed off at Leslie and they're taking it out on her."

"Aunt Gladys—"

"Damned if the people in this town aren't just as pea-brained as always," she continued as she came and sat at a table next to Akiko. "Bunch of superstitious morons, the lot of them."

"Aunt Gladys, please. This is no time to worry about the past," Lexie said.

"Everyone hereabouts called me a whore and a tramp when I was a girl," Aunt Gladys went on, ignoring her, tapping her red-nailed arthritic fingers on the plastic tabletop. "Said I was no good, when really they were all just green around the gills because I was a real looker. They don't understand it when people have ambitions or don't fit their cookie-cutter mold. Moose Creek Junction is nothin' more than a hole-in-the-wall-town. Leslie, you should move away."

Akiko looked around the room. "This house have bad aura," she said. "I feel it. I give your place a Japanese crensing to chase away evil spirits, OK?"

"A *cleansing*?" Lexie asked.

"*Hai*, that's what I say. A cleansing—a special prayer. I say it right now." Akiko closed her eyes, bowed her head and started chanting softly in her native tongue, hands pressed together.

A loud crashing sound exploded around Lexie, then something slammed into her head. Pain shot through her temples as the sound of tinkling glass splattering against the floor assaulted her ears.

Everything went black.

CHAPTER 12

"LEXIE, LEXIE . . ."

As if from a million miles away, Lexie heard a voice urgently calling her. Someone prodded her shoulder. "Wh . . . what?" she asked, her mind foggy as the docks of San Francisco's Fisherman's Wharf at midnight. She couldn't move, couldn't think straight.

An agitated voice shouted, "Aliens! We've been invaded by a bunch of douche bag aliens! They've bombarded us with one of their evil offspring!"

That's Aunt Gladys, Lexie thought as she struggled to the surface of consciousness.

"Lexie, wake up!"

Lexie dragged her eyes open to see Sister Lucy crouched down beside her holding something to her forehead. The cool, hardness of the towel revealed it was full of ice. It felt good in a way, but also bad because the ice pack pressure caused such intense pain to radiate through her frontal lobes she wouldn't have been surprised to see pink elephants dancing on the bistro tables in spike heels.

Pushing herself to a sitting position, Lexie grabbed for the pack. "Give that to me," she snapped at Lucy and pulled the towel away from her face. Red splotches covered the terry cloth. *Blood*. The pain returned with even more intense throbbing. Lexie groaned and pressed the ice pack against her forehead to keep the bleeding under control. "What happened? What hit me?"

"Good question. Something flew through the window and slammed into your head." Lucy's voice shook and her face was creased with concern. "Thank the good Lord you're all right. I was worried."

"Rook! Rook!" Akiko crouched in a corner with one arm raised defensively over her face and the other arm outstretched, her index finger pointing toward the middle of the floor where a round, dark green object covered in yellow paper had landed. Several of the bay window panes near her table were broken, making it look like a gaping mouth full of shark's teeth. Chunks of splintered glass scattered messily across the floor and a warm breeze filled the room.

The age-spotted skin on Aunt Gladys' arm flapped as she shook her fist at the broken window. "You'll never take me alive, you little puke-green bastards! I know Elvis personally. He'll cut off your heads and shove 'em down your throat if you touch a hair on any of our heads!"

Lexie decided Aunt Gladys seemed fine except

for being pretty pissed off and back to Looney-Toons land.

"Akiko, are you all right?" Lexie rose to her feet with Lucy's assistance, glancing at the small Japanese woman.

Akiko took several deep, shuddering breaths and stood, tears in her wide brown almond-shaped eyes. "*Hai*. My eyes closed when I say special prayer and sudden-ry, ah, how you Americans say . . ." She hesitated a moment as she searched her vocabulary. "Ker-plew!" She threw her hands in the air to demonstrate.

"It was probably just a bunch of bored teenagers looking for trouble. " Lexie moved next to Akiko and patted her on the back. Figure the odds Akiko would ever come back to the café. She and Lucy had probably lost their last and final customer. Just peachy.

Akiko again pointed at the thing on the floor. "Rook at that—what is it? It not rook so good, Rexi-*san*."

Lexie hadn't paid much attention to the object that had nearly knocked her into yesterday, but she now examined it closer. "Oh, my gosh, it looks like a—"

"Grenade, grenade!" Aunt Gladys shoved past Lexie and did a sort of running shuffle toward the door. "Fire in the hole! Retreat! Everyone out!"

Lexie, Akiko, and Lucy wasted no time following Aunt Gladys. Outside, standing in the middle of the street, the ladies looked at each other in utter surprise.

"What do we do now?" Lucy asked.

"Call the police." Lexie fished the cell phone

out of her jeans pocket and dialed 911.

Everything after that was a blur.

Otis was first to arrive and he did not look happy. What else was new? His deputy, Cleve Harris, trotted dutifully alongside wearing a rumpled uniform on his thin frame, looking as though he'd slept in it for five nights in a row. He had a long, pockmarked horse face and bug eyes with a mop of stringy brown hair on top of his head. Lexie had known him in school and he had always been the king of nerds. Looked like he still held the title. And he still reminded her of Goofy; all he needed was floppy ears and a long dog's schnaz.

Harris trundled up and hooked his thumbs in his belt. "Hey, ladies." He tipped his hat at everyone and gave Lexie a dopey look, big teeth dull and yellow. "How's it goin', Lex?"

Otis hitched his striped sheriff's pants over his portly belly as he came up behind his deputy. Then he popped Harris on the back of his head. "Not too good, numbskull. Otherwise she wouldn't have called us. Get to work."

Notepad in hand, Otis questioned Lexie and Lucy while Harris questioned Aunt Gladys and Akiko.

When ambulances and fire trucks blazed onto the scene a short while later, sirens blaring, Lexie figured the neighbors would take up a petition to have her removed from the neighborhood. Peacefully or forcefully. As they all stood on their door stoops, observing the scene unfolding before their eyes, they looked none too happy. Lexie had a good idea what they were saying. "That Lexie always did cause trouble and look what's been going on! Nothing's changed a bit."

The police walked around gathering evidence while the bomb squad, dressed in special attire, went inside the house to investigate the grenade. The question in everyone's mind was why the grenade hadn't exploded. After the bomb squad had looked everything over, one of the men came out to talk to them. He said his name was Jake Cordova. He spoke in a deep, gravelly voice and had just a fringe of silvery hair on his head.

"It was a grenade, all right. A World War II-vintage Japanese grenade. It was too old to detonate. You folks were lucky." He rocked back and forth on his heels, hands clasped behind his back. "Just the same, we're taking it down to the lab for safe keeping." To Lexie he said, "Your house has been given the all clear signal."

"Thank you," Lexie told him, still a little dizzy from the blow to her forehead.

"Japanese, eh?" Otis gave Akiko a hard look. "You know anything about this?"

Akiko's hands fluttered to her throat. "Oh, no."

"What about your husband? Maybe he collects this war memorabilia. Wasn't he in the army?"

She shook her head. "*Hai*, Vietnam War. But he no do this. He go Westonville to buy new tractor parts. He not in town."

"I'll be by to question him anyway," Otis said.

Cordova mopped his brow with a handkerchief. "I wouldn't get too excited just yet, Sheriff Parnell. From the looks of everything this appears to be a prank. Maybe played by a disgruntled customer." He pulled a piece of yellow lined paper from his breast pocket. "Take a look at this. It was rubber banded around the grenade."

He handed the paper, splattered with the blood from Lexie's wound, to Otis who read it, grunted and said, "Whether it was intended as a prank or as an assault, I'm getting to the bottom of it." He handed the note to Lexie. Lexie looked it over and her mouth went dry and cottony.

Lucy took it from her, her face set in solemn lines. *"You will pay, you witch,"* she read aloud. She flipped the paper over and looked at the front again. "Hmm, this looks like it was written in nail polish."

"Nail polish?" Lexie cleared her tight throat and glanced at the blue glittery brush strokes on the paper. "Must have been a woman who wrote it."

"Maybe," Otis said. "Or maybe a man with a nail polish fetish or someone just wanting to throw us off. It's hard to say."

An ambulance attendant came up to Lexie and touched her arm. She was a small, blond woman with a perky, upturned nose covered with freckles. "Ma'am, would you like us to look at that cut on your forehead?"

"Is my Aunt Gladys all right?"

The attendant nodded. "Mrs. Maplethorpe is sedated and someone's taken her up to her room to rest."

"I appreciate it," Lexie told her.

Akiko made her apologies and left hastily. Lexie wished she could have sent her home with one of those apple pies and some of the stew. Otis told Cleve to go on home, and he pulled Lucy aside to lecture her in a stern voice. Lexie decided now was as good a time as any to have her wound attended to.

"Show me where to go," Lexie told the attendant, followed her over to one of the ambulances and sat down on the tailgate. After wrapping a blanket around Lexie's shoulders, the attendant took her vital signs, and began to poke and prod on her bruised forehead.

Hearing the roar of an engine, Lexie watched as a Jeep pulled up and parked nearby. Gabe stepped out and sauntered toward her, wearing his usual attire of jeans jacket, button down shirt, and Levis that hugged his long legs. "Just can't stay away from trouble, can you, lady?"

"You know what happened?" she asked, catching a whiff of his spicy cologne.

He nodded. "Heard it on my police radio."

Even though his words were harsh, Lexie saw the lines of concern crinkling at the corners of his eyes. She decided Gabe survived his line of work by putting up this tough-as-nails appearance. He witnessed too many awful things and couldn't let the world see how the crime and tragedy affected him, otherwise he might not be able to perform his duties. Indifference had become his fortress against the world.

"This time trouble came looking for me, Gabe," she told him. "I was in my house minding my own business when someone threw a grenade through my front window." She winced as the attendant put ointment on her cut and bruised flesh. "Guess I got in the way."

"You're lucky it didn't go off."

"That's what the bomb squad guy said."

"He was right." Gabe folded his arms across his chest. "Are you going to be all right?"

"Yes. I just had an unexpected surprise, but I'm over it."

"Do you want anything for the pain?" the attendant asked her, standing back and cocking her head to the side to examine her handiwork.

Lexie put up a hand. "No, I'm fine. I'll take some aspirin later."

"You might want something to help you rest," Gabe commented. "Shock can do funny things to you. It could still settle in later."

Lexie thought about it for a minute, then remembered her date with Jack. She wanted all her faculties about her when she met him at the Jefferson. "Honestly, Gabe. I don't need anything."

A muscle ticked in his jaw. "Take care. Like I said before, keep your nose clean. We're getting

close on this case and you need to keep a low pro-
file." He touched her hand lightly, sending a stream
of sparks up her spine, then walked over to Otis and
struck up a conversation, during which Otis handed
him the note from the grenade. Lexie wondered
what it was about Gabe that stirred her blood. She
was certain it wasn't good. The man condescended
to her and she hated it. He was just doing his job,
but she didn't like being pandered to.

By the time Lexie was done with the attendant,
Gabe had left. All the other emergency vehicles had
disappeared and the ambulance took off as well. She
joined Otis and Lucy, who immediately hugged her
and patted her on the back.

"Go inside and get some rest, dear. I know I'm
going home to put my feet up. We've all had quite
an upset."

"I agree. I'm definitely going to enjoy the time
off tomorrow. I think I'll stay in bed all day with my
head under the covers." Lexie knew it would be impossible, but it sounded good.

Otis indicated the broken front window. "You
can use duct tape and a piece of cardboard until you
get it fixed."

"I'll do that," Lexie said.

"Maybe you girls ought to think about closing
the café until the heat dies down," he suggested. He
removed a handkerchief from his pocket and blew
his nose. "It's not safe anymore."

A wave of dizziness swept over Lexie and she

blinked, then stepped back to lean against the porch rail. "You don't have to worry. Akiko was our only customer and from what I gather, everyone in town believes our family has a curse on it. Nobody wants to eat at the Saucy Lucy right now anyway."

"Lexie, are you OK?" Lucy rested a hand on her arm.

"I think I just need to go in and rest like you said."

After discussing the incident a few moments more, Otis and Lucy got in their family sedan and drove off, leaving Lexie standing on the Victorian's porch in front of the broken shark's teeth window, mulling over a lot of unanswered questions.

Once the dull roar in her mind quieted, Lexie went inside and cleaned up the mess, all the while wondering who would do such an awful thing. Had someone really intended to hurt her, or was it just a prank? Her head was really starting to hurt. She scrounged aspirin from a cupboard by the sink, took two and slugged them down with a glass of water. After she swept up the broken glass, she went into the pantry and found a roll of duct tape and a piece of cardboard.

She'd just finished the temporary repair job when the bell on the front door tinkled. Hearing someone's muffled footsteps in the hallway; she immediately remembered she hadn't put up the CLOSED sign.

Could Eva be home? She'd agreed to keep an eye

on Aunt Gladys tonight. But no, Eva always parked in the old garage out back and entered through the door in the kitchen. Had Barnard Savage dropped by to harass her? Maybe he'd decided to brave her wrath and would try and squeeze out a story.

"Hullo?" Lexie put down the tape.

A middle-aged man and a woman stood there scowling. Maybe they weren't pranksters, but they looked angry. They were, however, quite well dressed. He was tall and wore a black, expensive-looking suit, and silk tie. The woman, who was slightly taller than Lexie, wore a dress and a fur coat, and her shoes looked as pricey as the man's clothing. Lexie felt inadequate in her jeans and simple top. The white apron with the ruffles she also wore didn't make her feel better.

"May I help you?" Lexie asked. For some reason, she got the impression they weren't paying The Saucy Lucy Café a visit because they'd heard about her good coffee and wanted to sample it.

The man, who towered intimidatingly over Lexie, cleared his throat and fixed her with a hard stare. "We're looking for a Ms. Alexandria Lightfoot."

Uh, oh, Spaghettios.

His tone wasn't friendly. Lexie nearly lied and told him she didn't know where Ms. Alexandria Lightfoot was. Unfortunately, she was too honest and accommodating for her own good, thanks to the Reverend Castleton's strict upbringing, so the fib wouldn't work. "I'm Lexie Lightfoot," she responded in an unnaturally high voice. Her throat had gone dry and her knees developed an annoying watery sensation.

"I am Dr. William Briarhurst and this is my wife, Olivia. I assume you know who we are?"

Yes, she did. They were Elton Briarhurst's very rich and influential *and* torqued off parents. "Yes," Lexie said with a nod. "I am so sorry about Elton's accident and I feel terrible about it. Would you like to sit down?"

She gestured at a room off to the right which she'd restored to an original old-fashioned parlor, complete with period antiques such as brocade settees, fern stands, statues, and an iron fireplace ensemble. A Persian carpet covered the polished wooden floorboards and replica velvet-flocked paper from the turn of the century adorned the walls along with a several old oil paintings.

The Briarhursts didn't answer, and William Briarhurst's nostrils flared. This was not good. Panic seeped through Lexie's pores and she began to ramble to fill the awkward silence.

"It's actually very comfortable in the parlor, you know. Some of my customers like to come in here and relax with their coffee and newspapers. It's a nice room, sunny and pleasant . . ." She hoped Mr. and Mrs. Briarhurst wouldn't notice how nervous she was. "I, ah—"

"You need to realize, Ms. Lightfoot, that we are not here to pay you a social call," Mrs. Briarhurst said sharply, raising a haughty brow as she glanced at the bandage on Lexie's forehead.

Oh, really? Lexie folded her arms across her chest, an ominous feeling creeping over her. "How may I help you, then?"

"We're here to talk about Elton," Dr. Briarhurst said.

Ah. Maybe they just wanted to find out what happened. So did she.

"Again, I'm so sorry. How is he? I've been worried." Lexie didn't think it would be a good idea to tell them the hospital had gotten wise to her and refused to give her any more updates on Elton's condition.

"He's finally on the mend, no thanks to *you*," his mother said with a sniff.

Lexie blinked. "I hope you don't think I had anything to do with the accident."

"Well, you certainly did not behave in a responsible manner with our son. How you could run over him? I don't understand," Dr. Briarhurst rumbled angrily.

"Run over him? What are you talking about? It was a hit and run. No one knows who did it."

"Don't try and cover for yourself, Ms. Lightfoot. Elton told us everything once he came out of his coma. Due to your irresponsibility, he will now need weeks of therapy in order to walk again," Dr. Briarhurst insisted.

Olivia Briarhurst began to sob softly and took out a flowered hankie to dab at her eyes.

"I haven't done anything wrong," Lexie protested.

"This is all a mistake."

"You, as his employer, should have known better than to have him repair your roof without the proper equipment," Dr. Briarhurst stubbornly persisted. "Why, it's outlandish and you know you're responsible."

Lexie's mouth dropped. "Elton told you he was repairing my roof?"

"Yes," Mrs. Briarhurst said with another indignant sniff. "And we'd like you to know we expect you to pay all his medical expenses. You'll be lucky if my husband doesn't file a lawsuit against you." She hooked her arm possessively through Dr. Briarhurst's.

Lexie was stunned. She figured Elton didn't want his high society parents to know he was moonlighting as a male stripper. She understood why he used her as the fall guy. She imagined the Briarhurst's gave their rich and spoiled son plenty of money to go to college and live on, but he apparently enjoyed doing something completely against his strict upbringing.

No surprise he'd kept his questionable employment a secret. It most likely would have raised his parents' gently born eyebrows as well as their hackles and they'd no doubt sever his allowance. Maybe even remove him from the family will.

"Mr. and Mrs. Briarhurst, please understand—I'm sorry about Elton's accident. But you have been misinformed about a couple of things. One of them is that I wasn't the person who ran over him, and another is that he wasn't here to repair my roof."

"Don't try to project blame," Dr. Briarhurst growled. "You are responsible for this tragic event and you know it. By the time I'm through with you, you will no longer have a business and you will suffer for your lack of foresight. You will have to forever live with the fact Elton might never walk again or could possibly have brain damage—"

"Or *die*." Mrs. Briarhurst sobbed, her furry shoulders heaving. She produced the delicate hankie again and dabbed at her watery eyes.

"All you need to know, Ms. Lightfoot," Dr. Briarhurst said, eyes flashing, "is that you will hear from our lawyer."

Dr. Briarhurst pulled his sobbing wife down the hall and out the door, shutting it with a loud bang.

Dumbfounded, Lexie stared at the entrance for a few numb minutes, during which time her mind replayed over and over the conversation with the Briarhursts. Was this really happening, or was it a dream? Pray God it's a dream, she told herself, pinching her arm.

"Ouch!" It was no dream.

Lexie's head was thumping like a washing machine that hadn't been loaded correctly. *Ka-thunk, ka-thunk*. Had the Briarhursts thrown the grenade through the window? No, that didn't seem like their style at all. But they could have hired someone to do it for them.

Despite Lexie's racing thoughts and her ballooning head, she knew one thing. If she didn't lose the café because small-minded and ill-informed people were afraid she was a murderess and refused to eat here any more, she could very well loose it to the Briarhursts' no doubt sharp-looking, smooth-talking and well-paid legal expert.

Time to go lawyer hunting.

Lexie finally managed to shuffle to the front door, flip over the CLOSED sign, then found her way into the parlor and sat down on a gold brocade sofa that had belonged to Grandmother Castleton. Her insides trembled and a dull roar of disbelief echoed in her brain. How could people be so cruel and thoughtless?

She glanced around. The room had once been a favorite family gathering place. During the Christmases of her youth, her favorite time of year, the large stone fireplace had been draped with festive swags and a large decorated fir tree dominated the northeast corner by another large bay window.

The parlor reflected a sense of warmth and comfort, from the knick-knacks her mother and father had placed around the room to the furniture and gilt-framed pictures her grandparents had arranged so lovingly when the home belonged to them. Lexie closed her eyes and reminisced about her childhood when all seemed right with the world, when her grandparents and parents had been alive and they'd enjoyed good times together.

She could almost smell the rich chocolate scent of Grandma Castleton's special cocoa and remembered how they used to make popcorn in an old-fashioned pan over the open fireplace. Her memories were a pleasant place to let her troubled mind dwell and they acted like a healing balm on her aching soul. She opened her eyes to the empty room that had once been filled with life and happiness, but now was full of memories and scents of days gone by. She rarely set foot in here except when townspeople reserved the room for meetings and events such as birthday parties and anniversary celebrations.

Even Lucy's book club, which typically rotated from one member's house to another's, had held meetings here on several occasions. Lucy hadn't scheduled one lately and Lexie imagined the persnickety literary ladies didn't want to discuss the latest book they'd been reading in the house of a suspected murderess.

Lexie felt like running away. She wanted to go somewhere—maybe an island in the middle of the Pacific Ocean—where no one knew her. It would be wonderful to disappear and leave all her troubles behind.

That was impossible. How could she up and disappear when her daughter needed her? Sister Lucy would be beside herself. It would be wrong.

She was left with the wreck that had become her life. Her business was going down the toilet because people stupidly believed she was capable of murder. She wanted to pay Lucy a salary this month, but was short on cash.

Then there were Eva's expenses.

The car payments on her Ford Escort still needed to be paid and spring tuition at the university would be due soon. Lexie also needed to buy food and gas and pay utilities and, unfortunately, her savings would only stretch so far.

Cousin Bruce's money had mostly gone to pay for the renovation on Aunt Gladys' attic quarters. She decided she'd better try to call his hotel in Singapore and see when he was coming to pick up his mother, or if he'd wire a little more *dinero*. There's only so much blood you can squeeze out of a turnip. It didn't seem very promising.

She could go down to MacGreggor's Pub and see if she could get a job waitressing. Maybe they needed help slinging hash. She doubted it, but she could give it a shot. Rats! She'd have to find someone to sit with Aunt Gladys while she worked. That could be a problem.

There was no excuse why she couldn't ask The Undertaker for help with at least Eva's tuition, but she refused to be humiliated again. He would repeat what he'd said many times before: I *paid my own way through college and Eva can too. It'll teach her what the real world's all about.* He'd make Lexie feel foolish for asking and remind her he had a new family to provide for.

The dimwit.

How could a man completely disown a child from a previous marriage like she never meant anything? Even if Eva was over eighteen, she was still his daughter. She still needed him. Lexie shook her head. The man was such a lost cause.

To top things off, the Briarhursts were acting like she had hurt their son, as though everything were her fault. They had even got her halfway believing it. Maybe there *was* something she could have done to prevent Elton's accident.

Lexie leaned back against the sofa and closed her eyes. Warm tears oozed from under her lashes and rolled down her cheeks. She hated to cry. Only silly women cried. Here she was, doing it. So be it. *She was a silly woman.* Finally a numb acceptance of her circumstances spread through Lexie's limbs and she relaxed enough to doze.

"Mom, wake up."

Lexie's eyes immediately flew open and she readjusted herself on the sofa, her neck kinked from the uncomfortable position she'd slept in.

Eva stood in front of her, hands on her hips. "What's with the duct-taped window? And your head!" She winced. "What happened?"

With a mouth as dry as dirt, Lexie explained about the old grenade being thrown through the window, hitting her in the head and upsetting Aunt Gladys so badly she had to be sedated. She explained how the Briarhursts had shown up, threatening to sue her.

"Nobody's coming to the café to eat any more because they're afraid. I've still got bills to pay and I can't afford an attorney. I'm in a real pickle, sweetie."

Eva sat next to Lexie on the sofa and laid a hand on her arm. "Remember, Mom, I've got part-time work. I can make my car payment and cover insurance." Eva knew better than to suggest they ask her father for help. Mother and daughter had gone that route too many times before and been burned.

"I hate you have to work," Lexie said. "How do you keep your grades up?"

"I'm fine, Mom. I'm a big girl. Besides, lots of my friends have jobs."

Lexie swallowed a sob. No matter how bad things got during the divorce and afterward, Eva had always managed to keep up her spirits, even through her ornery teenage episodes.

"Don't worry about Elton's snobby parents. They're only trying to scare you. Call Bruce, too. He needs to haul his b-u-t-t back here to get Aunt Gladys. This is too much for you."

Lexie pulled a tissue from her apron pocket and blew her nose. "I guess so. I let myself get overwhelmed instead of thinking."

"It happens to all of us," Eva said maturely, no doubt enjoying the fact that for once she was able to give advice to her mother.

Strange how your kids grow up and the roles reverse at times, Lexie thought. She remembered when Eva's biggest worry was not being invited to a friend's birthday party, or thinking that her rear end was getting too flab-ulous.

"Thanks," Lexie told her daughter. Eva leaned her head on Lexie's shoulder for a moment.

Eva pulled back and looked at her mother earnestly. "Hey, didn't you tell me on the phone the other day you have a big date tonight? Don't you need to get ready?"

In her misery, Lexie had completely forgotten about Jack Sturgeon and the movies. She glanced frantically at the grandfather clock. "I don't have much time."

"Then get a move on." Eva pulled her up and prodded her out the door into the hallway.

"There's stew in the kitchen for dinner and Aunt Gladys is resting in her room—"

"Would you stop already? Aunt G and I will be fine." Eva pointed at the staircase. "March!"

CHAPTER 13

Up in Lexie's bedroom, hairbrushes, make-up, and clothing flew as Eva helped her get ready. From the items in her closet she selected a black skirt, a black, low-cut sweater, and black heels. She topped off the ensemble with her mother's pearl earrings and necklace. Eva insisted she wear her hair down instead of pulled back in her standard ponytail and helped her arrange the ginger-colored mass into soft waves that fell to her shoulders. Next Eva applied foundation, putting extra on Lexie's bruised forehead. With a soft brush, she expertly applied cheek color, eye color, and finished her masterpiece with mascara. Eva also insisted Lexie borrow the Escort so she wouldn't have to deal with the old truck clunking along and possibly breaking down.

Unaccustomed to wearing a dress and heels, let alone makeup, Lexie glanced at herself in the bathroom mirror, completely unprepared for what she saw, but pleasantly surprised. *Not bad looking for a thirty-seven-year-old broad if I do say so myself.* Maybe there was hope for her yet.

"Thanks for everything, Eva," Lexie told Eva downstairs as she slipped on a light jacket and put Eva's car keys in her pocket. "I just wish I could quit thinking of all the nonsense going on in my life right now. It's distracting."

"Mother!" Eva rolled her eyes. "OK. Listen up. Tonight I'm . . . I'm like your fairy godmother. And I command you to have a good time." She removed an umbrella from a wall hook and tapped Lexie on the top of the head with it. "Just be back by midnight or you'll turn into a pumpkin. Got it?"

Lexie laughed. "Got it."

Stars twinkled above like a million diamonds splayed on a blanket of black velvet as Lexie backed the Escort out of the garage and drove down the street. The sound of an engine revving drew her attention and she saw a dark car whip around the corner and out of sight when she drove past her house. Her blood froze in her veins. Was that the mysterious car she'd seen parking in front of her house lately? The one that disappeared every time she came out to investigate?

She stepped on the gas, zoomed down the street and around the corner, determined to follow the vehicle. Sighting taillights up ahead in the distance, she pressed harder on the accelerator. Intent on her mission, she never noticed passing the one squad car belonging to Moose Creek Junction's finest parked off the road in the shadowy bushes. One second later, a red light flashed in her rearview mirror and the sheriff's cruiser pulled up alongside the Escort.

"Crap!" Lexie couldn't see inside, but she could imagine if it was Otis in there, he was furiously shaking his fist at her and swearing up a storm. She pulled over and the cruiser parked behind her. Furious, she got out and marched up to the sheriff's vehicle just as Otis slid his portly form out of the driver's seat.

Yellow streetlights provided enough illumination to reveal the irritation written on Sheriff Parnell's face. "I thought you were Eva, Lexie. Where the hell were you driving so fast? And why did you get out of your car? I'm supposed to come up to yours."

"Whatever," Lexie said. "I'm in pursuit of a suspect. I've got to go—"

Otis put a restraining hand on her arm. "Hold on there, girl. What suspect? What in Sam Hill are you talking about?"

"That car I told you about. It went that way!" She pointed down a dark street.

"It's long gone by now," Otis said in a firm voice.

"Yes, no thanks to you," Lexie snapped back.

"Lexie, you are not an office of the law, so quit acting like one. You should have called me, not gone after the damn car yourself. You could have gotten yourself hurt."

Lexie pulled her arm loose from Otis' firm grip and rubbed it. "There was no time!"

He snorted. "I'm only giving you a warning

ticket this time because you're my wife's kid sister. But don't let me or Cleve catch you driving like an idiot again or I'll have your license yanked. Who do you think you are, anyway? Columbo on steroids?" He shook his head, then looked her up and down and whistled, as though he really hadn't seen what she was wearing before. "All dressed up and some-place to go? That's not usually your style, is it?"

"Whatever, Otis," Lexie said, ignoring him. "At least I'm trying to get somewhere on this case. Admit it. You're not much good at your job, are you?"

"You're good at getting yourself in hot water is what, missy." Red in the face, steam practically coming out his hears, Otis scribbled on a pad, ripped off a yellow ticket, and shoved it at her. "By the way, did you get a glimpse of who was driving? A license plate number or maybe even part of it?"

"No." Scowling, Lexie snatched the ticket from her brother-in-law's meaty grip and stormed back to her car.

"I'm warning you, Lexie. Keep your nose out of trouble," Otis shouted at her.

Lexie ignored him, got into the Escort and drove off. Maybe it was a dumb stunt to go chasing after the mystery car, but like she told Otis, at least she was trying. What if she had managed to get the li-cense plate number or see who was driving? She'd be a hero. OK, maybe not a hero, but at least the car chase would have been worth her time.

It wouldn't be easy to convince herself to have a

pleasant evening. Putting the mysterious vehicle from her mind and her humiliation at patootiehead Otis' warning, she sailed down the street in Eva's Escort.

A few minutes later, she pulled into a parking space in front of the Jefferson Theater, shrinking in her skin when she saw Jack pacing outside the building. This was so embarrassing.

"Wow," Jack exclaimed when he saw her, eyes lighting up. "My date's a knockout. What happened to your head?"

Lexie's face got warm and she touched the bandage. "A minor accident at the café. I'll tell you about it later. Your knockout date is late. I'm sorry."

He chuckled. "No harm done. We've probably only missed a few boring previews." He took her hand and they went inside to purchase tickets. In the lobby, he bought popcorn and soda and escorted her up to balcony seats.

The theater was an old relic, probably dating from sometime in the 1930s. Ornate maple woodwork, red brocade wallpaper, plush carpeting, and vintage light fixtures gave the place a feeling of a time gone by. The interior had been renovated, but the restoration maintained the original flavor.

Lexie recalled coming as a kid to the Saturday afternoon matinee. Lucy usually brought her and of course, being the older sister, Mom and Dad put her in charge. For treats, the girls bought popcorn and sodas, Pay Day, Baby Ruth, and Look candy bars. It was a good time, a pleasant escape from reality.

Except for Lucy's bossing. Since Lexie was the younger sister it had come with the territory.

Lexie relaxed in her seat next to Jack, feeling a familiar sense of anticipation as the lights faded. It was a fun movie about a boy wizard, which was actually meant for children. But Moose Creek Junction didn't exactly get first run movies. There wasn't a large selection to choose from and they were usually several months old. As they said, beggars couldn't be choosers, so the audience was packed with adults and children alike. Despite its shortcomings, the old Jefferson Theater was a major attraction.

Jack leaned over and whispered another compliment to Lexie about how good she looked and how much he enjoyed being with her. Lexie shivered with delight at the feel of his strong arm when it came down gently around her shoulders. Instinctively, she snuggled closer, feeling safe and protected. Though the black car incident was still in her thoughts, it was way in the back of her mind. She'd think about it later.

It had been a long time since Lexie dated anyone, if you didn't count the tragic Henry Whitehead fiasco. Going to the movie with Jack was different. He had a pleasant personality and was very nice looking. He smelled like Irish Spring soap, not dirty diapers, which was a vast improvement over Violet's ex.

When the movie was over, Lexie and Jack walked through the Moose Creek Junction Park hand in hand, enjoying the silvery moonlight and warm October evening. Bushes rustled softly in the light breeze and late autumn flowers and trees had a magical quality. Also magic was having a nice man paying her compliments and speaking sweetly to her. Not yelling and slapping her around like Dan. How different this was. How . . . wonderful.

Jack Sturgeon was someone special.

"So, what's with the bruise on your noggin?" Jack asked.

Lexie frowned. "Some kid threw a rock through my front window. Unfortunately, I got in the way. The police think it was probably just a prank."

"Little punks." Jack stopped walking and took her face in his hands, staring at her in earnest. "Are you all right? Maybe you should be home resting?"

"Oh, believe me," she told him, smiling up at the angled planes of his attractive face, her skin prickling. "This date has been the best medicine. I'm right where I need to be."

Jack leaned into her and gave her the most exquisite kiss. Later, when he'd walked her to her car, he said, "I had a very nice time, Lex. You'll go out with me again, won't you?"

"Of course."

"Good." He leaned over and lightly kissed her forehead, then stood straight and smiled. "How about next Sunday you come with me out to my cabin on Gun Smoke Lake? We can spend the day fishing and grill up some trout for dinner. Then we can head back to town and catch another movie, if you like."

"Sounds like fun." Lexie smiled. "And thank you for tonight. I really enjoyed myself."

"So did I. I'll pick you up about seven-thirty on Sunday. The fish don't sleep in too late, you know. Remember to wear old clothes. Fishing's a dirty business."

Lexie got in the Escort and drove home through the dark streets, her whole being alive. How could she have been so lucky to meet Jack Sturgeon? He actually liked her, wonder of wonders. Tonight, nothing could bother her. Any time a problem broke surface in her mind, she fought it back into a deep, dark corner. She had all week to think of a way out of her dilemma. Tonight she wanted to bask in the after-glow of her date with Jack.

Another customer-less week dragged by. Lucy decided they needed to take advantage of the break, instead of moping around, so they took inventory of the café supplies: canned goods, flour, sugar, salt, and the list went on. They cleaned and organized all the cupboards. They decided to make their Saucy Lucy fruitcake for the church bake sale that was held in November, just in time for Christmas. It was an old recipe and wasn't one of Lucille Castleton's, but actually came from Grandmother Castleton, who the family claimed, had brought it over from England. The cakes were filled with a multitude of dried and candied fruits, the crimson, green, and gold of the ingredients being representative of the holiday season. It was also filled with spices such as cloves and cinnamon and the baking scent was so heavenly you could nearly float away on it.

As the week dragged by, Lexie had the strangest experiences. She went from elation when she thought about Jack Sturgeon to fretting endlessly about her predicament. She kept waiting for the Briarhurst's attorney to call and give her bad news, but he never did. She knew, deep down, the Briarhursts had merely been behaving like distraught and confused parents. There was no case against her because she'd done nothing. It bothered her, however, to have people mistrust and dislike her.

At the moment she was like the pariah of Moose Creek Junction with no customers and no friends. Everywhere she went people shunned her, except for Jack, and behaved as though she had a contagious disease, sending her narrow-eyed, sidelong looks. It was downright awful and Lexie briefly considered sewing a scarlet letter of some sort on her apron. Possibly "M" for maligned, or "P" for pissed off. She vacillated between the two ideas.

It was Thursday and as they prepared the day's minestrone soup special—why they bothered, Lexie had no idea—Lucy finally came up with an idea she thought would help Lexie clear her name. "For Pete's sake, people simply couldn't be mean spirited to you if you attended church services with me," she proclaimed. "It would be extremely uncharitable. And besides . . ."

Lexie and Lucy were standing at the kitchen

sink, peeling carrots. Lexie turned to Lucy and gave her a long look. "For God's sake, Lucy, they'd stone me. Either that or put me under a door and pile rocks on it until they crushed my chest."

Lucy rolled her eyes. "There you go again, getting all melodramatic. Why, you should have gone into acting, even though Mother and Father would never have approved."

"Leslie's right," Aunt Gladys piped up. She sat at the kitchen table, which was covered in newspapers, doing one of the paint-by number pictures Lexie had purchased at the Loose Goose Emporium. She actually enjoyed it, or so she said. Today she wore her zebra-striped caftan, about fifty strands of huge black beads looped around her neck and about a thousand jangling bracelets. "There's a bunch of teeny-tiny pea brains around here. Lucille, you've spent entirely too much of your life in Moose Creek Junction. *Born yesterday*, if you know what I mean."

"What in heaven's name do you mean by that?" Lucy asked indignantly as she turned from the sink to glare at Aunt Gladys, carrot peeler held in mid-air.

Aunt Gladys cackled as she used her paintbrush to dab rich green color on a tree. "Take off your rose-colored glasses, girl. People are mean and ignorant. When they get even the slightest thing on you, they'll tear you apart like a pack of wild dogs."

"Moose Creek Junction is our home," Lucy protested. "People wouldn't hurt their friends and neighbors like that."

"Lucille, your sister has been gone too many years to be one of them any more. To them, she is an outsider. They have no loyalty to her."

Lexie had to agree with Aunt Gladys. Occasionally the old bag of wind actually had some wise counsel although Lucy didn't think so.

"You're delusional again," she said. "I think it's time for you to take a nap."

Aunt Gladys stuck out her tongue at Lucy and made a farting sound.

Lucy snorted with indignance and turned back to the sink to peel carrots with a vengeance. "Lexie, if you would just go with me to church this Sunday, you would see how forgiving people are."

Lexie sighed. "Sorry, I can't. Jack and I are going fishing."

"On Sunday?" Lucy was flabbergasted. "Really, what would Mother and Father think? Sunday is a day of rest."

"Fishing is very restful," Lexie said. "Besides, Jack is a wonderful guy. Mom and Dad would be happy for me."

"I don't know this Jack Sturgeon fellow, but he doesn't seem like the best influence on you. Taking you out to cavort in the wilderness on a Sunday, no less."

"Oh, leave her alone, Lucille," Aunt Gladys called out as she lit up a cigarette and blew smoke into the air. "Your mother and father would have liked knowing Lexie's enjoying herself with a nice young man like Jack. Let her kick up her heels a little. 'Make hay while the sun shines', they say."

Lexie frowned at Aunt Gladys and her cancer stick. She had all but given up trying to control the old woman's smoking. It was impossible.

"You're not much for maintaining decorum, are you?" Lucy asked Aunt Gladys.

Aunt Gladys blinked. "Maintaining *what*? If you mean do I like to have fun, you sure as hell better believe it. Now I know why your father named you after your mother. You are exactly like her. A friggin' stick in the mud."

Miffed, Lucy ignored Aunt Gladys and turned to Lexie. "If things get serious with this Jack fellow, he'll need to join the church so you can be married there. You and Dan ran off to get a quickie Las Vegas wedding and that could have been part of the problem. The marriage was never a church sanctioned union."

"Lucy, lighten up, will you?" Lexie finished chopping the last of the carrots and frowned at her sister. "We're only dating. OK? Nobody said anything about a wedding." Not yet, anyway, she thought.

Lucy pouted, her face melting into lines of defiance.

Lexie hated that look. It always meant Sister Lucy was on the warpath. "Just because you didn't hand pick Jack Sturgeon to date me doesn't mean he's not a good man. Trust my judgment for once, will you?"

"You didn't do so good picking out Dan, Lexie."

Lucy's lower lip quivered. "I don't want to see you hurt again."

"I'll be all right. At the moment we need to worry seriously about our lack of customers. While I'm sure the homeless shelter loves it, we can't keep giving all our leftover food to them. We'll go broke. You have Otis to fall back on. I only have the poor house."

Lucy nodded. "I'll talk with my friends and encourage them to come back to eat at the café. Besides, I still haven't been accused of anything and I'm part owner."

Lexie patted Lucy's arm. "That's right."

The telephone rang and Lexie seriously considered not answering. She was pretty certain it wasn't a customer asking what their hours were. More than likely it was Barnard Savage, or another reporter from Westonville, or maybe even one from Timbuktu, asking more questions about Henry Whitehead's murder.

"I'll get it," Lexie finally said, on the outside chance it might be someone ordering a pie or maybe a dozen cinnamon rolls. She picked up the receiver and put it to her ear. "Hello?"

Click.

Lexie slammed the phone down, furious.

"Another hangup?" Lucy asked.

Before Lexie could answer, the phone rang again. "What do you want? Why do you keep calling and hanging up? We're getting pretty sick and tired—"

"Lexie?"

It was Jack.

Lexie felt completely ridiculous. "Gosh, I'm so sorry. I've been getting a ton of prank calls. I got one right before you called."

"I understand," he said. "Have you told the police?"

"Yes. My phone's supposedly tapped. It drives me crazy that whoever is calling doesn't stay on long the line long enough to be traced."

"Of course," Jack said. "That's the game they play. I was calling to check and see if Sunday is still good."

"I'm looking forward to it," Lexie said.

"Great. I'll pick you up at seven thirty. Fish don't sleep in."

Lexie laughed. "I'll be ready."

Lucy took off her apron and set it on the counter, then smoothed down her lavender- and blue-flowered housedress. "You're going to burn in hell, Lexie."

"At least I'll have a nice tan," Lexie responded.

Aunt Gladys gave a loud hoot. "Good one, Leslie!"

Lucy shook her head. "I hate to peel and leave, but I've got to go vacuum the church and dust the pews. I figured since we're not that busy, I could get it ready for Sunday services."

"That's fine," Lexie said. "I really doubt the café will get slammed."

She was right. The remainder of the week dragged by in a similar fashion, and by Saturday afternoon, Lexie was ready to throw in the towel. She felt like trotting downtown and standing in front of the old granite courthouse wearing a sandwich sign that said, *There is nothing wrong with eating at the The Saucy Lucy Café. You will not get ptomaine poisoning, no one will not put a curse on you, and you will not die.*

That, however, was absurd.

Instead, for the second Saturday in a row, Lexie and Lucy closed the café early. Once again, the soup kitchen regulars were fed well. Lexie and Lucy discussed their budget and decided that before long, they would have to shut down the café. Something had to give, and fast.

While Lexie and Lucy's business was suffering, on the contrary, Aunt Gladys' love life was blossoming. Frenchie, Aunt Gladys's rich boyfriend from the Sunrise Center, had been coming by in the evenings, courting the ex-Las Vegas dancer in an old-fashioned and quaint sort of way. It amazed Lexie he could put up with the loon, but they seemed to get along famously.

Aunt Gladys was annoying with her chain smoking and incessant gabbing, yet had an outlandish, eccentric wisdom that was appealing in a shunts-under-the-fingernails sort of way. Lexie admitted, grudgingly, she'd taken a shine to her. Whether she liked it or not, she could see they held similar ideas about life. They identified with each other on a certain quirky level.

Frenchie, the leprechaun man, was pleasant enough. He was kind to Aunt Gladys and kept her occupied so Lexie could have a break once in a while.

That was something to be happy about.

Sunday dawned bright and unusually warm for mid
October. Outside Lexie's partially open bedroom
window, birds twittered to each other in the cotton-
wood and aspen trees and neighborhood dogs barked
in the distance. Yawning, she stretched lazily in her
double, four-poster bed, enjoying the idyllic morning. For the first time in a while, she'd had a decent
night's sleep, though her ravaged forehead was still
tender to the touch.

Wincing at the dull throb still threading through
her temples, she sat up and looked outside into the
azure blue, cloud-studded Wyoming sky. That was
one nice thing about living in this state. Since the
wind blew incessantly, there was never a trace of
smog obscuring the horizon, a far cry from Los An-
geles, or even Tidewater, where she'd spent the last
years before moving home. Down there, a person
could believe it was normal for the sky to be a muddy
brown color all the time.

Standing, Lexie performed isometric exercises
to work out the kinks in her lower lumbar. She
twisted her torso, rolled her arms and did circles with
her neck. Yawning, she padded over to the window,
opened it further, inhaling the fresh air. It seemed
like a fine summer day, not autumn. Hard to believe
this part of the country was still in the clutches of
a severe drought, a drought that had lasted for the

last few years. Despite its devastating effects on local economics, the warm weather was good for one thing.

Fishing.

Slipping out of the white nightshirt with a nasty looking Chihuahua on the front that said, *Bite Me*, Lexie took a long, hot shower, letting the silken water sluice over her skin. Boy, she sure needed to get a softer mattress. Unfortunately, as the years marched on, her body was beginning to demand she relinquish the punishing firmness and give her old muscles a break. As she let her mind wander in the mist of steam, a thought occurred to her.

I need to call Bruce.

She had no idea what time it was in Singapore, but what the heck. It was worth a try. Exiting the shower, Lexie wrapped up in a large bath towel and sat on her bed. She picked up the phone and dialed the group of numbers Bruce had given her to reach his hotel. It'd probably cost a fortune to talk with him for a minute.

A series of beeping sounds filled the airwaves and finally a person actually came on the line. "Singapore International Hotel, how may I help you?" a man with a clipped voice answered.

Lexie asked for Bruce's room and the operator connected her. The phone rang and rang and finally someone picked up, but didn't say anything.

"Hello, Bruce? It's Lexie."

A high-pitched giggle echoed from the phone

receiver. "Brucie?" A pause. "Ah, he no here. He working."

Lexie rolled her eyes. *Right*. "When will he be back?"

Another giggle. "I not know."

"Thanks." Lexie hung up. Bruce either wasn't there, or wasn't talking. No use wasting her thin dime talking to his bimbo.

Damn. She'd e-mailed Bruce several times, but he hadn't responded. Now he probably wasn't going to answer his phone calls. She punched her frustration into a pillow. *Knock it off, Lex. Don't ruin what could be a fantastic day.*

She sighed. Eventually, if she kept plugging away, she should be able to catch up to Bruce. Maybe he really was onto something with his new scheme and had been busy working the last few weeks. *Fat chance*, Lexie thought. She knew better.

She donned a pair of old jeans, an old flannel shirt and sneakers. Tying her hair back in a ponytail, she went downstairs to make coffee. The caffeine was bound to put her in a better mood.

Aunt Gladys was already up and dressed in tight Pepto Bismol colored satin slacks, pink sneakers, and a blouse with bright orange, green, and yellow geometric shapes. Several strands of large beads hung around her neck along with a pink chiffon scarf she'd knotted around the wrinkled column of skin. Long dangly earrings with a pink ball attached to the ends hung from her ears. Her heavy makeup, which looked as though she'd applied it with a trowel, was firmly in place.

Though she was all powdered, rouged, and mascaraed, her white hair was still in pink sponge rollers. In one hand she clutched a large glass Lexie was certain must hold her special drink, and in the other she held a cigarette. She alternately took a drink or puffed as she read the morning paper.

When she saw Lexie enter the room, she snapped, "Are you the maid in this joint?" She pointed upstairs with a crooked finger. "I need my sheets changed. And I need some more towels. The room service around here is lousy."

Lexie sighed. "Aunt Gladys, I'm Lexie, your niece. I changed your sheets and put out fresh towels yesterday."

"They stink like dirty feet. The towels, I mean. Junior was up all night, dancing on the roof. I barely slept a wink."

"I'll check on the towels," Lexie told her, ignoring the part about Junior. How was she supposed to do anything about the imaginary culprit Aunt Gladys had conjured in her mind?

"Hey, you read the newspaper yet?" Aunt Gladys pointed to a column on the front page. "There's a story in here about some broad who keeps dating all these guys who wind up dead. Could be my life story, except," she snorted, "I married all the bums I dated."

Lexie shot over to the table and read the front

page over Aunt Gladys' shoulder. The headlines made her shrink into her shoes. *Dying For a Date: Local Woman's Love Life Shrouded in Mystery*. The story, written by Barnard Savage, went on to document everything that had gone on lately in Lexie's love life, including her divorce from Dan, Hugh Glenwood's untimely and still unsolved murder, Henry Whitehead's demise, and Elton's accident, including the rumor that she'd run over him.

Lexie moaned and put a hand to her aching forehead.

"Hell's bells, Leslie." Aunt Gladys patted her arm. "Don't worry about anything that butt wipe Barnard Savage has to say. He's a first class idiot. Why, I knew him when he was a snot-nosed kid who used to eat his own boogers."

Lexie didn't say a word. The story was really going to bury her business. Actually, bury it further—ten feet under. And there was no telling how Jack would react. Maybe he wouldn't want to go out with her again.

Numb, she went over and made herself hazelnut flavored coffee, her favorite. The day simply had to get better. She couldn't let events get her down. A few minutes later, she poured herself a cup of the nutty smelling liquid, liberally doused with cream and sugar. She sat down at the table next to Aunt Gladys, sipping the hot java and nibbling on a bran muffin.

She glanced at Aunt Gladys who had resumed reading the newspaper. "I forgot, where did you say you and Frenchie are going today?"

Aunt Gladys snorted. "Criminy. Everybody tells me I have the bad memory."

Lexie swallowed the bite in her mouth. "Sorry."

"Frenchie's driving us over to the pioneer museum in Westonville." She pulled the rollers out of her hair and plopped them on the table. "Then he's taking me out for a little shopping. Afterward we're going find a place that will serve up some juicy steaks. I'm sick and tired of your mullet soup."

Lexie ignored the barb. Aunt Gladys typically didn't mean anything by her sharp tongue. Age had made her a little uncouth and she merely let loose with whatever came to mind. "Sounds nice."

Aunt Gladys rolled her tongue around in her mouth and began to suck her teeth. "Frenchie's . . ." *slurp, slurp,* ". . . a very nice fellow," *slurp, slurp.* "Just like that fellow of yours, Jack what's-his-name." *Slurp, slurp, slurp.*

"He kicked you out of the Sunrise Center." Lexie handed Aunt Gladys a toothpick and she poked at her teeth, flinging tiny chunks of food particles across the room.

"Oh, hell, that wasn't his fault. It was that batty old hag Alice Leone. She's the one who started it, calling me a cheat."

"Alice Leone? She any relation to Carma?"

"Her aunt. She lives in Snow Village up by the Ice Queen Resort. Used to work at the resort as a waitress, though I imagine she's got too many varicose veins to sling hash any more" Aunt Gladys quickly removed the curlers and ran be-ringed fingers through her crimped hair. "She comes down here to Moose Creek Junction once in a while to visit."

The doorbell rang and both Lexie and Aunt Gladys went to answer it. It was Frenchie, dressed impecabbly as ever in a pair of tan Dockers, a white button down shirt and a shiny black leather jacket that didn't quite zip around his paunchy belly. An old-fashioned bowler style hat sat atop his head and the scent of Old Spice wafted from his clothing as he gave his leprechaun grin.

"Ready, darlin'?" he asked Aunt Gladys, green eyes twinkling.

"Just let me get my purse and run a comb through my hair, Frenchie," Aunt Gladys exclaimed. She disappeared into the other room.

"Please, come in and have a seat," Lexie said.

"No, we'll be on our way shortly. I'd just as soon stand on the porch and breathe the fresh air."

Lexie folded her arms across her chest. "I'm so glad you could spend some time with Aunt Gladys today, Mr. Duckworth. There are just a couple of things I need to tell you. She'll need another dose of her blood pressure medicine in the afternoon. Don't be surprised if she gets a little ornery and forgetful at times."

"Frenchie, please call me Frenchie." He patted her arm and gave her another toothy smile. "Don't worry about your aunt, Alexandria. She'll be right as rain with me."

"Thanks." Lexie liked the dapper old fellow even more than she had before.

Aunt Gladys shuffled back into the room a few seconds later. Frenchie gently gripped her elbow and guided her to his Mercedes-Benz parked along the curb in front of the house. The shiny black car, obviously expensive, gleamed in the morning sunlight. It appeared Aunt Gladys had found yet another rich old codger to sport her around. As outrageous as she was, she continued to have a way with the men and probably would until the day she passed over.

Aunt Gladys was nearly a head taller than Frenchie, but it didn't seem to bother him. Like a little peacock, he strutted beside her, opened her car door and helped her inside. Frenchie waved at Lexie before he got in and drove off.

The Mercedes-Benz was barely fading in the distance when Jack Sturgeon pulled up to the curb in his Ford F-250. After parking the rumbling vehicle, he jumped out and sauntered up to Lexie. He wore Levis that hugged his long legs, a green workman's shirt, a tan Carhart jacket, and work boots.

"Bet the fish are biting like crazy." He winced when he looked at Lexie's bruised forehead. "How's your head?"

"Good." The smell of Irish Spring soap drifted into Lexie's nostrils and she stiffened. "Did you read the paper this morning?"

"Why?"

"That story in there by Barnard Savage. What did you think?"

"He's a straight up fool. You ought to sue him."

Lexie relaxed. "You still want me to hang out with you today?"

He grinned. "Hell, yes."

She smiled. "Come on in. I need to get a couple of things."

Jack followed Lexie into the kitchen where she grabbed her purse, a jacket, and a small cooler with macaroni salad and sodas in it.

"This is a neat old house," Jack said.

"It's been in the family for many years." Lexie glanced around lovingly. "I grew up here."

"Lucky you. I was a city brat, born and bred." He grinned. "Guess that's why I love the outdoors so much."

The drive up to the cabin revealed the landscape's glorious autumn hues of russet, gold, and burnt-orange. Lexie had been on old Highway 40 many times as a kid, and back then was used to the way things looked. But after years of living near seascapes, scrubby gray-green trees and ice plant-covered sand dunes, she found the mountain scenery refreshing.

The higher the truck climbed into the foothills, the more wild and tangled the foliage became. Green pine and blue-green spruce trees carpeted the slopes in gentle waves with the quivering yellow leaves of aspen trees folded in. Sunlight refracted sparkling white diamonds off the rippling surface of

Crazy Woman Creek that meandered like a serpent along with the road.

Nature didn't seem to be affected by the drought one bit. It was still putting on a typical fall display with all the splendor of past years.

Lexie enjoyed her conversation with Jack, as well as her proximity to him. He was well-educated and passionate about conservation. "We simply can't keep taking our environment for granted." He waved a hand at the forest splendor outside their windows. "The planet's resources will only go so far."

"I agree," Lexie said. "I'm doing my part. Like when I brush my teeth. I always shut off the water until it's time to rinse. Don't want to be wasteful."

One brow raised, Jack glanced at her to see if she was being serious or being a smart aleck, which of course she was.

Laughing, Jack pulled off onto a bumpy gravel road lined with clumps of dusky green sagebrush and yucca. Wildflowers of blue, yellow, red, white, and purple rippled along with tall prairie grass in the mountain breeze: Indian paintbrush, sunflowers, vervain, coneflowers, and Canadian milk vetch. Even this late in the year, they clung tenaciously to life, unaware that according to the calendar, they should be long gone.

Jack had driven about a mile when Gun Smoke Lake appeared in the distance, glimmering like blue jewel in a sea of gold, russet, and green trees. Dry brown peaks of mountains rose in the distance beyond the water, craggy and immense as they brushed against the sky.

A small log cabin appeared, nestled amongst pine, spruce, and aspen trees. Jack pulled up to it and parked in the gravel drive. "This is it," Jack announced. "Home away from home."

"It's breathtaking," Lexie told him. "If I could paint, I'd spend forever up here doing nothing but that."

"Next time we come bring your canvas and oils," Jack said.

Would there be a next time?

Lexie's cheeks tingled with warmth as Jack came around and opened her door and guided her toward the cabin. He unlocked it and they went inside. It was a typical mountain log home and had a definite masculine flair. A kitchen with a willow branch table and chairs took up space on the northeast side of the room and a living area filled the other side with heavy pole furniture, Navajo wall hangings, and sturdy brown carpets. A stone fireplace with iron candleholders on the mantle dominated one corner and wooden blinds covered the windows. A collection of antique oil lamps filled a wood table in another corner. Several stuffed wildlife figures were positioned strategically throughout the room, along with a couple of sets of mounted antlers.

"You're a hunter?" Lexie asked.

Jack nodded. "Pheasant, elk, deer—nothing ⸱th shattering."

"But you got these?" Lexie pointed at the taxidermied items.

"Sure. I like a little sport now and then."

"Wow. This is a great place."

"There are a couple of bedrooms upstairs, too." He pointed to a wooden staircase. "Unfortunately, I don't get here as often as I'd like. It's kind of lonely to come up by myself. But I think I'm going to start coming more often." He smiled at Lexie.

Lexie cleared her throat. "Like you said, fish are early risers. Guess we'd better go sink a line."

"Right on." Jack pulled fishing poles from the wall. Outside, he collected a metal box from the back of his truck. Lexie assumed it contained bobbers, hooks, bait and the like. As they walked toward the lake, Lexie breathed in the fresh pine scent and basked in the warm sun caressing her face. This was the way to live.

At the water's edge, Lexie could see crumbling white rings where the water depth had slowly receded over the dry years. Hopefully, this winter they would get some decent moisture. It was a shame to see the lake like this.

Jack handed Lexie one of the fishing rods. He pulled out a small white carton of night crawlers and baited his hook. No longer afraid of the wriggling worms, Lexie squished one on her hook, wiped her slimy fingers on her jeans and sailed the line into the sparkling lake. She heard the responding splash as it landed in the water. It gave her a thrill she hadn't felt in a long time.

"It's been forever since I've fished," she told Jack.

"How long?" He smiled over at her as he cast out his line, causing ripples to radiate toward the middle of the lake.

"Mom and Dad used to bring my sister Lucy and I up here when we were kids. I loved it, though my dad always baited the hook and gutted any fish we caught. That was not a fun part for little girls."

"You don't seem to mind it now," Jack commented.

"I used to bring Eva to visit Mom and Dad and we'd go fishing. Since I had to bait her hook, I got over my squeamishness. Being a mom does that to you." Memories flooded her mind and she sighed. "Lucy and Otis brought Carl, too, and the cousins would have a blast trying to see who could catch the biggest fish." She paused a moment. "I miss that a lot."

"Things change," Jack said. "Not always for the worst. We just learn to make new good times."

Lexie felt a tug on her fishing line. Feet planted firmly, she jerked the line up and began to reel it in. The fish surfaced and splashed, struggling to free itself. Lexie wasn't about to let it go. At last the good-sized fish dangled at the end of the line.

"Whoo, hoo!" she shouted. "I still have the touch!"

Jack pried the hook from its mouth and held it out by its gills. "Good girl. You've earned your supper."

As the day wore on, the sun rose higher in the sky, taking away the morning chill. Between the two of them, they had caught several fish that were tethered to a sturdy fishing line Jack had staked in the water. Definitely a feast fit for a king or at least a very hungry cat.

Lexie pressed her sleeve to her damp forehead. "Man, it's getting warm."

"Sure is." Jack found a forked stick and propped his fishing pole up on the shore. "Watch this, will you? I'll gut what we've caught so far and put them in the refrigerator."

Slowly he pulled in the line of fish staked in the cool shallows and moved down the shore a ways. One by one he slit their bellies and cleaned them, tossing the guts into the water. Seagulls flew past, their eyes on the delectable fish entrails gleaming in the sun. Once Jack finished his job and moved out of the way, the birds dove down to gobble up the treats. They took to the wing again, crying out their pleasure.

Jack hefted the string of fish over his shoulder. "I'll be back with some sodas."

"See you in a bit." Tired of standing, Lexie sat on a boulder and watched Jack until he disappeared into the tree line. She glanced at her watch, noting it was nearly noon. The fish weren't bitingg any more

A familiar honking drew Lexie's attention to the sky. Shading her eyes from the sun, she watched a flock of geese flying south in a V-formation. Her stomach grumbled and she put a hand to her abdomen. The muffin she'd eaten at breakfast wouldn't last much longer. She was more than ready for a fish fry.

Closing her eyes, she let the warm sun relax her.

The smell of fresh pine was intoxicating. It would be wonderful to come here when life got overwhelming. Jack was lucky. There was no better place to worship God than the great outdoors.

Jack's angry shouts broke the reverent silence and Lexie's eyes flew open. She dropped her fishing pole, slid off the boulder and ran through the brush and grass up the shore. "Jack," she called. "Jack!"

No answer.

Breathing heavily, Lexie plowed through the trees and arrived at the cabin. At first all she could see was the string of fish splayed in the dirt beside a bush. Her heart froze in her chest. Pivoting on one foot, she continued to look for Jack. In a split second, she saw him. He was standing against a pine tree, his midsection pinned to the trunk with an arrow. Blood covered his shirt, jacket, and jeans with a reddish stain.

"My God, Jack—"

"Lex," he said as blood dribbled down his chin. Barely breathing, he raised his head and looked at her, eyes glazed and pain-filled.

"What happened?" Tears ran down Lexie's cheeks. She felt so helpless.

"Sh-shot me . . . look out . . ." Jack coughed, his body spasmed and he slumped.

Frantic, Lexie checked for a pulse. Nothing.

"No!" Lexie cried. It had all happened too fast. Jack was gone. In a split second. Just like that.

Who had done it? Were they still here?

She looked around frantically. She didn't see anyone, but did notice a blue object in the dirt at Jack's feet. She had just leaned down to pick it up, noticing footprints at the base of the tree, when she heard a noise behind her. Whirling, she saw the bushes on the other side of the clearing move slightly. A flash of movement rustled the trees.

Look out, Jack had told her.

If someone had killed Jack, they'd want to kill her. Panicked, she ran for the safety of the cabin. As she passed by a pine tree, a loud *thwak* sounded above her head. Stumbling backward, she fell and felt the sting of a rock slicing into the back of her hand. Quickly she stood and looked up, gripping the bleeding hand in which she still clutched the blue object. Barely a foot above her, an arrow was embedded in the tree.

Crying out, Lexie scrambled toward the cabin again. Hiccoughs erupted in her diaphragm and racked her frame. Something primal and black rose within her. Her heart pounded until she thought it might burst from her chest. Finally she reached the cabin, slamming the door shut and locking it. The second it closed, another *thwak* sounded on the outside of the door and an arrow tip pierced the wood.

Hiccough, hiccough . . .

Lexie's chest heaved with each frightened breath and she stared in horror at the door, expecting the killer to smash it down. She stuffed her fist in her mouth and bit back bitter sobs intermixed with hiccoughs.

Disorientation and fear clouded her brain. She couldn't focus her thoughts. Glancing at the small round disk in her hand, she noted the black lettering on it: *Ice Queen Resort and Casino*. A gambling chip. Had the killer dropped it?

The killer.

Lexie slid the chip inside her pocket. Heart hammering, she grabbed her purse and scrambled for her cell phone. Dialing 911 with shaking hands, she said to herself, *please let it work up here, please, please, please . . .*

An operator immediately answered and Lexie blurted, "My friend's, *hiccough*, been murdered. And now, *hiccough*, someone's trying to kill me!"

CHAPTER 14

THE FRONT DOOR RATTLED LIKE IT HAD BEEN hit by a freight train. Someone was out there. Someone sinister — trying to get inside. *Trying to get me.*

Blood hammered in Lexie's temples and shot to her fingertips, making them tingle. The cell phone nearly fell out of her numb hand before she could slide it into her jeans pocket.

Hiccoughs still shaking her frame, she pivoted, looking for a weapon. She spied the butcher block on the counter and grabbed the biggest knife. A door on the other side of the cabin beckoned her. Get out fast, she thought.

Wait.

She paused, hand trembling hand on the doorknob, as a horrid thought flashed in her mind. She could run, but what if the killer chased her? She was far from being the world's fastest runner. Considering she wasn't in the best shape and unfortunately carried around a few extra pounds of fluff, trying to make a run for it was probably a bad idea.

Better hide.

She locked the sturdy dead bolt on the door, and went around the room closing all the window shutters and locking them. More rattling at the front door, then pounding. Finally, it sounded as though someone was heaving himself or herself against the frame. *Over and over.* Lexie shook so badly she could barely stand and her knees literally knocked together.

Hide. Fast.

Her gaze moved to the closet under the stairs. Hiccoughing madly, she raced over and got inside, shutting the door. Coats hung from a rod, boots, and shoes were lined up on the floor, and sports gear hung from several hooks.

She noticed what appeared to be a trap door in the wooden floor. Shoving aside a mop and a broom, she lifted it up and looked inside. It was dark and forbidding.

When a splintering sound came from the pummeled doorframe, Lexie grasped a flashlight sitting on a shelf. Flipping it on, she shed illumination into the musty darkness, sighting a wooden ladder and a small concrete cellar full of slatted crates. And lots of gooey spider webs. Chock full of arachnid vermin.

Lexie abhorred spiders. Black, brown, white, green, or whatever color, they were squirmy, icky creatures. Small spaces gave her claustrophobia. A shiver of disgust ran up her spine.

Bite the bullet.

No time to worry about creepy crawlies. Or cramped spaces. Setting the flashlight aside, she yanked a long wool coat from the rod and spread it over the top of the trap door. Then she lifted the door and climbed down the ladder far enough to reach around the edge of the opening to make sure the coat covered it. She left the lid slightly ajar so she could see out, clutching the butcher knife tightly in her good hand. Just in case.

From outside the closet, she could still hear un-nerving racket of someone slamming against the door. The wood splintered one last time and a loud crash reverberated throughout the cabin, shaking the floor.

They broke it down.

Lexie swallowed hard, over and over, trying to rid herself of the hiccoughs. It didn't work. The cold dampness of the cellar seeped into her bones. She shivered. Her muscles twinged. The old concrete walls seemed to close in on her.

The floorboards squeaked with heavy footsteps. Dust drifted down in little puffs, tickling Lexie's nose and throat. She alternately swallowed both hiccoughs and sneezes.

The footsteps came closer and closer to the closet. The door creaked open. Lexie held her breath as the sound of ragged breathing came from the person standing above the trap door. Through the small slit she'd created between the floor and the wool coat, Lexie could see two dusty black boot tips. Could be army boots, Lexie thought. They were large, like a man's.

She swallowed again when her nose began to twitch wildly. She was going to sneeze. And hiccough. And get herself killed.

No!

Lexie took another deep breath and held it, praying she wouldn't give into those natural urges. She thought about Eva, dear precious Eva who still needed her. She wanted to live to see her grandchildren. She thought about Lucy and patootie head Otis and Carl. Even batty old Aunt Gladys.

God help her, she wanted to see them again, too.

Eeeeeek! Eeek! Eeek A tiny mouse scurried from its hiding spot in the cellar and skittered past her feet. Lexie bit her lip and kept her gaze riveted on the black boots. They stayed where they were a while longer, then disappeared. The closet door banged shut.

Thank heaven.

Lexie closed her eyes and took a shaky breath of relief. Now she *really, really* had to sneeze and hiccough. Instead, she took a big gulp of air, held her breath, and prayed. Hard. The intruder stomped around Jack's cabin for a bit, then the sounds stopped. Hopefully, the killer had left. *Please God, help me. Help me be strong . . .*

Off and on, Lexie looked at her digital watch in the darkness, pressing the little button for light. About twenty minutes later, she heard someone else enter the cabin. She tensed until she heard the voice.

"Westonville police," a man called out. "Is anyone in here?"

"I'm here," she called out into the darkness. Dropping the butcher knife, she pushed open the trap door and shoved aside the coat. Climbing out of the cellar, she slowly opened the closet door and walked into a room full of police.

Several burly uniforms stood near the gaping doorframe, guns drawn and pointed at the interior of the cabin. An ambulance with flashing lights was parked in front and squad cars sat haphazardly in the gravel drive.

Gabe strode through the open door, his presence reassuring. "Put your guns away," he told the officers, his detective's star flashing on his belt. "Secure the area and start looking around."

As the officers re-holstered their weapons and went about their business, Gabe walked over to Lexie, face lined with concern. "You all right?"

"Yes," she answered, then immediately began to shiver, sneeze, and hiccough, all at the same time.

"No, you're not." He took Lexie's hand, pulled a white handkerchief from his pocket and wrapped it around her palm. "You're bleeding."

"It's just a scratch." She blinked back tears and hiccoughed, feeling like a quivering mass of jelly. The strain of what she'd just experienced was taking its emotional toll. "Jack Sturgeon, he's out there by the tree—"

"The paramedics are taking care of your friend," Gabe told her.

"Is he . . . ?" *Hiccough.*

A muscle twitched in Gabe's cheek. "Yes, Lexie. He's dead. I'm sorry."

She swallowed several times, letting the awful knowledge sink in. She'd known Jack was gone, but it was still shocking to hear. A wave of dizziness washed over her and she swayed.

"Whoa there." Gabe grasped her elbow to steady her and gently led her over to the leather sofa. Removing his jacket, he placed it over her trembling shoulders.

"I know this isn't the best time. But I need to ask some questions." He took out a notepad and pencil. "OK?"

Miserable, Lexie nodded, glad that at least her hiccoughs seemed to have stopped.

"What happened?"

Lexie told him everything that had gone on from the time she and Jack left the house until now.

"Were you two dating?" he asked.

Lexie blinked. "We'd been seeing each other. Just a couple of times, though."

He scratched on his pad. "Did Sturgeon have any enemies?"

"No. As far as I could tell, he had a lot of friends and is . . . er, *was* well respected." Her throat was suddenly dry and she swallowed convulsively.

"We've talked before about your enemies," Gabe said. "Whoever they are, they seem to be getting bolder. Like the grenade incident."

"People hate me. I have no business left to speak of, I've been getting odd calls and that black car's been hanging around."

Stevenson scribbled in his notebook. "Did you tell Otis?"

She nodded. "I've never been able to see the car close enough to get a license plate number or a make and a model. There's not much he can do." She paused as a thought occurred to her. "Do you think whoever killed Jack is the same person who killed Whitehead and Glenwood? And hurt Elton?"

"Don't know. But I'm going to find out." Gabe wrote some more in his notebook, then flipped it shut. "You drive up here?"

"Jack . . ." Lexie's voice broke and she cleared her throat. "Jack did. It's his truck outside."

"Give me a few minutes to talk with my boys. Then I'll give you a ride home."

Later, as Gabe drove Lexie back to town, she closed her eyes and leaned against the head rest. She didn't feel like talking. All she wanted to do was go home, wrap up in one of her mother's quilts and sleep. Maybe the pain that squeezed through her heart when she thought about Jack would eventually go away. *Maybe not.* She felt as though she'd lost something before she'd even had the chance to grasp onto it.

When the car slowed, Lexie opened her eyes and saw they were at her house. Gabe pulled up in front of the old Victorian she'd called home all her life. The only thing different from when she was a kid, was the *The Saucy Lucy Café* sign tacked above the porch.

Lexie collected her purse and the cooler. "Thanks," she told Gabe.

He nodded. "You need anything, you call."

She got out and shut the car door, then walked up the sidewalk, feet dragging like sacks of flour. On the porch, she turned to watch Stevenson drive away, then went inside. Thank heavens Aunt Gladys was out with Frenchie. She didn't want to talk with anyone. The phone rang and she didn't answer it, figuring if it was important they'd leave a message.

Setting everything on a hallway table, she trudged up the stairs to her room, shut the door, and flopped on the bed, kicking off her shoes. *Amazing.* The carved ceiling patterns seemed to move in front of her eyes, she was so keyed up. One of her eyelids began to twitch.

Thump . . . ahhh . . .   Squeak, squeak, squeak . . .

Lexie pushed up on her elbows. *What the heck is that?* She stayed very still, straining to hear.

Thump . . . ahhh . . .   Squeak, squeak, squeak . . .

Someone was in the house. *The murderer?* Had he or she come looking for her? She thought about calling Gabe's cell phone. Or maybe she should call Otis. Maybe not. What if she got them over here for no reason? She'd better check it out herself.

Lexie slipped into the hallway. Tiptoeing, she followed the strange thumping and squeaking up the staircase to Aunt Gladys' living quarters. She paused at the attic door, ear pressed against the wood. The noises were definitely coming from inside. She grasped the doorknob and slowly turned it.

As it she poked her head inside, she noticed the curtains were pulled tightly around Aunt Gladys' bedroom alcove and the noises had stopped. However, an unusual odor wafted through the room. Lexie wrinkled her nose and sniffed. It smelled like oregano or . . . *incense?* Something was burning. Knowing Aunt Gladys' penchant for starting fires, she became concerned.

"Aunt Gladys?" She walked inside and looked for signs of mischief. "Are you up here? What's going on?"

The curtains jerked open and Aunt Gladys popped her head out, her cap of white curly hair in disarray. Frenchie was stretched out beside her in bed and they had the top sheet pulled up and tucked beneath their armpits. Both of them clenched what appeared to be joints between their thumbs and forefingers.

Lexie planted her hands on her hips. "Who said the two of you could do that up here?"

"Do what?" Aunt Gladys pretended to be innocent of any wrongdoing. "Have sex?"

Lexie's face prickled with warmth. "No, smoke."

Lexie sniffed the acrid smell again. "Is that . . . marijuana?"

Frenchie grinned. "Yes, indeed, or what the peasant folk quaintly call *weed*."

"But . . . but that's illegal," Lexie sputtered.

What kind of a mess was she going to have to clean up for Aunt Gladys now? In her mind, she saw Otis and his doofy deputy Cleve Harris doing a drug raid on the café. *The final nail on the coffin.* Barnard Savage would have a real heyday with this scoop. Another murder and a drug bust on top of it.

"Not at all, my dear," Frenchie said. "My doctor's prescribed this for medicinal purposes."

"And pigs fly," Lexie said. Still reeling from Jack's death, she decided this was the last straw—coming home to find her aunt romping in the hay with Prince Valiant and smoking dope to boot. Even her teenage daughter had never even given her so much trouble.

"Why are you two home so early? I thought you had a full day planned."

"We did." Aunt Gladys giggled, took another toke and exhaled. "But we ran into a bit of trouble at Dillon's department store."

Lexie could only imagine.

"But it was all a ridiculous mistake," Aunt Gladys continued. "Those silly security people insisted I'd taken a pearl necklace from the jewelry counter."

"How did that happen?"

"It was utter nonsense," Aunt Gladys insisted.

"It must have fallen in my pocket somehow and when we were leaving every alarm in the store started to screech. Hell's bells, there was such a fuss you'd have thought I was escaping from Alcatraz. It was all a terrible misunderstanding."

"Yes, indeed," Frenchie joined in. "The very idea that my little poopsie would shoplift is insane. Why, I could buy a hundred pearl necklaces for Gladys if I wanted to."

"As it was, he just bought that one." Aunt Gladys lifted the pearls around her neck, leaned over and gave Frenchie a smack on the cheek.

Lexie nodded. "So after you two got the matter settled—"

"We decided to come back here for a little slap and tickle, if you know what I mean." Aunt Gladys gave Lexie a knowing wink.

Lexie shuffled backward to the door, shaking a warning finger at Aunt Gladys. "No more shopping at Dillon's. And please put out the *medicinal* cigarettes before you burn my house down."

"Party pooper." Aunt Gladys took another puff and waved the smoke away from her face. "By the way, how was your date?"

"It was great. Right up until the point where someone killed him."

Aunt Gladys and Frenchie's mouths dropped open and they gave her shocked looks.

Lexie didn't wait to explain. She left the attic and hurried down to her room. She crawled back into bed, threw the covers over her head and huddled into a fetal position. Misery shrouded her like a veil.

The café was in the toilet.

There'd been another murder.

Everyone in town hated her.

Aunt Gladys was a loon.

She had no life.

Tears burned at the back of her eyes, but she refused to let them flow. Crying didn't accomplish a damn thing. She wanted badly to blame all of this on Dan for his lies and disloyalty. If he'd only been a decent husband she never would have moved home to Moose Creek Junction. But the time for blaming him had passed and she was trying to move forward with her life, not back.

Even if it meant living through this hell.

CHAPTER 15

T HE DAY OF JACK STURGEON'S FUNERAL TURNED out as dismal as the weather. It was actually cool and the sky was filled with dark gray clouds everyone hoped would give the parched autumn landscape some much needed moisture. More than likely not, though. Lots of teaser storms had passed over town, sometimes releasing a few drops of rain. Then nothing. The wind would pick up and blow the clouds north to Montana or South Dakota.

Anywhere but Moose Creek Junction.

Which is exactly where Lexie would have preferred to be at the moment. She'd been walking around like a zombie since the ill-fated fishing trip. She and Lucy had agreed to close The Saucy Lucy for the time being, a frightening, but sensible move. There was really no point in making all that food since no one came to eat at the café any more.

Lexie stewed about the situation all week. She simply couldn't get over the fact that yet another one of her dates had been eliminated. Lucy tried to offer moral support, but she hadn't actually been much help—going on about how there were lots of fish in the sea and Lexie would find someone new. *Blah, blah, blah.* Platitudes served up on an unappealing platter.

That wasn't the point. At all.

Her life had gone topsy-turvy. The café wasn't providing a living for her anymore. There was a murderer running loose in Moose Creek Junction. Lexie wasn't simply being blamed for all the mishaps, she was a prime target. As unlikely as it seemed, somebody wanted her dead.

Who?

Reluctantly, she got ready for the funeral by choosing a black dress, dark hose, and heels, strongly suggesting to Aunt Gladys that she also dress accordingly. When she was finally ready, thinking herself stable enough to face the solemn event, she went downstairs. She determined Aunt Gladys must be ready and waiting to go because she was singing, "Jingle bells, Batman smells, Robin laid an egg . . ."

Lexie followed Aunt Gladys' voice into the kitchen. "Let's go or else we're going to be . . ." she blinked. Aunt Gladys stood in front of the kitchen window wiping a stack of kitchen knives with a towel. That wouldn't have been quite so bad if she hadn't been naked. Well, not completely naked. A lacy bra encased her droopy breasts and a garter belt and hose covered most of her saggy hips and legs.

"Aunt Gladys, what are you doing?"

Aunt Gladys turned to Lexie, a knife in her hand, her eyes wide. "Don't ever sneak up on me like that, Leslie! You nearly scared the bejabbers out of me."

Lexie tensed her jaw. "Aunt Gladys, please. The knife—put it down."

Aunt Gladys blinked at the knife in her hand, then placed it and the towel on the counter. "Hell's bells. What on earth am I doing?"

"I don't know. You'll have to tell me." Lexie grabbed an apron and hurriedly tied it around Aunt Gladys, thankfully covering most of her unmentionables. "Have you taken your medicine yet this morning?"

Aunt Gladys shook her head. "No. I was too busy levitating over my bed. My shoulder's still a little sore from when I fell. I have to learn to land better."

Lexie rolled her eyes. "Let's go upstairs and finish getting you ready for the funeral."

Aunt Gladys snorted. "Funerals suck, Leslie. Who died, anyway?"

"Jack Sturgeon, Aunt Gladys. A friend of mine. Remember I told you?" About a million times, Lexie thought.

Aunt Gladys snapped her fingers. "That's right. I was nearly ready to go, but that panty thief has gone and snatched all my undies again."

"The panty thief? Wasn't it the boy-man?" Lexie asked.

"No, no, no. The boy-man's gone right now. I'm talking about the panty thief. No one knows his name. But he likes to sniff the crotches and wear the panties on his head and—"

"OK," Lexie interrupted, not liking where the panty thief talk was going. "Let's get you dressed. Lexie grabbed Aunt Gladys' bottle of pills from the windowsill. "But first, you need one of these."

Later, Lexie and Aunt Gladys, now dressed in a subdued brown dress, serviceable brown shoes, a bright orange scarf, and orange basketball earrings Aunt Gladys had insisted upon, met Lucy outside the First Community Church of the Lamb of God.

Flowers filled the podium area where Jack's coffin rested and a pianist played somber music on the other side of the riser. People who stood in small groups talking to one another stopped and stared when Lexie and Lucy walked in with Aunt Gladys. She could hear them whispering when they passed by, despite her attempts to ignore them.

Lexie was instantly uncomfortable. Not only because of Jack's untimely death, but also because she hadn't been to church in years. Her head started to ache excruciatingly and she winced, knowing she would have to bear the pain until she got home to take aspirin.

She looked around and noticed a man, a woman, and two children seated in the front row. It must be Rick Sturgeon, Jack's brother, and his family. Lexie was glad they were here.

After paying their respects at the casket, which was closed, Lexie, Lucy, and Aunt Gladys found a spot in one of the back pews. When Reverend Lincolnway got up to speak, Lexie realized several people kept turning in her direction, giving her pointed looks.

A shuddering sigh tore through her and she tried her best to ignore the accusatory stares. Instead, she lowered her head and concentrated on the healing cut on her hand. This wasn't about her and what people thought of her. It was about Jack Sturgeon, a kind and considerate man who hadn't deserved to die so young. Sometimes not even a funeral could get people to set aside their judgmental natures.

Lexie caught Carma Leone's eye. For some reason, she noticed her nails were painted bright blue. She squinted harder. Darned if that polish didn't look similar to the color of the writing on the grenade thrown through her window. That wasn't possible though, was it? Could Carma be behind the incident?

Confused, Lexie focused on Reverend Lincolnway's memorial as the sounds of weeping and sniffling rose from the assembled mourners. Unable to stop the tears that squeezed from her eyes and ran down her cheeks, she was thankful she'd remembered to bring along a tissue. Lucy kept her arm around Lexie the whole time, offering solace which, although well intended, seemed empty and meaningless.

After the service Lexie managed to shake hands

with the grieving family members and mutter her condolences. Then she helped Aunt Gladys shuffle back to her truck and she drove them home.

At least Aunt Gladys was patient with the truck's backfiring and chugging. Usually sassy and outspoken about everything, she remained subdued. Finally she turned to Lexie and said, "Tell me again, Leslie. Who was it that died?"

Lexie sighed. "It doesn't matter, Aunt Gladys. It really doesn't matter."

The rest of the week passed in a blur. On Sunday morning, Lexie awakened still sad, but slightly more prepared to deal with the real world. It seemed as though she'd been in a cocoon for days and was slowly forcing her way out, slowly becoming human again. Her sadness still lingered, needling her with the stinging loss of someone who could have become a good friend. The looming questions—mainly why—remained.

Despite the fact that life seemed easier to deal with after a week of retrospection, Lexie was still left with the frustrations of her life: the unsolved murders, the café's dwindling business, Eva's unpaid spring tuition and a Loony Toons aunt breathing down her neck day and night. It seemed almost too much to bear.

Better get to work, girl. According to her late father,

keeping busy was a cure for almost everything.

Getting out of bed, she yawned. Standing in the bright sunlight pouring through the curtains, she did her morning stretches, reaching to the ceiling and then to the floor, twisting her torso, executing shoulder rolls. Then she did a few push ups, pelvic tilts, and yoga positions. It felt good to get back into her routine, something she'd dismissed all week while she wallowed in self pity.

The time for that was over. She was a survivor, and survive she would.

She dressed in a pair of old jeans, a T-shirt, and knotted her hair into a ponytail. Slipping upstairs, she checked on Aunt Gladys who was still in bed, snoring away like a chain saw with a thread of drool running down one side of her chin, her face slathered in a mint green mask. Pink sponge rollers peeked from her scalp where they clipped her wiry white hair into tightly crimped curls. More than happy to let the septaugenarian troublemaker sleep, Lexie went downstairs and out into the back yard where birds twittered endlessly in the golden sun.

Autumn, with its earthy scents and russet landscape had always been Lexie's favorite time of year. It symbolized a new beginning, not an end. As the earth slowly went dormant, causing brilliantly colored flowers and lush green trees to fade with frost, seeds dropped from petals and leaves, burrowing deep in the soil. There they remained snug and warm, preparing for the moment when they would burst forth once again in all their glory. Not until the time was right, not until the calendar promised the sun's warmth would allow them to grow.

Breathing in the crisp fall air, filling her lungs full with the sweetness, Lexie felt a heightened sense of vitality and purpose. Even in this quiet period of her life, when it was best she burrow away until the storms of life blew over, there were things she needed to do. She would make preparations until the time arrived for her to resurface. Nature had many lessons to offer, lessons she would be wise to heed.

Hands on her hips, Lexie surveyed the garden, from which she had harvested fat, juicy tomatoes, carrots, cucumbers, peppers, corn, beans, and zucchini. She'd canned and put up enough vegetables for most of the winter, though her gardens the last few years hadn't been as prolific. It was hard enough trying to coax foliage from the high plains climate soil when they had normal rainfall. The drought turned the garden her mother had tended so lovingly into a shadow of its former self.

Full of tangled weeds and dried husks of plants, the vegetable bed looked sad and lifeless. Except for the pumpkin patch. The basketball-sized orange gourds lay barely hidden beneath fat brown, prickly leaves, their vines snaking across the ground. They thrived because they were one of the last vegetables to be harvested. They ripened just in time for Halloween.

Halloween.

Lexie recalled way back in June she'd reserved

a booth at the Trick-or-Treat Festival tradition-
ally held every year at the Moose Creek Junction
Community House. Mom and Dad always encouraged her and Lucy to spend Halloween night
trick-or-treating there rather than wandering the
neighborhood in schlompy costumes begging for
candy. Even back then, in a small town like this, it
had seemed a safer option.

Lexie had loved attending the event to hand out
treats to the children because it reminded her of a
kinder, gentler time. It also reminded her of when
Eva was a little girl, when she had lovingly hand
sewn the costumes and goodie bags and walked her
daughter around their neighborhood, pretending
to blend into the shadows. Even then, things had
seemed simpler.

Halloween was tomorrow. Would she have the
guts to brave the gossips and go to the festival, as she
had done since she'd moved back, with treats for the
little goblins and ghouls?

"Peter, Peter, pumpkin eater . . ."

Lexie turned to see Aunt Gladys wearing the
leopard print caftan and feathery slippers. Her face,
still covered with the mint green facial mask shell,
cracked at the corners of her mouth as she sang.
Lexie rolled her eyes. It could be worse, she thought.
At least the silly old gal hadn't come out naked.

Seeing she had caught Lexie's attention, Aunt
Gladys lifted the sides of her caftan and did a merry
jig as she continued with her song. ". . . had a wife

and couldn't keep her. So he put her in a pumpkin shell and there he kept her very well."

"Nice morning," Lexie said.

Aunt Gladys stopped cavorting, cocked her head to the side and batted her eyelashes. "Excuse me? Do I know you?"

Here we go again, Lexie thought as she sank down in an old lawn chair. "I'm your niece, Aunt Gladys. Lexie. Don't you remember?"

Aunt Gladys put a finger to her lips and looked thoughtfully into the distance. "You wouldn't try to fool an old woman, would you?"

Lexie shook her head.

Aunt Gladys snapped her arthritic fingers. "That's right! I know who you are. Forgive me, I've suffered a momentary lapse in memory."

Lexie smiled. "I think we need to go inside so you can take your medicine and have some breakfast."

"Good idea," Aunt Gladys said. "I need my power drink. Stimulates my brain cells, you know. Helps me think a lot clearer."

It would stimulate my puke reflex, Lexie thought.

"Did you hear Junior last night?" Aunt Gladys asked. "He was making such a ruckus on the roof I had trouble sleeping again."

Lexie stood and took Aunt Gladys' elbow, steering her toward the back door. "I'm afraid I've never seen Junior."

Aunt Gladys stopped and her eyes went wide. "You're not in cahoots with him, are you? I couldn't live here any longer if you were."

"Of course I'm not," Lexie said. "Now please, come inside."

"What are we going to do today?" Aunt Gladys asked innocently.

Hide out, Lexie thought. Then, in her mind's eye, she saw a flash of all the smirking townspeople's faces. She considered how they were gossiping mercilessly about her. Fabricating lies and distorting the truth. Wickedly putting her out of business for no good reason. They should all be ashamed for making a difficult time in her life even worse.

She needed to show them. Show them she wasn't afraid. Remembering the apples she'd picked from a tree in her yard that now sat piled in two bushel baskets in her pantry, she suddenly knew what she and Aunt Gladys would do today.

"Have you ever made caramel apples, Aunt Gladys? Or carved a pumpkin?"

Aunt Gladys scratched her head. "My housekeeper, Irene, used to do all that for Bruce when he was a little boy."

"What about when you were a girl?" Lexie prompted. Aunt Gladys shrugged and her eyes filled with tears. She looked at Lexie with a panic-stricken expression. "Hell's bells, Leslie. I . . . I don't remember."

Lexie felt a sliver of compassion for the old woman's fading memory. "That doesn't matter because today we're going to do all of those things.

Tomorrow evening, you and Lucy and I are going to the Trick-or-Treat Festival."

"Yipee! I promise I'll be good, too. Cross my heart and hope to die." Aunt Gladys crossed her heart with her forefinger. "I know exactly what we can wear. I've got some costumes from a number I did in Vegas years ago."

Lexie experienced a moment's flicker of hesitation. If Aunt Gladys wore them in Las Vegas, no doubt they were X-rated. She wasn't so sure they'd be appropriate for a bunch of anal-retentive pilgrims and their offspring. Then again, with a little tailoring, maybe the costumes were just the thing to wake up the town and make them realize they couldn't keep her down.

The next day, Lexie, Lucy and Aunt Gladys took turns examining themselves in a full-length mirror in Aunt Gladys' room. From the ex-Las Vegas showgirl's costume trunk, they had fished out gauzy yellow, purple, and orange satin tutus complete with matching tights, spotted butterfly wings, and curly black antennae.

As Lexie had feared, the showgirl outfits were revealing up top, especially since she had a fair amount of cleavage. After discussing the problem for a while with Aunt Gladys and Lucy, Lexie produced several colorful T-shirts from Eva's dresser drawer. Putting them on and knotting them at their waists worked. *Voila*, the exotic tutus instantly became more acceptable for the family event.

Aunt Gladys, Lucy, and Lexie loaded the Halloween treats into a large Tupperware container and put it in Lexie's truck. Lexie also threw in the Halloween decoration box from the garage, a roll of masking tape, and the two pumpkins she and Aunt Gladys had carved.

"For Pete's sake, Lexie," Lucy said as they drove to the Community House in the bumping and grinding truck, "can't you afford a new vehicle yet? This one is hideous." Her fingers gripped the seat with white knuckles and her antennae slipped askew on her head when the vehicle lurched and backfired.

"Not unless you've won the lottery and want to share," Lexie said.

Lucy sighed heavily.

"I've kind of gotten used to it." Aunt Gladys adjusted a gauzy wing on her back. "It's like the Tower of Terror ride at that theme park in California—Fantasyland isn't it? Anyway, it takes you way up in the sky and drops you back down . . . *ker-plunk, ker-plunk, ker-plunk.*"

Ignoring their complaints, Lexie watched as the Community House, a large white clapboard building near the city's small recreational reservoir, Buffalo Lake, came into view. In the parking lot, people had stopped their cars and walked their excited children to the entrance, adjusting their costumes.

When Aunt Gladys, Lucy, and Lexie arrived, business people were festooning their wooden booths with spooky Halloween paraphernalia. They stopped what they were doing to stare at the three women and talk amongst themselves. Lexie ignored their catty comments, which were whispered just loud enough for them to hear, and went over to the Chamber of Commerce's check-in desk.

With Aunt Gladys and Lucy right behind her, she marched up to the president, Morton Frost, a tall man with old-fashioned brown and gray mutton chop whiskers. Standing there in his pin-striped three-piece suit, he reminded Lexie of the Wizard of Oz, working his evil behind closed doors and curtains, trying to fool everyone.

"I reserved a booth for the Saucy Lucy Café," she told him.

He nonchalantly flicked lint from his expensive suit and perused a piece of paper on the table in front of him. "Hmmm, I'm afraid I don't see you here."

"There's got to be some mistake," Lexie said, feeling like a complete idiot in her purple butterfly costume and antennae. Her face surged with warmth. "I made the reservation months ago."

He gave her a smug look. "I'm sorry to say it's not here."

"Let me have a look at that, you pompous ass wipe." Aunt Gladys grabbed the paper from his hand and held it under her nose.

"Aunt Gladys," Lexie mumbled, afraid she was

going to get them kicked out.

Aunt Gladys stared at the paper for a second, making faces. She elbowed Lucy hard in the ribs and shoved the paper at her. "Quick, read this crap for me. I can't see a blessed thing."

Lucy grasped the list and squinted at it. "Ah, there's the Saucy Lucy. We're assigned to booth G." She tapped a line on the paper with a fingertip. "Mort, you simply must get yourself reading glasses."

Aunt Gladys snorted. "Reading glasses my ass. He's just being a c—"

Lexie cupped her hand over Aunt Gladys' mouth and nudged her away. "We'll just clear out of here, Mr. Frost. Sorry for the trouble."

Red as a persimmon, Frost glared at the women as they toted their boxes to the designated booth and set everything down. "What's his problem?" Lucy nodded at Frost. "Mort's usually not like that."

"It's the murders," Lexie responded. "I told you, people are giving me the cold shoulder. They think they'll get their hands dirty if they associate with me. That's why they're not eating at the café. That's why we're shut down."

"Sons of perdition," Lucy snapped. "Let those without sin cast the first stone, let the—"

"Hey, gabby pants," Aunt Gladys said to Lucy as she struggled to lift a carved pumpkin out of a box. "Could ya quit flappin' your jaw for a minute and give me a hand here?"

With a frustrated grunt, Lucy went to help Aunt

Gladys.

Ignoring Frost's snub and the business people's whispered comments, Lexie busied herself hanging up orange and black crepe paper and ghoulish cardboard jack-o-lanterns, black cats, spiders, and witches. In one corner, the city hall organizers had arranged a spook alley, complete with creepy graveyard with headstones, cobwebs, and scary looking creatures of the night. An array of candlelit jack-o-lanterns sat on a crooked stone fence, their faces flickering in the dimly lit room.

Finally, it was time. Someone opened the double doors and ghosts, witches, and goblins of all sizes shuffled into the main hall, their goody bags ready, excitement practically crackling in the air. Squealing with delight, they trooped from booth to booth in small groups, chanting their, "Trick-or-treats," in exchange for goodies. Parents stood at the back of the room, talking amongst themselves and keeping a watchful eye on their little ones.

Aunt Gladys, Lucy, and Lexie each had a bowl of caramel apples to hand out, but the children took one look at their booth and steered clear. Lexie became angrier and angrier by the minute. It appeared the children, having been properly briefed by their parents, were purposely avoiding their booth. "I think we should go," Lexie said. "We're wasting our time."

"Don't give the old battleaxes the benefit of seeing you defeated," Aunt Gladys said. "Show 'em what you're made of. You are a Castleton, after all, even if you did go and marry that numb nuts boy who knocked you up."

Lucy, who was drinking punch from a paper cup, coughed and sputtered. Turning as red as the punch, she wiped her mouth with the back of her hand and glared at Aunt Gladys. Another pearl of wisdom from the peanut gallery, Lexie thought. Aunt Gladys was right. She needed to stand her ground. Come hell or high water.

Finally, one little boy of about eight, dressed like a vampire, approached their booth. "Tre-e-e-k-or-tre-e-e-e-at," he muttered through long white fangs, his brown eyes sparkling with mischief.

Lexie smiled and plopped a caramel apple into his outstretched bag. "Are you Count Dracula?"

"Uh huh," he murmured.

"Thanks for coming to our booth," Lexie told him.

"I like caramel apples," he said.

"So you're not a 'fradie cat like the other kids, eh?" Aunt Gladys settled one bony hand on her orange, silken hip.

He nodded and Aunt Gladys plopped another caramel apple in his bag.

"Can you tell us what they're afraid of?" Lexie asked.

Count Dracula looked around the room, as though checking to make sure no adult saw him talking to the enemy. "You guys are bad. And Theresa's mom says you are both witches. Lots of the moms are saying that."

Aunt Gladys snorted while Lexie and Lucy exchanged concerned glances.

"Why?" Lexie asked.

"I dunno. That's just what they say." He pointed at Lexie with one of his black-clawed fingers. "They say you . . ." he peered around again, then said in a whisper, "kill your boyfriends."

Lexie's heart wrenched. "That is absolutely not true."

He shrugged. "I think they're all goofy. Everybody knows witches are just make-believe. Thanks for the apple!"

With that, Dracula ran off, cape flying behind him, and joined the rest of the costumed children in the surging crowd.

Aunt Gladys shook her head. "I told you this town was full of backwater hogwash."

Lucy slammed her bowl on the counter. "I've had about enough of this nonsense. I think it's pointless to stay here any longer—the kids are all dodging us."

Lexie was no glutton for punishment. They packed up their things, but left the apples and jack-o-lanterns. They removed the decorations and started to leave. Suddenly a tall woman in a red and white polka dot clown costume shouted in Lexie's direction, "Go home. Nobody wants you here."

"Uh, if you haven't noticed," Lexie snapped. "I am leaving."

"I mean nobody wants you here in town." Her bulbous red clown nose twitched. "You need to move away and take your trouble with you."

"Shut up, Bozo." Aunt Gladys snapped back. "Unless you want Elvis to knock your block off."

"Shhh, Aunt Gladys," Lexie said. "Let's just leave."

The clown's eyes opened wider and her bright red mouth dropped. "Back off, Gladys whatever-your-last-name-is-this-week. You're a menace to this town, too."

"I'll get to the bottom of this right now." Aunt Gladys stormed toward the clown and yanked off her orange wig. She glared at the dumbfounded woman, her butterfly wings fluttering. "Why, Mazie Bannister, as I live and breathe. You always had a double chin as a baby, and I believe it has gotten fatter. You can't cover that up with white paint, no matter how much you cake it on."

"You old fool," Mazie sputtered indignantly. "How dare you speak to me like that?"

Aunt Gladys threw back her head and snorted. "Because I see right through you. You're pretentious and petty and frigid. Always have been. Why, I'm amazed Andy Bannister still keeps a lazy, pain-in-the-ass, bony shrew like you around."

A primal growl came from the depths of Mazie's diaphragm and she leapt from her booth onto Aunt Gladys. Aunt Gladys' box went flying and crashed on the floor. Polka dotted and gauzy orange arms and legs tangled as the two women mixed it up, scratching, kicking, and biting.

Lucy's hands flew to her bright red cheeks. "Dear Lord, Lexie. Do something!"

Lexie put down her box and shouted, "Aunt Gladys, stop! *Both of you, stop!*" She might as well have been yelling at the wind because they didn't pay one bit of attention.

People stared open mouthed at the cat-fighting old women. Children jumped up and down, thinking it great fun to see two elderly ladies in a brawl. "Fight, fight, fight!" they chanted.

Lexie looked around, desperate for help, but realized quickly it wouldn't come from the holier-than-thou citizens of Moose Creek Junction. This was a fight she was going to have to break up herself before either of the women got hurt.

Mazie was on top, her painted clown's face smeared with red and white as she tore at Aunt Gladys' butterfly tutu. As for Aunt Gladys, her wings were already in shreds, her antenna bent beyond repair and skewed atop her white crimped hair. The women's grunts and shrieks filled the air as they knocked over chairs and smashed into tables, spilling candy everywhere.

Lexie hurried over and grabbed Mazie's shoulders, trying to yank her off Aunt Gladys. But Mazie swung around and ripped the sleeve on Lexie's T-shirt, then smacked her hard in the face.

"Owww!" Lexie howled as a major sting exploded in her cheek. She staggered backward from the force of the blow, unable to gain her balance before she fell into a table. When she knocked it over, she tripped and landed hard on her backside, emitting another winded squeak when a basket of potato chips dumped on her head.

Stunned, she sat there for a moment, fighting to catch her breath. Amazed an old woman could hit that hard, she shook the chips out of her hair and heard them skitter onto the floor. She rubbed her aching cheek, ignoring all the rubber neckers staring wide eyed at her, mouths agape.

Hearing the old women's labored breathing and angry snarls, she caught sight of them rolling across the floor, hands locked in each other's hair. This nonsense had to stop.

Right now.

Sister Lucy had finally taken action. She had grabbed a pitcher of lemonade. Taking careful aim, she sloshed the old ladies with the pale yellow refreshment.

Hit by the largest blast of icy liquid, Mazie squealed, jumped off Aunt Gladys and stood, spitting and sputtering. Lemonade dripped down her painted nose and face, leaving behind a flesh-colored trail. She shook loose the silvery ice cubes nestled in her costume and they clinked to the floor. Pieces of popcorn clung to her smashed-gray-hair-sans-orange wig, and a red sucker was still stuck to the front of her polka dot clown suit. Looking around at everyone in the room staring at her, her face puckered up like a dried apple and she started crying like a big baby, shoulders quivering.

Aunt Gladys stood to her full height and smoothed her rumpled butterfly costume covered in wet spots, bits of hay and whatever else she'd rolled in. With one wiry black antennae hanging in front of her eye, she took a deep breath and set her chin squarely. "That will teach you, Mazie dear, to keep your cake hole shut and your mitts off me and mine. Got it?"

Lexie felt something warm dribble at the corner of her mouth. She swiped at it with the back of her hand and saw it was blood. *Brother.* What a mess this had turned out to be. They never should have come. It had been a bad idea.

"Come on Aunt Gladys." Lexie took her aunt's arm. "Let's go."

As Lexie, Aunt Gladys, and Lucy left, Mazie made another run for Aunt Gladys, growling. Just then, Gabe Stevenson pushed his way through the crowd. He grabbed the crazed clown by the arm. In his deep rumbling voice, he said, "Whoa there. What's going on?"

Otis and Cleve elbowed their way through the throng as well. Neither of the local lawmen looked very happy, especially Otis, who glared at Lexie like she'd just blown up a childcare center.

Mazie thrust a wobbling finger at Lexie and Aunt Gladys. "Those two started it. They have disrupted our entire Halloween Festival."

Gabe frowned. "Somebody called Sheriff Parnell's

office to report a brawl. And from what they said, all four of you ladies were involved. So, guess what?"

Lexie did not want to ask; it was too humiliating.

Aunt Gladys, still sputtering and dripping, asked the burning question for the rest of them. "What?"

Otis produced a huge ring of keys from his belt and rattled it with an evil grin. "You're all going to jail, girls."

"For what?" Mazie asked, aghast.

"Disturbing the peace and destroying public property," Stevenson said.

Lexie closed her eyes and groaned.

Chapter 16

"CHIPPIE."

"Harlot."

"Hussie."

"Jez-e-beeeel—"

Lexie was about to tear her hair out. She was tired and sweaty. She smelled. Like stale caramel popcorn and rotten apples.

"No more cat fights, you two." Lexie stopped pacing and glared over at Mazie and Aunt Gladys who were sitting on straight back wooden chairs, barking at each other like Nazi stormtroopers over their tuna sandwiches and green Jell-O, the unappetizing prison lunch.

Mazie's clown costume was wrinkled, torn, and covered with blotches of food. Her makeup was completely destroyed and consisted of only of red and white streaks. She kept sniffing and wiping her nose on her droopy sleeve. The more she wiped, the more she streaked.

Aunt Gladys' butterfly costume, which had once upon a time graced Las Vegas floorshows in hotels such as the MGM Grand and The Flamingo, looked like Jack the Ripper had shredded it. Food smeared her tutu. She'd removed her smashed and tangled antennae headpiece long ago and discarded it in a corner where it lay like a mangled bug.

"Lexie's right," Lucy told the elderly ladies from her bunk. She settled herself more primly and properly on the covers. "You're making it worse than it is." She had also removed her antenna, her usually tidy bun was askew atop her head, and her outfit was spattered with food stains.

For some reason, she seemed to be taking the incarceration calmly and had barely spoken since they arrived the previous evening. She appeared to be patiently waiting for the moment when they would be sprung from this hell on earth. Lexie wanted the whole episode to end. This place sucked. The whole reason they'd wound up here sucked. Otis had ignored her protests at being locked up. Turning tomato red, he'd stormed out, leaving the ladies to their own devices in the stuffy cell. Snickering, Cleve had trotted obediently after his boss, hiding the smile on his long horse face. Gabe had merely chuckled and told them, "Make yourselves at home, ladies, and if you need anything, call."

So much for her indignant show of bravado.

Lexie watched closely as Mazie and Aunt Gladys resumed eating, staring daggers at each other over gray trays clutched in their knotted fingers. She scratched her head and looked around. Practically everything in the Moose Creek Junction jail, or the "pokey" as Aunt Gladys called it, was the same bland color. Gray food, gray cups, gray sink and toilet, gray blankets on the gray bunks, and gray walls. Even Otis and Cleve and Gabe seemed to have a creeping gray tinge spreading across their flesh whenever they brought in meals or checked on their "prisoners."

Lexie resumed pacing the cell, her crumpled butterfly wings flopping. She refused to eat or sleep, so trays of her food remained untouched and her bunk was barely rumpled. It was demoralizing, disgusting, and demeaning. She didn't deserve to be in jail. She wanted out.

Now.

"Psst, hey you," one of the women from the cell across the way called. Lexie looked over at her. Last night she hadn't paid much attention to their neighbors. She'd been too outraged.

"That's right, sister," she said with a toss of her head. "I'm talkin' to you."

The woman's voice was unusual, Lexie thought, like a cheese grater scraping on a chalkboard. She walked over to the bars and studied the woman and her *compadre* a little closer.

The woman who had spoken was dressed in a tight, short, black leather skirt, a tight green blouse, boots, and a fur coat. She had poofy, long blond hair that had been teased into proper submission, but probably housed tons of illicit secrets.

The other woman, who was passed out on one of the bunks with her voluptuous rump covered in tight purple satin Capri slacks, was snoring like a buzz saw. She wore her purple-red hair in a punk rocker style and a tight purple crop top, a feather boa, and a fringed, black suede vest.

Both wore tall black boots, about a pound and a half of makeup, plenty of gaudy jewelry. The women had so many tattos and piercings, Lexie winced looking at them. The blonde's Adam's apple caught her eye. *Tell me it ain't so.* Lexie wasn't sure, but it looked like the blonde was a man, or a man becoming a woman, or however it went.

Transvestites. In Moose Creek Junction?

Holy moly.

The blonde tossed her head again and put one hand on her hip. "What are you staring at, girlfriend? These?" She squeezed the ample breasts that were about to bust loose from her top. "I paid an arm and a leg to a doctor in Denver to have these puppies latched on." She gave a falsetto giggle as she continued to stroke her creamy flesh.

"No, I . . . um . . ." Lexie's face prickled with heat.

"Never mind," the blonde said. "I just wanted to tell you and your girlfriends you'd better not plan on moving in on our territory."

"Territory?"

"Is there an echo in here or are you just deaf?" The blond shook her head. "Bambi and I have been working this town for the last six months. And there's no room for anyone else. Got it?"

Lexie's ears burned. Prostitutes, *transvestite* prostitutes, no less, had moved into little old Moose Creek Junction and set up shop. *Incredible.* "My aunt and my sister and I have no intention of moving in on anybody's territory," she said emphatically.

The blonde sat on the edge of the bottom bunk and crossed her long, shapely legs. "That's what they all say, honey." She pointed at herself with a long red nail and rolled her eyes. "Believe me, Trixie's heard it all."

Lexie's mouth went dry. This was the final straw. She turned to Aunt Gladys, who had resumed grousing at Mazie. "Are you done eating?" Lexie asked.

Aunt Gladys blinked. "What crawled up your butt and died? I don't like it here, either. The room service is crappy. We have absolutely no view."

Lexie walked over and took her plate, then went back to the bars and scraped the gray plastic along the rungs. *Thunk thunk thunk thunk thunk . . .*

"Lexie, what are you doing?" Lucy asked, her expression horrified. "You're going to get us in more trouble."

"No, I'm going to get us out of here," Lexie returned. "I'm tired of being a jailbird."

Trixie covered her ears and squealed. Aunt Gladys and Mazie did the same. Amazingly, Bambi on the bunk continued to snore.

A few seconds later, Gabe sauntered from the

sheriff's office into the detainment area. "Hey," he said to Lexie, irritation chiseled on his face. "What's the problem?"

"This place." Lexie quit scraping the plate across the bars. "We want out. Now."

"No can do. You're under a 24-hour lockup."

"For what?"

"Disturbing the peace."

Lexie cleared her throat, seriously missing her early morning caffeine fix. She had a headache, her mouth was as dry as a desert and tasted like metal. She lowered her voice to a harsh whisper. "Those *women* in the other cell are . . ." she looked over to make sure Trixie wasn't listening and lowered her voice even further. "Prostitutes."

"That's a fact," Gabe acknowledged, folding his arms across his chest.

"They're hardened criminals, for cripe sake." She gripped the plate harder. "Why are we in here with them?"

He shrugged. "You broke the law."

"I told you my aunt's disturbed and she got confused yesterday. Lucy and I were trying to break up the argument she and Mazie were having. That's all."

"Really?"

Lexie clenched her jaw. "Let me take Aunt Gladys home. We'll be out of your hair."

He lifted a dark brow. "You're no bother at all."

"Don't be smug, detective," Lexie shot back when she heard the patronizing tone in his voice.

"There's no reason to keep us here any longer."

"I suppose you ladies *have* learned your lesson."

Lexie rolled her eyes. "I told you, Aunt Gladys is a disturbed old woman who—"

He held up a hand. "Save it. I'll see what I can do."

"How hard could it be to let a crazy old woman and her nieces go free? She tried to look past Gabe's large frame and out the door into the office. "Anyway, isn't Otis in charge? Where is he?"

"I'll see what I can do," Gabe repeated firmly.

Anger shot through Lexie, right down to her toes. "Why are you in town? Why aren't you out solving the recent crime wave?"

He chuckled. "I heard about two grannies in a brawl at the Moose Creek Junction Community House on my police radio. Couldn't resist checking it out."

"It is absolutely not funny," Lexie said, frowning.

He raised a brow. "Maybe not to you."

She tapped her toe anxiously. "You ought to be hound-dogging the murderer instead of terrorizing little old ladies."

"What makes you think I'm not?"

Lexie clenched the plate so hard her knuckles turned white. "You're taking your sweet time about it. Meanwhile, my life's become a living hell."

"Solving a murder is no piece of cake. We're talking two here, along with Elton's assault."

"I think you're in over your head, Gabe Stevenson. I think *I* could do a better job of getting to the bottom of this. It is my town, after all."

Gabe stiffened. "Don't even think about doing anything stupid, Lexie. Let the law handle things."

"In the meantime, how do I survive? My business is ka-put-ski and the whole town hates me."

"You're a resourceful woman. You'll think of something."

Lexie glared at him. "How dare you be so condescending? You have no idea what I'm going through."

He was silent for a while, as though mulling over what she'd said. "I will tell you this and only this. Someone doesn't like you, Lexie. Someone I think is very strong and driven by jealousy. I believe they're responsible for all the recent crimes and they may be after you."

Lexie shivered. "What do you suggest I do? Hire a bodyguard?"

"Tell me who might want to hurt you and why. In the meantime, lay low and be careful."

Who would want to hurt me?

Lexie's mind was a blank. Soul weary, she rested her head against the bars. This was terrible. Like a nightmare. Deep down, she feared it might never end.

"Hey."

Miserable, she glanced up at Gabe.

"I know you love to hate me. But I'm your friend. Not the enemy. OK?"

Despite her irritation, Lexie relaxed at the sound

of Gabe's smooth, reassuring voice. *Smooth and reassuring like the devil's forked tongue.* With her index finger, she rubbed the ache between her brows. "I'm tired of all this."

"I know." He smiled. "If you're really good, I might get you out of here in a couple of hours."

"Oh, joy," Lexie said.

"By the way." Stevenson's hazel eyes twinkled mischieviously as he looked her up and down. "Nice tutu."

Lexie's face prickled with heat as she watched him stride back to the sheriff's office.

Everything was quiet.

It was nearly midnight and black as ink outside in the crisp November air, except for the bright stars and luminous moon that covered the sleeping neighborhood with a silvery cloak. Dark branches on the old elm tree outside Lexie's bedroom window scratched the glass, like the fingernails of a night creature tapping to gain entrance.

She sat back in the dainty chair at the writing desk in her bedroom and snapped her journal shut. The only light was the small lamp on her desk, an amber glass antique that had been in the family for years. Originally kerosene, someone along the way had wired it for electricity. Shadows from furniture danced around the room, creating an eerie atmosphere.

Lexie shivered—why, she didn't know. Maybe a goose had walked on her grave. There was no reason for her to be so jumpy, but she felt funny. She and Aunt Gladys had stayed close to home since the jail incident and everything had been fine. With the café closed, Lexie had too much time on her hands and Aunt Gladys whined with boredom. She'd kept both of them busy cleaning the house, weeding the backyard, and painting the restaurant area. Since Christmas was right around the corner, they'd made several batches of Grandma Castleton's suet pudding and put it in coffee cans to steep with age.

Always, niggling at the back of her mind, was one unsettling fact. Her savings were getting low. After the attic renovation, Cousin Bruce's bribe money was nearly gone as well. Gabe had told her to lay low and she was doing her best. Sooner or later she and Aunt Gladys would run out of mundane chores and cash.

Then what would they do?

One thing was certain, they couldn't starve. She'd have to go out in public and try to find a job. Or try to get a hold of Bruce again. Cousin Bruce— the great escape artist.

Lexie sighed with weariness and recalled her mother's quilting frames. She could dig them out of the garage and set them up to make a quilt. That would kill some time and Eva would get a new cover for her dorm bed. Whether she needed it or not. There was fabric and batting and yarn in one of the hall closets where she stored her craft items. She wouldn't even have to leave the house to gather sewing notions. Making the quilt would probably kill them with sheer boredom, but it'd keep them busy.

For the moment, at least, Aunt Gladys was asleep upstairs. Everything was peaceful, though a creepy sensation continued to tingle Lexie's spine. With difficulty, she ignored it. It was not the time to give in to unease. It was the time to concentrate on where she was heading with the mess that had become her life. And when she wrote in her journal, she had the chance to reflect on things.

Wearing her comfortable old gray sweats and slippers and sipping a cup of chamomile tea, she'd written about the Halloween Festival/jail fiasco. While it had been frustrating to live through, in retrospect, it was funny.

Two old ladies in a cat fight? Transvestites in Moose Creek Junction? She smiled, despite all the damn trouble her aunt could manage to brew up. She was, however, extremely glad it was over. She didn't want to think about what mischief the old gal might get into next.

Lexie's journal was a relic of the divorce class she'd taken right after she and Dan had broken up. The therapist had encouraged the group to write down all their feelings of rage and sadness in order to vent them. Hopefully, instead of allowing negative emotions to remain bottled up, if you wrote them down and aired them, you could get rid of the hate and keep it from festering.

She'd felt foolish at first, writing about her deepest inner thoughts. Afterward, she became hooked. The journal became a journey of her soul and she realized things about herself. She found out that since she was a little girl, she'd felt overshadowed by her powerful preacher father and outspoken sister. She'd never felt good enough, no matter what she tried to achieve, so she'd quit trying.

That's the reason she'd so easily latched onto Dan Lightfoot, even though she'd sensed in her young heart he would be difficult. He was strong and commanding and believed in her. At the time, his attention was intoxicating and addictive. As the years rolled by, Lexie let herself believe she needed him to exist and overlooked his transgressions: the physical abuse, his controlling attitude, and his extramarital affairs.

She glanced down at the slightly bent joint on her right ring finger. She'd injured it during a particularly bad argument with Dan in which she'd dared to fight back. Her fighting back hadn't accomplished a thing: she'd only managed to injure herself.

The fight had finally knocked some sense into Lexie, however. A woman shouldn't have to be hit in order to be loved. It wasn't right. It was physical abuse, pure and simple, even though Dan believed it wasn't. To him, he was just letting her know who was boss. *It's my way or the highway*, he'd told her. His words had extinguished the light in Lexie's soul and her love for him had withered and died on the vine. Her bent finger symbolized her determination to get her life straight again.

Lexie's nostrils twitched and she wrinkled her nose. *Sniff, sniff.*

An odor tickled her nostrils and made her sneeze. *Smoke?*

It really did smell like that. It seemed to be coming from somewhere in the house. A smoke alarm's loud, piercing shriek pierced the stillness. It sounded like it was coming from downstairs. Lexie's frayed nerves snapped.

She stood and saw a curl of gray mist coming in under her door.

Aunt Gladys.

Random thoughts flashed through her mind and she started to hiccough. Either Aunt Gladys had lit candles for another Ouija board ceremony and one had fallen over and caught something on fire, or Frenchie had snuck upstairs and they were having another medicinal smoke and had caught the sheets on fire. She grabbed her purse and checked the door to make sure it wasn't hot, then slid from her room out into the hallway. Holding an arm in front of her mouth and nose, she made it up the night-lit stairs to the attic, coughing and hiccoughing alternately. She flung open Aunt Gladys' door, hurried to the bed and shook the elderly woman's shoulder.

"Wake up, Aunt Gladys!" *Hiccough.* "Fire!"

Aunt Gladys moaned and rolled over to stare at

Lexie with bleary eyes. "Tired? Yes, of course I'm tired . . ."

"No, we've got to get out of here," Lexie urged between hiccoughs. "The house is on fire."

Aunt Gladys sniffed and coughed. "Oh, my . . ." She sat up and reached for her robe and slid on her slippers. She also managed to grab her glasses before Lexie threw a protective arm around her shoulders and dragged her down the smoky stairs and out into the frosty night air.

Standing on the sidewalk, Lexie shivered as the smoke alarm pierced the chill night like a finely sharpened sword. Through a fog of disbelief, she noted most of the smoke was billowing from her kitchen, on the west side of the house. Distressed, she struggled to recall whether she was paid up on homeowner's insurance.

What a ridiculous thing to worry about!

Shock had taken hold of her, clenching her tightly in its grip. The smoldering house in front of her wasn't just any house. This was her parents' house. Her grandparents' house. No amount of insurance could replace the sentimental value of the heirloom Victorian.

Another loud shrill pierced the night air—a fire engine.

"Hell's bells. This is all my fault," Aunt Gladys sobbed as she slipped on her robe. "I left a candle burning in my room." A fit of coughing overtook her and she bent over to wheeze.

"Who knows, *hiccough*, how the fire, *hiccough*, started, Aunt Gladys." Lexie patted her aunt's shoulder reassuringly, shivering mightily in the cold air, glad someone had called the fire department. Her head still swam with confusion, but it wasn't the time for blame. "The important thing is we weren't hurt."

"You mean you're not mad at me?"

"Heaven's no."

"You're a good egg, Leslie." Aunt Gladys began to cough again, her shoulders trembling.

Lexie held tightly onto Aunt Gladys until the fit passed. The fire could have been caused by an electrical problem, she thought to herself. Or someone could have started it.

The question was, *who*?

The neighbor from next door, Al Whitcomb, a tall, elderly, barrel-chested man with a thick black beard hustled out of his house wearing his sweats and a heavy jacket. Lexie thought he must look a little like Blackbeard. "Are you two all right? I saw the smoke when I took out my trash and called the fire department."

"Thanks, Al. We're fine." Lexie wondered why Whitcomb was taking out the trash at such an ungodly hour of the night. She shivered when an icy breeze sliced into her and she curled her cold toes in an attempt to keep them warm. It didn't work. They were slowly becoming ice cubes.

Trying desperately to suppress hiccoughs, Lexie looked around, noticing several people stood on their porch steps talking excitedly. Did someone set the fire in order to burn her out and run her out of town?

Was it one of her neighbors? Were they that devious and desperate? Or was it the person Gabe said wanted to hurt her out of spite and jealousy?

The murderer?

Despite her paranoia, all Lexie could process was that she and Aunt Gladys were safe. Eva was safe in her dorm room at college. The fire department was on its way. Everything would be all right.

She hoped.

"I know who did this." Aunt Gladys held up a crooked index finger. "It was that boy-man. Junior. He's been fooling around up on the roof and I knew he was up to no good."

Lexie patted her aunt on the shoulder. "It doesn't matter."

Siren blaring, the Moose Creek Junction volunteer fire fighters rounded the corner in a well-outfitted red and gold ladder truck and barreled toward the house. Within seconds, fire fighters in hats, rubber boots, and yellow jackets poured from the rescue vehicle, unleashed long hoses, and headed up to the smoking house. Like a well-oiled machine, the men hoisted their hoses and doused the licking orange fire, daring it to stay alive under a good wet shower. The stubborn flames lit the sky with a sick, unnatural glow and Lexie's stomach sat in her abdomen like a lump of bread dough.

Before long, the fire seemed to be under control.

A fire fighter, his yellow rubber slicker covered with ash, walked up to Lexie, Al, and Aunt Gladys. He was a tall, burly man with a sandy-colored handlebar mustache. The crinkled lines around his eyes were lined with gritty soot and dirt. Lexie got the impression of a mad hornet coming their way.

"I'm Chief Bob Plowman," he said sternly as he walked up to them. "Was everyone out of the house?"

"Yes," Lexie said.

One of Chief Plowman's eyebrows cocked. "You the owner?"

Lexie nodded and hiccoughed. She took a deep breath and swallowed.

"You're lucky," Plowman said. "Fire's out. Were you cooking anything?"

"No. Is the house . . .?" Lexie was almost afraid to ask the question. "Salvagable?"

"Sure. Damage was contained to the kitchen. You'll have to hole up somewhere while the fire marshal conducts his investigation and your insurance company can get someone out to do repairs."

Plowman nodded at an ambulance. In her shock, Lexie hadn't noticed its arrival. "They'll check you folks out," he said.

One of the ambulance attendants walked over to Lexie, a short, rotund fellow with a serious expression. "You all right, ma'am?"

"I'm fine." *Hiccough.* "But my aunt isn't."

Aunt Gladys clutched Lexie's arm as another paroxysm of coughing racked her frame.

"Smoke inhalation," the attendant said, taking Aunt Gladys' elbow. "And let's check you out, too. Just to be on the safe side," he said to Lexie as he took Aunt Gladys to the ambulance.

The bustling EMT crew asked both Lexie and Aunt Gladys questions as they sat in the back of the ambulance. They covered them with blankets and took their vital signs. Lexie's hiccoughs finally stopped, but Aunt Gladys' cough didn't seem as though it was going to quit any time soon.

One of the paramedics had Aunt Gladys lie on a gurney and covered her mouth with an oxygen mask. Then he approached Lexie and said in a low voice, "Your aunt's condition has us concerned. She'll need to go to the hospital in Westonville for observation for a few days. Her lungs may have been burned slightly by the smoke. That coupled with her age and high blood pressure . . . well, we'd better be safe than sorry."

"Of course." Lexie clasped her blanket more tightly, angrier by the minute about who would have the nerve to burn her house down. Then she thought of Bruce and his callous attitude toward his mother. She'd told him to come and collect his mother, hadn't she? It wasn't safe for Aunt Gladys to be here. Now look what had happened.

The EMTs continued to fuss over Aunt Gladys and Lexie tried not to think the worst. They were doing their jobs, doing everything they could for her.

"Leslie?" Aunt Gladys clawed at her oxygen

mask, staring at Lexie with questioning eyes.

Lexie held her wrinkled, age-spotted hand. "Don't worry, Aunt Gladys."

"What's happening?"

"They'd like you to go to the hospital for a few days for observation."

"I don't want to go." Her eyes filled with tears. "I hate hospitals. The doctors and nurses are all such schmucks."

"I promise you'll be fine."

"Don't let them keep me there," Aunt Gladys pleaded. "It'll kill me if I have to go back and live in a place like that."

"It's only for a short time, then you can come home," Lexie assured her, though she wondered where home would be until the house was repaired. *Take it one step at a time, Lex.*

Aunt Gladys gripped her hand tighter. "Promise me, Leslie. Promise me you won't put me away again."

Lexie's heart melted. She knew despite the old woman's penchant for driving her crazy, she couldn't let her down. "I promise. I'll bring you home as soon as you're well enough. Now you've got to rest."

"Thank you." Aunt Gladys closed her eyes. "That's more than my son, the idiot savant, ever offered to do."

After the ambulance had hauled Aunt Gladys off to the hospital, red light atop the vehicle blinking in the swirling night mist, Plowman approached Lexie again.

He removed his hat and wiped the sweat from his brow with a handkerchief. "You won't be staying here tonight, ma'am. You'll want to call family or find someone to stay with for now."

"You can use my phone," Al offered.

She nodded.

"Me'n the boys will be working here a little longer checking for hot spots and making sure nothing starts to cook again," Plowman explained.

"What happens next?" Lexie asked.

"We'll get the county fire marshal over here in the next couple of days to determine the cause of the fire."

"What if it's arson?"

"The fire marshal will file a criminal report and turn it into the police for investigation."

A lot of good that will do, Lexie thought. So far, they hadn't been much good at ferreting out a murderer. She was certain they wouldn't have much luck tracking down an arsonist. "Thank you, Chief."

He gave a sooty grin. "Just doin, my job, ma'am. Just doin' my job."

CHAPTER 17

"FOR PETE'S SAKE. THIS IS AWFUL," LUCY TOLD Lexie the next morning as they discussed the fire. She had immediately come to fetch Lexie at Al's after the fire, and they sat in Lucy's front room, decorated in Mom and Dad's hand-me-down Cold War furniture, along with Nana McCool's ancient vacuum tube television with a dead spider in the screen. Of course, it no longer worked, but Lucy had covered it with one of Mom's handmade doilies and placed a plant on it. A spider plant. How fitting, Lexie thought every time she saw it.

Lexie had called Eva to let her know about the fire and also to insist she stick around the dorms for a while. Eva, bless her heart, wanted to come home and make sure everything was all right, but Lexie convinced her to stay put. At least until all the trouble blew over.

"I'm not sure if someone set the fire or if it was faulty wiring," Lexie told Lucy. "We'll have to wait and see what the fire marshal says after his investigation."

"What about Aunt Gladys and her candles?" Lucy asked.

Lexie shook her head. "Aunt Gladys was upstairs sound asleep. Chief Plowman said the fire started in the kitchen."

Drained by all the commotion and emotion and befuddled by the bizarre events, Lexie sat on her sister's couch. Numb. That's all she felt. Hands wrapped around the thick ceramic mug of coffee, she stared into the steamy brew—not drinking, just thinking.

That's it, she told herself. *I've had enough. I will find out who is behind all of this nonsense and make them stop. Otherwise, I have no life left in Moose Creek Junction. In fact, I may have no life at all.*

People around her had been hurt or murdered. She'd been stalked by some unknown person and attacked numerous times. Her business had slowly been ruined by innuendo and suspicion, and now the fire had put the final nail in the café's coffin. She had her family's safety to think about, not just her own. It was obvious the police weren't going to solve the situation any time soon, despite their good intentions

To hell with Otis' warning to stay out of it. And to hell with Gabe's hints that she'd best not get involved. It was her life, her future. At the rate things were going, either she was going to have to take matters into her own hands or something far worse than the fire could happen.

She refused to wait and see what it might be.

"Hello? Earth calling Lexie." Lucy swayed back and forth in Grandmother Castleton's antique rocker. "I asked you a question. Do you think someone set the fire deliberately?"

Lexie set her jaw. "Gut instinct—yes. I think they did. Gabe thinks someone's trying to kill me."

"Good heavens, why?"

"Jealousy or spite."

"For what?"

"Who knows?"

Lucy held her face in her hands and took a deep breath. "This is not good. I think I need to give your name to Reverend Lincolnway for prayer circle. We need a miracle."

Lexie stood and paced—something she'd been doing a lot lately. "While you and the sisters bow your heads and rub on your beads, I'm going to take action."

"Alexandria Kathleen." Lucy shook her finger and her scolding tone transported Lexie back to when she was a kid and Lucy had gotten upset with her. "Don't you even think about hunting down the killer. You got yourself clobbered a couple of times already. Lord knows what could happen next time."

Lexie threw her hands in the air. "I've already been targeted, no matter what I do. Remember the rock that smashed my front window and my forehead? And now the fire? I don't have a choice. I'm damned if I do, and I'm damned if I don't."

"Lex—"

"If I don't find the person who hates me, Lucy, I will have no life left here. I'll have to move away."

"No, never again." Lucy stood, her face a mixture of apprehension and anger. "This is your home and this is where you'll stay."

"Then tell me, what choice do I have except to conduct my own investigation? The police aren't getting anywhere."

Lucy frowned. "You're trying to rope me into some sort of new scheme, aren't you?"

"I need your help."

"You know I promised Mom and Dad I'd take care of you. That's not fair. You're taking advantage."

Lexie stopped pacing and met Lucy's gaze. "Look, you don't have to do it. I'll take care of it on my own."

"Over my dead body," Lucy said. "I'm in this with you, whether I like it or not."

"Only if you're sure."

"I'm sure. What about Aunt Gladys? You'd better call Bruce again and see if he'll come get her."

"I've tried that already: it's impossible to reach him. Besides, for the next few days, Aunt Gladys is in the hospital."

"What about after that?"

Lexie snapped her fingers. "I bet Frenchie will babysit her."

Lucy shook her head. "I can't believe that at her age she's got another boyfriend. It's really disgusting."

"Comes in handy for us, though," Lexie said.

"We still better call Bruce and let him know what's going on. Maybe he'll feel guilty enough to come home." Lucy handed her the phone.

"It's not likely, but here goes." Lexie fished Bruce's phone number out of her purse and dialed. After about a million clicks, buzzes and rings, someone finally answered.

"I'm calling for an American guest of yours, a Mr. Bruce Slickman. This is an emergency." As Lexie waited for the connection to Bruce's room, she recalled the times when Aunt Gladys brought him to visit in Moose Creek Junction. Even as a boy, he'd been high strung and hard to pin down. He'd get into mischief, like frying snakes on electric fences and tying rubber bands around stray cats' tails. What a joy he was to have in the family.

A few seconds later, an Oriental woman's voice came on the line. "Hu-rr-o? Who this?"

Lexie tried not to imagine who she was, though she had a good idea. Probably she was one of Bruce's *comfort girls*. "Lexie Lightfoot, Bruce Slickman's cousin. Is he there?"

"Why you need speak with him?"

Lexie gritted her teeth. "It's a family emergency."

The woman must have handed the phone to Bruce because he came on the line. "Lexie? What's this all about?"

"Sorry to bother you, cuz. There's been an accident."

"My mother?"

"She's fine, but she is in the hospital."

"My God, what happened?"

"My kitchen caught on fire last night. Your mother has a slight case of smoke inhalation and the doctors want to watch her for a few days. Bruce, you really need to come and get her." Lexie decided there was no reason to go into all the additional complicated reasons. The phone call was costing enough as it was.

"I can't," he said. There's a big deal going on Tokyo next week. I'll make a million. I just need you to keep Mom for a while longer."

Lexie rolled her eyes.

"He's said no, right?" Lucy said softly.

She nodded. "Bruce, I can't explain all the details right now. It's not safe for Aunt Gladys around here."

"What do you mean? Is she causing trouble?"

"It's not so much that," Lexie said. "This is just not a good place for her right at the moment." Her stomach twisted. She had a bad feeling.

"But I'm flying to Tokyo in a few days and after that I'm off to the Philippines. There's no possible way I can come home."

"Bruce," Lexie squeaked, gripping the phone so hard her fingers hurt. "You are not treating your mother very nicely. Remember, she carried you in her womb for nine months."

"You don't understand, Lexie. This is the deal of a lifetime. It's worth millions and I already have several investors lined up. I've got to get offices arranged and staff hired. The good news is when I'm through with this, I'll have the money to put Mom up in the Taj Mahal for the rest of her life if she'd like."

"What she'd like is for you to be a caring son. Quit leaving her with relatives or dumping her in assisted living centers. It's inconsiderate and rude. You're breaking her heart."

"Lexie. It sounds like you're running into some financial difficulty."

"That is part of the trouble, but not everything. Your mother needs you."

"I'm going to wire you some money. How does fifty thousand sound? Maybe you can hire an old folks' sitter to watch her."

"Bruce, I don't want your money. I want you to come home. *Your mother* wants you home."

"I can't, cuz. Tell you what, though. I'll make it seventy thousand."

"This is not an auction, you moron! This is your mother we're talking about. You can't just pawn her off like an heirloom watch."

"OK, eighty thousand, tops. That ought to take care of you and the old girl for a while. You could even do some traveling. Maybe go to Hawaii. I'll be back to collect her as soon as I can."

Lexie released an exasperated breath and started to speak again, but Bruce cut her off.

"I'll wire the money first thing in the morning to the Moose Creek Junction Savings and Trust."

"But Bruce—"

Click.

Lexie's entire body tingled with rage at the sound of the phone disconnect and a clawing headache thrummed through her temples. She put the phone down.

"He hung up, didn't he?"

"Yes. He's sending more money, which I do need in light of recent happenings, and to pay you back for this call that probably cost an arm and a leg. But he doesn't give a damn about his mother."

"That's Cousin Bruce for you. Don't count on him changing."

"Whatever," Lexie said. "In the meantime, we have a job to do, so we'd better start making plans."

"What do we do first?" Lucy asked.

"Create a list of everyone in this town we know and what possible reasons they might have to hate me."

"We're going to be at this for days." Lucy pulled a pad of paper and pencil from a magazine rack. "We have a population of 1,200. Actually, 1,201 if you count the Greensboro's new baby."

A sudden thought occurred to Lexie. "We also need to make a trip up to the Ice Queen Resort."

"You're going to drag me to a gambling den?" Lucy templed her hands in prayer and looked heavenward. "God forgive me—why must we go there?"

Lexie ignored Sister Lucy's goody-two-shoes repentance speech. "I forgot to tell anyone this. But on the day Jack died, I found a gambling chip from the casino at his feet. I believe the killer dropped it."

"Maybe the killer's a gambler."

"Or maybe they work up there. Either way, it's a good place to start looking."

CHAPTER 18

SOMEONE ONCE SAID THAT IF THE WIND ISN'T blowing, you're probably not in Wyoming. Well, it was blowing and howling like a banshee when Lexie and Lucy went to clean the First Community Church of the Lamb of God later that morning. Good old Wyoming, Lexie thought wryly, combing her fingers through her mussed ginger curls as they walked through the front doors.

Women were fools to try and have decent hair styles around here. Gusts ripped through fashionable styles like nothing, leaving them in a shambles. No one should ever waste money on big hair in Moose Creek Junction. It wasn't worth it. How amazing Winkie Hightower had done so well as a hair stylist. Lexie figured folks at least liked to maintain the illusion they were getting their tresses dressed.

Lexie looked around the church, half expecting the roof to cave in while she studied the simple lobby furniture and the portraits of Jesus on the walls. It smelled the same as when her father had presided over the congregation—like dust balls and perspiration.

Beyond an arched doorway was the chapel area with a raised dais and the pulpit where her father had given many a sermon. Lexie remembered as a little girl squirming through morning church services every Sunday. Back then, she'd have rather had all her teeth pulled, one by one, than sit through those sessions. She still felt the same way.

"What's wrong?" Lucy asked. "You look like you just saw a ghost."

"I did," Lexie shot back, hiking up the pants on the too-large green sweat suit she'd borrowed from Lucy. "Me. At eight. What a geek."

"You did have some bad teeth," Lucy said. "Thank goodness for braces."

Lexie rolled her eyes at Lucy. "Not everyone was born perfect like you."

"You're just jealous."

Laughing, the sisters retrieved cleaning supplies from a closet in the deacon's room and set to work. While they cleaned, they discussed the townspeople and possible murder suspects among them. They bantered ideas back and forth and discussed minor details. Before long, the grilling process was even more tiring than the housework. Their conversation had covered nearly everyone in Moose Creek Junction by the time they'd finished vacuuming, scrubbing, mopping, and dusting.

Lexie wiped the back of her hand across her

damp forehead. She and Lucy had gone over everything until the chapel, lobby, the classrooms, and the little kitchen were spic and span. Jesus would have been proud. Hopefully, the hypocrites who came every Sunday to wash away their sins would think it was good enough, too.

"Where do we start?" Lucy rubbed a little harder on one of the wooden chapel pews with her polishing cloth, then stood back to inspect her handiwork.

"Start?" Lexie blew hot hair through her teeth. "Aren't we about done?"

Lucy met her gaze. "I mean with your investigation. We flubbed it up the last time. How are we going to do it better?"

"We've reviewed a whole town of suspects, now we need to focus on the most likely ones."

"How?"

Lexie sat down and tapped her fingers on the polished wood. She curled her toes in the too-large sneakers she'd also borrowed from Lucy. "First off, someone murders Hugh, then Henry, and finally Jack. Why?"

"You said Henry smelled awful," Lucy mused.

"I don't think that's enough motive for someone to want to murder him."

"What about Violet? Maybe she was still upset about their divorce."

"Gabe believes the same person who killed Henry also killed Hugh and Jack. Violet wouldn't have a reason to murder any of them."

"Does Detective Stevenson think the same person who killed your dates also ran over Elton? By the way, have you heard how he's doing?"

"Eva told me Elton's recovering nicely. Gabe thinks it was the murderer who ran over Elton."

Lucy lifted a brow. "How come you know so much about what Detective Stevenson thinks? You two seeing each other behind my back?"

"Knock it off, Luce. He mentioned his theory to me when we were in jail."

"Oh."

Lexie wanted to take the heat off her love life before Lucy started in again so she said, "Does Otis have any theories?"

"Not really."

"I bet he's too busy getting ready for the election this month. Right?"

Lucy shrugged. "I won't speak ill of my husband. It's uncharitable."

"I am right. Oh, well. I guess if I had a decent husband like Otis, even if he was a goober, I'd want to stand up for him, too. But I can't even keep a steady date . . ." Lexie snapped her fingers. "That's it!"

"What?" Lucy's eyes opened wide.

"The murdered guys were all dating me."

"What about Elton? You weren't dating him. He was far too young for you, for Pete's sake."

"Gee, thanks, sis."

"I'm just trying to be practical."

"I know, I know. But back to Elton . . . My idea

falls apart with him. Regardless, it's all we've got to go on."

"Someone's killing your dates. A jealous woman?"

"Or a jealous man," Lexie added. "Whoever attacked me at the tavern was big and strong. Someone in man's boots nearly found me hiding in the cellar at Jack's cabin the day he was killed."

"What about Dan?"

"Believe me, I've considered that," Lexie said. "I think Dan's too busy with dizzy Davina and the baby."

"That's right. I forgot the current Mrs. Lightfoot is a new mommy. How lucky for Dan. Changing dirty diapers and doing midnight feedings at his age, for Pete's sake."

"The Undertaker? Get his hands dirty or lose sleep?" Lexie chuckled. "No, he'll have her doing all the hard work."

Lucy removed her apron and sat down beside Lexie, her housedress with the big splashy orange flowers settling around her. "Did you or Dan have any enemies while you were in California? Someone who would be angry enough to come all the way up here to cause you trouble?"

"Not that I know of."

"I don't like this detective business," Lucy said. "It gives me a headache."

"Me, too," Lexie agreed. "I keep thinking about the gambling chip from the Ice Queen Resort I found by Jack's body. I'm convinced our killer has a gambling problem."

"Folks around here say Henry spent plenty of money up there. Probably lots of people around town go up there to gamble."

"Aunt Gladys told me the old gal who got her booted at the Sunrise Center, Alice Leone, is Carma Leone's aunt. She worked up at the Ice Queen for years as a cocktail waitress. She still lives in a trailer up in Snow Village and only comes to Moose Creek Junction to visit Carma once in a while and go to the grocery store."

"Hmm, interesting. I seem to remember Carma mentioning at church that she had an aunt. I didn't realize she lived up there."

Lexie's mind was bursting with ideas. "Remember the dark tinted car I told you about that hit my truck the night Whitehead was killed and has been skulking around my house? It's a fancy sports model, probably way too expensive for anyone around here to afford. A lucky gambler could buy it. Or they might have even won it."

"Definitely possible," Lucy said.

"I think we need to take a trip up the mountain. Especially while Aunt Gladys is at the hospital. When she comes back, I won't be able to get away."

"If I just take off, Otis will suspect we're up to something."

Lexie paced in the oversized sneakers, the gears in her brain spinning. She didn't have a very high opinion of her brother-in-law, but she didn't need to start a family feud. "We won't tell him we're going to the Ice Queen. We'll say we're going to attend the Christian retreat in Burns Valley for the weekend. What's it called?"

"Revelation Camp."

"Tell Otis I've been so stressed I need some time away."

"Where do we get the money for this little expedition, Lex? Otis keeps the checkbook locked up tight and you're not in the best financial position."

Lexie grinned. "Bruce is wiring me more hush money to keep Aunt Gladys, remember? We'll have plenty for a field trip up to the Ice Queen Resort."

Lexie and Lucy spent the rest of the day preparing for their mission. First, Lexie needed some clothes since no one was allowed in her house until the fire inspector had done his report. That might be a few more days and until then, she couldn't keep borrowing Lucy's clothes.

When they'd finished cleaning the church, they drove downtown to the Loose Goose Emporium where clothing was of the L.L. Bean kind. Lexie said, "Hi," to Bertie, who was busy stocking some of her shelves with cans of string beans and peas. She nodded to Violet who sent angry looks her way, but thankfully didn't cause another scene.

Wanting to get underway up the mountain as

soon as possible, Lexie quickly scooped up a couple of pairs of jeans and some plaid flannel shirts, hiking boots, and thick cotton socks. The next item she snagged was a heavy down jacket with red flannel lining and a pair of mittens.

There was still no sign of storms even though they were a couple of weeks into November. The drought had other things on its mind and had changed the weather patterns. By now, they should be knee deep in snow. Still, the weather in Wyoming had always been unpredictable. Folks claimed there were only two seasons: snow and wind. Blink and the weather could change.

After Lexie had changed into a pair of her new jeans and a flannel shirt, Lucy drove them past the Victorian and sat parked across the street for a while, staring at the charred kitchen area jutting out into the dead brown yard. "Who in heaven's name would start a fire in someone's home? It's purely evil." Lucy shook her head. "I'm glad the fire department arrived in time to keep the entire house from burning down."

"I know." Lexie's insides twisted. "A lot of Castleton ancestors would have been rolling over in their graves if the house had gone up in flames. That Victorian is kind of a family heirloom, you know?"

Lucy nodded. "Remember how Grandmother Castleton used to fuss over those roses by the porch? And Mother . . . Her favorites were the tiger lilies. How she babied them. This place was Dad's pride and joy, along with his congregation." Lucy wiped a stray tear with the back of her hand.

"I miss them all, too." Lexie patted Lucy's shoulder. "Sometimes I wish we could go back in time to when we were kids and the grownups took care of everything."

"Wouldn't it be great?"

"If Dad were here now, he'd probably stand up at his pulpit one Sunday and give a lesson about the commandment, 'thou shalt not kill'. If the murderer was in the audience, he or she would feel so guilty they'd stand up and confess."

Lucy smiled.

"We may not be as commanding as Dad, but we'll get to the bottom of this mystery, Lucy, if it's the last thing we do."

"For Pete's sake, I don't want it to be the last thing *I* do." Lucy's eyes flared with concern. "Don't talk like that."

Lexie stared heavenward. "It's just a figure of speech, Luce. You don't need to get your support hose in a twist."

Lucy clutched her orange-flowered abdomen when her stomach growled. "Meanwhile, I'm starving."

"Let's go grab something to eat."

Lexie and Lucy bought wrapped sandwiches and sodas from a vending machine at the Conoco gas station. Lexie wrinkled her nose at the taste: cardboard and rubber. No wonder people had eagerly welcomed her soup and sandwich café. This stuff was rotgut. It sufficed to silence the stomach growls while they prepared for their mission.

The next stop was the bank where Lexie collected Cousin Bruce's donation to the cause and deposited it in her account. She would have much preferred Bruce come home and take care of his mother. That wasn't likely to happen any time soon. Since she was in no financial position to pretend she didn't need the cash, she decided she would spend it wisely and try to make Aunt Gladys happy.

Lucy was surprised at the large amount he'd wired, but Lexie wasn't. How much did it cost to ease a guilty conscience these days?

Since her cell phone was still at the house charging in its little stand, she used Lucy's to call Eva. She must have been in class, so Lexie left her the message she and Lucy were going to Revelation Camp on a three-day retreat. She also instructed Eva to please call the hospital every day to visit with Aunt Gladys.

Lucy drove them to the Westonville hospital to see Aunt Gladys before they left. The old gal was sitting up in the bed watching television, but her complexion was pale. She was attached to monitors and had breathing tubes in her nose. She'd apparently managed to convince an attendant to purchase some gift shop items for her.

She wore red lipstick and bright spots of apple-shaped rouge on her cheeks. Her mystery shopper had also found a pair of chunky purple earrings, several gold clinking bracelets, and a paisley bed jacket, all of which Aunt Gladys wore with her typical regal confidence. To top off her ensemble, someone had even painted her nails a hot pink.

No doubt dressing up, despite the circumstances, was meant to impress the man who'd come to visit. Frenchie sat next to her in a comfortable-looking hospital chair with a footrest, reading a magazine called, *The Millionaire's Guide to Money Investments*.

He smiled at the sisters and put down his reading material. "I came as soon as I heard about the fire," he explained. "I had to make sure my little sugar bun was all right."

"Winkie's already been here," Aunt Gladys said. "He brought those. Everyone's been so nice." She pointed at the bouquet of mixed wildflowers on a nightstand. "Frenchie brought these." She nodded toward a vase on the other nightstand that looked like, and probably was, cut crystal. It was full of at least a dozen deep red roses with perfect petals.

"Thank you for coming, Mr. Duckworth," Lexie said.

"Of course," he said.

Lexie and Lucy, who was holding the vase of flowers they'd purchased downstairs in the gift shop, exchanged knowing glances. They both knew their floral arrangement didn't hold a candle to either Winkie or Frenchie's bouquets. Lucy quietly set the pink carnations and daisies on another table.

"Thank you for the flowers, girls. How did you

know pink carnations are my favorite?" Aunt Gladys coughed, holding a lacy-edged hankie to her mouth. "The most wonderful thing has happened. Frenchie has offered to let me stay at his house after I get out of here. What do you two think?" She looked adoringly at the leprechaun fellow seated next to her.

Lexie couldn't even process the idea of Aunt Gladys living with Frenchie. She sat down in a molded plastic chair beside Aunt Gladys and took one of her age-spotted hands. "We'll talk about it later."

Aunt Gladys wrinkled her brow. "Has anyone called Bruce? He should know what's going on. I have no idea where to reach him. Isn't he over in one of those countries where they eat dogs?"

Lexie and Lucy exchanged another glance. "I got a hold of him," Lexie said. "He's worried sick about you. He'll come as soon as he can. But he's in the middle of a big business deal so it could be a while."

Aunt Gladys silently nodded and laid her curly white head back against the pillows. Lexie could tell by her aunt's pursed lips she was disappointed. Bruce is a rat fink, Lexie thought. Shame on him.

"How is the hospital treating you?" Lucy asked Aunt Gladys, thankfully changing the subject as she dragged another chair next to the bed.

"They say my lungs aren't clear yet and they are worried about my blood pressure. I told them it was Frenchie here who got me all excited but they didn't buy it." She winked at him. "I'll be staying for a while longer."

"The doctors will take good care of you," Lucy said.

"I'm bored," Aunt Gladys said. "I'm so sorry about the fire. I really think the boy-man is responsible. I warned you about him."

"I'm sure it was faulty wiring," Lexie told her, though in her heart she knew it was arson. "The house is old."

Later, when Aunt Gladys nodded off while they watched television, Lexie whispered to Lucy they needed to be on their way.

Lucy stood and picked up her purse.

"Please let Aunt Gladys know we'll be gone for a couple of days," Lexie told Frenchie as she pushed to her feet.

Lucy wrote down her cell phone number on a piece of paper and handed it to him. "If something comes up, call us."

Frenchie nodded. "Don't worry, I'll keep an eye out for Gladys. She's kind of special to me."

"We appreciate it," Lexie returned.

By the time they drove into Lucy's gravel driveway, Otis' sheriff's car was parked in the garage. *Otis.* Explaining their little excursion to him was not going to be fun. The sisters found him plopped in front of the TV with a remote in one hand and a can of beer in the other. Lucy explained they were going to a retreat in Burns Valley and, surprisingly, he didn't question them. He merely grunted and kept his balding noggin focused on the screen.

Lexie's internal alarms flared. Her brother-in-law seemed way too interested in whether the Broncos would win against the Green Bay Packers. That meant once he processed Lucy was leaving him to deal with the big bad world on his own for a while, there would be hell to pay.

After dinner, the sisters went up to Lucy's bedroom where she packed a suitcase full of housedresses, girdles, support hose, and sturdy waffle-heeled shoes. Lexie spread out her purchases from the Loose Goose on Lucy's bed and stuffed a few items into the blue athletic bag she'd purchased.

Suddenly Lucy turned to Lexie with a look of surprise. "My goodness, what car are we going to drive? Someone might recognize mine."

"My bucket of rust is out of the question," Lexie said. "It'd die trying to climb the mountain."

Lucy's expression was skeptical. "I don't think this will work, Lexie."

"Wait a minute now. Don't back out on me. What about the used car dealership where Carl works? Could he loan us a vehicle?"

"Hmmm. It's possible. Let me check." Lucy picked up the phone and called her son.

As Lexie tucked away a few new cosmetics she'd purchased, along with new toothbrush and toothpaste, she heard bits and snatches of Lucy's conversation.

Finally Lucy hung up and turned to her. "Carl really wants to help us, but he said his boss would have a cow if we borrowed one of the cars on the lot."

"Crap," Lexie said.

"Language, sister dear."

"Sorry."

"Carl said someone just traded in a van Big Daddy hasn't seen yet. He said we might be able use that."

"Big Daddy?"

"That's his boss. He owns Big Daddy's Used Vehicles."

"Ah hah. I see."

"Carl says to come by Big Daddy's about ten o'clock tomorrow morning and he'll 'hook us up with some wheels'."

Lexie put her hands on her hips. "Looks like we're ready to rock."

Otis was his usual grumpy, unpleasant self the next day as he shoveled Lucy's breakfast of eggs, bacon, and sliced cantaloupe down his craw, followed by about a gallon of coffee. It seemed he'd had time to process the fact his wife wouldn't be around for the next few days to answer his beck and call. He was not happy and let the sisters know it by the way he slammed down his silverware and glared around the table.

Still out of sorts, he helped Lexie and Lucy load their luggage for the trip. Grumbling under his breath with a toothpick between his teeth, he checked the oil on Lucy's car and kicked the tires.

"This is a shitty time to be leaving, Lucy, with the election and all. I need you here. Taking off like this is plain selfish."

Lucy winced at the emotional blackmail. "It's just a couple of days, Otis. You'll be fine. Call me on my cell if you need anything."

He ran his hand through the sparse fringe of hair he had left around the edges of his head. "You'll be miles from here. How can you help me?"

Lucy shot Lexie a pleading look.

Lexie, who was feeling guilty, shrugged. How do you deal with a grown man who whines like a baby because he can't deal with the real world on his own? Otis barked and snarled a lot at people, but inside he was a scared little man who couldn't do much of anything without his wife's help. He couldn't even see what a petty fool he was acting like.

Patootie head.

"Come on, Otis grow a pair," Lexie commented, in a braver tone than she felt. "You're all grown up now and the boogie man won't get you if Lucy leaves for a couple of days. Besides, how would you like your voters to know their trusty sheriff can't even make his own breakfast or wash the skid marks out of his shorts?"

He immediately turned a bright tomato red that clashed with his tan uniform. "I still think the two of you taking off to a Bible thumper rally is pretty shitty." He spit the toothpick from his mouth for emphasis. "But go on. Don't let me interfere."

"See you in a couple of days, Sheriff Parnell." Lexie crawled in Lucy's car and shut the door. To hell with him, she thought as she brushed off her jeans. She was getting to the bottom of these murders once and for all. No one, not even her whiny brother-in-law, was going to stop her.

Once they were on the highway, Lexie said, "I'm sorry we had to lie to Otis, Lucy."

"It's not him I'm worried about so much," she said stiltedly, her hands white-knuckled as she gripped the steering wheel. "We've just told a whopper of a lie. Lies in my book are about as bad as murder."

"Lucy, don't you know the difference between white lies and malicious lies?"

"Lies are lies. God hates all liars." Lucy glared at her.

"This lie may just save my life."

Lucy relaxed her tensed shoulders. "That will be the one saving grace. Regardless, I'll still be repenting of this lie for years to come."

Lexie turned to watch the passing landscape filled with brown rolling hills and dark skeletal trees that had lost their brilliant autumn leaves. It was dreary and dry in this part of Wyoming, adding to her current state of depression.

Maybe she'd pushed Lucy too far. Maybe she should have gone up to the Ice Queen Resort on her own to snoop around. Lucy had insisted on going with her. It was a catch twenty-two situation. Whatever, she thought to herself, using one of Eva's favorite phrases.

When they reached Big Daddy's, she studied the sea of vehicles in the lot with prices painted across their windshields. Flags of orange, red, and yellow were strung out to utility poles. Standing guard above it all, a statue of a cowboy wearing enormous chaps clutched a sign that said: Howdy Pardner.

It positively reeked of cornball and hillbilly, but this was the only place Carl could find a job after he'd graduated from high school. And far be it from Aunt Lexie to make any derogatory comments about her nephew. The kid had to start somewhere, and since his dream was to eventually buy the car dealership from Big Daddy, she figured the time he spent here was an investment in his future.

Lucy parked and the sisters dodged a couple of gangly, hungry-looking salesmen as they walked toward the office located in a small trailer. Stepping onto the rickety wooden porch, Lexie noticed two planters in the shape of cowboy boots. The stone containers held skeletal Mugo pines. Looked like Big Daddy needed to do more watering.

"Watch out for Mitzi," Lucy said in a hushed voice, her hand gripping the doorknob. "She's a vicious snake. She'll snap your head off given the chance."

"Who's she?"

"Big Daddy's daughter. She works in the office. Or rather, she paints her toe nails in the office. Unfortunately, she and Carl were dating, last I heard."

Lucy opened the door and they walked inside.

Garish red carpet covered the floors and dinged-up Venetian blinds hung lopsided at the windows. A young woman with big blond hair and large hoop earrings sat in the corner. The smell of cheap nail polish, strong perfume, and bad coffee hung in the air as Mitzi, one long leg propped up on an old metal desk, painted her toe nails a ruby red color that matched the carpet.

The first thing that came to Lexie's mind to describe Mitzi was: vicious poodle woman. She was the type of girl Aunt Gladys would call a chippie, especially since rumor had it she danced topless at her other job. Lexie folded her arms across her chest and watched what was certain to be a curious exchange.

Finally taking notice of people in the office, Mitzi popped her gum and rose, bouncing out from behind the gray monstrosity. Black vinyl slacks clung to her youthful thighs and she wore a bright red and very revealing sweater that would have made Daisy Duke blush.

"Big Daddy ain't here and the assistant manager's busy in his office," she said importantly. "You gals want somethin'?"

Lucy cleared her throat, obviously trying to squelch her disgust. "I'm here to see Carl."

Mitzi popped her gum again and batted her false eyelashes. "You got an appointment?"

"He's my son." Lucy gave Mitzi a stern look. "And he's expecting me."

"Oh, howdy, Miz Parnell. Long time, no see,"

Mitzi drawled. "Sorry I didn't recognize you in that dress. Them flowers on it are awfully big."

Lucy ignored her. "Please tell Carl I'm here."

"You two can have a seat if you like while I go get him."

Lexie glanced at a dusty black leather couch strewn with rumpled newspapers and wadded up napkins. The coffee table held the remains of an old doughnut and its accompanying crumbs along with several dog-eared magazines and a sad looking Boston fern, also in dire need of water.

She and Lucy exchanged a glance.

"No, thank you," Lucy told Mitzi.

"Sure." Mitzi popped her gum again and shimmied her curvy little backside down the hallway. She returned a few moments later walking closely beside Carl, her big, doe eyes staring worshipfully at Big Daddy's assistant manager.

Carl's wavy chestnut hair had the same texture as his mother's and it was the color of Otis's back in his younger days. When he still had hair. Carl also had an athletic build that would put Adonis to shame. He was a handsome young man. No wonder Mitzi the poodle was hanging onto him for dear life.

"Mom," Carl said and walked over to give his mother a hug. "And Aunt Lexie." He hugged her also. "What's up? You two have been keeping to yourselves lately."

"There's been a lot going on, dear." She glanced at Mitzi, then back at her son. "Can we talk privately somewhere?"

"Let's go outside," he said.

When Mitzi started to follow them out the door, he turned to her and said, "Stay and listen for the phones, Mitzi."

Her lavishly made up face fell. "But—"

"I'm expecting a call from a very important customer, sweetie. Be a nice secretary and listen up for him, OK? You'd be doing me a huge favor."

She grinned broadly. "Of course, Carl." Twirling, she flounced back to her seat and plopped down.

Outside the trailer office at the feet of the giant cowboy, Lucy took her son's arm. "Please tell me you two aren't still seeing each other."

Carl glanced around to make sure no one was listening. "I know Mitzi can't add two-plus-two, Mom. But she is the boss's daughter. I have to be nice."

"Do you have to date her, for Pete's sake?"

He shrugged. "Once you get to know her, she's not so bad."

Lexie, who had been quietly standing by, imagined Carl was thinking if he married Mitzi and became Big Daddy's son-in-law, he'd stand a better chance of inheriting the dealership. He wasn't such a dumb kid, but sacrificing himself to Mitzi the poodle was a pretty big move. It would be interesting to see what the future held.

"What's up with you two?" Carl walked them past rows of vehicles. "Why do you need to borrow a car?"

"It's a long story," Lucy said. "I'll let your Aunt Lexie explain."

They stopped beside a small red Miata with a ragtop and Lexie told Carl from start to finish about the murders, the threats on her life, and finally the fire and how the police even seemed stumped. She could feel perspiration clamming up her skin by the time she'd finished telling her story. Either the sweatshirt she'd worn was too heavy in the warm autumn sunshine, or she was nervous. Either way, she wished she didn't have to do this.

"Your mother and I need to go up to the Ice Queen Resort and check out some leads," Lexie said. "I'm tired of waiting for the cops to do their job."

"It's not smart to interfere in police business," Carl said. "I can't believe Dad agreed to this nonsense."

Lucy put a hand on Carl's arm. "Your father doesn't know. We told him we were going up to a religious retreat in Burns Valley. You *have* to keep this quiet."

Carl groaned. "Dad's not going to like it."

"It's not up to him," Lexie said. "Besides, he's busy with the election. He doesn't need to know anything."

Carl scratched his head. "You two have no clue what you're getting into."

"We'll be careful," Lexie promised. "We need a different car to drive up the mountain so we won't be recognized."

"The police are probably working as hard as they

can on the murders," Carl warned. "They don't always tell everything otherwise it might compromise the case. If you two go snooping around, it could make things worse."

"What could be worse?" Lexie exclaimed. "Aunt Gladys is already in the hospital and someone nearly burned down the café Someone obviously wants me dead."

"I understand you two are wigged out, but it's pretty hare brained to chase after dangerous criminals."

"We're only trying to get information to help the police," Lexie said. "I think they'll appreciate it in the long run."

"Damn," Carl said after a few minutes of stewing. "I shouldn't do this, but I'm going to. I'll loan you a vehicle. I'm warning you though, it's not the fanciest transportation."

"Doesn't matter," Lexie said. "We need wheels."

Carl directed them down another row of cars and into a large, dirty white garage where the clank of tools and buzzing equipment punctuated the air. Greasy men worked diligently on all makes and models of cars, rotating tires, doing bodywork, and changing oil. Carl led them past the busy mechanics and up to a van parked in a stall.

Lexie's jaw dropped as she stared at it. The first thing that came into her mind was the old hot dog commercial and the accompanying jingle. *Oh, I wish I were an Oscar Mayer weiner . . .*

The vehicle, originally white, had been painted

with murals of cookies, doughnuts, bags of peanuts, popcorn, and every type of junk food imaginable on the planet. The most outstanding food of all rested on top of the unsuspecting van. A giant hot dog sat nestled in a bun, complete with mustard, ketchup, and relish. It must have been three feet long, Lexie figured.

"Oh, my Lord," Lucy muttered, her face drained of color.

"I told you it was bad." Carl knitted his brows.

"It's perfect." Lexie shoved her hands on her hips. "How well does it run?"

"She's still in pretty good shape. She'll get you up the mountain."

"That's all we need," Lexie said.

"It's hideous," Lucy complained.

Lexie turned to her sister. "Look at it this way. Who would ever believe it was the two of us riding around in a weiner-mobile?"

Lucy groaned. "For Pete's sake, the things you get me into."

CHAPTER 19

THE WEINER-MOBILE WAS THE PITS, BUT LEXIE, who had opted to drive, wasn't about to admit it.

It could definitely have used more soup, more squirrels or something under the hood. It ran like a little old lady in a marathon, chugging slowly up the mountain past meadows, spruce and pine trees and aspen groves in fading autumn hues of russet, orange and brownish yellow. The mountains in the distance seemed light years away.

Lexie ignored the strange stares and glares of fellow travelers when they pulled around and zipped past the hot dog truck. "Rubberneckers," Lexie grumbled. So what if their mode of transportation was somewhat questionable. It was none of their business. When a man in a hunting cap roared past in an old Ram Charger shaking his fist at them, Lexie stuck out her tongue.

"Alexandria Kathleen," Lucy barked. "You're going to get us in trouble. Ever heard of road rage?"

Lexie shrugged. It wasn't a terribly long drive up the mountain, but she was anxious. The bottom of the van might drop out at any minute. Then they'd really be in trouble. Hopefully, they'd make it safely to their destination. *Please.* To pass the time, she counted sagebrush and antelope. The herds thinned out as the weiner-mobile climbed lofty heights to the Ice Queen Resort, leaving sagebrush the winner in Lexie's counting contest.

On the passenger side, Lucy sat ramrod straight, looking neither right nor left. As though if she moved, something would jump out at her and attack. Lexie knew exactly what was bugging her. Lucy regretted lying to Otis. To top it off, she was going to spend time at a gambling resort. Two major sins committed in one day.

No doubt Sister Lucy would have a stiff penance to pay once she confessed her transgressions to Reverend Lincolnway. He might even take away her church-cleaning privileges.

Lexie glanced at her long-suffering sister. "Are you all right? Do we need to stop so you can stretch your legs?"

"Keep driving. I want to get this over with." Lucy set her mouth in a firm line.

"You look like you swallowed a skunk."

"I might as well have," Lucy said. "I feel sick to my stomach. It smells like stale ketchup and mustard in here."

The nose knows.

Lexie wasn't aware that ketchup had a smell. "We're almost there—"

"Stop!" Lucy shouted, her face white as cauliflower.

"But—"

"Now!"

When Lucy clamped a hand over her mouth, Lexie quickly veered onto the shoulder. After the van had rolled to a halt, Lucy jumped out, leaving the door swinging. Lexie watched as she hustled her support-hosed legs through the brush and finally leaned over a bush, her shoulders heaving.

Lexie winced. *Now she's really going to be pissed about coming up here.*

A few minutes later, Lucy climbed back in the van and slammed the door. She pulled a wet wipe from her purse and washed her face and mouth, then popped a breath mint onto her tongue. Leaning back, she rested her head against the seat.

"Are you all right?"

"This hot dog van is completely ridiculous. I may have to walk the rest of the way."

Lexie bit her lower lip. "It's not much further. Can you hang on?"

Lucy sighed. "God help me, I'll try."

The silence between the sisters was intense as Lexie drove on. Finally, she rounded a bend and drove into Rawhide City. *Only a few miles more,* Lexie thought. *Any longer and Sister Lucy might just kill me before anyone else gets the chance.*

Rawhide City was a typical mining town from the 1880s. False front buildings had been restored along with solid brick buildings of the era, complete with gingerbread outcroppings. These sentinels of yesteryear lined the narrow streets, teasing tourists with promises of antiques, tourist gadgets, and gambling parlors. Everything in the town was Old West themed and Lexie knew the city council along with the historic preservation society reviewed every new business' building plans to make sure all structures retained the flair of Rawhide City's frontier beginnings.

The town itself had not started with such careful planning. Initially, prospectors had climbed up to the remote spot and searched for gold, finding only small amounts, but staying around long enough to establish mercantiles, bars, and blacksmith shops.

One die-hard, Potato Creek Tommy, despite many grubstakes, hadn't been so lucky at the start of his mining career. He spent years looking for the mother lode and had only come up with small bags of gold dust. Tommy never found that elusive gold. He did find a silver vein and became an instant millionaire.

Like many successful prospectors who hit pay dirt, he bought himself a mansion in Rawhide City and imported only the finest food and wine for his dinner table. However, he had an eye for ladies of the evening and spent a large portion of his fortune on the sporting houses on Hobble Street. Eventually, he irritated the wrong person and wound up getting himself shot at the Thin Dollar Saloon. By that time, he'd nearly spent himself broke.

It was your typical rags-to-riches-to-rags story and Potato Creek Tommy was only one example of a miner who got caught up in the glamour of a high lifestyle and fast women, only to lose all his hard-earned cash and ultimately his life. The sad scenario happened over and over in mining towns across the West.

Rawhide City relied on gambling casinos and tourist shops to stay alive. It also served skiers from the Ice Queen Resort a short distance up the gulch. The atmosphere was charming and yuppie. People came from miles around to vacation, either for the gambling or for winter and summer sports.

The typical tourist season ended in October, so it was quieter this time of the year. People browsed the shops and wandered into gambling establishments, but not the surging crowds usually associated with summer.

"Dens of iniquity," Lucy muttered as she looked at casinos lining the narrow street.

Lexie noticed a café called the Buffalo Steak House. "Want to stop and rest? You still don't look so good."

Lucy shook her head. "No. Keep driving through this heathenish place. The sooner we get this trip over with, the better I'll feel."

Lexie wondered how someone born and raised in Moose Creek Junction could be so snobby. It was amazing to think her sister was also married to Otis Parnell who could win a Corny Sheriff of the Year award hands down. Not to mention her son worked for Big Daddy's where a giant cowboy statue stood sentinel and big-haired Mitzi smacked her gum as she answered the phone and painted her nails blood red.

Oh, well. That was Lucy.

Lexie tooled the van higher up the mountain toward the Ice Queen Resort. She shifted the weiner-mobile into a lower gear. Ignoring the alarming whine and click the engine emitted, she concentrated on the road that climbed past dilapidated mine shafts planted on the reddish brown hills.

Groves of aspen with sparse, rusty orange leaves dotted the mountain ridges like melted butter, interspersed with spruce and pine trees and old cabins with mossy, caved-in roofs.

Crazy Woman Creek, which crossed Potato Creek further up the gulch, gurgled at the bottom of the ravine lining the steep, narrow road. Ancient tailings raised mounds along the water's edge. Lexie could tell by the old waterline the creek was down, no doubt because of the drought. A prick of alarm touched her, but what could she, a mere human do against the ravages of nature? Nothing.

So, Miss Know-It-All, what do you think you are going to do about a crazed murderer? Lexie shrugged off the unsettling thought.

"For Pete's sake." Lucy vigorously rubbed her ears with her fingers. "My ears are ringing."

"Mine, too," Lex agreed. "It's the altitude. Swallow hard a few times."

The sisters began a swallowing session during which they both admitted their ears had "popped" and felt better. Lucy rescued gum from her purse and they chomped and swallowed, chomped and swallowed.

While concentrating on pushing her tongue into a gum bubble, Lexie noticed the line of vehicles stuck behind them. Too bad, so sad. What was she supposed to do? There was no making this beast of a van go any faster and she couldn't pull over. She did her best to ignore them until the road leveled out.

They dropped into a broad bowl of land where the Ice Queen Resort, a large brick edifice with pine shutters, wooden porches, and railings dominated the grassy meadow. The Grand Tetons rose in the distance, ringing the resort with mountain majesty. Lexie noted the drought had been just as severe up here.

Dry brown ski runs slashed down the slopes next to areas clotted with dry, scrubby bushes, stands of aspen and the usual pines and spruce. Only a few dirty patches of snow had accumulated in hollows of ground. It was not a good sign for the economic hopes of the ski resort. Last year had been bad, and this year it looked like it could be worse. It was November. The resort should be knee deep in snow. However, it looked like the South Dakota badlands.

Off in the distance she could see the rooftops of Snow Village, a small town that had grown up around the Ice Queen Resort. Kind of like a castle with a village where all the commoners lived to serve the royal skiers, Lexie thought. Most of the resort staff and their families lived in Snow Village in modest clapboard homes and trailers. They went to Rawhide City for groceries and supplies, or to visit the small medical clinic. If they needed anything more substantial like new furniture or clothing, they drove to Moose Creek Junction or Westonville.

As if she, too, were thinking about the drought and its devastating effects on the mountain resort, Lucy pointed to some purple clouds mounding over the Tetons. "There's a storm brewing."

Lexie nodded. "That would be good for everyone. We haven't had any decent snow in . . . how many years?"

"Not since you moved back," Lucy said.

When Lexie pulled the chugging van off the main road and drove toward the hotel, the line of cars and trucks behind her quickly motored ahead and a few people honked.

"Ah, get over yourselves," Lexie complained. "People are always in such a blasted hurry." She pulled under the wooden awning at the front of the hotel and parked. "We may not have had the fanciest vehicle to drive up here in, but thanks to Bruce's guilt money, we can . . ."

Lexie trailed off, unable to believe what she saw.

Lucy raised a concerned brow. "What's wrong?"

Lexie pointed. "That's the car that's been following me!"

"Heaven's to Betsy." Lucy looked at it parked

by the curb for a minute, then fumbled in her purse and produced a pen and a notepad. "Pull over there and let me write down the license plate. Detective Stevenson and Otis might be angry at us for coming here, but at least we'll bring home something for them to investigate."

Anxiety niggled at Lexie as she and Lucy settled into their room. Neither she nor Lucy wanted dinner. Lucy's stomach was still upset and Lexie's mind was definitely not on food. She wanted to march right in to the hotel staff and see if they could track down who owned the mysterious car parked out front.

Then she wanted to confront the individual and demand they explain why they'd been following her. Was he or she responsible for the murders? The personal attacks on her life? The fire at her home?

Going up to someone and asking if they were a killer would not be wise. It would be crazy.

As Lexie and Lucy unpacked their belongings, Lexie's mind worked overtime. She remembered the day when she and Lucy had talked to the insurance company about the café fire. It might be some time before they got reimbursed for the damage. After that, it would also take a while for them to get the fire damage repaired and get the café up and running. What she would do with herself and Aunt Gladys in the meantime was the question. On a final note, there was the dilemma of Aunt Gladys wanting to move in with Frenchie.

Brother.

Lexie's head started to ache. It was too much to think about. She'd have to sort it all out later. The first order of the day, she told herself, was to snoop around. She and Lucy had already located the mysterious car that had been following her. There was no telling what else they might find to help with the murder investigation.

"Let's go check out the casino," Lexie suggested.

"That den of iniquity," Lucy said with a sniff. "You know Daddy would have a fit if he knew we were here."

"Dad always said God gave us brains to think and to help ourselves. He would understand we drove up here for a good reason. It's not to gamble our lives away."

"Oh, very well." Lucy set her lips in a frown.

Downstairs, as they walked through heavy wooden double doors into the casino, Lexie heard the loud *ka-ching* of gambling machines and the rat-a-tat-tat sound of coins spitting into metal trays.

"For Pete's sake." Lucy stopped in her tracks. "This is sin at its worst."

"Not everyone thinks like you do," Lexie said. "Relax. You don't have to convert anyone here. Come on." Lexie took Lucy's arm and pulled her forward.

The casino had been decorated with a mining theme. Train tracks lined the periphery of the inside walls and antique ore cars along with a couple of narrow gauge trains dotted the rails. The walls themselves had been given a *faux* cave-like appearance to replicate the inside of a mine and rusty tin candleholders clung to the rock, giving off dim electric light. Huge wagon wheel chandeliers hung from the ceiling, illuminating the gambling area.

Banks of one-armed bandits, lights flashing, swallowed up the gambling pit. People sat on high-backed stools in front of Game Kings and other machines plugging dollars, quarters, dimes, and nickels into slots. Lexie noticed one man in particular sitting in a wheelchair smoking a cigarette. Oxygen tubes were threaded up into his nose and a canister of oxygen perched next to him. Funny he didn't blow himself up.

Most of the gamblers stared stone-faced at the readouts on the machines. Not being familiar with the gambling life, Lexie was amazed at the intensity with which everyone pursued their sport.

Bells chimed and wild musical jingles clanged as individuals, old and young, held out hopes for hitting the jackpot. Cocktail waitresses in short skirts and fishnet stockings meandered past stony-eyed patrons, bringing drinks and emptying ashtrays. Cleaning staff quietly wiped down and swept up messy areas and tellers in cash cages handed out money to lines of customers.

Lucy dug in her purse and fished out her fan. She swooshed it back and forth in front of her bright red cheeks.

Hot flash, Lexie thought. "Are you all right?"

"For Pete's sake, no," Lucy said. "I told you this was an awful place. I'm burning up."

"Why don't you go back to the room and rest?" Lexie suggested.

"Over my dead body."

As Lexie and Lucy passed by rows of machines, Lexie was amazed. She'd heard that for some people, gambling wasn't simply a pleasant hobby. They were addicted. Elderly people actually blew entire social security checks on the habit and young parents spent grocery money that should have gone to feed their kids. Sad, but true.

Lexie and Lucy both turned to look at one lady who was sobbing so loudly she could be heard over the casino clamor.

"Who cries at a casino?" Lucy asked.

Lexie shrugged. "Let's go see."

They walked around a bank of machines toward the woman who wore a purple silk blouse, a tan leather skirt and high-heeled boots, all expensive looking. She sat in front of a dollar machine with Elvira, Mistress of the Dark depicted on the front. The woman's shoulders heaved tragically; sorrowful gulps tore from her throat, and she'd covered her face with her hands.

"Excuse me," Lexie said when they walked up to her. "Are you all right?"

The woman moved her hands away from her

eyes, but not completely away from her face. Her eyes were red and swollen from crying and black mascara smudges gave her a raccoon-ish appearance. She made a surprised squeak, slid off her stool and stood, knocking over her plastic cup that spilled a couple of quarters on the plush carpet. Hands still covering her face, she stumbled down past the bank of machines and out of sight.

Lexie furrowed her brow. Something about the woman intrigued her. Maybe it was the hands with the perfectly manicured red nails, or the sleek black hair combed back in a ponytail. Lexie wasn't sure.

Lexie and Lucy exchanged awkward glances.

"I swear that was Carma Leone." Lucy fanned herself furiously again.

"I thought she looked familiar." Lexie planted her hands on her hips. "She was obviously upset. I wonder what she's doing up here?"

"Maybe she's visiting her Aunt Alice.."

"Possibly. Did I tell you she was the old dingbat who got Aunt Gladys tossed from the Sunrise Center?"

"I don't remember." Lucy rubbed her forehead. "Lexie, let's call it a night. I have a bad headache and my bunions are killing me."

"I want to look around a little more."

Lucy sneezed and pulled a lace-edged hankie from her housedress. "The cigarette smoke in here is kicking up my allergies, too. Please, let's go back upstairs."

Lexie shook her head. "You go on. I'll be up in

a bit." She fingered the gambling chip in her pocket, wondering what in the world she'd been thinking to drag Lucy up here. She should have turned the chip over to the police, not try and be a super sleuth on her own. She had no idea how to go about this sort of thing.

"Are you sure you'll be all right?" Lucy dabbed at her watering eyes and coughed.

"I'll be fine."

"Don't be gone too long or I'll worry." Lucy shuffled over to the elevator and disappeared inside.

Curious, Lexie decided to visit the blackjack tables. She knew absolutely nothing about gambling. It had been strictly forbidden in the Castleton home.

Lexie's father had warned his congregation about the sins of gambling and drinking. He refused to allow his daughters to be subjected to any of those vices. His rules had been strictly enforced. The Castleton home never had a deck of cards or a pair of dice.

Lexie wasn't gambling. She would remain an interested observer. She dodged bodies and got slammed into once or twice by people with zombie-like stares before finally reaching the gaming area. Men and women from all walks of life leaned over green felt tables, placing bets with live dealers in tuxedos, versus computerized video poker.

None of it made a lick of sense to Lexie. People pushed chips, like the one in her pocket, toward the dealer. Anxiously, they awaited the fateful roll of the dice. Only one happy person would win, after which the remaining players would slurp their drinks and grumble to each other. On the next round they tapped their cards and nodded at the dealer again.

This is pointless, Lexie told herself, tucking her hair behind her ears. Wandering around staring at blackjack players would prove nothing. She'd have to question someone. See if they could offer useful information. Otherwise, the whole trip had been a waste of time and Lucy would be right. She was forever getting into ridiculous situations for no good reason.

She thought of the hell she'd been through the last months with people around her being murdered, the police considering her a possible suspect and getting attacked herself. The café fire was another painful reminder her life had become a fiasco. Eva and her Aunt Gladys, innocent bystanders to all of it, could be hurt or worse if something wasn't done to stop the nonsense. Unfortunately, her foray into the detective business hadn't proven very productive.

What did she know about conducting an investigation, anyway? She must have been out of her mind to cook up the scheme in the first place.

Lexie noticed at one table the dealer was being relieved by a new one. When the dealer stepped away from the table, probably to take a break, she made a beeline in his direction and tapped him on the shoulder. He was an older gentleman, probably in his fifties. His graying sideburns and dark hair were streaked with silver and white. Lord, he must have stood seven feet tall.

"Sir?" Lexie tilted her head back to look up at him.

He turned and looked around, completely missing her, a perplexed expression on his face.

Lexie's cheeks burned with embarrassment and she tapped his arm. "Down here," she said, feeling like Thumbelina.

His glance grazed across her ample chest. "Yes?"

Lexie spoke loud so Mr. Friendly could hear her up in the ether zone. "May I ask you a few questions?"

"Why? Are you a reporter? I hate reporters." He glanced around.

Probably expects me to have a camera, Lexie thought. "I had a friend who used to come up here to gamble," she said quickly. "It's possible you might have met him."

"Why do you want to know?" One of Mr. Friendly's bushy brows lifted.

She cleared her throat. "He was murdered."

The man held up a hand. "Whoa. Are you a cop, or something? No comment." He turned and swiftly walked away.

Frustrated but determined, Lexie took long strides to catch up. "I'm not a cop," she insisted. "My friend's name was Henry Whitehead."

He stopped and gave her a thunderous look. "What do you want from me?"

"Did you ever talk to Henry? Did he ever mention an argument with someone in the casino? Maybe another player was angry with him—"

"Look, lady. There are plenty of folks who come up here and I never get their names. They drink, they smoke, they blow entire paychecks. It's their business. Usually, they aren't in a mood to mingle." He stalked off shaking his head.

Lexie felt like a fool. So what if Whitehead had made enemies up here? What did that have to do with Hugh Glenwood and Jack Sturgeon's murders? Elton's accident and the attacks against her?

What a stupid idea to come up here. Sometimes life, as her daughter would have said, was a total suck fest.

A deep weariness sank into her soul as she dragged herself to the elevators and pressed the up arrow. Inside, she punched the cherry floor button. Each floor of the hotel had been assigned a fruit, like the ones on gambling machines: grapes, lemons, watermelons, etc.

As the elevator swooshed upward, Lexie contemplated how she would admit defeat to her sister. It had been a waste of time to drag Lucy here in the weiner-mobile, sucking rancid ketchup and mustard fumes all the way. She had been out of her mind to think they could solve anything. Who did she think they were, anyway?

Starsky and Hutch?

Once the elevator reached her floor, she plodded down the hall and stood in front of the door to her and Lucy's room. With a sigh, she produced her card key. As she shoved it into the thin slot, the door swung wide. What was going on? Lucy wouldn't leave the door open like that.

"Lucy?" Lexie called as she entered the dark room. No answer. She ran her hand over the wall, looking in vain for a light switch. Her heart pounded a warning in her ears. Something was definitely not right.

"Lucy what's going on? Are you in here? Is everything all—"

Whack!

Something slammed against the back of Lexie's head. Dizzy and in excruciating pain, she stumbled forward, crumpling to her hands and knees. Funny, she didn't see birds circling her head, like in the cartoons. Her temples pinged with clawing sparks and pain gripped her senses.

In the darkness, she could barely see something stretched out in front of her. Reaching out, she groped it with her fingers.

Arms . . . a body . . . and legs encased like sausage in support hose.

"Oh, God . . . Lucy!"

Another crack on the back of Lexie's skull sent her tumbling into complete blackness.

Then there was nothing.

CHAPTER 20

I'M COLD. I CAN'T MOVE MY FINGERS. I CAN'T move at all. And, oh, my God, my head hurts.

Remember those old Salem witch trials where villagers weighted down the accused with a door covered in a ton of rocks? That's what it feels like.

What happened? What do I remember?

The café. My murdered dates, my ruined business, the fire at my house, the trip to the Ice Queen Resort. I went back to my room and someone clobbered me hard.

Lucy . . . is she all right? Oh, God. It's all my fault.

Lexie opened her sticky eyes and lifted her head despite the terrible pain. She blinked, attempting to focus. She tried to lift a hand. Impossible. Despite her impaired vision, she eventually fathomed the fact she was sitting tied to a chair.

Something moved in front of her and she shook her head to clear it. Finally the blinking and shaking worked and the room came into view. It was a musty old cabin, possibly one of those she'd seen along Crazy Woman Creek as they drove up the mountain. The fireplace was mossy and the rocks were crumbling, cobwebs hung from the ceiling like strands of silk and the dirt floor was covered with leaves, old rags, and other musty-smelling debris.

An ancient table and three chairs occupied one corner. Lexie assumed she was seated in the fourth chair to the set. A sagging, broken down iron bed hulked in another corner and the one window in the whole place had smudged and broken glass lining the frame, like a child's crooked teeth.

Outside the broken glass, Lexie stared at the dark, swollen purple sky that spit occasional snowflakes and sent them fluttering to the ground. It figures, she thought. Maybe now the curse of the drought would end and people could rejoice. She, however, was tied to a chair against her will.

What had happened to her? Who had brought her here?

Who was definitely the million-dollar question. More importantly, why?

"Hello," she called out as shivers racked her body. Even her nose was icy and she sniffed. "Is anybody here?" When no one appeared, Lexie began to scream. "Help! Help! Somebody help!"

The door flew open and a squat, mannish figure walked in.

Lexie's heart leapt and tears sprang to her eyes, obscuring her vision again. "Oh, hello, can you help me? Can you untie me? Someone smacked me over the head and—"

"I know. My mom hit you," a slurred voice said.

The figure lifted its sandy blond head and gave her a crooked grin. Lexie's eyes cleared and she nearly choked at who stood before her. It was Danny, the young man who worked at the senior citizen center.

"Your . . . your mother hit me? Why?"

"Shhh." He pressed an index finger to his lips. "My mom says you are a very bad person. She says you hurt us."

"Hurt you?" Hiccoughs ricocheted through her frame. "How?"

He shrugged. "Dunno. All I know is she told me to watch over you until she got back."

Hiccough. "Where did she go?"

He shrugged again and sat on one of the chairs. "Dunno. You got pretty hair. I like it."

"You should untie me and let me go. I'm a good person. Your mother's wrong. I didn't hurt anyone."

Danny stood up so fast he knocked over the chair, his expression darkened and his eyes blazed. "My mother is not wrong. Don't ever say she is wrong. Take it back."

Lexie shrank in her seat and swallowed more hiccoughs. "I'm sorry, Danny. I didn't mean it."

"Honest?" His eyes got rounder.

"Honest."

"OK. My mom will be back soon. You can talk

to her."

Lexie chewed her lower lip, wondering exactly who Danny's mother was and why she hated her so much. Her whole body had become a giant ice cube and the hiccoughs continued to tear through her. Stop it, stop it, stop it, she told herself. It hurt too much to hiccough. She swallowed in a desperate, spasmodic rhythm. Amazingly, the hiccoughs went away. Although hiccoughs-from-hell were the least of her worries.

She didn't have to think long before she heard car tires crunch on gravel. The door opened and in walked Carma Leone with a blast of cool wind, dressed in one of the Ice Queen Resort's black maid uniforms with a white sweater.

Lexie's mouth dropped. "Carma? You're Danny's mother? Why are you dressed that way?" Her blood ran even colder when she glanced outside and saw the mystery car parked by a fallen log. The same one that had rammed her old POS truck as she was on her way home from Whitehead's house. The same one that had been following her for months. The same one she and Lucy saw parked outside the casino.

"Ah, I see you recognize my little sports car. How astute you are." Carma cocked her head to the side.

What was Carma up to? Lexie licked her dry, cracked lips. "You're the one who's been doing all these things to me? And murdering people?"

Carma stood beside her son, setting her purse

and a brown paper bag on the table. "You got it right, sweetheart."

"But why on earth? What do you have against me? And what did you do to my sister?"

"I beaned her pretty hard, but she'll probably live. I'm not after her. I'm after you."

"Why?" Lexie choked back tears and fought another wave of hiccoughs.

"I guess I might as well get it off my chest." Carma thoughtfully examined her perfect red nails. "You see, back in high school, I had this boyfriend named Dan Lightfoot. Remember him? Tall blond football player with the cute dimples?"

"*Your* boyfriend? Carma, I never knew you went out with him."

"No one knew we were together. It was a secret. My mother didn't like him and we weren't allowed to date. But I loved Dan with all my heart." Her gaze drifted off into memories, and she rested a hand on Danny's head. "Dan was my first, you know. Danny is our son."

Flabberghasted, Lexie stared at Danny. Could it be?

Maybe that's why his features seemed so familiar the first time she met him at the senior citizen's center. Lexie and Dan hadn't started dating till their junior year. He and Carma must have had their fling before then.

Lexie's head reeled with disbelief. It was difficult to concentrate. *Carma and Dan.* The entire concept was alien to her. Could they really have been in love? It was hard to believe, but appeared to be true.

Dan had a son. What would The Undertaker think if he found out? What would Davina think?

"I never heard rumors you were pregnant, Carma. You know high school kids are brutal about gossip."

"My mom and I covered it up pretty good, didn't we? Why do you think I slouched and wore all those big, dumpy sweatshirts when I was a sophomore? At the end of the school year, my mom shipped me off to live with my Aunt Alice. I spent most of the summer before Danny was born ratting around in her tiny little trailer. Let me tell you, that was true murder." She gave an unnatural, high-pitched laugh.

Lexie shifted uneasily in her rope bindings. She had to keep Carma talking until . . . until what? She had to buy time. Before Carma did something desperate. Again. "You didn't give Danny up for adoption?"

"The kid had Down's Syndrome." She stroked his head and he grinned up at her admiringly. "No one would want him, so my aunt raised him up here, away from prying eyes. I came up to visit as much as I could. No one in Moose Creek Junction ever knew about him."

"Carma, I'm confused. What does your affair with Dan have to do with me?"

"I always believed once Dan and I graduated from high school, we could get married and the three of us would be together. I'd be eighteen and it wouldn't matter what my mom thought. But you came along. You bitch. He fell for you, then you got knocked up with Eva. That was the end of my dreams. You stole him from me. Eva got everything my Danny deserved."

"How could I steal him from you when I never even knew you two were together? It doesn't make sense. You should have told Dan you were pregnant. You should have made him take care of things properly. Maybe he would have married you. Don't you see?"

Carma blinked, seemingly contemplating for a moment, then she began to pace. "Don't confuse the issue, you whore. It was plain and simple. You stole Dan away from me and ran off to California with him. You had everything. Nice clothes, a home, and a car. A daughter who was normal and had everything she ever wanted: friends, good schools, and now even college. My Danny will never have any of that."

"That's not my fault, Carma. Don't fool yourself into thinking my life with Dan Lightfoot was all wine and roses. He was abusive and violent. He had numerous affairs throughout our marriage and in the end he left me for another woman. Do you see the pattern? He can't commit to anyone. He doesn't love people . . . he only uses them. He used *both* you and me, Carma. He hurt us both. Blame Dan Lightfoot for being irresponsible, not me."

Carma started to shake and she closed her eyes. "It wasn't his fault. It couldn't have been. You were the one who changed him, made him think he loved you and not me. You must have hurt him some-how so he wanted to be with someone else. If he would have stayed with me, I would have been the only woman he ever wanted. He'd have loved me forever." Carma glared at Lexie, her dark eyes flash-ing. "You ruined it all, you tramp. You don't deserve to live."

Lexie swallowed hard. It shocked her to real-ize how desperate and confused Carma had become when Dan jilted her. Now it was all becoming clear. "You ruined every attempt I had at being happy once I moved back home. Right?"

"Bingo." Her eyes narrowed into angry slits. "I killed them all. Hugh Glenwood, Henry Whitehead, and Jack Sturgeon. Of course, I couldn't have done it if my grandfather hadn't shared so much of his mili-tary training with me. The army teaches men to be killers. Danny's help made everything possible." As she stroked his head, he once again glanced ador-ingly up at her.

"And Elton? What about him?"

"Ah, Elton was a true accident. I was driving past your house that night and I had Danny with me. I thought it might be fun to let him take the wheel. When Elton came barreling out of your house, poor Danny tried to swerve. Since it was his first time driving, he turned the wrong way and *ker-splat*." Carma shrugged nonchalantly.

Lexie shivered at Carma's callous attitude. "Someone attacked me at MacGreggor's Pub, then threw the rock through my window and set the fire at the café."

Carma laughed, another high, unnatural laugh. "We did it all, Danny and I. Right down to stealing the butcher knife from your kitchen to kill Whitehead. You really ought to think about putting deadbolts on your doors. Locks are too easy to pick. Of course, you won't be around much longer to worry about it."

Lexie sensed she was running out of time and strained at her bonds. They wouldn't budge. "Carma, you need help. It's time you admitted it and—"

Carma waved her off and began again. "Every man you went out with was marked for murder, Lexie. Unfortunately for them, they got involved with you. Since you so conveniently came up here and found me, I've decided to end it once and for all. I'm tired of keeping up with your whoring. I'm tired of having to kill every man you date." She snickered. "I'm going to finish you off in flames, the way it should have happened days ago." She grabbed the brown paper bag on the table, reached inside and produced a box of wooden matches. "The brush and grass around here is extremely dry. No one will think twice about a forest fire burning down this cabin. You, unfortunately, will be inside."

Lexie strained once again at her bindings. They wouldn't budge. Anguish sifted through her soul. The ropes were so tight she could barely move. They sawed painfully through her clothing and into her skin reminding her she would die soon. No one would know the truth behind the murdered men. No one would suspect she'd been murdered. Carma's plan seemed perfect.

Keep her talking, a small voice persisted in Lexie's head.

"Carma, back at the casino, why were you crying?"

Her dark eyes flashed again and she rattled the box of matches warningly. "None of your business."

"If I'm going to die anyway, why does it matter?"

Carma paused thoughtfully, then relented. "Do you think it's been easy trying to take care of myself and Danny, too, on a nail technician's salary?" She snorted. "Danny's medical bills have been enormous. Since he was born, he needed expensive doctors, surgeries, and medicine. I've had to support myself by gambling. I've done a pretty good job of it, too."

Ah ha. So Carma Leone was addicted to gambling. It was a disease, Lexie knew, like alcoholism. A debilitating disease. No wonder her father had preached against the sinful habit. "So why were you crying?"

She frowned and her mouth trembled. "Lately I've run into a streak of bad luck. My bank account is cleaned out, both checking and savings, and my credit cards are all maxed to the hilt. I'm broke on my ass. Before long, the bank will repossess my car, my house, and my life. I don't suppose you'd know what that feels like, would you?"

"You'd be surprised."

"Right, Miss High-and-Mighty. You've never suffered a day in your life."

Lexie decided to get Carma's train of thought onto something positive, rather than her venomous hatred. "I can tell you love Danny very much. Why would you involve him in all the murders? You're hurting him. I know you don't want to do that."

"Danny doesn't understand, you see," Carma said. "He only knows you are a bad person and I can do no wrong. He agrees with everything I say and do because I am his mother." She patted Danny's shoulder. "Right, Danny?"

"Right, Mom." He grinned up at her with his innocent, freckled face. "You are the best."

"That's so wrong, Carma. To use your son as you have: you've taken advantage of an individual who doesn't know any better."

Carma shrugged. "I take care of Danny just fine. He's helped me these last months as I've needed, doing things I couldn't physically accomplish. Like, for example, who do you think lifted you up and dumped your ass in the laundry cart after I beaned you on the head in your room? It was my sweet child, assisting me with my dirty work."

"That's right, Mom," Danny said. "I always help you. I am a good boy."

"Of course you are, sweetie." Carma pinched his dimpled cheek. "Now it's time to say good-bye to the bad woman." She nodded at Lexie. "Let's put her out of her misery."

Danny looked solemnly at Lexie. "She gave me candy once. It was good."

"Danny," Carma said sternly and gave her son a reprimanding look.

He shrugged. "OK, Mom."

Tears streamed down Lexie's face. This was it. She was going to die because of Dan, that bastard who was no good for any woman and no good for anyone else. Yet, Carma in her confused, lunatic way loved him and always had.

Carma took Danny by the hand and led him, just like a little boy, out of the cabin. Standing beside the doorway with her son, Carma said, "Light a match, Danny. Do it just the way Mommy taught you."

"Sure, Mom," he slurred.

He tried to light the match, but it sparked out. Frustrated, he tossed the ruined match aside and tried another. This one flared into life.

Lexie whimpered and strained against the ropes tying her to the chair. It was over, her whole life. She'd never see her daughter again, never see Lucy or patootie head Otis or Carl.

God damn you, Dan Lightfoot. God damn you, Carma Leone.

Horrified, Lexie watched the match fall to the cabin floor, instantly igniting the pine needles and debris. Flames leapt into life. Carma and her son stepped back. Through the wall of orange fire, Lexie saw them wave, then disappear from sight.

Smoke crept into Lexie's lungs as she struggled to free herself. She coughed spasmodically. Her eyes began to sting and water. The fire licked her face with heat. She knew she'd die from smoke inhalation first, but the thought did not comfort her. She cried harder, amazed it could end this way. With one woman's hatred and one stinking match.

"Lexie! Lexie, are you in there?" a voice shouted.

Though she felt ready to pass out and her throat was dry as a dead leaf, Lexie lifted her head and managed to stammer, "Yes—" Smoke clogged her lungs. She coughed and gulped for air.

Through the crackling flames a loud crash resounded as the back door burst open. In the swirling gray smoke, Lexie saw a tall figure race in her direction. *Gabe.* Deputy Dog had made it in time. Thankful for his timely arrival, Lexie made a mental vow never to call him Deputy Dog again.

Gabe lifted her up, chair and all, and carried her swiftly outside away from the cabin. As he put down the seat and sliced through Lexie's bindings with a pocketknife, she watched the ancient cabin explode into licking flames. Trembling, Lexie felt the sweet relief of knowing she would live. She should have been overwhelmed with joy to be alive, to see another sunrise. Instead, she cried harder.

It's the emotion of the whole thing, she told herself. The murders, the attacks on her life, the café fire. She was probably in shock, and no wonder.

As the ropes fell away, circulation slowly

returned to her fingers, causing them to tingle painfully. Taking her numb hand, Gabe dragged her up a weed-choked hill, far away from the smoky, crackling inferno. Lexie cried and coughed alternately, leaning against the detective and glad of his strong arm around her shoulders. Slowly, relief flooded her limbs as she watched a yellow fire truck, siren wailing, pull up to the cabin. Fire fighters jumped out and aimed a fat hose at the crumbling structure, dousing the orange glow.

"Look down there." Gabe pointed at a dirt road that snaked toward a stand of fir trees. Two uniformed police officers had pulled over Carma's fancy sports car. As Carma got out of the driver's seat, they handcuffed her, then loaded both she and Danny into their squad car and drove off.

"The ambulance is on its way," Gabe said, stroking her aching head and holding her against his side.

Sure enough, Lexie could hear another shrill siren piercing the chilled air. A horrible thought hit her. "Lucy—"

"Is fine," Gabe reassured her. "One of the hotel maids found her and called an ambulance. She's down at St. Mary's Clinic in Rawhide City."

Lexie relaxed, yet knew she owed a big apology to her sister. That would come later, after they returned home safe and sound. Lucy would forgive her, just like Lexie forgave Lucy whenever she goofed up. That was the thing about families. You might get upset with each other, but you had to forgive and forget. As a kid, Lexie had never understood the concept when her father preached it from the pulpit. She did now.

Through her sniffles and shivers, Lexie allowed Gabe to comfort her. And gosh darn, she actually liked it. It bothered her on a certain level, but now was not the time to question her feelings. Later, she would think about it. For now, standing on the cold, windswept hill and having Gabe's arm around her was wonderful.

She had survived.

When the detective produced a clean tissue from his pocket, Lexie used it to wipe away her sniffles. She looked around, realizing it was snowing hard. Tufts of fuzzy flakes swirled around the forested area, blanketing the rocky, uneven ground with a shroud of white. They'd been in a drought for years with barely a drop of water. Now it was snowing like crazy. That was Wyoming. Unpredictable and wild.

Lexie hugged herself and tried to quell her shaking and chattering teeth. "How . . . how did you know where I was? I thought I was going to die."

"Not while I'm around, lady." Gabe removed his heavy overcoat and wrapped her in it.

Lexie wondered what it was supposed to mean, but immediately dismissed it. It wouldn't be good to put a lot of meaning into his comment. Instead, she snuggled against Gabe's warm, broad chest. Her shivers immediately lessened. Warning bells went off in her head, telling her not to get too comfortable. She knew she could really get used to Gabe's protective presence. That wasn't very wise. She had no idea how he felt about her or how she felt about him.

"You're lucky I found out where you and Lucy had gone," Gabe admonished. "When I saw Lucy and Otis' car at Big Daddy's, I stopped to talk with them. I intended to let Otis know the investigation was coming along fine. You see, I was already onto Carma, but I was taking my time to make sure I had all my evidence in order."

"You knew she was the killer?" Lexie fought back annoyance as she glared up at him. "You never told us about any evidence."

"There's *always* evidence," Gabe said.

"You were certainly in no hurry to see justice done," Lexie groused. "My life was in danger."

"Which was why I told you to lay low and let me do my job."

Lexie stubbornly remained in a silent pout.

"Lexie, these things take time," he added, lifting her chin and staring into her eyes. "You can't go busting people without clear cut proof. Otherwise, you compromise the case."

"Yeah, yeah, yeah," Lexie said, relenting as she stared into Gabe's handsome face and saw the concern in his eyes.

"Anyway," he continued. "Carl told me you and Lucy had come here. I had a gut feeling you two were up to no good."

"So my nephew ratted us out," Lexie said. "Thank God. I'll have to give him a big hug the next time I see him."

"You did a dangerous thing, Lexie. Lucy was hurt and you nearly got yourself killed."

"You brought the cavalry in the nick of time. Though for a moment, I thought it was all over." Lexie shivered again, even though Gabe's overcoat and warm embrace had made her quite toasty. "Carma blamed me for getting the life she thinks *she* deserved. She and Dan were lovers back in high school and she swears I stole him from her. Danny's their son."

"I've done my homework, Lexie. I know all about it. It's over now. She's going to jail."

She gave a shuddering sigh. "What about Danny? What will happen to him?"

"The state will put him in a good home. I'm sure the courts will realize he was coerced into helping his mother commit the crimes."

"He won't get in trouble?"

"More than likely not. Because of his condition, he can't be held responsible for what his mother influenced him to do. He'll get the psychological help he needs."

"Good."

"I stopped at Big Daddy's for another reason." Gabe stroked the hair back from her bruised and swollen face. The ambulance sirens were wailing louder and he glanced anxiously at the road.

"Why?"

Gabe turned his attention back to her. "I thought you might be there, too."

Lexie's heart caught in her throat. "So?"

"I, um . . ." He trailed off and shuffled anxiously at her side. "I wanted to ask you out."

"You're kidding, right?"

"Nope." His face turned red and he grinned. "I've wanted to ask you out for a while. But I'm a big doof when it comes to women."

"The big, strong detective has a fatal flaw."

"So, what do you think?" He chuckled and squeezed her shoulders. "Will you have dinner with me sometime?"

Lexie smiled up at him. "Why not?"

CINDY KEEN REYNDERS

CINDY KEEN REYNDERS WAS BORN IN PORTLAND, Oregon and has lived all over the United States and also in Japan. She has visited Canada, the Philippines, Samoa and New Zealand and the travels have given her an appreciation of other cultures.

Cindy enjoys crocheting, reading, garage sales and other hobbies along with volunteer work, which she performed with the Red Cross and numerous other charitable organizations. Writing has been, and always will be, the one true passion that lights a fire deep down in her soul. Growing up, she discovered she loved words and found that she had an aptitude for stringing them together into sentences.

Over the years, she has won or placed in various writing contests. She has also written for and edited numerous newsletters. Additionally, she has sold several non-fiction magazine articles to "True West" and "Wild West." As she raised her children, she always found time to read to them and tried to instill her love of the written word into their lives. She hopes to carry on this tradition with her grandchildren.

Cindy currently lives in Cheyenne, Wyoming with her husband Rich whose family has lived in the state for generations. She has a grown daughter and son-in-law, two grown step-daughters and two grown sons. ▶

At one time, she had three poodles that matched the color of her carpet. She now has one poodle-shitzu mix that likes to "eat" the carpet. Add to the mix two granddaughters who keep everyone in stitches and as you can imagine, her home is filled with lots of love and laughter.

In addition to keeping track of her extended clan, which includes three sisters, two brothers, her father, step-mother and numerous nieces and nephews, Cindy works for Laramie County School District 1 (LCSD1) in Cheyenne. She is a marketing specialist in the district's Community Relations department and writes feature articles for the LCSD1 Public Schools Chronicle, which has a circulation of approximately 40,000 readers. She has found that her family and friends inspire her to explore human nature and she believes this has enabled her to draw out all aspects of human behavior in her books.

Her future goals include being able travel more as time allows and to write, write, write. She constantly challenges herself to develop more entertaining plots, characters and settings. Nothing pleases her more than to be able to tell a good story. If it touches someone's heartstrings and makes them laugh or cry, then she knows she's done her job.

PAWS-ITIVELY GUILTY

CINDY KEEN REYNDERS

After a difficult divorce, Lexie Lightfoot moves home to Moose Creek Junction, Wyoming, to start a new life with her teenage daughter, Eva. Lexie and Lucy open a small business, The Saucy Lucy Café. Lexie begins the process of assimilating herself back into a small town full of gossip and secrets.

Lucy is a staunch, churchgoing woman who believes her sister must remarry in order to enter the kingdom of heaven. After several disastrous blind dates arranged by her sister, Lexie is ready to give up in the dating department. Especially when her relationship with Detective Gabe Stevenson, the handsome lawman from Westonville, goes south. She is determined to live her life without a man and without her sister's interference.

When her friend goes missing and Lexie and Lucy find her buried in her garden, Lexie is devastated. Moose Creek Junction's inept sheriff, and Lucy's husband, Otis Parnell, is no help. With Gabe on vacation, the Westonville police are having a hard time finding the murderer.

Lexie grows impatient and decides its time to lend a helping hand. With Lucy's assistance, the sisters begin questioning the townspeople in order to conduct their own investigation. When things start to cook, Lexie and Lucy find themselves in a heap of hot water!

ISBN#9781933836614

Mass Market Paperback / Mystery

US $7.95 / CDN $9.95

DECEMBER 2008

www.cindykeenreynders.com

Dolores J. Wilson's

Big Hair and Flying Cows

Bertie Byrd is unique. To say the least.

She calls Sweet Meadow, Georgia, home, where she works for her father doing auto repairs. She also drives the tow-truck, although Sweet Meadow's rather colorful denizens tend to treat Bertie more like the local, free taxi service. You know, someone has to get to a doctor's appointment or pick something up at the dry cleaners.

Bertie's favorite day of the week is Friday, when she leaves the wrecker with her father for the whole weekend and joins her friends at the Dew Drop Inn for a night of dancing. Her best friend, Mary Lou, sometimes fixes her up with dubious dates, although Bertie has to remind her friend not to tease her hair too high for those occasions. Like the time when they went to Carrie Sue's open house, and a ceramic cow with angel wings hanging from a ceiling fan locked its hooves into Bertie's big hair and refused to let go. She had to wear it all night, dangling chain and all.

Bertie's nearly perfect life is about to take a downhill turn, however. It starts when her landlord, Pete, currently a resident in a nearby nursing home, starts showing up at her house. In his birthday suit. A very badly wrinkled birthday suit. And then she goes to her mailbox, a rubber large mouth bass, and finds a notice from the zoning commission saying she can no longer park the wrecker in her driveway. The notice is signed by George Bigham. But when she goes to the courthouse to take care of her little problem, it is only to discover George Bigham is deceased. And Mary Lou's pregnancy test just came up positive. Can it get any worse?

In a word. . . yes.

ISBN#9781932815979
Mass Market Paperback / Fiction
US $6.99 / CDN $9.99
Available Now
www.doloresjwilson.com

Dolores J. Wilson

Barking Goats and the Redneck Mafia

Bertie Byrd Fortney never thought she'd be spending her wedding night in a maternity ward. But her best friend went into labor right in the middle of the conga line at Bertie and Arch's wedding reception, and it wasn't until her friend's son made his entrance into the world that Bertie, her husband, and her stepdaughter could leave on their motor home honeymoon. The trip's trials, however, leave Bertie wondering if a honeymoon is some kind of test a woman must pass before becoming a wife.

To add to her tribulations, Bertie returns to Bertie's Garage and Towing to find Linc, her tow truck driver, is being threatened by the Redneck Mafia. The mob boss has told Linc to return to Atlanta to marry his daughter, or he will move him there himself . . . one body part at a time.

And then Bertie is taken hostage by a man who has taught his goats to bark and his twins to talk. A mistake on both counts, in Bertie's not-so-humble opinion.

Finally, a bizarre accident involving an elderly drunken citizen Linc mistakes as a hit man, a golf cart, a trip to the hospital, and a positive pregnancy test has tongues wagging in Sweet Meadow, Georgia. Did Bertie really get knocked up on a golf cart by her tow truck driver?

Will Bertie be able to douse the rumors? Will she be able to save her faithful employee from the mob? More importantly, will she pass the wife test?

ISBN#9781932815634
Hardcover Fiction
US $24.95 / CDN $33.95
Available Now
www.doloresjwilson.com

Dolores J. Wilson's

Jail Bertie and the Peanut Ladies

Bertie is at it again.

It starts when she wants a traffic light at a dangerous intersection. But because the purchase of an automatic traffic counter would cut into the city council's Christmas party fund, Bertie is forced to count each car personally and present a report. Then Bertie, in her inimitable fashion, gets into it with one of the council members. When he dies of a heart attack, she's accused of causing it. Goaded into running for the now-open position, an unlikely political career is launched. That's not all.

She finds herself running against Booger Bailey, he of barking goat fame. That's going to be interesting. Who, for instance, is the mysterious donor financing his campaign?

And then there's the two octogenarians who talk Bertie into backing them in a business venture: street vending their boiled peanuts. But what are they really up to?

Seemingly insignificant events once again twist Bertie's life into a series of improbable, and hilarious, misadventures. Because Bertie is off . . . and running.

ISBN#9781933836119
Hardcover Fiction
US $24.95 / CDN $33.95
Available Now
www.doloresjwilson.com

BLOOD TIES

LORi G. ARMSTRONG

Blood Ties. What do they mean?

How far would someone go to sever . . . or protect them?

Julie Collins is stuck in a dead-end secretarial job with the Bear Butte County Sheriff's office, and still grieving over the unsolved murder of her Lakota half-brother. Lack of public interest in finding his murderer, or the killer of several other transient Native American men, has left Julie with a bone-deep cynicism she counters with tequila, cigarettes, and dangerous men. The one bright spot in her mundane life is the time she spends working part-time as a PI with her childhood friend, Kevin Wells.

When the body of a sixteen-year old white girl is discovered in nearby Rapid Creek, Julie believes this victim will receive the attention others were denied. Then she learns Kevin has been hired, mysteriously, to find out where the murdered girl spent her last few days. Julie finds herself drawn into the case against her better judgment, and discovers not only the ugly reality of the young girl's tragic life and brutal death, but ties to her and Kevin's past that she is increasingly reluctant to revisit.

On the surface the situation is eerily familiar. But the parallels end when Julie realizes some family secrets are best kept buried deep. Especially those serious enough to kill for.

ISBN#9781932815320
Mass Market Paperback / Mystery
US $6.99 / CDN $9.99
Available Now
www.loriarmstrong.com

LORI G. ARMSTRONG
HALLOWEd GROUNd

Grisly murders are rocking the small county of Bear Butte where Julie Collins has spent the last few months learning the PI biz without the guidance of her best friend and business partner, Kevin Wells. Enter dangerous, charismatic entrepreneur Tony Martinez, who convinces Julie to take a case involving a missing five-year-old Native American girl, the innocent pawn in her parents' child custody dispute. Although skeptical about Martinez' motives in hiring her, and confused by her strange attraction to him, Julie nevertheless sees the opportunity to hone her investigative skills outside her office.

But something about the case doesn't ring true. The girl's father is foreman on the controversial new Indian casino under construction at the base of the sacred Mato Paha, and the girl's mother is secretly working for a rival casino rumored to have ties to an east coast crime family. Local ranchers — including her father — a Lakota Holy group, and casino owners from nearby Deadwood are determined to stop the gaming facility from opening.

With the body count rising, the odds are stacked against Julie to discover the truth behind these hidden agendas before the murderer buries it forever. And when Julie unwittingly attracts the attention of the killer, she realizes no place is safe . . . not even hallowed ground.

ISBN#9781932815740
Mass Market Paperback / Mystery
US $6.99 / CDN $9.99
Available Now
www.loriarmstrong.com

LORI G. ARMSTRONG
SHALLOW GRAVE

Surveillance on an insurance fraud case in Bear Butte County unfolds tragically for PI Julie Collins and her partner, Kevin Wells. The reappearance of a mysterious hole—cause of the fatal accident—brings about the landowner's unsettling confession; bones were recently uncovered on that remote ridge. Fearing repercussions from their illegal off-season hunting, the hunters reburied the remains and kept quiet.

Now the hole is back, but the bones have vanished.

Were the bones part of an ancient Indian burial ground? Connected to the unsolved disappearance of a Native American woman? The overworked, understaffed sheriff asks for Julie's help.

But the case opens old wounds, and she finds herself at odds with the Standing Elk family, discovering they withheld information from her in the months before Ben's death. And Julie's relationship with Tony Martinez hits a rough spot when she agrees to go undercover in his strip club.

On the wrong side of tribal politics, family disputes, and employee rivalries, Julie continues to dig for answers...while the personal stakes climb. In a brutal fight for her life, Julie finally comes face to face with her brother's killer...and realizes not all deceptions run deep.

ISBN#9781933836188
Mass Market Paperback / Mystery
US $7.95 / CDN $9.95
Available Now
www.loriarmstrong.com

IN STEREO
WHERE AVAILABLE

BECKY ANDERSON

PHOEBE KASSNER didn't set out to be a 29-year-old virgin, but that's how it's worked out. And, having just been dumped by her boyfriend, she doesn't see that situation changing anytime soon.

Meanwhile, her twin sister Madison—aspiring actress, small-time model, and queen of the short attention span—has just been eliminated on the first round of Singing Sensation.

Things aren't looking so great for either of them. But when Phoebe receives a surprise voice mail from some guy named Jerry, victim of a fake phone number written on a cocktail napkin, she takes pity on him and calls, setting in motion a serendipitous love story neither of them ever saw coming.

And suddenly Madison's got a romance of her own going, as one of twelve women competing for two men on a ruthless, over-the-top reality show. As Phoebe falls in love with the jilted high school English teacher who never intended to call her in the first place, Madison's falling in love, too—after a fashion—clawing and fighting her way through a tide of adorable blondes. Could it get any crazier?

Stay tuned . . .

ISBN#9781933836201
Trade Paperback / Fiction
US $15.95 / CDN $19.95
Available Now